Praise for the novels of

Maggie Shayne

"Maggie Shayne delivers romance with sweeping intensity and be-
witching passion. Readers will lose themselves in her dark, en-
thralling brew of love, danger, and perilous fate."

—Jayne Ann Krentz

"Maggie Shayne's gift for melding the mystical and magical into
her novels has made her one of the preeminent voices in paranor-
mal romance today."   —*Romantic Times*

"Maggie Shayne is a reader's joy. Fast-paced, witty, delightful, and
shamelessly romantic, her stories will be treasured long after the
book is done. A remarkable talent."   —Teresa Medeiros

"Ms. Shayne definitely knows how to keep you guessing . . . Her
characters come to life in a way that makes you feel as if you know
every one of them. A wonderful romantic suspense with edge-of-
your seat tension, steamy passion, and real emotions with which a
reader can identify."   —*Rendezvous*

"Maggie Shayne proves she has what it takes to shine with a work
that combines elements of gothic melodrama and romantic suspense and turns the mixture into something rare and precious."

—*Affaire de Coeur*

"A hauntingly beautiful love story that endures through time itself."   —Kay Hooper

Immortal Desire

MAGGIE SHAYNE

BERKLEY SENSATION, NEW YORK

THE BERKLEY PUBLISHING GROUP
Published by the Penguin Group
Penguin Group (USA) Inc.
375 Hudson Street, New York, New York 10014, USA
Penguin Group (Canada), 90 Eglinton Avenue East, Suite 700, Toronto, Ontario M4P 2Y3, Canada
(a division of Pearson Penguin Canada Inc.)
Penguin Books Ltd., 80 Strand, London WC2R 0RL, England
Penguin Group Ireland, 25 St. Stephen's Green, Dublin 2, Ireland (a division of Penguin Books Ltd.)
Penguin Group (Australia), 250 Camberwell Road, Camberwell, Victoria 3124, Australia
(a division of Pearson Australia Group Pty. Ltd.)
Penguin Books India Pvt. Ltd., 11 Community Centre, Panchsheel Park, New Delhi—110 017, India
Penguin Group (NZ), 67 Apollo Drive, Rosedale, North Shore 0632, New Zealand
(a division of Pearson New Zealand Ltd.)
Penguin Books (South Africa) (Pty.) Ltd., 24 Sturdee Avenue, Rosebank, Johannesburg 2196,
South Africa

Penguin Books Ltd., Registered Offices: 80 Strand, London WC2R 0RL, England

IMMORTAL DESIRE

PRINTING HISTORY
Destiny: Jove mass market edition / February 2001
Immortality: published in *Out of This World* by Jove / August 2001
Immortality: Jove "great reads" edition / September 2005
Berkley Sensation trade paperback omnibus edition / December 2007

Berkley Sensation trade paperback ISBN: 978-0-425-21748-1

PRINTED IN THE UNITED STATES OF AMERICA

10 9 8 7 6 5 4 3 2 1

Contents

Destiny

This book could not have happened without the help of some special people: My friends. They didn't help me with the research, or the plotting or the character development. They did something far more important than that. They came through for me when I was in trouble. They were there for me when I needed them. With kindness and wisdom they reached out when I was drowning and pulled me onto the shore.

It shouldn't surprise me. They always do.
So here's to you, dear ones: RomEx Rules!

Special thanks to Justine Davis, Anne Stuart,
and Gayle Callen

It also couldn't have happened without the support of my personal hero, who put up with my whining, tears, and hysterics over this project, and stepped in as he always does to take care of everything in the known universe so I could do what needed to be done. (And who dragged me off into the wilderness for a mental health weekend afterward.) Thank you, hon. You're my rock.

Author's Note

Research on the civilization known as Sumer has been a hobby of mine for almost a decade now. I knew that one of these days I'd find the right time to use it in a book, and now I have. The culture, the customs, and the religion of the time are accurately portrayed here, right down to the manner of greeting a respected friend, the clothing, the names, and even the description of the queen's headdress.

However, as happens in fiction, sometimes the author has to take a few liberties, and I want to be clear about those. First of all, two of the characters you meet in this novel, King Eannatum and Queen Puabi, were real Sumerian rulers. She was the Queen of a city-state called Ur, and he was the King of Lagash, and later all of Sumer. They both ruled around the same time—2500 BCE, and Eannatum truly was credited with unifying Sumer and ending threats from the nearby land of Umma. However, there is no historical record of Eannatum and Puabi ever meeting, much less having the relationship depicted here.

The other bit of poetic license I took was in stating that a priestess of the temple had to remain unmarried and chaste until and unless she was chosen to perform the Sacred Marriage Rite with the king. I have no way of knowing if that was the case. No source yet has said one way or the other, and indications are that the Sumerians saw sex as normal, healthy, and even sacred, so they may not have forbidden their holy women to engage in it, married or otherwise. However, the Sacred Marriage Rite itself was very real, and was common practice in Sumer.

The observations I've made in this book about the changing roles of women during this pivotal time in history are absolutely true. Women are still struggling to regain the status and power they had prior to 2500 BCE.

I've sprinkled a few Sumerian phrases through this book. These are guesswork at best, as pronunciations and meanings change with every new research book that comes out. Translating the old cuneiform tablets is one thing—trying to figure out how the language sounded is a great deal more difficult. Even the name "Nidaba" has been given as "Nisaba" in some sources. So nothing is certain.

All that said, I will add that any mistakes you may find in the research were obviously put there by evil typesetters intent on ruining my credibility. < grin >

Maggie Shayne

Prologue

When she opened her eyes, there was a sheet over her face.

She sucked in her next breath, her *first* breath, the breath of life itself, and it rushed into her lungs with a force powerful enough to burst an ordinary set. The power jolted through her, arching her back, electrifying her every cell for just an instant. Then she went limp again and released the air in a slow, shuddering sigh. Slowly, awareness returned.

She was in a vehicle that moved wildly and wailed like a hyena. An ambulance, she realized dully. Disoriented still, she tried to clear her mind, to recall what had preceded this latest death and re-vival, and found only vague memories; a struggle on a rooftop, a gun, the sense of plummeting downward, and the shattering im-pact at the bottom. She lifted a hand, to push the sheet away from her face. But her hand moved mere inches, and no more. She was strapped down.

Strapped down!

The emotional dam she had so carefully built broke open wide to let ice-water panic flood her veins. A pulse beat in her temple and repeated itself, magnified, against her chest. Memories she had long ago buried clawed their way out of their graves, deep inside her mind, and a few gnarled fingers emerged to scratch at her hard-won sanity until they drew blood.

She had been strapped to a contraption like this one before. No details came just then, thank the Gods. Her control had been too hard won for that. Only sensations, feelings and emotions. Pain. Rage. Despair. Pain. Rage. And a tormentor who had savored her suffering.

"Release me."

The voice she heard was her own. It was deep, and low, and bore a tone of command, even though it shook with the force of the emotion it sought to conceal.

"What the hell . . ." someone said. And her mind heard: *Young. Male. Confused. Afraid.*

"Release me," she said again, louder this time, more firmly.

The sheet was yanked away from her face, and the wide brown eyes of a young man blinked down at her. "My God, she's alive!" he called, apparently to whoever was driving the screaming vehicle. He wore a uniform, a badge like a policeman might wear. Lights flashed from without, but the vehicle never slowed. "For the love of Christ, she's . . ."

"Loose the straps!" She commanded, twisting and tugging at the bindings that held her down.

"Easy, now," he said, hands to her shoulders, voice lowering to a soothing tone. "Take it easy. The straps are just to keep you from falling off. You need to lie still. You've been—"

She tugged harder, and one of the restraints snapped in two, lashing backward like a whip and slapping the young man's face even as he jumped away. He pressed a hand to his cheek, and his eyes widened. She could taste his fear but cared nothing about it. Reaching to the strap at her other arm, she ripped it free as well. Then the young paramedic found his courage and leaned over her again, grabbed her shoulders, pressed her body down.

"Calm down!" he ordered. "You'll hurt yourself!"

She shoved him away from her with so much force that he flew off his feet, and his back smashed into the paraphernalia lining one side of the vehicle. He was shouting now. The ambulance skidded to a stop even as she tore at the one remaining strap at her waist, snapped it easily, and surged to her feet. She couldn't stand upright in the vehicle. Bent over, she lunged toward the back of the ambulance, wanting only escape. Freedom.

All her life, it seemed, she had been made to fight for her freedom. She valued it above all else, in a way she imagined few others ever had.

The second man clambered in from the front and came rushing at her even as she reached for the doors. Escape was so close! He grabbed her shoulders. Turning on him like a cyclone, she flung him away. Items crashed and broke and spilled. Both men swore and grappled for her.

She lunged toward the doors again, but the younger one was right behind her now, having recovered himself. He jabbed her hard with something before she could fling him away, and the stab of the needle's fang pierced her flesh. She felt her eyes widen as she looked down at the hypodermic in her arm.

Drugs, her memory whispered.

Experiments.

Living death, mired in inky blackness with no hope of escape.

She would not go back to that place! She *must* not! Yet she felt it creeping up on her even now. Reaching for her. Coming to pull her back into its cold embrace. "No . . ." she whispered.

She whirled on the young man, but dizziness made her sway. The man caught her in his arms. "Easy."

"Gods, what have you done to me?" She pressed a hand to her head as if she could slow the dizziness, the weakness, push it away somehow. "The drugs . . . you mustn't . . . give me drugs . . ." Her knees bent against her will. Her legs turned to water.

"It's just a sedative," he said, bearing her weight now, cradling her carefully. He was cut, bleeding in several places. The other one behind him held his arm oddly. Vaguely, she realized it was broken. He shouldn't have tried to stop her. He should have just let her go.

"You're going to be fine, I promise you," said the one who held her. "Come on, now." He eased her down onto the stretcher and she tried to push his hands off her, to resist, but she had no strength.

Darkness closed in around the edges of her vision. Her body was slowly going numb. "Lie down, now," he said. "Relax."

"I . . . cannot . . ."

She moved her mouth, but no further words emerged. Hazy outlines now, the two men leaned over her, shaking their heads. One ran his hands over her legs, her arms. "I don't understand it," he was saying. "She was as bent and broken as—"

"Broken, hell," said the other, still clutching his arm to his chest. "She was *dead*. We were going through the motions, but we both knew we'd lost her."

"It was a mistake. We messed up—"

"She was dead, Jerry. You know it and I know it."

"That's not possible."

Her vision faded even as she saw the man shaking his head. He said, "Damn, I think she broke my freaking arm."

"Can you drive one-handed?"

"Yeah. Yeah, I can manage it. Can you handle her?"

"I can *now*."

She heard the driver move away while the other man remained beside her, checking her for injuries. She felt the vehicle lurch into motion again, heard the siren begin to wail once more . . . but then it, too, faded into nothingness. She felt herself slipping away as well, and she fought to cling to her soul.

"I cannot let go," she whispered, sensing that if she did, she might never find her way out of the darkness again.

She needed something . . . something to cling to. Something to keep her anchored.

It came to her slowly, like a gentle, loving hand curling around her own. Her memories. Not the horrible memories she had buried so deeply, but the better ones. The real ones . . . of the life before.

"Yes," she said, though she never knew if she had spoken the word or only thought it. Four thousand, five hundred years and more had come and gone . . . but though the ages in between faded like morning mists, that *before-time* was as clear to her as if she were living it still. It was *her* time. She had known nothing of what she truly was then. She was a child, innocent, young, with so much ahead . . .

More than she ever could have guessed.

2501 BCE
City-State of Lagash, Kingdom of Sumer

Her little *kaunake* dress was white and made of fine linen, just like the ones the grown-up priestesses wore. It reached to mid-calf. Her feet were bare, at the moment. She wore the fringed shawl that was reserved for sacred occasions, and in her tiny hands she carried a large pottery bowl brimming with lush ripe fruits. The priestess beside her was dressed in the same manner, except that she also wore a golden band about her head, in deference to her station. Her arms were bare, save for the gleaming gold and silver bands wrapped around her coppery skin like vipers. Her hair was dark as night, and long and gleaming. The little girl thought the priestess Lia was the most beautiful woman in all the world.

Soberly, the two entered the *cella*, the room at the very top of the ziggurat tower. The little girl tried to concentrate on being serious and appropriately solemn as they crossed the dim room that was lined with stone statues, all winking their lapis lazuli eyes in the flickering torchlight. But the entire never-ending rite seemed so silly to her that she battled a smile, and finally a giggle emerged despite her best efforts.

The priestess looked down at her, a frown etched in her dark brows. "Hush, Nidaba! This is the most sacred room in the temple, the home of the Gods themselves! Show some respect."

Biting her lip, Nidaba stopped giggling. Instead she spoke. "The home of the Gods is in the heavens, is it not, Lia?"

"You know it is."

"Then how can they also live here, in these figures?"

"The Gods are everywhere, child. Now, come, we must attend them."

Nidaba sighed, but obeyed. The two walked forward, side by side, their feet whispering through the dried rushes that lined the floor and filled the *cella* with their green fragrance. They passed by all the smaller stone figures, which represented worshippers, for the Ancient Ones must never be left unattended. At the front of the room were statues created to house the essence of several deities. Enlil Lord of Air, Enki Lord of the Fresh Waters and the *Abzu*, Nidaba, Goddess of the Sacred Script, for whom the little girl had been named. And standing in the center, larger and more beautiful than any, was the Queen of Heaven, Inanna.

Bowing deeply, the priestess Lia held her bowl of fruit before the Great Goddess, and chanted, *"Inanna me en, Inanna me en. Inanna duna agruna ka me en."* She placed the bowl of fruit at the feet of the statue.

"She won't eat it, you know," Nidaba said, eyeing the statue. "She *never* eats it."

"The offering is only symbolic," Lia said, obviously struggling now to keep the impatience from her tone. "You'll understand when you're older."

Nidaba sniffed. "The High Priest will eat what he wants of it, and we will get his scraps."

"That's enough, child. Now, go. Place your offering."

With a sigh, Nidaba walked to the statue depicting her namesake, held up her bowl of sweet-smelling fruits, and heard her stomach growl as she chanted the sacred words. Then she set the bowl at the feet of the Goddess, licked her lips, and snatched a plum, taking a big, juicy bite before Lia could stop her.

"Nidaba, you *mustn't*!" Lia pressed her hands to her mouth as Nidaba chewed and swallowed, smiling all the while. The priestess's wide-eyed gaze darted into every corner of the room around them, as if fearing witnesses to such blasphemy.

Nidaba only shrugged and took another bite, then wiped the luscious juice from her chin with one hand. "Why mustn't I? There is more of the Goddess in me than in this statue. And I am named for her, am I not? I will learn the sacred script one day soon. And then I will fill a thousand tablets with the reasons why it is wasteful and silly to feed delicious fruit to stone statues." Crossing her arms over her chest, she nodded once for emphasis. Her long, dark hair fell into her eyes, ruining her powerful declaration, she thought, but she simply stuck out her lower lip and blew the hair aside.

The priestess Lia seemed to stifle a smile, but it was a sad one. Kneeling, she gripped the little girl's shoulders. "You know that only boys are allowed to attend the *edubba* school and learn the sacred script."

"It's not fair, and you know it," Nidaba said, her chin coming up higher. "The Goddess never made that rule! I'll bet some . . . some *boy* did!"

Lia lowered her head a bit, conceding the point, but not aloud. Never aloud. "It is the way of things," she said. "It was not always so . . . but . . . well, it is today, and there is nothing to be done. I'm sorry, Nidaba."

"It was the Goddess Nidaba who gave us the script," the girl said slowly. "And *she* is not a boy."

"No, she is not."

"And it was Nidaba who gave me to you, as well, and gave me her name," the child went on.

The priestess nodded. "That is what some believe. You were found in a basket on the doorstep of the temple, with only your pendant, and the Goddess's name was etched in its face."

Remembering the tale she loved best, Nidaba softened her stance and her tone. "And you were the one who found me there," she said.

"Yes. There was a terrible storm that night. I found you howling with rage, your little face just red with fury. I brought you inside, and all the priestesses gathered round to see you. We wrapped you in dry clothes, fed you warm goat's milk sweetened with honey, sang to you until your wrath seemed to ease. And as it did, so did the storm. With your first smile, the clouds skittered away and the full moon beamed down on the city of Lagash. And that is why some believe you to be the daughter of the Goddess herself."

Nodding slowly, Nidaba smiled. But then she recalled the beginning of the conversation, and her smile became a frown. "Then . . . who would *dare* forbid me from attending the *edubba* school?" she asked.

Lia sighed. "It is as it is, Nidaba. We can only accept and be content."

"I will *not* be content. I want to go! I want to learn! I want to go to *edubba*!" Nidaba made fists of her hands, stomped her foot, and grated her teeth as a flood of rage washed through her. Her face heated and her heart pounded.

The floor beneath her bare feet began to tremble as she ranted and raged. The shaking intensified; the entire room, perched high atop the ziggurat tower quaked and shuddered violently. The stone images themselves rocked back and forth, some of the smaller ones tumbling onto their frozen faces.

Screaming in fear, Lia fell to her knees, prostrating herself before the image of the Goddess Nidaba, even as the tremors faded. "Forgive me!" she cried. "The child *will* learn the sacred script! I vow I will make it so!"

The rumbling stopped. There remained only silence as the little girl stared at the bowed form of her beloved priestess and felt sorry for her outburst. Quietly, Nidaba went to where Lia still knelt trembling, her face damp with tears. The child touched the priestess's shoulder. "Don't be afraid," she said softly.

"I have angered the Goddess!"

"But . . . you didn't," Nidaba whispered. Moving in front of Lia, she cupped the priestess's cheeks in her small palms and looked right into her dark eyes. "The Goddess didn't make all that fuss, Lia. *I* did."

Lia sat up slowly, looking at the child with eyes as wide as the sky over all of Sumer. "You . . . *you* did?"

Nidaba gnawed her lip. "Sometimes . . . when I get very angry, things . . . *happen*." She sighed and bent her head. "I'll try not to do it again."

Chapter 1

Of all the men he'd ever been, he thought he liked Nathan Ian King best.

He sat on the veranda, sipping strong Nepalese tea as the sun rose. Orange with a pink hue, its upper curve licked at the sky over the Atlantic. This veranda, on the back of his house, looked out over the sea from on high. It was the view that had made him choose this place . . . had made him want to stay. All that water . . .

It still seemed incomprehensible to him.

Nathan King was a collector and dealer in antiquities. He was an expert in his field, though few would venture to guess how he had come by his expertise. Even fewer would believe he had acquired most of the pieces in his personal collection long before they'd been considered old.

Nathan was at ease and content with his life. And why shouldn't he be? He had established his gallery in a "historic"—the term made him smile—two-story brick building on the narrow, cobbled streets of old Boston. Then he had purchased this estate, an hour's drive from the city. The house was a sprawling one, built of red brick in the Victorian style: flat roof, tall, narrow windows, endless rooms lining long hallways, all of it set on fifty acres of lush meadows and secluded woods against the backdrop of the mighty sea.

He had created Nathan King, and his *kingdom*, some ten years ago. He'd been tired, then, of caution, tired of living in anonymity, of keeping to himself, of moving around so frequently. Enter Nathan, who in a very short time had become known and loved by hundreds. Nathan, who contributed yearly to homeless shelters and scholarship funds. Nathan, who had even been known to speak to local students about various historical periods, at the requests of their teachers.

Nathan Ian King was a model citizen. He never so much as ran a red light. His life was so perfectly ordinary that it was almost boring. Almost.

Too good to last, this persona. Already he knew his time as Nathan King would eventually come to an end. In ten years he hadn't aged a day. In ten more people would begin to wonder about that. And while he had cut off all contact with others of his kind, they were bound to find him out as soon as tales of a man who did not age began to surface.

Then again, he thought, lifting the porcelain cup to his smiling lips, there was always makeup. A drastic measure, perhaps, but possible. He was really going to hate to give up his mundane life as Nathan King. It had been peaceful, tranquil . . . and not a single immortal Witch, Dark or Light, had tracked him down in all the time he'd been living it. The past decade had healed some of his oldest wounds, he thought. Like an overworked laborer after a long vacation, he felt renewed. Almost . . . reborn. Which was a miracle in itself.

"Got the mornin' paper for you, Nathan."

Nathan inclined his head without taking his eyes off the spectacular sunrise in progress over the ocean. So much water. The abundance of so precious an element still amazed him, even after so much time. You could take the man out of the desert, he mused . . .

"Come, George. Watch this with me. It's incredible."

"Aw, you say that *every* mornin'," George said, obviously unimpressed but with a touch of humor in his childlike voice. He closed the French doors behind him and lumbered onto the veranda to take a seat at the round glass-topped table. He tossed the newspaper down in front of Nathan, but Nathan didn't so much as glance at it. Not yet.

The sun rose still higher, its neon-orange glow spreading now over the face of the water, reflected in a million glowing ripples. And higher still, beaming warmth onto Nathan's face, spilling light and heat over his body. "It's glorious," Nathan whispered.

A deep, booming laugh escaped George. "You say *that* every mornin', too."

"I do, don't I?" Nathan finally dragged his gaze away to look at George. As always, his right-hand man was dressed . . . interestingly. Today he wore a stylish brown suit from the Big and Tall Shop over a pink tie-dyed T-shirt that he must have picked up at a garage sale. Glancing down, Nathan saw the ever-present Air Jordans on George's size 12 feet. He managed not to smile. He wouldn't hurt the big man's feelings for the world.

"So tell me what's on the schedule for you today, George," Nathan began.

But before George could answer, there was a thump on the French doors. Nathan looked up to see Sheila, her pudgy arms weighed down by a cluttered tray, standing on the other side of them. Nathan jumped up and flung the doors open.

"About time, too!" Sheila huffed, handing him the tray. "A lady could die of old age by the time you two *gentlemen* got around to opening a door for her."

Nathan smiled at her. He knew full well her name wasn't Sheila. Not really. She used to wait tables at a diner where he liked the tea. Until they caught her stealing leftovers to feed the pigeons outside and fired her. Just an excuse, really. She was getting on in years, and maybe someone had learned, as well, that she hadn't given them her real name and that her green card was a fake.

If you asked her who she was, where she was from, her reply was always the same. "Just a sheila from Down Under. Born in the bush and raised with the joeys."

She sank into a chair at the table and fanned her face with one hand for dramatic effect. "I swear, you two will work me to death one of these days."

She was kidding. It was a running joke how hard the two men of the house tried to *keep* her from overdoing. When Nathan thought about the way she had been living when he'd met her—the condition she had been in . . . ah, but that was over now. She was part of his own, odd little family. She kept pigeons of her own up on the flat roof of Nathan's house.

"Breakfast smells fantastic," he told her, carrying the laden tray to the table and scrutinizing her weathered face, as he did every morning. She would never say a word if she was feeling poorly. She couldn't know it, of course, but Nathan would pick up on it anyway. His gift was empathy. He tended to pick up on and oftentimes internalize the pain—physical or otherwise—of others. He'd had to learn to shield himself, block it out, for the most part, or live in misery. But he often lowered his guard to experience the feelings of those closest to him. It was probably why, when he loved at all, he loved so much.

Today Sheila was well. Her cheeks were pink and plump and freckled, eyes bright and blue. Her carrot hair, just starting to line itself with silver strands, was pulled into a 1950s-style ponytail high atop her head.

"My breakfasts *always* smell fantastic!" she declared with a wink. She reached for his newspaper, moving it out of the way as Nathan deposited the tray in the middle of the table. Then she said, "Oh, my, now, is this a sorry-looking beauty!" She turned the paper toward him, and Nathan glanced down with feigned interest as he took his own seat.

Then he went still, staring at the small photo in the sidebar on the front page. The caption read, "Do You Know This Woman? (Story on page 10)"

Nathan's throat went dry. His eyes seemed to burn and his vision blurred. Even as he stared, trying to make sense of something he knew to be impossible, George and Sheila were taking their plates from the tray, removing the shiny stainless-steel lids, and digging in.

"Today we'll get those new bulbs planted in the front garden, won't we, Georgie?" Sheila was saying. "It's gonna be turnin' cold before we know it. We'll soon be fresh out of time for fall gardening."

"I like to plant things," George said with a smile.

"Will you have time to pick us up some more mulch on your way home from the shop tonight, Nathan?" Sheila asked.

Nathan didn't reply. He was lifting the newspaper now, staring down at the photo, unable to look away, even to read the story that went with the hauntingly familiar face in the photograph.

"Nathan?" Sheila asked.

He finally tore his gaze away from the photo and turned to Sheila. "I . . . Sorry, I . . ."

"Say, now! Is it the unknown beauty who's got you so dumb-struck?" She was using her motherly tone. From time to time she tended to do so. More often with George than with Nathan, how-ever.

She leaned closer, looking over his shoulder, and Nathan smelled the ever-present scent of Ben-Gay on her shoulders. "She's a looker, she is. All that long, dark hair. Do you know her, then?"

"I . . . No, I don't believe so."

"Couldn't tell from the look on your face, love. Crimey, you've gone chalk white."

He shook his head in denial, because, of course, it was not possi-ble. "She resembles someone I knew once."

It was George's turn to become curious. He got to his feet and limped around the table to lean over and stare as well. "I know who she is," he announced, as if it should be obvious to them all.

His words made both Nathan and Sheila stare up at him.

George smiled. "She's the lady in the picture," he said, looking toward the French doors with a nod. "The one in the front parlor, over the fireplace."

Nathan closed his eyes. Neither of them could know he'd painted the piece himself. Neither of them ever would, if he had his way. His secrets were his own. And knowing them . . . could be dangerous. Fatal.

"Well, now, you know, George, you're right. She *does* look a good deal like the woman in that painting! Isn't that curious?" Sheila asked, and her eyes narrowed on Nathan. "Turn the pages, Nathan, love. Don't keep us in suspense."

He pried his numb fingers loose and managed to turn the pages. He found the article beneath the headline

MIRACLE IN MANHATTAN.

Yanking her bifocals out of her apron pocket, Sheila perched them on her nose and read aloud in her Aussie accent. "'An uniden-tified woman survived an apparent suicide attempt in Manhattan last week.'" She clucked her tongue. "Oh my, such foolishness! 'Witnesses claim the woman jumped from the rooftop gardens of the Hotel Tremayne on Wednesday night and fell four hundred feet to the street below. Paramedics at the scene were astounded. The woman, who they said appeared to have been near death, regained consciousness en route to the hospital. She became disoriented, and even violent, breaking the arm of one paramedic in her panic.'"

Tilting her head, Sheila frowned. "My, now, but she don't look strong enough to break a twig, does she?"

Nathan gently took the newspaper from Sheila's hands, and she let him, looking at him with worry in her eyes.

Nathan read on, silently. The woman had been sedated and taken to a nearby hospital. Despite what should have been a lethal plunge, the article reported, she was unharmed but catatonic, and had been moved to a mental hospital in New Jersey.

"'No identification was found among her personal effects,'" Sheila read, the sound of her voice startling Nathan by coming from so close. She had run out of patience and was now reading over his shoulder. "'Police are asking for help in establishing her identity and locating her family. She is approximately five feet nine inches tall, of slender build, with black hair and eyes, and an olive complexion, perhaps indicative of Middle Eastern descent. The only other possible identifying features, police said, are a pierced left nostril, in which she was wearing a ruby stone—'"

"A ruby stone," Nathan echoed.

"'—and an unusual birthmark,'" Sheila read on. "Odd, they don't say what the birthmark might be."

Nathan swallowed the lump of sandstone that seemed to have lodged in his throat. "They'll keep that quiet. A genuine relative would know. That way they can filter out crackpots."

"Makes sense," she said. "Lord knows, this sorry world has enough of those."

Nathan stared at the story, willing it to tell him more, but the final line was nothing but the number to call should anyone have knowledge of the woman's identity.

He folded the paper closed, staring again at the fuzzy black-and-white photo on the front page—the one that looked so much like a woman who had been dead for well over four thousand years.

She couldn't possibly be the same person.

And he couldn't possibly rest until he knew that for sure.

He gave his head a shake, closed his eyes. Gods, it had been so long. He told himself it was an illusion, a trick of a faulty memory. But he knew better. He could never forget her . . . could never forget the woman she had been, the woman he had loved.

Or the girl he had known first . . .

The young prince removed the royal cloak with its fiery crimson fabric and gold-threaded edging the moment he got beyond the palace doors. It was cool within, but far too hot outside beneath the blazing sun to wear such heavy garments. Besides, the cloak set him apart. When he went to the *edubba* school for his daily lessons in the art of the scribe—as his father insisted he must—he preferred to look more like the other boys.

Not that it did much good. They all knew who he was. And they avoided him as if he were an outcast. No twelve-year-old boy would wish to befriend the son of his king.

And now, Eannatum thought glumly, his father had decided that he needed still more lessons to prepare him for ruling Lagash of Sumer one day. Lessons in *religion*, of all things.

And he had no choice but to obey.

He walked the hot paths from the *edubba* through the center of the city. Grasses grew lush on either side of the well-worn paths of Lagash. Palms and *hashur* trees shaded his way, growing between and around the frond-covered roofs and sun-bleached mudbrick stalls of merchants and tradesmen. He passed countless people, many with bundles on their backs, farmers come to trade and crafts-people of all kinds, some with so many crops or wares that they came with donkeys or oxen pulling laden carts along behind them. Others displayed sculptures and jewelry, pottery vessels and new clay tablets, wrapped in wet leaves to keep them moist. And even more vendors hawked fruits and vegetables and grains, costly fabrics and more. Anything you might desire could be found in his father's kingdom. The city was a thriving one, gleaming like a jewel on the banks of the Euphrates. A lush oasis in the midst of the wild desert. It made young Eannatum lift his chin a bit higher and straighten his spine as he walked.

The path wound further and then, towering before him, was the mighty ziggurat. A huge structure, a man-made mountain, bleached white by the sun and reaching into the very heavens. It was built with a massive square base. Each succeeding level was a smaller square, all the way to the sacred *cella* at the very top. It resembled a giant stairway on all sides, one that might seem to lead to heaven itself.

This was his destination, and he mounted the steps with some trepidation. Learning the ways of the temple priests and priestesses—the ways of magick, divination, healing—was a frightening prospect. Far more difficult, he suspected, than learning to make the symbols of the written language on the moist clay tablets at school. But more than the lessons themselves, Eannatum feared he might disappoint his father. And above all, he did not wish to do that. He often felt burdened by the weight of his father's expectations. He disliked being set apart from the other boys his age. He disliked being held above them, and often wished he could put on a disguise and run away to live the life of a normal boy.

Much as he might fantasize about that, though, he knew his duty. And he took honor seriously. He would do what he should . . . what he must.

He opened the door at the top of the stairs and stepped out of the blazing sun into the cool, dim corridors of the tower's lower levels. The door groaned as it slowly swung closed behind him.

Eannatum swallowed hard, looking around.

Then the flickering of a torch appeared in the distance, and a female voice said, "This way, my prince."

With a nod, he followed that dancing torchlight, barely glimpsing she who carried it. Brief flashes of her white robes, and the gold bracelets adorning her arms were all he was allowed. He was led to a small room, where baked stone tablets lined the shelves on the walls. In the center was a table of wood, with three chairs around it and a rack of unlit candles in its center.

"Sit. Light the candles and wait," the woman said. She then anchored the torch she carried in a chink in the wall and vanished like a shadow.

Eannatum sighed, wondering what would become of him were he to wander off into the depths of this massive structure. He'd been inside before, of course. During ceremonies and on the High

Holy Days. But then he'd been in the company of his father and a dozen servants. The halls had been alive with people and chanting and alight with candles and torches.

It was different now. Dark. Lonely. So dim and hollow that every step, every breath, echoed a thousand times. Haunted, he thought. His footsteps in the corridors had bounced from the walls over and over again, and it had sounded as if he were surrounded by netherworld ghosts.

He took the candlestick to the torch in the wall, lifted the wicks to the dancing flames, and lit them one by one. Then he carried the softer candlelight to the table and replaced it in the center. Waiting had never been his favorite thing to do. As the son of the king, he rarely had to tolerate it. But today he must. So to pass the time, he removed the moist clay tablet from the sack he carried, and took out the stylus reeds as well. He might as well work on his lessons as sit here wasting time.

He was still bent over the tablet, pressing symbols into clay with the reed, when the priestess stepped into the room. At her side was a girl, younger than Eannatum by two years, at least.

The priestess was beautiful, as was every priestess Eannatum had ever seen, be she young or old, plump or poor. There was a kind of emanation from women who served the Goddess. A glow that seemed to come from within, making them beautiful to any eye that beheld them. What they might actually look like seemed to Eannatum to have very little to do with that beauty.

But the girl . . . the girl was different. Stunning. Her eyes were large and round, thickly fringed with extravagantly long, curling lashes and gleaming black in the candlelight with an intensity that took his breath away. Her brows were thick and dark, her lips, lush and red. And there was something else about her . . . something invisible, yet real all the same. It was something that went beyond that inner light that all priestesses possessed. He didn't know what it was, but he was certain it was real. She made his stomach clench tight and his skin heat and tingle. The feelings confused him.

The priestess bowed slightly. "Welcome, my prince," she said. Then she nudged the little girl beside her.

The girl looked startled. "Prince?" she asked. "Are you Prince Eannatum?"

"Yes," he said, smiling slightly when her eyes went wider.

Again the priestess nudged the girl, and this time the girl bowed, but only halfway. She never took her eyes from Eannatum's. And when she straightened, she looked up at the priestess, a question in her eyes. "Lia, what is the prince doing here?"

The priestess smiled at the girl. It was obvious to Eannatum that the woman loved the child very much. He wished yet again that his own mother had lived beyond the day of his birth, that he might have known such love. But regrets were a waste of his thoughts.

To distract himself, he answered the girl's question himself. "My father feels that if I am to be fit to rule one day, I need more education than just that of the *edubba*. He wishes that I learn all the tales of the Gods and of creation. All the rites and divinations mastered by priests and priestesses. And all the secrets of magick."

"Yes," the priestess said. "All the very same things you are learning here with us, Nidaba," she told the girl.

"The king is very wise," the girl whispered.

Her name was that of a goddess, and Eannatum remembered hearing talk about her, but just then he was too busy watching her to recall it. He had placed all his stylus reeds into a pottery vessel on the table, and the girl's eyes kept darting to them. He saw eagerness and longing unmistakably gleaming from their ebon depths.

"This is my charge," Lia said to him. "Her name is Nidaba."

He nodded, noticing for the first time the onyx pendant the girl wore around her neck. As shiny and black as her eyes. And it came to him what he'd heard of her before.

"You are the one they say is born of a goddess," he said.

"That is what some say, yes." She moved forward without being asked and sat down at the table, her eyes still flicking over the stylus reeds every few seconds and over the clay tablet on which he'd been doing his assignment.

"I was hoping you might allow Nidaba to join us in your lessons, my prince," the priestess Lia said. "She is truly the most gifted student we've ever had here at the temple. She will be a powerful priestess one day."

At the praise the girl smiled, bowing her head slightly but beaming with pride all the same.

"I thought you two might become friends," Lia continued. "Learning is always easier with a friend at your side."

Eannatum looked warily at the girl. "Are you not afraid to be my friend?" he asked.

Her chin came up. "I am not afraid of anything. Why should I be?"

Such a spirited reply surprised him. He tried not to smile, because he thought it would offend her. But he found her truly amusing. So small, so pretty . . . and yet obviously not the least bit intimidated to be in the presence of her future king. "Not afraid of anything?" he repeated, lifting his brows.

"No."

"I don't believe you. What about a lion? Surely you would be afraid of a lion?"

"What could a lion do to me?" she asked, tilting her head to one side.

"Kill you and eat you, of course!"

Nidaba looked very thoughtful. "Then perhaps I should finally be able to know my mother and my father."

Eannatum fell silent for a moment. He could see the sadness in her eyes, hear it in her voice. His own voice was softer when he said, "They are dead, your parents?"

Nidaba shrugged. "They must be dead. Or else why would they not have kept me to raise for their own?" She looked down at the table. "Unless they simply did not want me."

"No," Eannatum said quickly. "It couldn't have been that." And he meant it, though he barely knew her.

"Why couldn't it?"

He smiled at her, seeing a slight moisture now glistening in her downcast eyes. "You are wise, your priestess says. It's plain that you arc brave as well. And you are quite the prettiest girl in all of Lagash. Only a fool would give such a child away."

The girl's head came up quickly, and she presseed her hands to her cheeks. They grew pinker, and she smiled. Eannatum saw the moisture in her eyes vanish and felt extremely pleased with himself.

"Why would you think I might be afraid to be your friend, Prince Eannatum?" she asked at length.

"If we are to be friends, you must call me Natum. I like it far better."

"All right—Natum, then. Surely the other boys at the *edubba* school are your friends. Aren't they?"

"My friends?" he asked, lifting his brows. "They are afraid even to sit too close to me, in case they might make some mistake and offend me, thus incurring my father's wrath."

Nidaba smiled at him. "More likely they're afraid you'll tell your father of the mischief they make." Then she leaned closer over the table. "But I *do* know how it feels, Natum. Girls give me a wide berth when I pass them in the streets."

"And why do you suppose that is?" he asked, fascinated by her even though he was not entirely certain just why.

She shrugged. "I think they fear that I really *am* part deity, and that I can incinerate them with my divine glare." As she said it she narrowed her eyes to slits, demonstrating what she perceived to be a frightening look. It only made him smile wider.

"And can you?"

Her smile was swift and brilliant, and so stunning he had to gasp for his next breath. She crossed her arms over her chest, and settled back into her chair again. "I have never tried. But I promise not to try it on you, so long as you promise not to report my mischief to your father."

"It's a bargain, then."

Reaching across the table, he clasped Nidaba's hand in his, and the feeling that went through him was like none he had known before. A tingling, jolting sensation that made no sense. Her eyes widened and leapt to his, and she drew her hand back quickly, staring down at her palm. So she had felt it too, then. How very odd. It had to be a sign. An omen.

"You will be my first real friend," he said, already sensing that it was true. And he reached out again to take her hand.

Warily she slid her hand into his, and again there was that jolt, but only briefly. It passed in an instant, and he closed his hand around hers, cradling it, and liking the feeling.

"And you will be mine," she told him in return, her hand warming beneath his as their fingers laced and their eyes seemed to lock.

Lia cleared her throat. Eannatum released Nidaba's hand quickly, and they both looked up at the priestess. "Nidaba can be a great help to you in your lessons," she told Eannatum. "She is already far more talented at divination and certain healing rites than many of the priestesses in the temple."

"Than *all* of them, she means," Nidaba whispered behind her hand, her eyes sparkling with mirth.

Lia sent her a quelling look. But the remark only made Natum like the girl more. "I'll be grateful for the help," he said. "My work at the *edubba* takes up most of my time, and for these added studies I will take any help offered. But . . . but I would wish to repay your kindness in some way, Nidaba. Is there anything you would like in return?"

Nidaba's gaze fell again upon the clay tablet, covered with wedge-shaped figures. Then she looked up at Lia. The priestess nodded once. Licking her lips, facing Eannatum once more, Nidaba said, "Yes. There is something. Something I wish for more than anything in all of Sumer." She reached out and gently took the reed stylus from the pottery cup. Staring at it, she whispered, "I wish to learn the script."

For some reason, the declaration seemed perfectly logical. It didn't surprise him in the least. Though he supposed it should have, since girls were no longer allowed to learn the script. It had always seemed an odd law to him, but it had been that way for his entire lifetime. His father said it had not always been so. "Then I will teach you," he said.

Her eyes widened as she looked from the pen to his face. "You will? Honestly, you truly will?"

Smiling, he bent down, reached into his pack on the floor, and pulled out a new tablet, still wrapped in moist leaves. Unwrapping it, he placed it on the table, took a fresh reed from the cup, and carefully inscribed the symbols that stood for Nidaba's name into the clay.

Fascinated, the girl came around the table to stand beside him, leaning over him to see what he had done. "That . . . that's my name," she whispered. "Just like on my pendant."

"Yes." He pushed the tablet sideways so it was in front of her. "Now you make the symbols. Just the way I did."

She stared at him, blinking, looking doubtful, but he nodded at her. She bent over the tablet, clutched the stylus awkwardly, and began. Eannatum watched, occasionally covering her hand with his own to help her guide the stylus reed. The result was clumsy, sloppy, but legible.

And her eyes were brighter than any two stars in the Sumerian
night sky. "I did it," she whispered, awestruck.

It amazed him that such a small thing could mean so much to
her. And it amazed him even more that seeing that light in her eyes,
and knowing he was the one who put it there, could make him feel
the way it did.

"Thank you, Natum," she whispered. "You have given me a gift
more precious than anyone ever has. And I will not forget. Not even
if I live forever."

"Don't be silly," Eannatum said with a grin. "No one lives forever."

Folding the newspaper and setting it carefully aside, Nathan
looked up at his two dearest friends. He had been living the life of a
mortal for a long time. He'd had no contact at all with others like
him. He loved this life of his. And he knew—dammit, he knew full
well—that he would be risking all he had built if he did what he felt
compelled to do.

And yet he had no choice.

"I can't explain this to you . . . but I need to go there."

"Go where, Nathan?" Sheila asked.

He cleared his throat. "To New Jersey. To . . . to this hospital. I
need to see her." Lowering his head, fixing his gaze on that fuzzy
photo once more, he muttered, "I need to be sure."

chapter 2

Masses of raven hair, uncombed, unwashed and tangled, spilled over the shoulders and down the front of her straitjacket. She sat on the floor in the darkest corner of her locked room. Knees drawn up to her chest, eyes focused on nothing and utterly vacant. Onyx eyes. Thick, dark lashes. She never blinked, seemed totally unaware of Nathan, peering at her through the tiny square of double-paned, mesh-lined safety glass in the door.

"So?" Dr. June Sterling asked. "Do you know her?"

There was a tight knot in Nathan's chest. This couldn't be . . . it couldn't be Nidaba. "Can I go inside?" he managed, though his voice came out hoarse and barely audible.

"It's your neck." The short, slender woman with her bobbed auburn hair and gold-rimmed glasses took a jangling key ring from her pocket and unlocked the door. "Just don't get too close."

"I don't imagine she could hurt me if she wanted to," he said, staring at the heavy-lidded eyes veiled by locks of matted hair. "It looks as if she's drugged to the point where she's not even lucid."

"Mild tranquilizers don't make people catatonic, Mr. Smith." Pushing the heavy door open, the doctor stood back to let him pass.

"Not most people, no." He walked into the room, saying nothing more. What could he say? That in immortals, certain drugs could have exaggerated effects? No, of course he couldn't. Not without ending up in the padded room next to this one. So he said nothing at all.

He stood there for a moment, just staring at the woman, torn between hoping she was Nidaba and hoping to the Gods she wasn't. Because he'd known Nidaba. Fiercely proud, stubbornly independent. She would hate the way he'd been living his life, he thought vaguely. She had been the opposite of this boring man he had created. Free. Unashamedly proud to be who and what she was and refusing to tone it down or hide her truest self for anyone. And let those who had a problem with that be damned.

No, the Nidaba he had known wouldn't like Nathan Ian King very much. Not the way she had liked King Eannatum.

And she would rather have been dead than reduced to this . . . this . . . shell of a woman. If she was aware of her surroundings, the confinement alone would have been enough to drive her mad. She had always been a free spirit. The freest he had ever known.

This woman could not be that fierce priestess he had known. She could not be his Nidaba.

His throat painfully tight, Nathan spoke without turning, his eyes on the pathetic piece of humanity curled into the fetal position on the floor in front of him. "Leave me alone with her, will you?"

"I don't think—"

"Just go out and close the door. I'll take full responsibility."

"Mr. Smith, that isn't—"

"For the love of God, *do it*." If he put some small portion of his power into the command, he couldn't help it. Manipulative it may be, but, dammit, he needed privacy. He needed to see her. To touch her.

To *know* . . .

Dr. Sterling said no more. She backed out, her steps echoing as she left. The door groaned as it closed again. Good. Nathan braced himself, took a deep breath, told himself this woman wasn't Nidaba. She couldn't be Nidaba. He crossed the room to where she sat on the floor, moving slowly so he wouldn't startle her. "Hello," he whispered, keeping his voice low, filling it with tranquility and calm. Whoever she was, the last thing he wanted to do was frighten her. "I've come to visit you. Is that all right?"

The woman didn't move. Didn't blink. Just sat there, her knees drawn up, arms wrapped around them, head tipped down against them, hair curtaining her face. Her hospital gown had bunched around her hips, and her underpants were showing. He couldn't see her hip. If she were immortal—and Nidaba or not, he suspected she must be immortal—the mark would be there. She was still rocking slightly back and forth, forehead to her knees. Her tangled hair was wild, and the room smelled of disinfectant and vaguely, urine.

Nathan moved closer, crouched before her, and very slowly lifted a hand to her hair. For more than a week she had been confined here. And he had to wonder if she had been bathed or properly cared for once in all that time. Her hair was matted, knotted, and dull. He touched that hair, pushed it aside and tried to see her face. But she tipped her head downward even more sharply, and she hunched her shoulders against him.

"It's all right," he whispered. "I just want to see you."

Her rocking had stopped. She sat rigid, tense. Trembling.

She was afraid of him. And while he was sorry for that, it made him even more certain that she could not be Nidaba, despite the resemblance. Nidaba had never been afraid of anything.

He lifted his hand again. She flinched.

"I'm sorry, I didn't mean to frighten you." Sighing, Nathan lowered his hand, and his gaze with it. And then he saw the edge of a berry-colored birthmark, just peering out from the bottom of the hospital gown, on her right hip. His mouth went dry as he moved his hand to the gown, touching only the fabric, not the woman, watching her the whole time and seeing not a flicker of interest in her unfocused, unblinking eyes. He lifted the edge of the gown. And he saw it—the crescent moon emblazoned on her right hip. His stomach heaved, and his back bowed with the force of it. Nathan bit his lip to keep the shock from taking over, tried to reason with his own mind.

Immortal. Yes, whoever she was, she was that. But he had already suspected that might be the case. For her to have survived the fall from the top of that building, to have revived in the ambulance, to have had the strength to fracture the arm of an attendant—she

would have had to be an immortal High Witch. She was one of the
Light Ones, obviously—if she were a Dark Witch, the mark of the
crescent would be on her left flank rather than the right. But that
didn't mean she was his Nidaba. It couldn't mean that.

It mustn't . . .

"Nidaba?" he whispered.

He touched her chin, to tip it up. The jolt sizzled through him at
the contact, as happened whenever one immortal High Witch
touched another. Like a static charge, only magnified.

She jerked away so fast that her head slammed into the wall behind her. Had the wall not been padded, he was certain she would
have split her skull.

"Easy, easy," he said, his voice low, soft, coaxing. "I need to look
at you . . . please . . ." Softly, very gently, he cupped her chin again.
She flinched, but not so violently this time. And, finally, he managed
to turn her face up so he could see her. Her tangled hair fell away, revealing her fully to him.

Sunken eyes, haloed in gray. Hollow cheeks, jaw too sharply de-
lineated. Despite all of that, he knew this face—knew it well. His
eyes drank in every bit of it, but only for a moment. Because his vision became clouded . . . with tears he thought he'd finished shed-
ding long ago. Seeing her hurt—*physically hurt*—like a blow too
powerful to withstand. It was a moment before he could even manage words.

"By the Gods, it *is* you," he whispered. "Nidaba . . . what's happened? What's happened to you?" Instinctively, he put his arms
around her shoulders, pulled her to his chest, rocked her slowly—
but it was like embracing a corpse. There was no response. No reaction. Barely any warmth at all. Nothing even to indicate that she was
alive. And yet he held her against him, held her close as he hadn't
done in too long . . . and realized he was trembling fiercely.

Finally he withdrew his arms from around her, settling his hands
on her shoulders instead. He stared into her expressionless face.
"Where are you, Nidaba?" he whispered. "Where have you gone?
Can you hear me at all? Do you even know I'm here?"

She didn't blink, didn't flinch. Just curled there limply, eyelids at
half mast, head heavy on a boneless neck. He had believed her dead.
He had mourned her to the point of madness. He had existed in living anguish for years before he had even begun to recover from her

loss. And he never had recovered from it—not fully. Now, his head was spinning—he was reeling with the realization that she had been alive all this time. And he had never known. Never . . . but then again, he hadn't known there *were* such beings as immortal High Witches when he'd known Nidaba. He hadn't learned any of that until much, much later. And by then she had been dead . . . her body burned to ash.

Or so he had been led to believe.

He didn't think Nidaba had known what she was back then, either. But she had learned all the secrets, in time. And when she had, she would have realized that he was immortal as well. Why hadn't she come back to him, then? Why hadn't she sought him out, found him, told him she was alive? Why would she have hidden from him all this time?

The door opened. He felt a cold draft but dismissed it quickly. "Well?" Dr. Sterling asked from the doorway. "Is she the woman you thought she was?"

Slowly, Nathan gathered his wits. He couldn't take his eyes off Nidaba. Sitting there, vacant eyes staring at nothing, mouth slightly agape and wet. If he took her from here now, openly, the papers would run the story. Nidaba had already become fodder for human-interest stories. The tale of the woman who had survived a fatal fall would be told, and they would track her down, track him down, despite his use of a false name. His haven, his perfect, anonymous life, would be ruined. And he would have gladly allowed it to be, for her sake. But it wouldn't end there. If her whereabouts were known, Nidaba would be in danger. She wouldn't be able to defend herself in this state. He needed to take her away from here, in secret. Protect her. Try to . . . try to reach her again, through that darkness into which she'd fallen.

"Mr. Smith?" Dr. Sterling asked.

"No," he said. "No, she's not the woman I knew. I'm sorry I wasted your time." But with his back to the doctor, he leaned close to Nidaba and whispered into her ear, "I'll be back for you. I promise. I'll take you out of here, Nidaba. I'll make you well again. It won't be long."

He thought there was a hitch in her shallow breathing. Perhaps a flicker in her eyes. But nothing more. From her, at least. The reaction in Nathan was nothing short of catastrophic. He was trembling even harder than before, from somewhere down deep. He felt it right to his bones. He brushed his lips over her cheek and got to his feet, but his knees seemed almost too weak to carry him. His steps were as uneven as a drunkard's when he started toward the door. Everything in him rebelled at the notion of leaving her behind, even for a little while.

"Thank you," he said to Dr. Sterling as she held the door for him.

She closed it, the locks clicked into place, and he thought he was going to vomit.

"It was no trouble at all," Dr. Sterling said. "The exit is that way, just down the stairs and—"

"I know where the exit is."

He walked away in a daze. He didn't know what had happened to Nidaba to bring her to this point. How she had survived this long, or why she had never sought him out. He only knew that when he took her from this place—and he *would*—he must leave no clue as to where she had gone. He wouldn't risk drawing hordes of reporters to his door. Because they would be followed, and in very short order, by hordes of immortals. Dark Ones. And his quiet existence would come to a violent end. As would Nidaba's life.

He hadn't recognized her!

Dr. Sterling stood in the hall, watching the man who called himself John Smith as he walked away. She waited. He rounded the corner, out of sight, and she heard his feet tapping down the stairs, then the closing of the doors to this wing. She let a few more minutes tick by, ensuring that he'd had time to leave the hospital, get into his car, and drive away. Then, finally, she pressed her palms lightly to the front of her face, heels of her hands curving just beneath her chin, and slid them slowly upward, over the top of her head, through her hair, and down to her nape, wiping out the glamour she had cast.

When she took her hands away, she once again appeared as she truly was. Dark. Small. Ever young.

She almost smiled as she thought that perhaps her most well-honed magickal skill might not even have been necessary. If John Smith—or rather Nathan King, as he called himself these days—hadn't recognized his precious Nidaba, then it wasn't likely he would remember her.

Ahh, but then again, Eannatum was a wise man. His name had gone down in history as one of the greatest leaders Sumer had ever known, and not without reason. His intelligence was legend—as was his cunning. It would not do to underestimate him.

She had been afforded precious little time to plan for this. Always she'd had to keep herself hidden from Eannatum, knowing he would have killed her with his bare hands if he had crossed her path again—*if* he had ever put it all together, realized the truth of what she had done.

Yet she had managed to see him from time to time. Sometimes from a distance. Other times, using her favorite spell—the glamouric. It had become something of a game, seeing just how close she could get without his seeing through the illusion. It was an occasional lark, a way for her to pass the time, all the while laughing at him from behind her borrowed countenance. She'd had conversations with him in one guise or another. She'd shared tea with the man. She'd even toyed with the idea of seducing him. Though if she had acted on the idea, he'd have known her as an immortal at her first touch.

But in all that time, she had never seen the priestess Nidaba. Until recently, the name of Nidaba had been unspoken among immortals. And she had become convinced that the harlot truly had died in that long-ago fire, her body burned to ashes.

She should have known that was a tale too perfect to be true.

Nidaba had been alive. All the while, alive. She had certainly kept her existence a secret. Until a year ago, when that detestable name began being whispered among the Dark Ones. She was old—one of the oldest, they speculated, their tones awed, almost reverent. Her heart would be a prize worth seeking. And many had begun doing just that. Hunting her. For a time, Puabi had convinced herself that was enough. That she could just sit back and wait for one of the other Dark Witches to destroy Nidaba forever.

But it hadn't happened. So Puabi had to take matters into her own hands. If you wanted a task done properly, she had mused, you must see to it yourself. And why should she allow some other Dark Witch to claim a heart with nearly four thousand years of power pounding within its chambers? Why not make it her own?

After hunting Nidaba for months, Puabi had finally found her in the city. And she'd thought that her lust for vengeance would finally be sated. She'd altered her appearance and followed Nidaba to the rooftop gardens of a hotel, and there, Puabi had attacked. Nidaba was strong—more skilled in battle than Puabi had expected. The bitch nearly defeated her! But the Dark Witch had been prepared for that eventuality. She pulled the gun she had brought along, just in case. She could easily carve out Nidaba's heart before the woman had time to revive from a gunshot wound.

Nidaba saw the weapon, and in the split second before the shot rang out—she jumped.

Jumped.

There had been a crowd. Police. Paramedics. And Puabi thought her chance at ice cold revenge was gone—that Nidaba had outsmarted her yet again

It wasn't until she had seen the article in the newspaper that she'd realized her chance was not lost after all. Her oldest enemy was imprisoned, drugged, helpless . . . all but gift-wrapped. Just waiting for Puabi to come and claim her heart, as she should have done a long, long time ago.

Puabi had arrived here only minutes before Nathan had. She hadn't expected to see him here. She'd planned to slip in, murder the bitch, and leave with her bloody prize beating endlessly in her hands. But Nathan's unexpected appearance had ruined her plans, and she'd had to act quickly.

Just as she would act quickly now—to take the beating heart from her enemy, and claim the wealth of power from the mindless shell where it awaited her blade. It would be easy, like taking a fledgling.

She slipped her hand beneath the draped fabric of the blouse she wore, closed her fingers around the hilt of the dagger at her side, and turned toward the door of Nidaba's padded cell.

"Excuse me?" a voice said.

Puabi let go of the blade, and looked up quickly—only to see the *real* Dr. June Sterling staring at her, her identification badge pinned neatly to her lab coat. "What are you doing here? This is a restricted area."

Too late now to cast a glamour and alter her appearance to the good doctor's myopic mortal eyes. The woman had already seen her. "I . . . seem to have got lost," she said, concocting a smile she hoped looked sincere.

Dr. Sterling peered through the glass at her patient, worry in her eyes, before looking back at her again.

"The doors to this wing are kept locked."

"I guess someone forgot that rule."

"No one forgot," Dr. Sterling said, her eyes narrowing. She lifted a hand toward her side. There was a small electronic box there, clipped to a pocket of the white lab coat. She knew Dr. Sterling would summon help by pressing the button on that box. She knew in an instant, and acted just as quickly. Her blade hissed from its sheath and slid cleanly between the psychiatrist's ribs. Blood bubbled when she drew the razor-edged steel out again, and Dr. Sterling, her mouth working soundlessly, slumped to the floor. Her eyes were wide, wet, but fading.

She started to smile . . . but then she saw the stubborn woman's fingers twitch on that little box in one final effort. *Damn her!*

Some sort of alarm went off, and the formerly silent hallways seemed to come alive with slamming doors, pounding feet. No time now to do what she had come to do.

Puabi, once the most revered queen of all Sumer, leapt over the fallen doctor, and ran. Nidaba's heart—the trophy she had come here to collect—would have to wait for another time.

The woman sitting on the other side of the mesh-lined, locked door, frowned at what was happening inside her mind.

For a moment there had been a ripple in the sky, and the young priestess-in-training looked up, tilting her head to one side.

"What is it?" Natum asked.

Nidaba frowned. "A voice," she said softly. "Did you hear it?"

"No. Was it a man's voice or a woman's?"

She shrugged. "A man's, I think."

"And what did he say?" Natum asked.

"That he was coming to take me out of this place." Nidaba frowned and tipped her head to one side. "But I don't want to go."

"Don't you?"

"No. There is only pain out there. And loss."

Natum tilted his head to one side at that. He was such a beautiful boy. His almond-shaped eyes were fringed with thick lashes. He had such a strong jawline, for a boy, and the nose of a king. Thirteen now, and she'd known him for a year and a day. "How do you know of this pain?" He asked her.

"I've lived it. We both have, Natum. Don't you remember? It is our future."

"How can I remember what hasn't happened yet?"

That question caused more ripples in the fabric of the world around her. She stared harder down into the waters of the Euphrates from where she and Natum sat on its grassy bank, their robes pulled up to their knees and their feet dangling in the muddy water. She searched the blue sky and examined blazing red sun. Then she focused on the palm trees, their fronds swaying slowly in the gentle, searing breeze. Part of the sky seemed to fold away, and beyond it Nidaba saw a door, with a glass window that had wire crisscrossing it and a wall lined with some kind of cushioning.

Don't look there. Don't!

"This isn't right," Nidaba said, averting her eyes from that tear in the world. "We never had this conversation."

"No, we didn't."

She concentrated, and the rippling stopped. The world around her solidified once again. The tear was gone, the sky sealed itself in place again. "That's better," she said. "I know what this is. It's our first rite together. You've been studying for a year and a day, so to celebrate, Natum, we shall conjure a boon from the Gods."

"I was afraid you'd forgotten."

Nidaba lowered her head. "I would never forget. I . . . I even made a gift for you."

Natum smiled broadly, his white teeth gleaming in his copper-skinned face. "You did?"

Nodding, Nidaba shyly opened her pouch and extracted a tiny piece of a clay tablet, already baked hard by the sun. She handed it to him.

Natum held it in his palm, and drew it closer. He looked down at it and read aloud the symbols she had inscribed. "'Nidaba. Eannatum. Forever Friends.'" He pressed his lips together and closed his hand around the small piece of clay. "Thank you, Nidaba. I will treasure this always."

She tipped her chin up. "Even when you are a great king and your people shower you with gifts of gold and lapis?"

"This bit of clay is more precious than any of that could ever be." He opened his palm and looked at it again. "And no mistakes!"

"I had a good teacher."

"As did I . . . I hope." He looked a bit nervously toward the area Nidaba had set up. Candles stood in a circle, and a libation of honeyed wine lay at the ready, beside a dish of salt.

"We'll soon find out. Have you decided what your request shall be?"

He licked his lips. "Does the priestess Lia know we are doing this, Nidaba?"

Nidaba shook her head. "The priests and priestesses of the temple are planning a stuffy initiation rite for you, to be held in the temple *cella,* as befits a future king of Lagash," she told him. "It will be very boring, and I assure you nothing of note will happen." She smiled. "I've learned many secrets, the greatest one being that magick works best when practiced outside, beneath the sky, bare feet in the grass. But if I told them I thought so, I would be condemned for heresy."

"So might I, if we're caught," he said.

"Are you afraid?"

Holding her gaze with his, he shook his head slowly.

"Come, then." She took his hand, and again the tingling bolt rushed into her, and into him. This they had taken note of, discussed, but neither could explain it. Nor could they explain what happened next.

"My petition to the Gods should be one made for the good of all the people of Lagash, rather than for my personal good."

"Kingly already, are you?" she teased.

"I am trying to be."

What a wonderful leader he is going to become, Nidaba thought, but she did not say it aloud. She wouldn't wish to fill his head with too much arrogance or pride.

"The fishermen have been complaining of dwindling catches," Natum said. "So I will petition Enki to send an abundance of fish into the waters of the Euphrates."

Nidaba lifted her brows. "It is a good request," she told him.

They walked together to the circle, and while Natum sat down in the center, preparing himself for the rite, Nidaba walked 'round, lighting the candles one by one. Then she moved to the center and sat down, facing Natum. He lifted his palms, and she hers, and the two pressed their hands together. And together they began to chant the incantation.

"*Enki me en. Uta am i i ki Enki* . . . I am of Enki. I conjure thee, Enki."

And the sky darkened, and thunder rumbled in the distance. The waters of the Euphrates began to lap against the shoreline.

"*Ana-am ersetam nara-am!* By Heaven, by Earth, by the river!"

The winds increased, and Nidaba felt a rush of power coursing through her body. She knew Natum felt it too when his fingers laced with hers, clenching tight.

"*Amesh ikiba ul ishu-u!* Water without taboo!"

Lightning flashed, striking so close by that she felt the jolt sizzle up into her body from the ground, and her eyes flew open. They met Natum's, and she nodded once. Together they stood, facing the now roiling black waters. They lifted their joined hands, extended their forefingers side by side to point to the waters, and shouted, "Fill the Euphrates with Fish, Enki! *Akalu!*"

Lightning flashed again, this time striking the water itself and causing a huge spout to arise in its midst. The force made the hairs on Nidaba's nape stand erect, and her skin tingled. Then, slowly, the odd wind died, and the sky cleared. And when it did, she stared, wide-eyed, as fish leapt and jumped amid the now calm waters in numbers she had never seen before.

Nidaba turned to Natum and said, "You must tell no one of our rite, Natum."

"But why?" He was breathless, his brows arched in wonder as he watched the fish bounding and diving about, where before the waters had appeared barren. "We—look what we did, Nidaba! *We* caused this. We *must* tell!"

"No." She shook her head firmly. "What do you suppose the High Priest of the temple would say of a child who could command such powers as we have just done? More powers than anyone in the temple? More powers than the High Priest himself can command?"

"The High Priest is my father's most trusted adviser!"

Nidaba swallowed hard and looked at him intently. "I know more of the man than you, Natum. Please, if you are my friend, you will not speak of this."

He stared hard into her eyes. "Is it so unusual, what we've done here today?"

"Unheard of, Natum. We are a powerful force, you and I."

He nodded once, smiled gently. "Yes. We are that . . . and more. Because you ask it, Nidaba, I will tell no one."

"Thank you, Natum."

Leaning forward, he kissed her cheek very gently. "We are friends," he said. "There are no thanks needed."

When he left her there, alone, she wondered which was the greater miracle. The fish splashing about in the water . . . or the warmth his kiss had left on her cheek.

Chapter 3

"Now, do you understand what to do?"

George was frowning at Nathan in absolute concentration. "I can do it. Just the way you said."

"I know you can," Nathan told him, patting him hard on the shoulder.

They were sitting in a parked car in a rural part of New Jersey, across the street from a century-old building that still had the words "Brooker Asylum" chiseled into its stony face. It was dark outside. Midnight, and neither the moon nor so much as a single star managed to pierce the gloom. A steady drizzle misted the windshield. And it felt damn cold outside.

In his pocket Nathan had a small bottle of ether and a gauze pad. He hoped he didn't have to use it, but if he did, he figured it was far better than the alternative.

George opened the back door with a gloved hand and got out of the car, bowing his wide back against that cold, misty rain. Nathan glanced beside him at Sheila, who sat behind the wheel. "And you, Sheila? Are sure you want to go through with this?"

She pursed her lips. "If you're determined to do this, then so am I. But that doesn't mean I have to like it. And I don't, you know. I don't like it a bit. This is completely unlike you, Nathan."

"It's more like me than you know." Like the man he'd once been, he thought vaguely. Not the one he'd become. Not the one Sheila thought she knew.

"Ah, you're talkin' in circles again. If you knew the woman in the photograph, Nathan, why didn't you just say so? The authorities would have let you take her—unless she's totally insane." Sheila widened her eyes. "Is that it, Nathan? Are you bringin' a lunatic into the house?"

Nathan took a breath to bolster his waning patience. "It wouldn't be safe for this woman if anyone were to know where she was. I can't explain any more than that, Sheila, and I'd appreciate it if you would stop asking me. Just . . . trust me on this."

"Oh, sure, and suppose you're caught? What then, I ask you? Is this crazy woman worth getting yourself thrown into the pen?"

He stared at the building in the distance, with its barred windows and safety glass, and he thought of the woman he'd seen yesterday, sitting inside, a captive of this place and, perhaps, of her own mind. And he nodded. "Yes, as a matter of fact, she is. She's worth . . . anything."

"They likely have security cameras," Sheila said, continuing the argument she'd waged all the way out here. "I don't suppose you've thought of that."

"As a matter of fact, I have. It's been . . . taken care of." He couldn't tell her that he'd called up a bit of the magick he'd learned from the very woman he was about to rescue. But he had. His magickal skills were rusty, but not forgotten. Some things, once learned, were never truly forgotten. He only wished he'd thought to disable the cameras when he'd visited here yesterday. Perhaps no one would make the connection.

Sheila tipped her head to one side. "I swear, I've never seen you like this, Nathan."

"I haven't *been* like this. Not—not in a long time."

"Maybe you'll explain that remark to me one of these days."

He turned toward her, touched her cheek. "It means a lot to me, you and George standing by me like this. Insisting on coming along when I would have done it alone."

"You couldn't get by without us, and you know it. Go on with you, now. Fetch your woman and let's be away with her." She glanced toward the hospital and shivered. "This place gives me chills."

Nathan nodded, pulled on his gloves, and got out of the car. "Keep it running, Sheila." Then he closed the car door and gave his lapels a tug. Hunching his shoulders against the frigid autumn wind and slashing droplets, he crossed the narrow drive and walked along the winding path up to the old brick building. It was grim, this place. Dead leaves skittered across its lawns and sidewalks. The bricks were uneven, chipped in places, and the bars installed when the structure had been built in the 1890s remained in the arching windows. They had never replaced them with the modern mesh equivalent. The place looked like a prison. Dirty and cold. A Gothic nightmare. No night sounds reached him beyond the rustling of the dead leaves and the whisper of the cold rain. No crickets chirping. No night birds singing. But he could hear, on another level. A deeper level, even though he tried to block his own empathic tendencies. Ghosts of this building's past lingered, howling and shrieking in their madness, their torment too powerful to filter out.

No such sounds pervaded the nights around the building anymore, he supposed. Today, the terror of insanity was drugged into slumberous submission. Just as Nidaba had been when he'd seen her here the day before.

The front doors opened easily, and he walked through a foyer that looked shockingly modern—so much so that he'd been startled by it when he'd first seen it the day before. There were padded chairs and magazine racks, and a reception desk with no one in attendance, since visiting hours were long since over. The main doors stood before him, and they too were unlocked. They led only to an admitting area, a nurses' desk, and a row of administrative offices. The patients were housed on the second through fifth floors, with every stairway and elevator inaccessible without a key. *His* patient, Nathan mused, was in room 419. For a bit longer, anyway.

He nodded toward the fire alarm on the wall in the dim reception area, and George followed his gaze and nodded back. They'd planned this. Rehearsed it. Gone over it. Nathan was as prepared for tonight's adventure as he used to be when leading his army into battle. He'd bought clothes, prepared a room for Nidaba, and researched this building. He'd even studied blueprints. He was ready.

Something stirred inside him. Deep down. Adrenaline, excitement even, surged in his veins, and he thought for a moment that he felt more alive than he had in years.

George backed into a shadowy corner to count silently to one hundred, just the way they'd planned, and Nathan went through the second set of doors. A nurse looked up from a folder at the desk and said, "Visiting hours ended at seven."

"Yes, I know. I wanted to see one of your doctors," he lied. "Dr. Sterling. Is there any chance she's still here?"

"You a friend of hers?"

"A . . . colleague, actually. I was hoping to discuss a case with her."

The woman's expression eased a bit. She had a pinched look about her, even then. Narrow nose, skin a hint too pale. She didn't get a lot of sun. "I guess you didn't hear, did you?"

"Hear?" Nathan's senses went on alert.

"Dr. Sterling's in the hospital—she's critical. One of the patients upstairs attacked her yesterday."

"*What?*"

Nodding hard, the nurse rose from her chair, smoothed her dress. "Stabbed her," she said. "It's a miracle she didn't bleed to death on the spot."

"I can't believe this." Nathan's mind raced. He pinched the bridge of his nose, fighting the certainty that there was more to this than he was just now hearing. "I just saw her yesterday afternoon. When did this happen?"

The nurse shrugged. "The alarm went off just after four. We found Dr. Sterling outside our Jane Doe's room on the fourth floor, but Jane was still trussed up nice and neat. All the patients were accounted for, in fact. I still can't figure it out." She rubbed her arms, gave a little shiver. "No one saw anything unusual. It's as if a ghost did it. I'll tell you, it makes you want off the night shift in this mausoleum."

The woman had been stabbed—right outside Nidaba's room. By someone who had managed to go undetected. And only minutes after Nathan's own visit. Could all that be coincidence?

"Did they . . . did they find a weapon?" he asked slowly.

"No, actually, they didn't. Whoever it was took it with them. But we searched all the patients' rooms and—I suppose whoever did it probably hid the weapon somewhere before running back to their room. You know, some of these psychos are sharper than we give them credit for. Obviously." She shook her head. "Poor Dr. Sterling."

Nathan was so shocked to hear all of this that he nearly forgot his plan. But his nerves were bristling, and he didn't like the feeling of static dancing up and down his nape and forearms. Like a storm in the air. Something was very wrong here.

He vowed to get to the bottom of it all later, but now he steered himself back to the subject at hand. He glanced at his watch, then pretended to sniff the air. "My God . . . is that *smoke* I smell?" he asked.

The nurse sniffed, frowning and tipping her head to one side. "I don't smell anything."

Right on cue, George hit the fire alarm in the waiting room. A bell went off, and the nurse flew out from behind the desk, her key ring in hand. Others came running. She raced to the stairway doors, to the control panel there. Inserting her key, she turned it and hit a button to release the main locks. According to the building's plans and renovations, the individual rooms would still be locked, and the elevators would go to the bottom floor and shut down. But now the stairways and all the exits were unlocked. They would not be that way for very long.

The nurse ran to the first landing. Nathan headed up, too, only a few steps behind her. He could hear others coming behind them, but he knew the staff would be thin at this time of night. Still, that wouldn't stop them from questioning his presence, if George didn't hurry up and . . .

Before he completed the thought, the lights went out. "Good man," Nathan muttered under his breath. He shrugged off his overcoat, revealing the white lab coat he wore underneath it, folded his overcoat over one arm, and continued up the stairs. At each landing the head nurse shoved open a stair door and shouted behind her, sending a handful of her staff onto that floor in search of the fire. The emergency lighting finally kicked in, but it was dim.

"Do we evacuate the patients?" someone asked at the first landing.

"Not yet. Let's just make sure this isn't another false alarm first."

Nathan bit back his instinctive response to that. He wanted to chastise the fools. If the fire had been real, their hesitation could have cost lives. But it wasn't real. And he was concerned only about getting one patient safely out of here.

At the fourth floor, he simply went in with the rest as they spread out to check the rooms. His eyes were sharp, even in low light. Years of immortality tended to hone all of the senses to new levels. He chose one nurse, a small blond woman who blinked like a mole at him in the darkness when he said, "I think it's coming from in here" and led her straight to Nidaba's door.

The nurse didn't even hesitate, and the others were racing down the halls, running from room to room, getting further and further away. She unlocked the door, and Nathan gripped her hand, tugged her inside, and closed the door behind them. "Don't you smell it?" he said. "Over there, by the window."

The nurse hurried forward, and he quickly moistened a gauze pad with the chloroform in his pocket, recapped the bottle, and moved up beside her.

A second later, his hand was covering her face, and she was slumping in his arms. He laid her down gently, carefully. "Sorry about this," he said. "I didn't have a choice." Mentally, he willed her to forget this incident, but he had to hurry. He had no idea if the command would take.

But there was just no more time. He hurried to the bed where Nidaba lay still, eyes closed, totally oblivious to the alarm sounding throughout the halls.

At least she wore no straitjacket now. They must put it on her only when forced to be in the room with her. He scooped her into his arms and headed to the door. He looked up and down the hall, but the searchers had moved past this point and the path to the open stair door was clear. Taking a deep breath, he opened the door and he ran. He reached the stairway, raced down it, and emerged at the bottom after three flights.

A burly attendant appeared as Nathan crossed toward the reception area. He hadn't seen Nathan yet, but he would at any second, unless . . .

Even as the attendant started to turn toward Nathan, George's shadow fell over the man. Sensing it, the attendant whirled, but not in time. George picked the man up by the front of his shirt and tossed him aside like yesterday's garbage. Then, even as the man struggled to his feet, stumbling toward the control panel to re-engage the locks, and even as the stampeding of a dozen pairs of feet thundered down the stairs, George ran ahead, opening the doors, and holding them as Nathan carried Nidaba through. Nathan heard the locks engage as he passed. They'd only just made it out in time.

Outside, they sprinted across the lawn for the car. George said, "Let me carry her, Nathan! I'm bigger than you are."

Nathan shook his head. "Can't do that, George," he panted. Nidaba's weight was a warm burden in his arms, and her body pressed to his, even limp like this, was something he had long thought he would never feel again. Silently, he heard a little voice telling him not ever to let anyone take this woman from his arms. Not ever. But he knew better than to think that way. She had changed—even if he *could* reach her and bring her back to him, she would still have changed. And so had he. Lifetimes had come and gone, for both of them.

George opened the back door, and Nathan cradled Nidaba closer to his chest and folded himself into the car. The single attendant stepped outside the madhouse doors, rubbing his head and looking around. He had probably mistaken George for a patient and won-dered where he'd gone. But no one had seen Nathan taking Nidaba away. And Nathan hadn't been stupid enough to leave the car in plain sight. He'd had Sheila park it in a well chosen spot, away from any streetlights and with a line of shrubbery between the car and the front door of the hospital. Between those precautions, the moonless night, and the steady drizzling rain, the car was all but invisible to mortal eyes.

Still, he had no doubt that the police were on the way, or would be shortly. George went still, crouching beside the car until the at-tendant walked back inside, shaking his head. Then George ran around and got into the front seat, and Sheila shouted, "Hold on!" and hit the gas.

The tires spun a little, caught, and the car lurched into motion.

The irony of it all was far from lost on Nathan. Particularly when he could hear the sirens in the distance and when Sheila took a cor-ner too fast and the car rocked up dangerously, flirting with a two-wheeled stunt before gripping the pavement with all fours again.

"It's all right, Sheila," he told her. "They're not chasing us. At least I hope not."

She slowed down, but not by much.

For a decade, Nathan thought, he had cultivated the most mundane, most placid, staid, uneventful existence any man had ever known. And now he was breaking into a mental hospital to kidnap a patient and then speeding through the night in a getaway car. All because of a single glimpse of Nidaba's face.

She had always had this effect on his life. Always.

He held her now. Her upper body lay across his lap, her shoulder against his belly, her head resting just above his heart. The car swayed and shuddered, even now that he'd told Sheila it would be all right to slow down a bit. Streetlights fought with shadows for the right to bathe Nidaba's pale face. He pushed her hair away.

"I've got you now, Nidaba," he whispered. "Can you hear me?" With one hand he stroked her cheek. "I know you can. If you want to, you can. And I'm going to keep talking to you until you do. You're coming back from wherever it is you've gone, Nidaba. Whether you want to or not. I'll bring you back."

The car slowed a bit, Sheila finally getting the idea that the police had been left far behind them, if they'd ever been after them in the first place, which was doubtful. Or perhaps she was only distracted by listening to Nathan's soft-spoken words.

"How are you goin' to care for her, love?" she asked him.

He glanced up, met her eyes in the rearview mirror. "Take her home, clean her up, put her to bed . . ."

"She needs nourishment, Nathan. She can't eat in that state. She ought to have an IV. She could dehydrate in short order without one. She can't go to the bathroom on her own. She needs a nurse, Nathan, and how you're goin' to hire one without answerin' a lot of uncomfortable questions is beyond me."

He swallowed hard. "I'm not going to hire a nurse. Whatever care she needs . . . I'll do it myself."

"And I can help," George announced, looking anxiously at the woman lying so still in Nathan's arms.

"You've got no clue what you're saying—neither of you."

"Yes, I do." Nathan looked down at Nidaba, at her long lashes, blackest velvet lying against her cheeks. She had always had the thickest, longest lashes . . .

"Besides," he said, forcing the words past the lump in his throat. "It will only be until the drugs have a chance to clear out of her system."

Sheila sighed. "They don't drug mental patients into a state of catatonia, Nathan. She's ill."

"No. No, you don't understand. Nidaba . . . she has a . . . *reaction* to certain drugs. Most tranquilizers have a magnified effect on her. As if she'd been given ten times the normal dose."

Sheila's silence made him look up again to see her frowning ferociously into the mirror. "How do you know all this, Nathan?" Then she blinked. "And didn't I once hear you say something similar about yourself?"

He nodded very slightly, averting his eyes as he did so. "We have the same . . . sensitivity to chemicals," he explained quietly. "For all we know, without all the drugs in her system, Nidaba could be perfectly sane."

"Or completely *in*sane!" Sheila said.

There was silence in the car for a long moment. Then George asked, "Didn't the newspaper say she jumped off a building?"

"They can't know she jumped," Nathan answered quickly. "*She* certainly didn't tell them so. She could have fallen . . . or been pushed." To his own ears his voice sounded defensive and childish.

"But . . . but, Nathan, didn't she break somebody's arm in the ambulance?" George pressed on.

Sheila caught Nathan's eyes again. And he could see that she was once again suspicious of him. She was not a foolish woman. She knew he was keeping secrets—that there was something about him that wasn't quite . . . normal. He'd seen this look in her eyes before. But she was also a woman with her own secrets to keep. So she had never pressed him to reveal his.

This time, though, he might have pushed her too far.

"We're just going to have to wait and see," Nathan said softly.

George turned around, one big arm anchored on the back of the front seat as he stared back at Nathan. "I hope she doesn't break *my* arm, Nathan. That would hurt."

"I won't let her hurt you, George. You're my friend. I don't let anyone hurt my friends." He lifted a hand, gave George's shoulder a squeeze. "You trust me, don't you?"

Nodding hard, George looked a bit more at ease. "My arms are pretty big, anyway. It would be awfully hard for her to break them, I think."

"I'll bet it would."

The remainder of the long ride back passed in relative silence. George fell asleep, his gentle snoring keeping an odd rhythm. Sheila stopped asking questions, but Nathan caught her eyes on him every now and then, wide with worry, and on Nidaba, narrowed in distrust. The next several days were not going to be easy.

Then again, nothing with Nidaba had *ever* been easy. Or calm, or boring. He sometimes thought the Gods had decided to give turmoil a physical body, and his Nidaba had been the result.

She feared nothing. She dared anything. Consequences be damned.

It had always been that way. Nidaba was . . . chaos.

She learned fast, the littlest novice priestess in the temple of Inanna at Lagash. At first, Prince Eannatum had simply thought her to be unusually brilliant. At first . . . but soon, he, like everyone else in the city-state, began to wonder about her origins. Particularly after witnessing her powers firsthand.

For more than a year after that secret rite they had performed together, fishermen had been hauling more bounty from the Euphrates than they ever had. So many fish that the excess had to be salted, packed in barrels, and shipped upriver to Nippur and Kish and downriver to Ur and Eridu. And Natum wasn't vain enough to believe *he* was responsible for the magick they had wrought that day. No. It had been *her* doing.

There was something *more* to Nidaba. A power that surged through her. Made her somehow . . . more than anyone he'd known before. More alive. More beautiful. More passionate, more inquisitive. Just more. As if she truly were the child of a Goddess.

Though she would have likely punched him in the belly if he said so aloud.

Yes, she would. Despite that he was a prince. That was one of the things he loved about her. She dared *anything*.

They had been studying together for more than three years, and she had become a far more talented scribe than he would ever be, when he one day set aside his tablet and stylus and stared at her across the table. "I am tired of lessons," he said.

"Then what shall we do?" She had seen thirteen seasons by then. He had seen fifteen, but she had already grown nearly as tall as he.

He shrugged. He didn't know what he wanted to do, but he was restless. His father said it was natural for a boy of his age. That did nothing to ease the feeling, however.

"Shall we attempt some divinations? Or visit the *cella*? We could drop pebbles from the uppermost windows onto the people as they pass below!" Her smile was as bright as her eyes. And her eyes were brighter than any he'd ever seen. But even their excited gleam failed to reach him today.

"We do those things all the time. I want to go outside. I want to swim in the river and roll in the dirt!"

Her beautiful smile faded, and she tilted her head to one side. "Perhaps if you ask the guards . . ."

"Pah, they would only tell me I must behave with dignity at all times!" He shook his head. "Everywhere I go, they follow. They watch. Soon I will be finished with the *edubba*, and my father says my lessons here will end soon as well. It is time for me to move on, now. To learn the skills of battle, and of war." He heaved a sigh. "My life is nothing but lessons and responsibilities. I would give it all to be free, like you."

Nidaba got up from her chair and came round to where he stood. "I know it is difficult for you, Natum, but don't assume it is any easier for me. I too have duties, responsibilities—"

"Oh, come! The priestesses let you do just as you please! They are too afraid of you to do otherwise!"

She took a step back as if he'd struck her, and he instantly regretted his words. He reached out for her, parted his lips to speak the apology he knew he should give, but she held up a hand to stop him. "So that is what you think, is it? Let me set your mind to rights, *my prince*. They *let* me do nothing, here. I do what I please because I *dare* do what I please. I am free because I insist on my freedom. It is too valuable to me to give it away without a fight. So I do what I want, and I break their silly rules. When I am caught, I am punished for it, believe me. But the punishment is the price of my freedom, so I take it without complaint."

He crossed his arms over his chest, certain that a slip of a girl such as she would not know punishment if she saw it. "Do you, now?"

"You doubt me?" she asked, eyes going wider.

"I doubt you know what real punishment is," he said. "I would be beaten were I to defy my father. Don't you doubt it. And if you faced such consequences as I, you would understand my frustration far better."

She lifted her brows. Then she turned her back to him, and before he could guess what she was about to do, she pushed the white gown from her shoulders, letting it fall, baring her skin to him and catching the garment again only just above her hips. Her arms, her back, were unclothed, and for an instant he felt an unknown pull in his groin, and a tightening in his belly. But only for an instant. For though her flesh was bared . . . it was also marred.

Natum leaned closer, eyes widening at the strips he saw criss-crossing her slender back. He lifted the candle-rack from the table, and the golden glow fell across her coppery skin, illuminating the angry red welts, and the darker places where the skin had been ripped and the blood had encrusted.

"By the Gods, Nidaba . . ." he said on a breath. Tears stung at his eyes, and his throat went taut, even as an unfamiliar rage rose like fire in his chest. Gently, he reached out, lifted her dress up, and righted it for her. Then, placing his trembling hands on her shoulders, he turned her around. "Who did this to you?" he demanded, surprised at the depth of emotion in his voice, and the churning in his belly. "Tell me and I will have his head on a pike by dawn!"

She smiled at him, very slowly. "Listen to you, already sounding like some mighty king."

He didn't like what he was feeling. The churning in his gut, the pounding in his chest.

"I am but an orphan child, and I belong to the temple—as much as I am capable of *belonging* to anything or any*one*. The priestesses are kind and loving. But you know how stern the old High Priest can be."

"Lathor did this to you?"

"Yes. Your father's most trusted adviser, the High Priest of the temple, has a fondness for the scourge that goes, I believe, beyond what is holy." She shrugged. "He enjoys it, I think. But for the most part, I am able to avoid him."

"And what grave offense brought about such a punishment?" Natum asked, his anger still seething.

She shrugged. "I took a date from the offering plate set before the stone image of a deity in the *cella*. I have done so for years, whenever I please. This time he saw me. And when he asked for an explanation, I replied that the goddess lives in me, and therefore I have every right to eat her dates."

"You *said* that?" He was amazed.

"Lathor called it blasphemy and took the scourge to me." Again, that slight shrug. "He is very lucky that I have learned to control my anger," she said softly. "I wanted to bring the entire tower crashing down upon his hairless head."

And for some reason, as she said it, Eannatum had the feeling she could have done exactly that.

"I still believe I am right and he is wrong," Nidaba went on. "And I told him so, when he finished whipping me."

Lowering his head, shaking it slowly, Natum tried to quell the nausea in his belly. "Gods, Nidaba, do you fear nothing?"

"What is there to fear?" She shook her head. "I wanted the date, I knew the consequences of taking it—*if* I were to be caught. I usually am not, you know." She shrugged as if it mattered not in the least. "You want to go outside without your guards, and you know the consequences of doing so—*if* you're caught. So tell me, is it worth the risk to you, Natum?"

"How can you even speak of this when your back bears the marks of Lathor's scourge? He must be made to pay!"

She rolled her eyes. "You do tend to change the subject, Natum. I am used to Lathor's scourge. It doesn't hurt so much after the first day or so. And if he deserves to be punished for what he does to me, the Goddess will see to that. Or, I will, when I am grown and no longer under his care."

"You will not have to. And this will not happen again. Mark my words, Nidaba."

She smiled very slowly. "Do you want to go out without your guards, my prince, or don't you?"

Looking into her eyes, he managed to put his anger aside. They glowed, her eyes, with a gleam of excitement, and somehow, despite his fury at the High Priest, he felt an answering excitement well up within him. One that only she seemed able to provoke. "Yes," he said, "I do."

"And do you dare to do as you please, despite the consequences?"

"I do," he repeated.

"Then come with me." She offered her hand. He took it, felt the tingling sensation he always felt when they touched, and let her lead him through the ever-darkening hallways of the ziggurat tower, down sloping passages and hidden stairways, into the very bowels of the place, and lower. He grabbed a torch as they passed. Otherwise, he thought she'd have gone in utter darkness and been content.

Truly, she feared nothing.

"Here," she said at length, pushing hard on a block of stone that was easily larger than she was. It moved a bit in the wall, and Natum joined her, shoving hard at it. To his surprise it gave, moving inward, sliding on its own once they got it started. It revealed a passage to the left and one to the right.

"This way," she said, grabbing his hand once again.

He followed her into the darkness, and the huge stone slid back into place behind them by means of some hidden mechanism. He'd seen similar passages in the palace, but he'd never explored them. She would have, he thought. Nidaba would leave no mystery unexplored.

They walked for a time and soon emerged from what appeared to be a cave, half covered in sandy soil and reeds, into a grove of trees and grasses on the far side of the river. Blinking in the light, Natum looked across the water and saw the pristine white tower and the palace with its jeweled roof gleaming in the sun.

"We crossed beneath the Euphrates!" he said in amazement.

"Yes, and none of your guards are in sight. And look how far away the temple is! They cannot even see what we do here."

No one could see them there, it was true. And that place, that grove of untended lushness on the far banks of the Euphrates, became their hideaway. Where they could run and romp, climb trees and splash in the water, behave as normal children instead of as a future king and a future priestess.

That was, he had thought much later, where he had first fallen in love with her.

They hadn't been caught . . . not that time at least. But he'd decided then and there that it would be worth the consequences even if they were. To him, anyway. As for the so-called punishments Nidaba had suffered . . . he vowed to see to that as well.

The opportunity came later that same night, in his father's palace. Natum saw the High Priest Lathor exiting his father's throne room, resplendent in robes threaded with gold.

"*Ea* Lathor," Natum said, "might I have a private word?"

Turning, Lathor cupped his right fist in his left palm and bowed slightly, a greeting of deepest respect among Sumerian men. "Of course, my prince," he said. But for all his show of respect, there was none in the man's patronizing eyes. His eyes looked at Natum as a boy, not a man.

But the prince did not *feel* like a boy just then.

He nodded toward a smaller room, and the priest walked into it, taking a chair only after the prince had closed the door and waved a hand toward one. Eannatum himself remained standing.

"What is it, young prince? Do you require counsel of a spiritual nature?"

"No, Lathor. I require an explanation."

Lathor's brows rose. "An explanation? Whatever for, my prince?"

"For the marks of the scourge I saw today, cut into the back of a girl in your care."

Lathor frowned, then gasped, making his eyes wide. "Do you mean Nidaba? But how could you have seen . . . Prince Eannatum! Have you . . . *known* the girl?"

Natum had not realized he was capable of delivering his father's very well-known glare, but he did it then, and saw the priest pale in reaction. "I owe you no answer to such a question, Lathor. I am your prince, and that you would *dare* ask a question like that one leaves me to doubt your judgment even more than I already did. But for the sake of the young priestess—"

"Nidaba is no priestess, but a foundling and a student," Lathor interrupted. "And an unruly one, at that."

"Nidaba is more priestess than any woman in the temple," Eannatum shot back. And again, the High Priest fell silent. Good. "For the sake of her good name, I will deign to answer your impertinent question, Lathor. No. I have not *known* the girl. But I have seen the marks of your scourge on her tender skin."

The priest seemed relieved. He smoothed his robes. "Punishment well deserved, I assure you. Her upbringing is in my hands, Eannatum. I must see to it as I deem appropriate."

"Just as I will see to running Lagash as I deem appropriate when I take my father's place on the throne one day," Eannatum replied. He walked closer, leaned over the chair in which the High Priest sat, and braced his hands on either arm, framing the man. "And I promise you, Lathor, that should I ever see a mark on Nidaba's flesh again, my first command as king shall be the one I give to your executioner, and I shall word it thusly: *'Use a dull blade, and take all the time you wish.'*" He said the words slowly, drawing them out.

Lathor gasped audibly. "You . . . you *dare* speak to me in such . . ."

"It is only a matter of time, Lathor. My father is not a young man. I warn you, when I am king you will pay dearly for every welt on Nidaba's body. Do not forget."

The door to the room opened, and Lathor looked past Eannatum, his face easing in relief. Natum looked behind him to see his father standing there. And from the look on the king's face, his son deduced he had been listening for some time. Eannatum straightened up away from Lathor and, turning, pressed his right fist into his left palm and inclined his head. Lathor scrambled to his feet to do likewise.

No one said anything for a long moment, as the king looked his son right in the eye. Natum returned the steady gaze, not blinking or looking away. Then finally the king met the eyes of his adviser instead, and he spoke. "Lathor, it seems your prince has issued his first royal command. I would advise you to heed it."

Lathor's eyes widened. He sputtered once or twice, then bit his lip, bowed low, and scurried away. Only when they were alone again did Natum's father turn to him. "She will one day be a High Priestess, my son."

"She's not even an initiated priestess yet," he said.

"No. But if the talk of her talents has even a grain of truth to it, she will excel in her studies and grow into a woman of great power in the temple. And as for you, you will one day be a king. Not just of Lagash, but of all of Sumer."

"Your dreams are bigger than the ziggurat tower, Father," Natum said.

"They are more than dreams. They are strategies, plans that are already unfolding, Eannatum. But you do not need to know of them now. What you do need to know is this: Nidaba must serve her Goddess and you your kingdom. Do you understand this, Eannatum?" he asked.

Natum lowered his head. "She is my only friend, Father."

The king nodded. "She is *only* your friend, Natum. You would do well to remember that it is all she can ever be. With . . . perhaps, the exception of one night—the night of your coronation, when you must perform the sacred rite with the High Priestess of your temple. If my plans to install you to the throne of all Sumer come to fruition, and if she advances to the rank of High Priestess in time. Do you understand what I am saying?"

Natum felt the blood rush to his face, hotter with every word his father uttered. "I have never thought of Nidaba in . . . in such a way!"

His father smiled, came closer, and tousled his son's hair in an almost playful manner. "Then we'll save this talk for another time, when you have. For you will, Eannatum. You surely will. Already you are becoming a man." He smiled. "A good man. You will be a great leader one day. And you will think of this priestess in exactly such a way."

At the time Eannatum had thought his father could not have been more wrong.

But later . . . oh, later . . . he knew that it had been all but inevitable that he would think of Nidaba in the terms to which his father had alluded. Soon, all too soon, in fact, he found he was able to think of little else.

Chapter 4

Nathan cradled her in his arms in the back seat of the car as it sped through the rain-glistened night, and he remembered the day everything had changed between them.

She was fifteen. They had been in their secret place, swimming in the waters of the sacred river. The sun blazed in all its fury, baking the city. So they'd slipped away together, to cool themselves in the life-giving waters. They'd been laughing, splashing each other, ducking underneath the waves. And then, breathless and giddy, they got out and stretched themselves out on their backs among the tall, lush grasses along the riverbank, to let the sun dry their skin and their clothes.

"So what did you learn today, little priestess?" he asked her. "Have they taught you any new rites?"

He glanced sideways at her, grinning. It was a running joke between them how the magick they could work together would shock those who claimed to be far more learned about such things. Ironic, he thought, that she spent each day learning about religion and deities and powers when she ought, perhaps, to be teaching her teachers.

She didn't smile back, however. Instead, a frown puckered her brow. "Today I was taught about the Sacred Marriage Rite of the king."

"Oh." He turned his gaze skyward. It was a subject he thought unwise to discuss with her.

"You know of it, don't you?" she asked.

"Well . . . yes, I . . . I know . . . enough."

Her brows rising, she turned on her side to face him, elbow to the earth, her head resting in her palm. "You're embarrassed to talk to me about this, aren't you, Natum?"

"No!"

"You are so."

"Am not." And to prove it, he too turned on his side, facing her, just as she faced him. "I'll be king one day. Why should I be embarrassed about the sacred rite conferring my rulership?"

"Because you have to copulate with the High Priestess of the temple. That's why." She grinned. "I hope it's soon. The current High Priestess is already an old woman. If she gets any older—"

"Maybe you'll be High Priestess by then."

He blurted the words in self-defense. But the moment they were out of his mouth, her eyes shot to his, widened, and remained there. And he couldn't look away. "Maybe I will," she answered, her voice barely a whisper.

His throat was suddenly dry, tight. "I shouldn't have said that," he managed to say. "I'm sorry."

"I don't know why. I've thought of it many times." She closed her eyes, perhaps to find the courage to go on. "Wondered . . . what it would be like to be . . . more than your friend."

His stomach tightened into a knot, and he felt another place tightening, stirring, and pulling as well. His gaze drifted downward while she lay there, eyes closed, awaiting his reply. Soaking wet, her white gown was all but transparent, and plastered to her breasts, so their full, soft shape was clear to him, even to the tiny nubs at their tips. The gown clung to her belly, so he could trace the well of her navel. Sex was normal and healthy, and not something whispered about or forbidden—except if a girl wished to advance to the rank of High Priestess. She must save herself then, for the time when a king would need her. Untouched, she must draw the spirit of the Goddess into her own body. And then offer herself to the new ruler, who could be anointed king only by knowing her. By having her.

And suddenly, he felt as if he were on fire.

"Natum?"

He jerked his gaze upward again, meeting her eyes, which were open now.

"Am I pleasing to you? As . . . as a woman?"

He swallowed hard. "You're the most beautiful woman in all of Sumer. You know you are."

"Then you would not mind so much, if it were me? I mean . . . in the role of High Priestess . . . when the time comes."

He couldn't answer her. His voice fled him. So instead of speaking, he obeyed his body's demands. He leaned a breath closer and pressed his lips to hers. He kissed her slowly, tenderly, and he tasted lips he had dreamed of tasting for many nights. "I pray it will be you," he whispered, and kissed her again.

It was raining. It had been raining a little harder with every mile they had driven, and by the time they got back to Nathan's haven, it was pouring. It didn't look as if it was going to let up anytime soon. The headlights gleamed on wet gravel and shiny fallen leaves, slick with water. Everything bore that unnatural sheen that comes only on rainy, moonless autumn nights. It rained on Nathan when he carried Nidaba up the flagstone path to the house. George raced along beside him, holding an umbrella that did little good, while Sheila ran ahead to open the front doors.

So Nidaba got wet, and maybe chilled too, on such a brisk night as this. If she became ill . . .

"One step at a time," he muttered.

"What, Nathan? I didn't hear you." George started to close the door behind them, then paused. "Nathan! Nathan, look."

"Close the door, George. It's freezing," Sheila chided.

"No!" George darted back outside, and a moment later he returned with a sopping-wet dog slogging in beside him. It stopped halfway through the door, and Nathan tensed with Nidaba in his arms.

"George, that's a Rottweiler. They can be dangerous, you know."

"C'mon, that's a good dog. C'mon, now," George crooned, and the beast, easily weighing ninety pounds on a dry day, slunk inside. George closed the door, and the dog shook, sending a spray of dog-scented droplets throughout the entire foyer.

"Dammit, George!"

"Nathan," Sheila said, her tone firm. And Nathan stopped him-self, knowing better than to scold the sensitive and childlike George. "We'll deal with the dog later. Let's see to your new charge now."

Nathan nodded, knowing she was right. "Get some towels and dry that beast off, George. And be careful. If it starts growling at you . . ." He glanced back at the pair. George was on his knees now, his arms around the soaked canine, his cheek resting on its wet fur. It didn't look as if he was in any danger of being bitten.

Nathan carried Nidaba forward, leaving wet footprints on the marble floor of the foyer, and on the plush carpeting of the front parlor, and on every step of the staircase as he carried her up. It was wide, this staircase, but steep. At the second floor, Sheila again ran ahead to open Nathan's bedroom door.

He carried Nidaba through it, and into the adjoining room, as Sheila flicked on lights. Technically a part of the master suite, this smaller room would serve as Nidaba's bedroom. Nathan wanted her close to him. He wanted to be able to watch over her every moment until she was well again.

If . . .

No. She *would be* well again.

Sheila pulled back the covers of the bed they had made ready. Nathan peeled off the now damp blanket he had wrapped around Nidaba in the car. She wore only a thin hospital gown beneath it. But at least it was dry. Gently, Nathan lowered her into the bed and pulled the covers over her, tucking them tight. Swallowing hard, he straightened, staring down at her, pushing a hand through his damp hair.

"Now what?" Sheila asked, sounding skeptical. "You've got her here, Nathan. But just what you intend to do with her is beyond me."

He drew a breath, sighed, and turned to the fireplace. Logs and kindling lay ready, and Nathan drew a long, slender match from the holder, struck it against the brick, and knelt to touch the dancing flames to the tinder. As the tongues of fire licked and spread, he dropped the match but remained kneeling there, watching the fire dance. Fire.

Fire was the hungry beast that had devoured his only love . . . and her only child, or that was what he had been led to believe lifetimes upon lifetimes ago. But Nidaba lived.

What of the child?

"Nathan?"

"Go on to bed, Sheila," he said, and his voice came out harsh, raspy. "Get warm and dry and get some rest. See to it that George does the same."

"You might follow your own advice, Nathan," Sheila said. "But I know full well you won't do it, so at least change your clothes. They're damp, and you're chilled through."

He felt his lips pull into an affectionate smile. "It's a wonder I ever survived before you came along with your mothering, Sheila." His tone was teasing.

"It's more than a wonder," she replied, in all seriousness. "It's a bloody miracle."

He glanced behind him to see her shrugging and turning to walk away, back through Nathan's bedroom, and toward the hall beyond its door. "Thank you, Sheila," he called. "Good night."

"Good night, Nathan," she called back. "Try and get at least a couple of hours' sleep, will you?"

"I will."

Shaking her head, she stepped into the hall, pulling the door closed behind her, and Nathan heard her mutter, "Liar."

She knew him a little bit too well.

Straightening up from the fire, Nathan went to the windows and parted the curtains to stare out at the falling rain. It beaded like liquid diamonds on the glass, melting and sliding downward in slow motion. Beyond the rain was only blackness. The pattering sound of the droplets on the glass and the low, distant moan of the wind were lulling. Soothing, somehow.

"What will you do to me this time, Nidaba?" he asked softly, letting the curtains fall back into place. He went to the chair beside the bed and sank into it. Hooking a forefinger under his chin, he studied her. "Sleeping Beauty," he murmured. "So peaceful, so tranquil, even if you do look a bit tousled and tangled right now. But you're not those things, Nidaba. You've never been peace or tranquility. You come into my life like a sandstorm in the desert. You rain chaos on my head, and everything inside me responds by joining in the madness. And then you leave me again."

His throat tightened on the final words. Leaning forward, he closed his hand around hers. "My life was turmoil for so long. I raged, Nidaba. For centuries I raged, and I'm not even sure I knew that you were the cause. Not then. But I fought with every Dark challenger I could find. I killed with a vengeance and a taste for blood that chills me now when I think back on it. I loved like a wanton, taking my pleasure wherever and whenever I wished and never letting it mean a thing to me."

He shook his head slowly. "But how long can a man live like that? I was a hurricane, Nidaba, and eventually all that anger, all that grief, blew itself out and left me . . . empty. Drained. It took a long time. A long time to reach that point. And it only heralded a new kind of existence for me. One in which I didn't care, didn't feel . . . anything at all. I killed if I had to. Felt nothing. If sex were offered to me, I would take it, and barely feel the pleasure of release. I was a shell. I closed myself off from every emotion, blocked my mind from the touch of any feelings not my own. But eventually, that too passed."

He ran his thumb over the back of her hand, slowly, in circles, wondering if she could hear him at all—or if she would give a damn about any of this even if she could.

"Finally I settled into this life. Calm. Placid. I learned how to care for people again. To connect. Even to open myself up a little. With George, and with Sheila. They're my family. I love them, but I've never—not in all this time—felt for anyone the way I felt for you. I made a conscious decision not to. Because I couldn't have survived that sandstorm again. The angst. The loss that crippled me for so long. I settled for a life without that kind of passion, that kind of need. And it's been . . . a good life."

He reached out, touched her cheek, smoothed her tangled hair away from her face. "And now you're back. And I have to tell you the truth, Nidaba. I'm scared to death of what's going to happen next. I don't even know if you'll recognize me after all this time. Or if you'll even remember the same things I do . . . like that night . . . the first time I told you I loved you. The first time you broke my heart . . ."

There was a voice.

His voice.

The words were not clear, but she recognized the tone even though he spoke English rather than the ancient Sumerian language he'd used when she had known him. And there was, just once, a touch. A warmth, surrounding her hand.

But her memories called, and they were so warm and good—so much more so than the reality that tried to encroach on her dreamworld—that she willed herself to ignore the interruption and returned to the bliss of her mind.

"I love you, Nidaba."

She had been sixteen when Natum had first said those words to her. They had been in their favorite place, the lush oasis on the far banks of the river. And she had been secretly dreaming that he would one day say those three sweet words to her. So fervently had she wished for it that she almost thought she must have imagined it.

But he took her hands firmly in his, and he said it again. "Do you hear me? I love you."

Her lips pulled into a tremulous smile, and her eyes grew moist as she stared up into his.

Natum frowned at her. "Have you no reply?"

"I . . . I . . ." She simply could not form words. So she didn't. Instead, she leaned closer to him, tipping her head back, pressing her lips to his.

Natum's arms closed around her at once. He held her close, and he kissed her for a long time. He tangled his fingers in her long hair, pulled her body tight to his, moved against her, and tasted her mouth in ways she had only imagined. And everything inside her seemed to come alive for the very first time.

When he finally lifted his head he said, "Do not attend the initiation rite, Nidaba. Do not take the final step in becoming a true priestess of Inanna. For when you do, marriage between us will be forbidden."

"Marriage?" She whispered the word, shocked to her core.

"Of course! Nidaba, there can be no other woman for me. Don't you know that?"

Blinking, she took two backward steps. "But . . . but Natum, your father has already chosen your bride! You're to marry the princess of Ur."

"A girl I've never so much as set eyes upon," he said, grimacing.

Nidaba's throat tightened. "I have heard tales of her beauty, Natum. If that is what you fear, then you need not."

"By the wings of Enlil, woman, are you even listening to me? Princess Puabi could be as beautiful as Inanna herself, and it would make no difference. It is you I love, and I will wed no other."

Staring at him in wonder, she felt tears brimming in her eyes. "Oh, Natum. If only it could be—"

"It can be. It will. I will be king of Lagash one day, Nidaba. And when I am, you will be my queen. None other." Then his face clouded slightly, and he searched hers. "That is . . . if you wish it."

"Natum, you know I do!" she cried, flinging herself into his arms, relishing the feel of them tightening around her. "I have loved you for always!"

She felt some of the tension leave him as he held her. He was so precious to her. Reed thin, tall and gangly now. He'd shot up in height so that he stood a hand's length taller than she. And he'd begun to sprout fine, dark hairs upon his face, which he seemed reluctant to scrape away. As if he were proud of the ever thickening whiskers. How she loved him!

"If you only knew," she confessed to him, "the tears I have shed lying alone at night and thinking that you would be married to some other girl one day."

"And yet you said nothing?"

"How could I?" Then she frowned. "How can I now, when wedding Puabi would be better for you, and for the kingdom itself?"

He leaned close, resting his forehead against hers. "It will never be, Nidaba. I vow to you, it will never be. And I will never give you cause to shed a single tear, ever again."

She sighed, and smiled at him as her doubts fled.

"I will speak with my father tonight," Eannatum said. "He will understand, I know he will."

Nidaba's lovely memory faded, and darkness began to creep in around the edges of her vision. She knew, sensed, that she was leaving now, the safe haven of her most precious memories . . . sailing into storm-tossed seas, where things she would rather not think about lurked beneath the surface, like sea monsters, with great snapping jaws and razor-edged teeth. She wished then for that voice from without to come for her, to call to her, so that she could cling to it and escape the darkness.

But the voice had fallen silent, and the dream she'd been relishing became the nightmare she had not wished to recall.

The High Priest came to her chamber that night, with Lia, her beloved Lia, at his side. The priestess who had been like a mother to her. Lia's gentle hand woke her, and Nidaba instantly saw the turmoil in the priestess's eyes.

"What is it?" she asked, instantly alarmed.

"You must wake, child. You've been summoned by the king himself."

Blinking in shock, Nidaba tried to quell her fears. But they rose up all the same. The king. What could he want of her? Only one answer came to mind. If Natum had spoken to his father as he had promised he would, then that must be what had instigated this midnight summons.

"Quickly, now," Lia said, handing Nidaba her finest white *kaunake* dress, and her fringed shawl. The High Priest turned his back while Nidaba donned the garments, but he never left the room, which was so odd that Nidaba wondered at it. Did he fear she would run away? Or was it that he did not wish Lia to have a private moment with her?

Her senses prickled. Something was wrong here.

Lia dragged a silver comb through Nidaba's hair and all too soon took her hand and led her down from the level where all the bedchambers were located, to the first level, and into the grand room that was used only for the visits of foreign dignitaries or religious officials. It was very much like a throne room, she thought. Two giant stone lions stood guard at either side of a dais, and golden animals and goblets rested at intervals atop marble stands. A goddess sculpture stood in the room's center, cradling a pottery vase, from which water flowed endlessly into a golden chalice.

The king sat in a thronelike chair upon the dais. Two soldiers stood on his left and two on his right.

Nidaba bowed deeply before the king and remained that way until he said, "You may rise."

She straightened. "Long life and health to you, my king," she

said in greeting, and she fisted her hand in her opposite palm, inclining her head.

"And to you," he replied. "Sit down, Nidaba. The matter about
which I must speak to you is of grave import to this kingdom. And
to my son."

She blinked in surprise, but took the seat the king indicated.

The king looked at her steadily for a long moment. His gaze was
powerful, his very visage spoke of authority not to be questioned. "I
understand the prince spoke to you today . . . of marriage."

Nidaba lowered her head to hide the heat that rushed into her
cheeks. "Y-yes."

"When my son spoke, Nidaba, he was not fully aware of the situation facing our kingdom. Nor of the threats to his rule."

"Threats, my king?" Nidaba's head came up, and her eyes
searched the king's face. He was dark, like his son. Thick, dark hair
and bushy brows. But his jaw was not so well defined, soft where
Natum's was hard. His cheekbones were not as sculpted, and they
hid beneath fleshy skin.

"Do you know that Ur and Lagash have long been enemies, vy-
ing for rule of all of Sumer?"

"Yes, of course I know this."

"Of course," he said, nodding. "But perhaps you do not know
that an allegiance between the two would create the most powerful
force in our land. Perhaps you did not know that he who rules over
Lagash and Ur would be in a position to declare himself King of
Kish, Ruler of all Sumer."

Nidaba said nothing. She knew suddenly why the king had come
here. He meant to prevent her from marrying his son. Her throat
burned, and her eyes grew hot with tears she refused to shed.

"I have been setting a plan in motion since before my son's birth,
Nidaba. We are being threatened by enemies from all sides—
particularly by the Ummamites. United under my son's rule, we
would be at peace, a land too powerful for even the king of Umma
to think of challenging, and Lagash would prosper as never before.
When he weds Puabi, princess of Ur, Eannatum's kingship will be
sealed. He will be king not just of Lagash, as I am, but of all Sumer."

The lump that rose in her throat was almost too large to speak
around. "But he does not *wish* to wed Puabi," she said very softly, in
a voice unlike her own.

"Perhaps he *did* not. But now that I have informed my son of what is at stake, he knows where his responsibility lies. And he is eager to accept the title King of Kish and to wear the crown of Sumer. Only one thing stands in his way, Nidaba."

Blinking away tears, she lifted her chin and looked the king squarely in the eye. "And what is that, my king?"

"Oh, I think you know."

Her voice reduced to little more than a dry rasp, she said, "Me?"

The king nodded. "You. He cannot bring himself to cause you pain. He cannot retract his proposal of marriage, Nidaba. His honor will not allow it. Though it is what he wishes, he will not betray his vow to you."

She nodded slowly, and the first of many tears finally spilled over and rolled down her cheek. "So you have come to me, to ask me to betray my vow to him instead," she murmured, understanding at last.

"Not to ask it," he said, his voice firm. "I am your king. My duty is to my country. As is my son's. Your duty is to obey. You will refuse my son's offer of marriage. It is the only way to free him of this promise."

Licking her dry lips, she battled a soul-deep tremor. "Respectfully, my king, how can I believe this is what Natum truly wants?"

"What he wants is of little consequence. His duty is to Lagash." He slanted a quick glance toward Lia, who stood behind Nidaba. "And what you believe matters very little. But your teacher knows the truth of this. Lia?" the king said. And he lifted a hand toward the priestess.

Nidaba turned and saw her, very pale, and trembling, one of the king's guards at her side, with a hand firmly around her forearm. Her heart raced as Lia, eyes cast downward, said, "The king speaks the truth, Nidaba. I heard it from the prince's own lips. He wishes to wed Puabi . . . for the sake of Lagash, if not for his own."

Every part of Nidaba's body began to quiver. "It's a lie!" She shot to her feet and ran toward the door. But Lathor, the High Priest, stepped into her path and blocked her flight. "You have not been dismissed, Nidaba. This is not finished."

She stood there, trembling, battling the sobs that were tearing at her breast. She squared her shoulders and stared defiantly at Lathor. "I believe none of this! Natum wants me, not some spoiled princess.

You force my own priestess to lie to me, and you expect me to believe it?"

"As your king told you, woman, it is of no concern to us what you believe. You will do as we command."

A cry was wrenched from Lia, and when Nidaba spun toward her, it was to see Lia forced to her knees, the king's soldier gripping her shoulder.

"If you don't," Lathor went on, "then it's painfully obvious that you've been taught poorly. A priestess who can't even manage to teach obedience to one orphan girl is not one we would reward."

Nidaba understood suddenly, vividly, clearly. If she did not obey, it would be Lia who would suffer the wrath of the king. Of Lathor. Oh, if the punishment were hers alone, Nidaba would gladly bear it. But she knew too well how cruel Lathor could be. And she couldn't bear the thought of him taking the scourge to Lia. Goddess, if he'd beaten Nidaba bloody so often over the minor offenses she had committed, what would he do to Lia over something this significant?

He might even kill her.

Lia's eyes met Nidaba's. And Nidaba saw the plea in them. The priestess was afraid. Bowing her head in despair, Nidaba sighed. "What must I do?"

"Ahh, much better. Perhaps you've learned something from us here in the temple after all," Lathor said. "It is very simple, really. Since you have been so eager to break the law and learn the script, you must compose a message to the prince. Tell him you have decided that your promise to the Goddess is more sacred than your promise to him, and that you intend to take your initiation as her priestess."

Nidaba lifted her head slowly. "He will never believe it."

"His belief will be my concern, Nidaba," the king said, his voice deep and none too steady. "Yours is only to compose the message."

A guard took Nidaba's arm, led her to a waiting chair, and drew a small table before her. Upon it was a moist clay tablet and a selection of stylus reeds. Apparently there had never been any doubt that she would comply with the king's wishes.

"Have I no other choice?" Nidaba asked, looking around the room as tears began to pool in her eyes again.

"None," the king told her. "But you will have compensation, Nidaba. You will be richly rewarded for your loyalty to my son."

"Your rewards don't interest me in the least. Nor does compensation from a king who would threaten a priestess to bring about his own ends."

"Be very careful with your words, girl."

Nidaba held his gaze for one long moment, then sat down and took up the stylus with a trembling hand. Then she put it down again. "No," she said. "I will do what you wish, but I will say my piece first. I may not yet be a priestess, but I have studied and learned, and I know the Goddess would not approve of these events. Conspiracies and threats, deceptions and cruelty. You are king. You rule by her favor. There was a time in this land when no one was more revered than a priestess of the Goddess. Now, we are treated as servants to the kings, rather than as his most valued advisers. Worse yet, we've become servants to the priests! Kings and soldiers talk of war and invasions and battles and conquests. Their concerns are of earthly power and might, rather than spiritual enlightenment and wisdom. I have studied our kingdom's history. I have seen the way these things have changed over the past century. It is wrong. And one day soon, mark my words, Inanna will have her vengeance!"

With every word she spoke, the king grew more pale, until he was on his feet and trembling with rage. He lifted a hand, pointed a finger at her. "Silence!"

"I will never be silenced."

He was quiet, staring at her, his lips thin. Then he sat down again, with a sigh as if of surrender. "So be it," he said. Then he glanced at the soldier who stood holding Lia's shoulder. "Kill the priestess."

The soldier's sword flashed in the torchlight as he yanked it free, lifted it high. Lia cried out.

"No!" Nidaba shouted. "No, no, please!"

The king held up a hand, and the soldier paused with his sword in the air. Looking at Nidaba, the sovereign of Lagash lifted his brows. "Well?"

Blinking in shock at the heights of cruelty she had never before perceived in the man, Nidaba sat down at the small table and finally picked up the stylus again. "I'll do as you wish," she said. But she told herself that this would not be all there was. She would speak to Natum herself. Privately, away from these authoritarian eyes. She would go to him just the moment she was out of their sight. She would explain to him that she had done this only to save the life of her priestess. She would give him one last chance to tell her that it was all a lie. That it was she he wanted. Not Puabi. No matter what his father said.

She *had* to do that much.

Bending over the clay, Nidaba pressed the symbols into its face, writing exactly what the king had told her to write, rather than risk any further trauma to poor Lia, who was shaking so hard now she could not even get up from her kneeling position on the floor. There was wetness spreading on the stone floor beneath the terrified priestess's knees and staining her robes, Nidaba realized, her heart wrenching in her chest.

Swallowing hard, she finished the message. Lastly, she removed the pendant from her neck—the small bit of onyx with the name "Nidaba" inscribed on its face. She rolled it gently over the clay, impressing the symbols there.

Then sitting up, she replaced the pendant at her throat. "It is done," she whispered. But she felt empty inside.

"Lathor," the king said.

At his word, the High Priest came to the table, turned the tablet around, and perused the symbols Nidaba had made upon it. When he finished, he nodded. "It is good," he said to the king.

Nidaba got to her feet, though her legs were shaking so hard with tightly leashed rage she could barely walk upright. Her back straight, furious tears leaking through despite the battle she waged against them, she wished only to flee to the haven of her chamber and let loose the torrent while she gave them time to go their way. And then she would slip out and find a way to see Eannatum—even if it meant scaling the palace wall to his chamber window. Unsteadily, she moved toward the doors.

But suddenly the king's soldiers were at her sides, gripping her arms and stopping her progress. She bit back a cry, and looked up with narrowed eyes from one to the other of them, then glared at the king. "What more do you wish of me?" she asked, as he rose and came forward. "I have done as you commanded! Why do your men treat me as if I am a criminal now?"

"Silence, Nidaba. You have served your king, your prince, and your kingdom well this day, despite your insolence. And you will be rewarded, for I am a man of my word. But you've shown me clearly that you are every bit as headstrong and stubborn as Lathor warned me you were. I need to do what is best for my kingdom."

"I don't under—" But even before she finished speaking, one of the soldiers was pulling her hands behind her back and binding them tightly while another wrapped a strip of cotton around her mouth so that she could not speak or cry out.

Nidaba struggled, casting her panicked eyes at the others in the room. The king kept his head lowered, his hand on his forehead, covering his eyes. The High Priest Lathor stood tall, watching, his lips pulling at the corners as though he battled a smile. Lia remained on her knees sobbing as she cried out, "Forgive me, Nidaba! Please, forgive me!"

Denial raced through Nidaba as the soldiers tugged her toward the back of the room, where another armed guard waited to open a small rear door. Beyond it she saw the camels waiting, packs dangling from their sides as if in preparation for a long journey. And she knew then that they were having her taken far away.

Fury welled up in her, and she felt the floor beneath her feet begin to vibrate, to tremble. The golden chalices and goblets teetered, and the king lifted his head to stare at her, his eyes wide, his face paling visibly.

"What's this?" he demanded.

Lia sent a desperate glance at Nidaba, and Nidaba saw and read it clearly. If she revealed the powers she had never understood, she would be more than banished. She would be killed. And so might Lia.

She fought to control the violence rising within her. The tremors eased and finally died.

"Perhaps, my king," Lia said, her voice choked and hoarse, "the girl was correct. Perhaps the Goddess is angered by this night's work."

The king looked toward the heavens, his face twisted in fear, and then Nidaba was hauled through the door, pushed and lifted onto the back of a camel. A soldier mounted right behind her, and held her in a cruel grasp as he urged the animal forward.

It began to run, its long legs and bouncing, bone-jarring gait soon putting miles between Nidaba and the lush city-state of Lagash, carrying her deeper and deeper into the desert night. Farther and farther away from her prince. Her Eannatum.

She vowed in silence that she would never love another the way she had loved him. And she would find him again—somehow she would tell him the truth of all of this.

She *would!*

Chapter 5

Nathan forced his tired eyes open, stirred to awareness by some sound or movement. He started when he realized he had fallen asleep.

And he knew something was wrong.

Nidaba's head twisted from side to side on the pillows, her face contorted, her breaths coming in short, sharp little bursts while her hands curled into fists and clutched at the covers.

Nathan shot to his feet and leaned over her, pressing a hand to her cheek. "It's all right," he said, and he tried to make his voice soothing and low, but feared that it came out hoarse with worry. "It's all right, Nidaba. I'm right here. You're safe. No one can hurt you here."

She only thrashed harder, and small sounds of anguish seemed torn from her chest now as she became more and more agitated. He put his hands on her shoulders, tried to still her frantic movements. "Nidaba, it's all right. Calm down now, it's all right. You're safe, do you hear me?"

Her legs began to twitch, her hands to swing in the air, and it was all he could do to hold her. She was strong, even in this state.

"Dammit, Nidaba, it's me! It's Eannatum!"

It was, he realized, the wrong thing to say.

Her thrashing ceased all at once. And her eyes flew open. Wide, wider than any eyes had a right to be, with tiny pinprick pupils drawn tight and irises like blue-black ice. Anger seethed in those eyes, so potent it hit him like a physical blow. The bed began to shake, to tremble and rock, as did the lamp on the nightstand and the floor under his feet. It shocked him so much that he drew back from her. His second big mistake of the night.

She swung her arms forward, her upper body rising from the bed even as she closed her hands around his throat. The force of the attack sent him reeling. He fell backward into the chair where he'd been sleeping, and Nidaba came with him, landing half sprawled atop him, her hands still clutching his throat with crushing force. The lamp on the bedside table crashed to the floor. He couldn't breathe.

But only for a moment. He quickly grabbed her hands to try to pry them away. But then Nidaba's death grip eased suddenly, and her body relaxed atop his. The violent shaking around him stopped. Her face fell to his chest, tangled hair veiling it from him.

He drew a ragged breath, then another as he carefully moved her limp hands away from his neck. Then he pushed her hair aside, cupped her face between his hands, and tipped it up to see that those fiery eyes had fallen closed once more.

"What the hell was that about?" he whispered to her unresponsive face. "By the Gods, Nidaba, was that hatred really directed at me? Or was it just mindless fury?"

No reply came. No clue whether he'd just been given a glimpse of the drug-induced madness possessing her or of the cold, harsh reality that lurked beneath it. He sighed and leaned forward to press his lips to her cool forehead. She couldn't possibly harbor that kind of hatred for him, could she? And why, for the love of the Gods? Then again, he thought slowly, she had attacked only when she'd heard him say his name. As if . . . as if just hearing it was enough to reach past the drugs still polluting her blood to the rage those drugs were supposed to suppress.

Rage against him.

But why?

The door flew open, and Sheila rushed into the room, then stopped and stared. And no wonder. He must have made quite the picture, lying across the chair with an unconscious woman draped over him. Behind Sheila that stray dog lingered in the hall like a shadow. Gorgeous beast it was, now that it was dry and clean. Its mouth wasn't drawn into a threatening snarl, but relaxed, almost smiling. If a dog *could* smile. Its hair wasn't bristled in warning, but instead, its tail wagged briskly. Nathan almost smiled at his earlier warning to George. This dog was anything but vicious. It almost bounced with friendliness.

"Nathan, what in the name of —"

He held up one hand, shook his head. "It's all right, Sheila. Nidaba just . . . it was some kind of a reflex." He gently closed his arms around Nidaba's waist, lifting her so he could get himself upright, and then scooped her up more carefully. "Get the covers, will you?"

Sheila came forward, straightened the mess of tangled covers, and pulled them back. "What in the world was that rumbling I felt, Nathan?" she asked, her voice tight. "Like an earthquake, it was."

"Must have been that thunder clap, just now. It . . . rattled the windows."

Sheila frowned, tilting her head sideways. "I didn't hear any thunder clap."

"No?"

Sheila's sharp eyes were raking the room, taking in the broken lamp, and then Nathan himself as he bent to lay Nidaba down. "She attacked you," Sheila said. "And don't bother lying to me. She tried to throttle you, didn't she?"

He glanced sideways at her as she spoke, saw the way her gaze was riveted to his neck, and reached up to touch the sorest places. His fingertips came away bloody.

Clucking her tongue, Sheila hurried into the adjoining bathroom, and he heard water running. He tucked Nidaba in, shaking his head as the dog came padding into the room and stretched itself out near the foot of the bed, as if intent on staying. "The drugs are starting to wear off," he said. "Enough to let her break through momentarily, at least."

"Oh, yes, enough so she can try to kill you, Nathan. No doubt you think it's a good sign." Sheila came out of the bathroom with a wet cloth and handed it to him.

"I *do* think it's a good sign, actually," he insisted. He thought he did, at least. "It didn't mean anything, Sheila. It was just some kind of . . . misfiring in her mind as the chemicals wear off. It was like a spasm—a reflex." He paced away from the bed, pressing the cool cloth to the scratches on his neck. It soothed away some of the sting.

"You can't be sure of that, and you know it," Sheila said.

"I'm as sure as I need to be."

"She was in that hospital for a reason, you know," she pressed on. "She jumped off a roof, for God's sake!"

"Or fell, or was pushed." He couldn't tell Sheila that even if she had jumped, it hadn't been an attempt at suicide. A forty-story plunge wouldn't leave so much as a lasting bruise on an immortal as old as Nidaba.

"She attacked a paramedic."

"Yes," he said, suddenly feeling a bit better about things. "Yes, she did, didn't she?" He even smiled a little. "That proves it was only a reflex, doesn't it? It wasn't me. She would probably attack anyone right now." He turned, taking the cloth away from his neck, and gazed at Nidaba, who had returned to a deep sleep.

"You sound glad about that," Sheila said. "She's violent, Nathan. This is not a reason for celebration."

He disagreed, but didn't say so.

"She needs a nurse here, someone familiar with mental illness, who would know what to do for her. You're doing her no favors by refusing to hire qualified caretakers for her, you know."

"If anyone finds out she's here—" he began.

"Listen to me. I'm your friend, Nathan. So for once, just listen to me."

Sighing, he turned to face Sheila, and forced himself to at least look as if he were listening.

"I know people," she said. "People . . . who can keep a secret." She came closer and put a hand on Nathan's arm. "Trust me, Nathan. I won't put you or your lady at risk."

He met Sheila's eyes steadily. "Exactly what are you suggesting, Sheila?"

"I have a friend. She was a mental health nurse Down Under. We

came here on the same ticket, Nathan. She's the only friend I have
from back home, and she can be trusted. I swear it. I've known her
all my life. She wouldn't betray her best friend." She shrugged. "And
even if I wasn't her best friend, she wouldn't betray me. I know
enough of her secrets that she wouldn't dare tell one of my own. Let
me call her. Let me ask her to come here and help us out for a few
days. Please, Nathan?"

He glanced down at Nidaba, then up at Sheila again. Nidaba
needed constant care. Sheila was right about that. She needed food,
liquids—she was thin as a rail, pale, weak. "All right," he finally
agreed. "All right, we can get her here. But be careful, Sheila. Please,
don't take any chances."

"I won't." She reached out and gave him a hug. "It'll be all right
now, you'll see."

Sheila left the room, but paused in the hallway when Nathan
called to her, saying, "You'd better take the dog with you. I don't
want anything around that might startle Nidaba if . . . when she finally comes around again."

The dog looked up at him, big eyes narrowing on Nathan's face
as if in some intelligent contemplation of his words.

"You heard the man. Come along, Queenie."

"*Queenie?*"

Sheila shrugged, holding the door as the big Rottweiler trotted
happily through. "George has already named her, love. I'm afraid
you're not the only one with a penchant for bringin' home strays."

Nathan rolled his eyes, muttering, "That's all we need."

Choosing to ignore him, Sheila closed the door. Nathan returned to his vigil beside Nidaba's bed.

The dog padded down the stairs behind Sheila, curled up by the
fireplace, and lay there relaxing and soaking up the heat as Sheila
telephoned a friend she called Lisette.

The conversation was exceedingly dull, until Lisette, it seemed,
tried to refuse Sheila's request for assistance.

"Don't you forget, girl, what you owe me," Sheila said, her
voice lowering. "You'd be rottin' in a cell in Queensland if not for
my help. I'm callin' in the favor, and you'd do well to honor the
debt."

It was obvious by the way Sheila's face eased that the woman had become more agreeable. "Right away, and not for more than a week. She may be well by then, or she may not, but a week is all I'll ask of you, either way. You'll be well paid, Lisette. Well paid. Nathan is a generous man." There was a pause. "That's fine. I can come pick you up, then. Noon tomorrow. No later. Good. Good. Thank you, Lisette."

Sheila hung up the phone. She sat back in the easy chair, looked at the telephone for a long moment, and then, pursing her lips, nodded. "It will be for the best," she told herself. "No better nurse on the planet than Lisette. Never was. Never will be." Nodding firmly as if to affirm that it was true, Sheila rose and walked back up the stairs.

The dog sighed and settled into sleep.

Morning came. And with it, another change. As the sun rose and slanted in through the bedroom windows, painting Nidaba's face with soft golden light, Nathan saw that her eyes were wide open. Dazed-looking, extremely unfocused, but wide open.

He got out of his chair and went to her, sitting on the edge of the bed. Taking her hand in his, he felt the jolting awareness shooting through his hand at the contact. "Nidaba? Can you hear me?"

She didn't respond. Didn't blink.

"Can you hear me at all, Nidaba?" He patted her hand gently. Still, no response or reaction . . . until her fingers moved just a little.

"You're coming back to us, aren't you? Bit by bit, the drugs are wearing off and you're coming back to us."

The bedroom door opened, and Nathan smelled the mingled scents of ham and eggs, and his favorite morning tea, ginseng and peppermint. "Mmm, that smells wonderful, Sheila," he said, not taking his eyes off Nidaba. Had her nostrils flared just now? Or had he imagined it?

"It's not Sheila," a voice said. Nathan turned his head as George came into the room with a tray in his hand. "She asked me to bring this up to you," he explained. "And to tell you that she would be back early this afternoon. By two, she said."

"Where did she go?" Nathan got up, took the tray from George, and put it on a table beside the bed. The dog at George's side kept

looking from Nathan, to Nidaba, to George, almost as if it was taking in the conversation, and maybe hoping for a scrap.

"She has a friend who's coming to help us take care of the lady,"
George explained. "She's gone to get her."

Nathan felt his lips thin, his gut tighten. Nidaba's stomach
growled noisily, and the dog's ears perked up at the noise.

"George, that dog probably shouldn't be in the bedroom,"
Nathan said.

"She's a *nice* dog, she really is." As he spoke, George stroked the
dog's head. The dog sent George an adoring look and wagged her tail.

George grinned from ear to ear.

Nathan sighed. "There's a fenced-in area off the garage," he said.
"If you truly want to keep the dog, she's going to have to stay there.
We'll rig up some kind of dog door so she can get in and out of the
garage. It's heated, so she'll be warm and dry."

"But she likes to be in the house," George said. "With me."

Nathan shook his head. "She's too big, and too new to us just
now, George. Give us some time to get used to her, and her to us,
and then . . . well, we'll see."

George's lower lip thrust out, but he would obey. He turned and
moped slowly out of the room, the dog going with him only after
he called her several times.

Nathan adjusted the bedside table, pulling it closer to the bed.
Then he sat down on the bed again, reaching for the stainless-steel
cover on the plate of food, but paused when he saw the morning paper there. Picking it up, he flipped through it and finally found what
he was looking for. A small story about the escape of an unidentified
mental patient during the confusion of a brief power outage and
false fire alarm at Brooker Hospital.

Escape. Not abduction.

Good.

He put the paper down and lifted the cover from the plate, eyeing the food. The ham would never do. But the eggs were scrambled, soft and fluffy. There was oatmeal, made extra thin. And the
juice—well, that would be the test, wouldn't it? If she couldn't swallow liquids all bets were off. He took the small glass of orange juice
from the tray and lifted Nidaba's head with the other hand. Those
wide black eyes stared unblinkingly into space. But her nostrils flared
at the scent of the juice, he saw it clearly this time.

"That's right, Nidaba. It's juice. I'm going to tip the glass up now. Try to sip. Just a little. All right?"

No reaction. He hoped to God he wasn't about to choke her to death. He tipped the glass up, just until the juice moistened her parched lips. Then a bit more, so some of the liquid slid between them, into her mouth. A small amount trickled down her chin.

And it happened. She swallowed.

Nathan lowered the glass and grabbed a napkin to dab her mouth clean again. "That was very good. Very good. Do you want to try something a little more solid?"

Nothing. He dipped up a spoonful of the oatmeal and carried it to her lips. Her mouth worked, accepting the food, moving convulsively to take it, grind it, swallow it. Oatmeal dribbled down her chin. It didn't matter. She needed nourishment.

This was not lucidity. Swallowing was a reflexive action. Her body was hungry, and her brain knew how to accept food. But it was progress. She was reacting, in physical ways, if not mental ones. It was progress.

By the time the bowl was empty, Nathan thought there was as much oatmeal on the outside of Nidaba as on the inside. It stuck in the long tangles of her hair, and coated the front of the hospital gown.

It was high time he get her out of that thing anyway. He'd done some shopping in preparation for her visit. The closet was well stocked. He set the rest of the food aside and hurried into the bathroom to insert the stopper and turn on the faucets of the clawfooted bathtub. The water flowed, covering the bottom and slowly climbing up the sides.

There was no one here to help him with this, he thought, knowing full well that Sheila would probably disapprove. George certainly couldn't deal with the task. No matter, though. It wouldn't be the first time he had bathed Nidaba. Only the first time in . . . forty-some-odd centuries.

Besides, maybe it would help pull her back to reality. Something had to. Because he damned well wasn't going to lose her again. Even now, the memory of the first time he suffered such a loss brought him close to despair.

Chapter 6

The message had been brought to his chamber early in the day by a temple servant. Eannatum had read the still moist clay tablet inscribed in Nidaba's unmistakable hand, signed by her own seal, which she wore around her neck. But he didn't believe it. He couldn't believe it. She loved him. She'd told him so, and by the heavens, he would make her tell him so again.

He threw his robes on haphazardly and ran through the halls of the palace to the rear doors, and through those to the worn roadways of the city. He didn't stop, not until he stood outside the temple doors, hands braced on his knees, panting for breath, his heart pounding like a *lilis* drum.

He caught his breath and stiffened his spine. She would see reason. He would only need to kiss her once to make her admit the truth. Tugging the doors open, he strode inside, only to be met in the entry corridor by the priestess Lia. She was as pale as a demoness, dark circles beneath her eyes, her skin drawn and taut. She rose from the chair in which she had been sitting, and said, "I have been expecting you, my prince."

"Where is Nidaba?" he demanded.

Lia's head lowered and her eyes never met his. "I am sorry. She is gone, Eannatum."

"Where?" She said nothing, until he gripped her arms and held them hard. "Tell me where she is, by the Gods!"

"I cannot. She refused to tell us where she would go, only that she would serve the Goddess as priestess in another temple, far from here. She took with her a tablet, with the mark of the High Priest Lathor, attesting to her rights to take the final initiation as a priestess of Inanna. And that is what she intends to do, my prince."

"No." He let go of the woman's frail arms and turned slowly away from her. "This is wrong. How could she leave Lagash on her own? I don't believe it. She couldn't have struck out on foot, into the desert, alone!"

"There was a caravan passing last night, my prince. She took a mule and rode out to join them."

He had not wanted the explanation to be so simple. Drawing a breath, closing his eyes, he asked, "Which way was this caravan moving?" His voice was softer now.

"East," Lia said, after a slight hesitation.

He looked over his shoulder at the woman and wondered if she was lying. And if so, why? "She will not leave me," he stated. "I will find her, and it matters not how far she has gone. I will have her with me again. And I vow, I will marry none other."

"I fear it is too late for that, my prince. I only wish it could be as you say."

"It can be," he said. "It *must* be."

But it wasn't. Oh, he tried. He ordered soldiers and messengers to every corner of Sumer in search of Nidaba. But to no avail.

He could barely tolerate food. Refused to take part in any revelry of any kind. Rarely slept. All he truly did was train for battle, and that simply because it was his only means of exhausting himself to the point where he was too tired to feel the pain. He trained with a sword until he could best every man in his father's army. He trained until his body looked like that of the mighty one of old, Gilgamesh, who some claimed was half god. And still the pain of losing Nidaba ate at his gut.

One day a trusted soldier, just back from yet another fruitless search, saluted Eannatum with his fist to his palm, bowed his head, and said, "I am sorry, my prince, but this journey, as all the others, has yielded no word of the woman you seek."

Natum frowned as suspicion tickled at the back of his mind. It had been weeks. *Weeks.* "How is it," he asked slowly, "that the most powerful army in all of Sumer can expend so much time and energy in such an extensive seach . . . only to find nothing?"

"Prince Eannatum, I—"

"No, no. Look up at me, face me as you speak," Natum commanded.

The soldier, Garon, was his own age. They'd attended *edubba* school together. Garon had been one of the few boys who'd tried to be Eannatum's friend when the others had shunned him. He knew this man well.

"I do not know how to answer your question," Garon replied. But when he said it, he looked away, just a quick flicker of his eyes toward the expanse of room behind him, and the doorway at its end.

He feared someone was listening! Eannatum realized it with sudden, startling clarity. And he would fear only one man above his prince.

His king. Eannatum's own father.

Realizing the danger to Garon should he press him here and now, Eannatum nodded slowly. "I am only frustrated at being thwarted. I know you and your men are doing your best. Go, Garon. Go on home to your pretty wife and your children."

Garon's lips pressed together tightly, and he couldn't seem to look Eannatum directly in the eye as he nodded, saluted again, and turned to leave.

An hour later, when Garon stepped out of his small white house with a water pail in hand, Eannatum was waiting. He stepped out of the shadows near the well, directly into Garon's path.

The soldier's head came up fast, and he sucked in a breath.

Eannatum held up a hand. "It's all right. We are alone now, my friend. No one listening at any doors, or lurking in secret palace passageways. You may speak freely."

Slowly Garon closed his eyes. "I am sworn to your father, Eannatum. I cannot betray him."

Eannatum shook his head. "I believe it is my father who has betrayed me," he said softly. "I believe he conspired to have Nidaba sent away, so that he could more easily convince me to play along with his ambitious plans. All of this is clear to me, Garon. The only thing unclear is where he has sent her."

Garon licked his lips, glancing from side to side nervously.

"If I were to lead a troop myself, Garon, which way would I lead them?"

Nothing. Silence.

Eannatum impaled the man with his eyes. "I have trusted you above others, Garon. I'll be king soon. And I'll need to know who of my men I can trust so fully. I believe you are one of the few. Prove to me that my faith has not been misplaced."

The soldier bowed his head, expelled his breath in a rush. And finally he spoke. "I have always heard tell that the city of Mari, far to the north, is a sight to behold, my prince. If I were to travel, I believe that would be my destination."

Nodding heavily, Eannatum closed his eyes. Mari. The temple of Mari was one of the most heavily guarded in all of Sumer. It housed great treasures, riches beyond compare. And it was a favored target of Sumer's enemies.

"Thank you, Garon." He clapped a hand to the man's shoulder. "No one will ever know of this meeting. You have my word."

"They may very well know already, my friend. For I've no doubt you were followed from the palace."

"You give me too little credit. I wouldn't risk you that way."

"Not even for her?" Garon asked, looking up. But then he smiled bitterly and lowered his head again. "By Enlil's wings, Natum, I can't even blame you. I'd have done the same."

That he'd slid into the old habit of addressing Eannatum by his casual name seemed to signal a shift in the conversation. A dropping of the pretenses and formalities of solidier and sovereign, a return to the conventions of two young friends.

"I promise that you'll be rewarded Garon, for your loyalty to me," Natum told him. "Tell me what you wish, and I'll see that it's granted."

Garon sighed as he looked Natum in the eye. "Fool that I am, I've but one wish, my friend. Take me with you on this journey north. Let me bring my regiment. You'll need us if you hope to return alive."

Eannatum tipped his head to one side. "Things are that bad in the north?"

"That bad and worse. Ummamite hordes have been gathering for months, just beyond the borders. They prepare for something momentous, Natum. And in the meantime, they amuse themselves with midnight raids on defenseless villages. Mari has had to become a veritable fortress to keep them at bay. The outlying areas have not been as fortunate."

Eannatum frowned. "Nidaba is not safe there."

"For a prince, your vision is narrow, Eannatum. *No one* in Sumer is safe just now."

Was this soldier chastising his future king? No, Eannatum thought slowly. No. This old friend was advising his comrade. And he was right. "My father has told me these things, but I thought he exaggerated the danger . . . better to persuade me to fall in with his plans."

Garon nodded. "I can see why you would mistrust him after all he's done, Natum. But while he's guilty of a great deal, on this score at least he gave you the truth. The situation is dire."

"We'll find a way to eliminate the threat of the Ummamites. Just as soon as I've found Nidaba and brought her back to Lagash."

Garon pursed his lips, as if he had more to say, but refused to say it. "As you wish, my prince."

Eannatum turned and left him there, his thoughts on his woman, not his country. Not invading hordes and not the security of his people. He was glad Garon had held his tongue, because he didn't want to hear what the man had to say. Deep down, he knew it full well.

The regiment, some fifty soldiers strong, marched northward with the dawn, much to the consternation of the king. For days they journeyed, marching on foot, a few mounted on the domesticated camels that were becoming an increasingly valuable mode of transportation, though they were still extremely rare in Sumer. Eannatum rode a camel. Garon rode beside him.

The journey was dusty, dry, hot. They crossed vast expanses of barren desert, too far from the shores of the blessed twin rivers to enjoy the life-giving kiss of their waters. By the time they neared Mari, Eannatum's dark skin had burned, even through the robes he wore. His lips were as parched as dried dates, and each time he blinked he felt sand scratch his eyes. And even then, he smiled when he saw the gleaming walls of Mari rise up in the distance.

"It is late, Eannatum," Garon said. "The men are tired, and the city gates will not open until dawn. Let us make camp here. There is a small village nearby. That means water, and perhaps even a meal of something besides hard bread and dried meat."

He stared at the walls ahead. So close. He wanted to ride to that city, to climb those walls and go to her. And yet fear gnawed at his belly. What if she really had left of her own volition? What if she really didn't want him?

He swallowed hard, refusing to believe it. Gods, it had been so long since he'd tasted her lips. He could almost taste them now.

"Eannatum?" Garon said.

Natum licked his parched lips. "We'll do as you suggest. It's a good plan."

Garon angled his camel toward a stand of *hashur* trees, where a spring bubbled with life. Then he held up a hand and shouted an order. The parade of men came to a halt, and the weary soldiers began to make camp.

It was near midnight, and the men's bellies were full, their thirsts sated, their tired limbs resting at last, when Eannatum *felt* something. He wasn't certain at first just what it was. Not a sound. The only sounds were those of the desert night. A jackal, yipping incessantly. A night bird's cry. The all but silent flapping of a pair of giant wings. The squeal of a bat. The bubbling of the spring. It wasn't a sound that woke him, made him sit bolt upright, frowning. It was something else.

A sense.

Then a vague vibration of the ground. As if a great thundering herd of cattle were pounding over it some distance away. He nudged Garon with his foot, and the soldier was on his feet instantly.

Only then did the sounds come. Shouts, battle cries, screams. Flickering torches took form in the distance, some arching through the night as they were flung.

"The village!" Natum shouted. "It's under attack!"

Garon's men came awake at once, as Garon shouted orders, and as one they rushed to defend the village. Of that battle, Eannatum remembered very little. He armed himself with a massive spear, a heavy shield, a club, and he surged into the fray. He recalled darkness, dust, smoke, fire. He recalled a wall of men, Ummamites, too many of them to number. And he recalled the blow to his head that rendered him useless.

He woke to the dawn.

Blinking his vision into focus, he managed to take stock. He was on his back on the ground, with the desert sunrise searing his eyes in their sockets. He was assailed by the scent of blood, of death. He looked around, and saw them, villagers, soldiers, women, children—bodies were scattered in every direction. The village was gone, except for smoldering remnants of what had been serene homes.

He heard sobbing, wailing, saw an old woman holding the lifeless body of a child to her breast.

"Eannatum, you're alive!"

He turned toward the sound of Garon's choked voice. The man limped toward him, his face black with soot and smeared with blood. "I seem to be," Natum said, as Garon grasped his hand and pulled him to his feet. "And I'm glad to see you are as well. But this . . ." He looked around again at the horror surrounding them. The anguish of the few survivors was heavy—a sodden blanket weighing him down, thickening the very air. They were his people, and their pain, his pain.

"This is happening daily up and down the northeastern borders of Sumer," Garon said, his voice grim.

More voices reached him now, and Eannatum saw a group of people approaching from Mari. Men, women, priests and priestesses. They fanned out among the dead and wounded to help the survivors. And at last, he saw the face he'd dreamed of nightly for so long—the beautiful, sculpted features of Nidaba, as she broke away from the others and ran toward the old woman who cradled the dead child. He heard her cry out. Heard the pain in her voice clearly, and felt it even more vividly in his heart.

His eyes burned as he watched her embrace the old woman and gently take the child from her arms. "See to your wounded, Garon," Natum said softly. And he moved forward until he stood behind Nidaba.

She lay the child down on the ground, her back to him, and she gently reached up to smooth a lock of dark hair away from the girl's still elfin face. "She did no wrong, this child! She did no wrong." Kneeling, Nidaba tipped her face skyward and opened her arms to the heavens. "Go in peace, child. Go into the bosom of Inanna, and there find healing and love. Go now. Linger in this pit of death no longer."

He couldn't remain silent. He put his hands on her shoulders and felt the tingling jolt of that contact. Nidaba lowered her arms. "Natum?" she whispered.

"Yes."

She rose slowly, turned to face him, and then suddenly, desperately, she flung herself into his arms and sobbed as if her heart had been smashed to bits. He held her hard, kissed her face, her neck, her hair. The ice encasing his heart seemed to melt at her very touch. "Gods, Nidaba, how I've longed to hold you again."

"And I, you," she told him.

He found her mouth, kissed her with everything in him, tasted the salt of her tears on his lips, and finally stared into her eyes. "Cry no more, my love. I've come to take you back with me. We won't be kept apart any longer. I promise you that."

Her expression changed. Her eyes widened just a bit, and her grip on him eased. Slowly she unwrapped her arms from around him and took a single step backward, out of his fierce embrace. "Eannatum, though I love you, surely you see now why we can never be."

He frowned. "I see nothing but an enemy to be defeated. I'll send my armies, and it will be done. It has nothing to do with us, Nidaba."

"It has everything to do with us!" She closed her eyes, bit her lip. When she opened them again, she seemed calmer. She took his arm. "Come with me."

They walked. Away from the scene of the battle, and all that carnage, far away, and up a hillside outside the city of Mari. Higher and higher they climbed, and though he plied her with questions, she never spoke a word until they reached the summit. Then, turning toward Umma, she pointed. "There."

He looked. And his heart seemed to freeze in his chest. Beyond the borders, just inside the land of Umma, he saw hordes—more soldiers than he had ever seen in one place before. Thousands of them, camp after camp, as far as the eye could see.

"Your armies cannot hope to stand against those masses. Within months, Eannatum, Sumer will fall to the Ummamites. And more innocent children will die at their hands. More young women will be enslaved by their soldiers."

"I'll find a way," he said, gripping her shoulders, staring into her eyes.

"Your father has already found a way." She lowered her eyes. "I didn't want to believe it either, but since coming here, I've begun to see the way things really are. Eannatum, Sumer will fall unless you can unite its cities. And you can do that only by marrying the princess of Ur and assuming the kingship of all Sumer. Then, and only then, will you have a chance to drive the Ummamites back and defeat them so soundly that they will not dare take up arms against Sumer again."

He shook his head in denial, even knowing her words were true. "It's you I love, Nidaba. How can I marry another when it's you I love?"

"You have no choice," she whispered, her voice growing hoarse. "I realized that after the third of these midnight raids that I witnessed. That's why I took the initiation. I am a priestess now, Eannatum. And you are a prince. We could not be together even if you were free. I serve the temple. You, your kingdom."

He swallowed hard. "We cannot wed. But we could be together. As king, it's my right to have any woman I desire. It's the law."

"An arcane law. No king enforces it anymore, Eannatum."

"This king will."

She closed her eyes, shook her head. "You love your people," she said softly. "I know you, Eannatum. I know you'll do the right thing. If you didn't, you wouldn't be the Natum I love so very much."

He closed his eyes. In a moment he felt her lips on his, light as a breeze. "Good-bye, Natum. Do not forget me."

And then she was gone. When he opened his eyes again, he saw her, running away down the hill, her white robes flowing behind her. It was a blade straight through his heart. But he knew she was right. He had his duty, and she had hers, and if they failed to play their parts, the blood of thousands would stain their hands.

Damn fate and all its cruel twists. Damn him, for falling so deeply in love with a woman he could never have. Damn the world, and everyone in it.

Chapter 7

The tab was full, and Nathan turned the water off, went back to the bedroom, and slowly peeled the blankets away from Nidaba. She lay still, unresponsive, her face sticky. She didn't look like a holy woman or a High Priestess, much less an immortal High Witch, just now. She didn't look like the queen she should have been. She looked like a messy little girl trapped inside a woman's body.

He knew better, though. He'd watched her grow from a child into a young woman right before his eyes. And what a woman she had become. He had seen her again, after she had left him on that bitter hillside. He had seen her on the day of his coronation.

He would never forget . . .

Nathan closed his eyes against the memories that burned in his mind and told himself to focus on the present, not the distant past. When he opened his eyes again, he forced himself to see not the sensual priestess he remembered, but the helpless, frail-looking woman lying on the bed, staring at nothing with eyes that seemed afraid.

"Forgive me, Nidaba. Even now, the memory of you burns in me as if it were fresh and new." He ran a hand across his forehead, reconsidered what he was about to do, then laughed at himself. There was no shyness in Nidaba. No humble, blushing virgin in her. There never had been.

He rolled her up onto her side, untied the hospital gown in the back, then laid her flat again. His hands at the sleeves, he pulled the garment off her.

Gods, she was so thin. The drugs in her system must be slowing everything down, including the restorative powers of their kind. He could see her ribs, and her belly was concave. The bones of her hips and her collarbones jutted sharply against skin that seemed to have thinned. He peeled away the white underpants, tossed them aside, and slid his arms beneath her.

His palms slid over soft skin, and his body came alive, not just with the jolt of immortal touching immortal, but with longing. A hunger that should have died long ago. And the craving wasn't in his body alone, but in his heart.

She was helpless right now. But she wouldn't be for long. Not Nidaba. When she was herself again, she would be fully capable of destroying him utterly. And if he didn't get his feelings under control, he would end up letting her.

He drew away from her, tugged the covers back over her, and contented himself with bringing a warm cloth from the bathroom and washing her face. Sheila would return with help. For once he was glad of her bossy ways and take-charge attitude. Sometimes, he admitted with a sigh, he needed to be protected from himself.

"Nathan! Nathan! Oh, Nathan, she's gone!"

George's frantic cries accompanied his feet clomping up the stairs at top speed several hours later. Nathan had been sitting with Nidaba, watching over her, reading aloud, talking to her about times long past, about his life today. Anything to pass the time. He'd made use of her bath himself, leaving the door open wide in case she should cry out or become afraid. It had been a quick bath. Exhaustion, mental as well as physical, had tempted him to linger in the hot water, to relax into its soothing embrace. His back and shoulders ached from the hours spent in the chair beside her bed. But he didn't dare linger He bathed, dried himself, put on fresh clothes. He didn't even take time to shave, because there was no line of sight from the sink to the bed where Nidaba lay, and he was sure something would happen if he took his eyes off her for too long.

There had been no significant change in her condition all morning, however.

It was after two when the door opened and George stood there, breathless and wide-eyed wearing a bright green pullover with a white tab collar and a chartreuse clip-on bow tie attached. "Nathan, she's gone!" he said again.

"Who's gone?" George was in pain. Nathan's empathic tendencies brought that pain and worry to him as sharply as if it were his own.

"My dog! My Queenie, she's gone! I took her to the fenced-in place, just like you said. And I put food and water out there, and I stayed with her for a long time. Then I thought she was getting bored. So I went up to my room to get her a ball to play with, and when I came back, she was just gone! Where could she be, Nathan?" As he spoke, George battled tears without much success.

Nathan was out of his chair and across the room before George finished speaking. He held George's big shoulders, felt like hugging the man, who was more childlike right now than he'd ever been. "She's all right, I'm sure of it, George. She's all right, wherever she is."

"But . . . but . . ." George's eyes filled with shimmering pools that would flood at any moment.

"Come on, sit down." Nathan led George to a chair near the window, settled him into it, pushed the heavy damask drapes open and looped the gold braided tie-backs around them. "Look outside, George. It's a beautiful day. That dog is probably running around, chasing rabbits, having fun. There's nothing out there that could hurt her. Is there?"

George looked out the window, his gaze intent. "Well . . . I don't *see* anything that could hurt her."

Nathan felt the big guy's worry easing just a little, and he pressed on. "There *isn't* anything. She's a big dog, George, a strong animal. Besides, I know you may not want to think about this, but you have to consider for a minute that she might have belonged to someone else. Maybe she went back to her home."

Innocent eyes searched Nathan's. "Do you think so?"

"Well, she was a purebred Rottweiler, George. A beautiful animal. It's hard to believe a dog like that didn't belong to someone."

Blinking, George pondered that for a moment. "She wasn't wearing any collar. No tags."

"No. Some dogs are pretty clever about wriggling out of their collars, though."

"They are?"

"Oh, yes. I've seen them do it. Listen, you take my advice and don't worry about her. Later on, when Sheila gets back with her friend, I'll ask her to drive you around looking for Queenie. And we can put an ad in the local newspaper if you want."

"We can?"

"Sure we can! Someone will have seen her. And even if she does belong to someone else, at least you'll know. And maybe you can visit her. And if she doesn't have a home, then we'll find her and bring her back here. Either way, there's no cause for you to be so upset. She's a smart, strong, healthy dog, romping around somewhere having the time of her life. I promise. She's fine."

George sighed, his shoulders slumping in obvious relief. "Thanks, Nathan. I feel better." He looked at the floor. "You always make me feel better."

"I'm glad." Nathan's throat felt inexplicably tight.

"I think I'll walk around outside for a while, see if I can find her."

"Just don't go too far, George. And stay out of the woods."

"I will," he promised. He got to his feet, glanced at the bed, then at Nathan again. "How is the lady doing?"

"Not much different than this morning, I'm afraid."

"She'll get better, Nathan," George said, and he patted Nathan's shoulder. "You'll see."

"Thank you, George. I'm sure she will."

George smiled. "Did I make you feel better?"

Looking up, Nathan saw the hope in his big, innocent eyes, and he forced a smile. "Yes, you did, George. Thank you."

"You're welcome, Nathan."

The sound of a car pulling into the driveway made them both turn to the window again. Nathan said, "There's Sheila now, with her friend." He almost sighed in relief. Gods knew, he needed the help. Just enough time to slip away for a shave and a bite to eat, knowing that someone was there with Nidaba, would be a blessed relief. Something moved in the woods alongside the driveway, and it caught Nathan's eye. His first thought was that he'd spotted George's precious stray running through the underbrush. But the shadowy form vanished. He watched, eyes narrow and searching, and caught one more glimpse of . . . something. But this time it looked like a person moving amid the trees, and then there was nothing at all.

A little shiver raced up Nathan's spine. He gave his head a shake, told himself he was overtired, his eyes were playing tricks on him. Still, he couldn't quite shake the ominous feeling.

"I swear, I don't know what's keeping Lisette," Sheila said, pacing the room once more. She'd spent the past hour telling Nathan about her friend Lisette's qualifications. She was an RN with experience in caring for the mentally ill, and she owed Sheila a favor. Apparently a very big favor, because Sheila was convinced she could trust the woman to keep quiet about Nidaba's presence here.

"Give her some time to get her bearings," Nathan advised. "She's probably unpacking, getting settled in. Besides, your word is good enough for me, Sheila. If she's willing to do the job, and you trust her, then she's hired. I'll pay her whatever she wants. Just so long as she does a good job." He glanced into the bathroom, where he'd started running another bath for Nidaba. "Tub's full." Walking in, he shut the water off.

"She's not the kind to dawdle, Nathan. I promise you that." Sheila frowned. "I'd best go and check on her."

"No need," a woman's harsh, raspy voice said as the bedroom door swung inward. "I'm right here."

Sheila's startled frown made Nathan wonder what was going on. He studied the woman standing in the doorway. She was small, slender, with silver hair in a swept-up style, and incredible skin for a woman of her age. Her eyes were vivid blue, and penetrating.

"Whatever has happened to your voice?" Sheila asked.

"I'm sure I don't know," she whispered. "It got this way only minutes after I arrived. I suppose I'm allergic to something in this house."

"Until this morning we had a dog running around the place. Could it have been that?" Nathan asked.

"Ahh . . . that's it," she rasped. "Dogs'll get me every time." Nathan smiled as the woman held out her hand. "You must be Nathan King." He had to strain to hear her. "Sheila has told me so much about you."

He reached for her hand, but she drew it back, looked at it, and shook her head. "Best not. If it's not from the dog, then this thing could be catching," she said, pointing at her throat.

"It's very good to meet you, Ms. . . . ?"

She smiled and said, "Call me Lisette."

"Lisette, then. I want to thank you for coming on such short notice. You're doing me a great favor by taking this on."

She shrugged, and he frowned. "But if you think you might be contagious, perhaps—"

"No worries," she whispered. "I'll use antibacterial soap and gloves with the patient. She'll be in no danger."

Nathan nodded, glancing again at Sheila only to see her still frowning at her friend in what looked like confusion. He wondered at that, but the woman was already moving forward, looking at Nidaba in the bed, glancing into the adjoining bathroom.

"I see you've got a bath run for her."

"Yes, she's in need of it. That is, if you don't mind getting started right away."

"Of course I don't mind." That sandpapery rasp scraped his nerve endings.

"I realize we haven't discussed terms yet. I'll pay you triple the going rate. All I ask is that you treat this patient with extreme kindness, be gentle with her, and see to it she has whatever she needs."

The nurse's eyes narrowed on Nidaba. "You care for the woman a great deal, then?"

For some reason, the question bothered him. "She's . . . an old friend. A very dear old friend."

"Don't worry, Mr. King. I'll take *very good* care of her."

He nodded as Lisette went to the bed, tugged at the covers, and then looked at him sharply. "Who undressed her?" she asked.

"She . . . dribbled oatmeal all over herself this morning," he replied.

The woman frowned. "Highly inappropriate, Mr. King," she said, and pulled the covers back around Nidaba. She rushed into the bathroom and returned with a large towel, then she yanked the covers down again, and proceeded to wrap it around Nidaba, rolling her up onto her side to do so. When Lisette touched her, Nidaba jerked, and her eyes widened.

Nathan jumped, but Lisette held up a hand. "It's all right. She'll need to get used to me if I'm to help her. Now she's ready. Carry her into the bathroom, Mr. King, and put her in the tub, towel and all. I'll see to the rest myself."

Sheila cocked her head to one side as Nathan scooped Nidaba up from the bed. She walked beside Lisette as they followed him into the bathroom. "I vow, Lisette," she said, "you're like a different woman when you're working. If I didn't know your face so well I don't think I'd recognize you at all."

From the corner of his eye, Nathan saw Lisette send her friend a smile. "I care very deeply about my work . . . but you know that, now, don't you?"

"Yes. Yes, that I do. But . . ."

"Hush, my friend. We'll talk later on, when the work is done. Save your worries, won't you?"

"Sure. Later on. And I'll brew you up something soothin' for that throat."

Lisette squeezed Sheila's hand and sent her a warm smile.

Nathan stopped beside the bathtub, staring down at Nidaba's wide, unfocused eyes. "Now, I'm going to put you into the bathtub, Nidaba. There's water. Warm, but not too warm. It's going to feel good to you, do you understand? There is no reason to be afraid, to be startled by this. No reason at all. This is good for you."

He continued speaking softly, telling her how good the water would feel, as he lowered her carefully into the tub. She started, just once, when the warm water touched her skin, but then she returned to oblivion again and lay back in the water.

Nathan knelt beside the tub, one hand always on her, to keep her from slipping. He had everything ready and within reach so Lisette wouldn't have to leave her alone for an instant and risk her drowning herself.

Where he touched Nidaba's shoulders he could feel the sharpness of her bones beneath her skin. And her thighs looked so thin, so slight, below the towel. Had they even fed her in that place?

Anger stirred in his gut.

"Go on now," Lisette said in that odd voice. "I'll take care of her from here."

He looked at the woman. Then he sought out Sheila's eyes.

"She's right, Nathan. Go on, have a shave, get some lunch. I saw the breakfast I made for you this morning, sitting cold and untouched on the plate. You need to keep yourself well or you'll never be able to care for this one. You know that."

"I . . ." He couldn't say it. He didn't want to insult Lisette or hurt Sheila, but he just couldn't bring himself to leave Nidaba alone with this strange woman. He barely knew her, after all.

"I'll stay," Sheila said, reading him so clearly it almost made him dizzy. "I'll be right here. I'll not let her out of my sight, Nathan, and if she needs you for anything, I'll call for you. All right?"

Meeting Sheila's eyes, seeing she wasn't angry with him for mistrusting her friend, he nodded. "I don't know what I'd do without you, Sheila."

"Oh, curl up in a corner and die, no doubt. Now go on. Out with you. This is woman's work."

Feeling slightly better, he left the room. But he didn't go far. He went into his own bedroom, just off Nidaba's, where his bed remained untouched, unslept in. He dug out a shaving kit he kept in the top drawer and stepped into the hallway to head to the guest bathroom, since his own was currently being used by the women.

He got only about ten steps when he heard the ear-splitting shriek and the crash. Choking on his own heart, he spun and raced back along the hall, through his bedroom, tossing his kit onto the bed on the way to Nidaba's room, and finally to the bathroom beyond.

Sheila was dripping wet, standing back and looking surprised, while Lisette gripped Nidaba's frail shoulders, attempting to hold her still while she thrashed and splashed and fought.

Nathan ran forward. "Let go—let go of her!"

Lisette did, and Nidaba instantly stilled. She sat stiffly in the tub, eyes wide, breaths rushing in and out of her parted lips in short panicky bursts. She was shaking. Visibly trembling.

Nathan knelt in the puddle beside the tub, but didn't touch her.

"It's all right. I'm here, Nidaba. It's all right." He watched her, wishing to the Gods he knew what sort of nightmares went on inside her mind where she was trapped. "What happened in here?" He asked without taking his eyes from her. Her collarbones poked up so sharply it seemed they'd pierce the thin layer of skin that covered them. Her small breasts rose and fell in time with her breaths.

"I'm not sure," Lisette said.

"Not sure, eh? Well, I am," Sheila cut in. "She started to get antsy as soon as you left the room, Nathan. Stiff, and jittery-like. Let me take the towel off, all right, and even wash her up a bit. But as soon as Lisette poured a bit of water on that hair of hers she went crazy on us. Thrashed about like a wild woman, she did."

Nathan nodded, his gaze slipping only briefly away from Nidaba. "I heard a scream."

"That was her, all right," Sheila said with a sharp nod.

"So you can speak after all, hmm?" He looked hard into those black eyes and they stared back, wide, but clearer than they had been before, he thought. Then he told himself that might be an illusion. Wishful thinking.

"I'm sure it was only the water on her head that set her off." Lisette was on her feet and beside the tub now. "Some mentally ill patients go into a panic when water touches their faces."

"And I think it was the fact that Nathan left the room," Sheila said.

"That's nonsense."

"Is it now, do you think?"

"I'm the one who's experienced with mental patients, Sheila," Lisette said in a harsh mutter that was closer to speaking in a normal tone than anything Nathan had heard her say thus far.

"Lisette's right," Nathan put in. "Besides, she didn't react right away, when I left her. You said yourself she let you wash her up a bit, didn't you, Sheila?"

Sheila's gaze narrowed. "That's right. Maybe it's you she dislikes, Lisette." She said it teasingly, the way a friend would to another friend, with a nudge of the elbow or a wink. But Lisette's scowl led Nathan to think she didn't take the comment in the same manner.

He hated to see tension brewing between Sheila and her longtime friend, so he stepped in. "Let's put it to the test, then, okay?" He looked around, not getting up from his knees, and spotted the small plastic pitcher Sheila had been using. Then he filled it and touched Nidaba's hair.

"Your hair is all tangled and dirty," he said slowly. "I'm going to wash it for you. All right?"

She didn't respond, just stared straight ahead. Nathan tipped her head back a little, to keep the water out of her eyes, and slowly poured. She didn't fight, didn't panic at all. So he dipped another pitcher full and poured that as well, and she tipped her head back farther. Her eyes fell closed.

He almost smiled. She liked this. He continued dipping and pouring until her long hair was thoroughly soaked. Then he applied a generous amount of baby shampoo and worked up a lather. He massaged her scalp with his fingertips, scrubbed gently and thoroughly, for a long time. Her hair, masses of it, tangled around his fingers as she lay back, relaxing more as he rubbed, eyes remaining closed. Her breaths came deep and slowly. He watched her chest rise and fall with it. And finally he began rinsing, pitcher by pitcher.

"You're very good at this," Sheila whispered, leaning close. "You must have the touch." She pressed another bottle into Nathan's hand. Conditioner. Guaranteed to remove all the tangles, so combing wouldn't be such a chore. He poured a quarter of the bottle over her head, and worked it in, rubbing it down to her scalp and out to the ends of her hair.

His patient was almost limp, she was so relaxed now. So he kept it up a little longer. She liked this. He hadn't thought Nidaba was capable of feeling anything . . . particularly pleasure. But she was doing precisely that, and he would keep it up just as long as it pleased her.

"I imagine the water is getting cold by now, Mr. King," Lisette said. And her tone, raspy, but louder still, made her disapproval very clear.

Too bad.

"It *is* beginning to cool down a bit." Nathan reached up and cranked on the hot water tap, then sent Lisette an innocent smile. "Easily remedied." And then he went back to massaging Nidaba's scalp while she reclined like a queen, relishing it, he thought. He made small circles with his fingertips, massaged her temples, and her neck just behind her ears, and then her nape, at the base of her skull. She let her head fall forward when he did that. And all her breath rushed out of her. When he eased her back again, he thought her face looked more placid than he had seen it in centuries.

Eventually, he rinsed the conditioner away. But she didn't sit up or move when he finished. A soft sound came from her throat, and if it meant anything at all, he thought, it meant that she wanted more of this. Fine, then. He would continue.

He reached for the sponge Sheila had put in here for him, the one he'd never bothered to use, and the scented body wash that he'd borrowed from the guest bathroom when preparing for Nidaba's arrival. Vanilla. Very slowly, he lathered one long, slender arm, lifted it, and rinsed it clean. Slow, soothing strokes up her outer arm, and then around to the more sensitive inner part. The well opposite her elbow. The hollow underneath. Her hand, her palm, and one by one each and every finger. When he finished with both arms, he washed her chest. He lathered and rubbed her small breasts, and her sunken belly.

Her eyes opened. Fixed on his hands. Darkened.

No. That couldn't be what it looked like.

Nathan rinsed the lather away, and pulled her forward just a bit, to soap and scrub her back and shoulders. And she seemed to like that so much that he continued far longer than was necessary. She acted as if the muscles of her back ached though he could barely see how they could. There seemed to be no muscle there to ache. There was nothing to her but skin and bone.

Sighing her displeasure, Lisette paced back and forth on the side of the room nearest the door. Sheila kept herself busy—she was wielding a mop over the spilled water right now. She seemed perfectly content to let Nathan perform this entire bathing duty.

When Nidaba finally leaned back again, Nathan moved along to the bottom of the tub, clasped one of her tiny ankles in his hand, and lifted it. Then he ran his hand and the soapy sponge over her leg, beginning at her foot, and moving slowly up over her calf, and down her shin. And then higher. He began to soap her thigh. And he watched her face, watched it intently. Her gaze seemed to heat as his hand neared the crux of her legs. And it was *not* his imagination. He was sure of it this time.

"You're in there, aren't you?" he murmured. "You're alive and kicking in there. Why won't you speak to me? Hmm?"

His hand edged closer to her center, but he moved past it and began working the other leg. Down the thigh, over the calf, to the foot. "Talk to me, Nidaba," he urged, massaging the small of her foot briskly. "Talk to me. Fight the grip of this darkness that holds you."

She didn't. But she was, in a way, responding to him more than she had since he'd found her in that hospital. Responding, Nathan realized, to his touch. He sponged a path back up the thigh, intending to bathe every inch of her . . . to *touch* every inch of her, if that was what it would take to draw a real response.

Dammit, he wished he'd gone with his initial instinct and bathed her himself when he could have been completely alone with her. But he hadn't expected this.

"Sheila, why don't you and Lisette go and get some clean clothes out of the closet for our guest?" His hand inched higher on Nidaba's thigh. He watched her eyes heat, felt her legs move just the slightest bit farther apart. That part of her hadn't shut down, then, had it? The sexual part. The hungry part. It was there he could reach her.

"Whatever you say, Nathan," Sheila chirped, merrily turning away. "I can see you've got things under control here." She walked past Lisette on her way, and Nathan hoped the woman would have the good sense to follow her out of the room.

"I'm not leaving this room," the nurse said. "It's inappropriate."

"You think I'm going to pull her out of the tub and rape her?" Nathan asked, his voice quiet, his eyes on Nidaba's. Hers, alive, feeling, wanting . . . but still staring off into the distance.

"It wouldn't be the first time a man had taken advantage of a mentally ill woman, Mr. King. But you can bet it's not going to happen on my watch. I'd be shirking my duty if I left you alone with her."

Nathan sighed, but his hand was still on Nidaba's inner thigh, and she was still sitting there, head tipped back, eyes burning. And Lisette was standing halfway across the room, too far to see what Nathan might be doing with his hands beneath the soapy water.

"I'll remind you who's paying your salary, Lisette," he said. "If you doubt my integrity so much, maybe I should look for someone else to—"

"I didn't mean to insult you, Mr. King."

He nodded. "If you insist on staying, fine. But could you at least get me some dry towels? They're in the small linen closet just down the hall."

With a muttered agreement, Lisette turned her back.

Watching Nidaba's eyes—her remarkably *clear* eyes—Nathan moved the soapy sponge higher, brushed it gently between her legs. Her lips parted and a breath sighed out of her. He rubbed again, up and down, soaping her, caressing her with the loofah. "Look at me," he whispered. "Look at me, Nidaba."

Her gaze faltered, shifted slightly, and her thighs parted further. She pressed against the sponge, and he rubbed a little harder.

"Look at me."

Suddenly, her gaze snapped to his, and locked on. Fire. Heat. Fury. Rage. So many passions boiled in that gaze. But it was clear, and it was focused on him.

Was this wrong, what he was doing? Probably. But suppose he could reach her, pull her out of the grip of her mind? Then wasn't it to her benefit that he do so, any way he could?

She arched her hips against the sponge he held, and he pressed, and moved it over her. Lisette would return soon, damn her to hell. Nathan dropped the sponge, moved his hand away.

Quick as lightning, Nidaba's hand closed over his and pulled it to her, pressed it against her, rocking her hips. Her eyes flared wider and held his with a fierce gaze.

Nathan swallowed hard against something that felt a lot like fear. But it couldn't be that. It made no sense to be afraid of her, despite the ferocity and the feral hunger in that gaze. And yet it made all the sense in the world. He was so close, so close to reaching her, yet not knowing what he would find when he did. But he was near, he could feel it.

Lisette's footsteps were coming back down the hall. Only seconds and his chance would be missed. All right, then, right or wrong . . .

Nathan moved his fingers against the woman, parted her folds, stroked her just a little. "Talk to me, Nidaba. Come on. Tell me your name," he whispered. He flicked his fingers over the core of her need. "Tell me."

Lisette's steps got louder, coming through the bedroom now.

"Come on, say it. Say your name." He rubbed her harder, faster.

She parted her lips, closed her eyes and whispered "Nidaba" on a trembling sigh.

Lisette went still just beyond the doorway.

Nathan smiled, and stroked her once more, pressed her between his thumb and forefinger, and she gasped in pleasure. He rolled that tiny nub of need, pinched and pressed and kneaded it. Lisette was coming into the room now. Three more steps and she would be through the door, and able to see where his hand was, what he was doing. He pinched her harder, rubbing the swollen kernel faster between his thumb and forefinger, and he leaned low, and whispered very close to her ear, "Let it go, Nidaba. Let it go for me."

Her body arched, and she cried out loud, going stiff in the water for a moment suspended in time. Lisette stopped walking, her frown dark and probing. Then Nidaba relaxed her shuddering body back into the bathwater, squeezed her thighs together around his hand, as if to keep it there.

He drew in a quaking breath, shivering with a desire that burned deep in his gut. "Good girl," he whispered, before he took his hand away. "That's my good girl."

He stopped touching her, and she stopped responding. Slowly, the veil he'd seen before took its place over her eyes. Her focus faded. She'd retreated again.

Chapter 8

"You'd best come down a moment, Nathan," Sheila said, as he sat his lonely vigil beside the bed once again, waiting for Nidaba to give some sign of being ready to come out of this catatonia. Her eyes remained open. He supposed that was a good sign.

Lisette lingered about the bedroom almost constantly. And while he had expected to be relieved at having some assistance, he wasn't. The woman made the hairs on the back of his neck prickle. He felt uneasy, but for no apparent reason.

"What is it, Sheila?" he asked as she stood in the doorway.

"There's a lady at the door." Sheila hesitated, shifting her stance uneasily. "Says she's looking for a relative of hers who spent some time recently at a New Jersey psychiatric hospital."

Nathan's head came around swiftly and he saw the nervousness in Sheila's face, and her stance. He glanced at Lisette, who was listening with apparent interest, and schooled his features to reveal nothing. "Odd that she'd think we would know anything about it. What did you tell her?"

"That we knew nothing about it, of course. But she refuses to leave until she's spoken to you directly." She pressed her lips together tightly. "I tried my best, Nathan."

"I don't doubt it." He rose, started for the door, then glanced back at Nidaba uneasily. "Stay here, Sheila. If she wakes, she could be more than Lisette can handle, and I don't want anyone getting hurt."

"All right, then." Sheila took the seat Nathan had been using.

He left the three women alone, hating to do it, but knowing he could not remain at Nidaba's side constantly. He just wished he could shake the constant feeling of impending disaster. His senses were too well honed to be mistaken—something was wrong. Nidaba was not safe, but he couldn't pinpoint the source of the threat. His disquiet about every stranger to enter the house, right down to that poor dog of George's, were irrational. He needed to find a focus for the feelings, isolate the danger, pinpoint its true source. Until he did, he couldn't banish this mistrust of every newcomer.

He walked down the stairs into the front parlor, and found a very slight woman perched uneasily on the edge of the settee. Her hair was cropped short, golden blond, and her eyes were huge and lustrous.

"I'm Nathan King," he said, and she was on her feet before he finished speaking, her big gaze turned on him, one hand flexing near her side.

She eyed him somewhat warily. "My name is Arianna Sinclair-Lachlan," she said. She didn't offer her hand, so he didn't offer his. But the fact that she didn't touch him put him on guard. Immortals rarely offered a hand to strangers—for fear of giving themselves away should the stranger turn out to be an immortal as well. Was she the threat he'd been sensing?

"I'm sorry to intrude, but this is a matter of some urgency. I'm looking for a dear friend."

"A relative—or so Sheila told me." He watched her, testing her.

"She's family to me." Her reply was not really any kind of answer at all.

"I'm afraid I'm not going to be of any help to you, either way." He sighed as if he truly regretted it and hoped he was convincing. "I sincerely wish I could."

"Mr. King, I know you went to see Nidaba at the Brooker Hospital the day before her disappearance."

He kept his eyes hooded, his tone flat. "And how do you know that?"

"Every car that enters the parking lot is caught on videotape, Mr. King. I got the tapes from that day, got your plate number, and had a friend trace your name through the department of motor vehicles."

He lifted his brows. "Are you some kind of detective?" he asked.

She didn't answer that question. "Your car came in only minutes before a male visitor signed in to see Nidaba. And while he signed himself in as John Smith," she said with a smirk, "the nurse on duty gave an excellent description, which you fit to a tee. And, as it turns out, you may very well have been the last person to see her before she was taken."

"Taken?" He tipped his head to one side. "The newspapers called it an escape."

Her slender brows rose. "Then you've been following the story?"

"Is that so surprising?"

"If she had simply escaped, I'd have heard from her by now," she said, her eyes narrowing on him. "I believe she was taken."

Nathan shook his head as if the woman made no sense to him. "Suppose she simply wanted to be alone? Honestly, I see no reason to jump to conclusions here, Miss . . ."

"Ms.," she said. "Sinclair-Lachlan."

"Yes, of course. Look, I'll explain myself to you if it will help ease your mind. I went to see your . . . *friend* because of the photo in the paper. She looked familiar to me. But when I actually saw her, face to face, I realized she was not who I thought she was, and I came home. End of story," he finished. He opened his mind, tried to reach out with the rusty tendrils of his empathy to see if she was swallowing a word of his story. But he was so out of practice. For too long he'd blocked out everyone. Other than Sheila and George, he had trouble picking up on anyone these days.

The woman paced across the room slowly. Nathan looked past her, and felt his heart leap in his chest. In the living room, just beyond the arching doorway at her back, the fireplace was clearly visible—along with the portrait above the mantel. The portrait he'd painted of Nidaba, in the flowing white robes of a Sumerian High

Priestess, with the golden circlet and its crescent bow upon her head. All the woman need do was turn and look . . .

"Come, let's go sit in the library. I'll pour you a drink and—"

"Are you aware that a doctor was killed that day, right outside Nidaba's room, shortly after your visit?"

He shook his head. "No. No I wasn't," he lied. But it wasn't lost on him that she'd said "killed." Not "attacked." So Dr. Sterling hadn't made it after all.

"I have reason to believe the person who killed her was after Nidaba," the woman said.

Right. And she probably knew that because she *was* that person.

"Another man was seen in the hospital the night Nidaba disappeared," the woman went on. "And according to the nurse who saw him, he also matches your description."

"So do several million other men in the world, I would imagine."

"Somehow I doubt that," she said.

He blinked, unsure whether he'd just been insulted or paid a compliment.

"Why did you go to see her?" she barked out without warning.

She was good. Sharp and quick. What she suspected him of, he could only wonder. What she wanted of Nidaba—well he had only two guesses for that. Either she was a friend, as she claimed, or she was a hunter, in search of an immortal heart more powerful than nearly any still beating. With the exception, perhaps, of his own.

If she were to succeed, this Arianna would have power beyond compare, because she would have to take his if she hoped to take Nidaba's. And with both, she would be nearly invincible.

"I'm trying to be patient with you, Miss, but you're pushing my limits here. I've told you already. I saw the photo in the newspaper, and it reminded me of someone I used to know. I went to see her. And once I did, I realized she wasn't the person I had thought she might be, and I left. I came back here that afternoon, and have remained here ever since. There are several people who can verify that for you, if you insist on it."

She watched him as he spoke. Watched him the way a critic watches a film. Narrow-eyed and probing, constantly searching for flaws in the storyline, or the acting.

It made him uneasy, that probing gaze of hers. He broke the

lengthening silence. "Tell me, what was she doing in the mental hospital, this friend of yours?"

It had the desired effect. The woman blinked and looked away from him. "Nidaba has had . . . a lot of trauma in her life. I think it finally got to be too much for her."

"What kind of trauma?" he asked, far too quickly.

Arianna stiffened, that sharp gaze shooting right back to him. "Why do you want to know? Why are you so interested, anyway?"

Shrugging in a careless manner, he shifted his eyes away from her. "Just curious, I suppose. I did visit her, and I couldn't help but feel pity. I am human, after all."

"Are you?"

He snapped his gaze to hers. She looked away.

"Believe me, Mr. King," she said, "if we had known where she was, we would never have left her there." She sounded slightly defensive now. "But by the time that article was brought to our attention, she was gone."

"*Our* attention? There are more than one of you?" He strode to the front door and looked outside.

"The others don't know I've come," she said. "They aren't as . . . reasonable as I am."

"You call this reasonable? You come to my home and practically accuse me of kidnapping a mental patient, and that's reasonable?"

"For me?" She seemed to battle a smile for just a moment. "A year ago I'd have kicked the door in, beat you senseless, and searched the place for myself, Mr. King. Some of my friends still would. You wouldn't believe how lucky you are that I've grown . . . calmer than I used to be. But I'm warning you, the others will follow the same trail I did, and it will lead them to your door. If they find out you've harmed Nidaba—"

"Harmed her?" He feigned deep offense. "What kind of man do you think I am?"

She just stared at him. So he went on with the righteous indignation routine. "I think maybe you'd better leave now, Ms. Lachlan-Sinclair." She felt guilty. He picked up on it, and thought his rusty skills might be freeing themselves up at last.

"Sinclair-Lachlan," she corrected, but her voice was softer now. "And I'm sorry. I didn't mean to come here and offend you. Especially if you really are . . . innocent in all this." Then her eyes narrowed. "But if you're not, I'll find out. And may God help you then."

Either she was sincerely worried about Nidaba, or she was a very good actress, he thought. And from everything he could sense in her, it was the former, not the latter.

Then she drew a breath, swallowed. "What . . . what condition was she in . . . when you saw her?"

He mulled that one over. How much to reveal? In the end, just to see her reaction, he said, "Catatonic."

Moisture sprang into the woman's eyes. A flash of her pain hit him—so much so that his resolve started to waver. "Oh, no," she whispered. "Even at her worst, she was never quite that far gone."

"Then, she's had these sorts of episodes before?"

"I thought she was over it. I thought . . ." She clamped her mouth closed, looking up at him sharply. "I've already said too much. You've made it quite clear that this is no concern of yours."

"The suffering of another human being is always of concern to me," he countered.

"That's a very pretty speech."

"But not a convincing one?" He shook his head, walked through the foyer, and yanked open the front door, praying she wouldn't look through the doorway and glimpse that portrait. "I wish you luck in finding your friend," he said. "But I have things to do."

"Don't think I won't be back," she warned. "If I get even an inkling you've been lying to me—"

"I haven't been. Good-bye."

"Hmmph." She stepped through the door, but before he could close it she said, "Wait." She dug in her pocket and pulled out a card and a pen. "This is my hotel . . . and the room number is on the back." She scrawled it as she spoke. "If you remember anything, or . . . whatever . . . call me."

Nodding slowly, he said, "All right. I will." He reached for the card. She didn't give it to him. Instead she set it down on the stand just inside the door, then turned and walked away.

Nathan picked the card up, looked it over as he closed the door, then carried it idly with him back into the living room, and put it into a drawer for safekeeping.

He stood still for a moment, wondering who in hell this Arianna really was and what she truly wanted from Nidaba. Immortal, she had to be. She had deliberately avoided touching him. She said Nidaba had suffered trauma. What trauma? Could this woman have known about his past with her? Or had there been something more?

And what kind of fool question was that, anyway? Of course there had been more. Centuries had passed since the anguish he'd rained down on Nidaba's head and she on his. Surely there had been more.

Footsteps on the stairs alerted him, and he turned to see Sheila coming down. His senses jumped. "Sheila, what are you doing down here?"

She looked at him with a frown. "Lisette asked that I bring up some broth for the patient," she said. "Whatever is the matter with—Nathan?"

But he was sprinting past her, taking the stairs two at a time. He raced down the hall, threw the door open, and saw the nurse leaning over Nidaba, her back to him so he couldn't see what she was doing.

"Lisette!"

She went stiff and still for just a moment. Then she straightened and turned slowly. The only thing in her hand, he saw, was a hairbrush. Even as Nathan blew a relieved sigh and called himself an idiot, Lisette pressed a palm to her chest, as if to calm her racing heart.

"My goodness, but you scared me half to death! What's wrong?" she asked him.

Swallowing his nervousness and feeling like a fool, Nathan said, "Sorry. Nothing. Nothing at all." He was going to have to stop being so irrational. The woman was a nurse, for God's sake.

Lisette sighed and resumed brushing Nidaba's hair. Nidaba lay stiff, jerking her head with each stroke.

"Why don't you let me do that?" Nathan asked.

"Oh, now, what did you hire me for, if you're going to do everything yourself?"

He didn't take no for an answer, though. "It's not you," he said. "I just like taking care of her." He stepped forward, took the brush away from the nurse, and waited for her to step aside. When she did he said, "Go now. Take a break. Get some dinner and rest. I'll handle her myself for a while."

"But—"

"Go."

With a sigh, she finally did.

Nathan watched her until she closed the door behind her. Then he turned to Nidaba, smoothed her hair with his hand, and whispered, "I'm here. It's okay, she's gone." He pulled his chair up and began running the brush through her ebony hair in long, slow strokes. And he thought she relaxed just a little bit. "You don't like Lisette at all, do you, Nidaba?"

Naturally, there was no reply.

"You're as bad as I am, then. I don't like her either. But I wonder why," he murmured softly. "I honestly do wonder why."

The woman who called herself Lisette lingered in the hall, pacing nervously and wringing her hands as she hoped to the Gods that Nathan King would not discover the drug-filled hypodermic needle she had shoved underneath the mattress when he'd burst in on her.

Dammit, she'd barely hidden the weapon in time.

Then she slowed her pace, calmed herself. A slow, knowing smile spread across her face. So what if he *did* find it? It wouldn't change anything. She would simply have to find another way to do what she had to do—what she should have finished centuries ago!

And she would.

She always found a way to do what must be done. And this time there would be no question, no deception, no mistakes. This time Nidaba would die by Puabi's own hand. As it should have been on that hotel rooftop. As it should have been over four thousand years ago.

Chapter 9

He fell asleep brushing Nidaba's hair, and he dreamed. Memories he'd locked deep inside long ago resurfaced now, to torment him again, as fresh as if they were new.

Eannatum sat at his father's bedside, clasping the old king's withered hand in his own younger, stronger one. "I am here, Father," he whispered.

The king lay still, swathed in coverings of the finest fabrics. Sacred incense burned, and tendrils of its smoke lingered in the air, like spectral dancers. The powerful smell of the smouldering herbs laced each labored breath his father took, but Eannatum knew the herbs would not save his father. Nor would the incessant chanting of the priest who sat on the chamber floor. Nor the prayers and supplications of the entire kingdom. Death hovered, waiting to take the once mighty king away. Natum could almost hear the Dark Goddess's raspy voice, whispering from the dim corners, from the hidden realms, from the underworld . . .

I am the Darkness behind and beneath the shadows . . .

I am the absence of air that awaits at the bottom of every breath . . .

"Silence!"

Eannatum's shout caused the priest to stop his chanting. "No, I . . . didn't mean you," Eannatum said, but it didn't matter. The young man got to his feet, bowed deeply, and left the room.

But Eannatum sensed he was not alone with his father, even then. The Dark Goddess was there, lurking, waiting. He could feel her cold breath on his nape, and smell her foul stench in the air. Ereshkigal.

I am the decay that fertilizes the living . . . the bottomless pit . . .

"Shut up, Crone. Let him live!"

"My son." The voice, weak but real, came from his father. And Eannatum bowed over the old man, tightening his grip on his father's hand. "Do not speak so to the Dark Goddess. For it is into her embrace I go, and she alone will see me to the other side."

"Father, you mustn't say such things. You'll be well. I've sent for more herbs, more priests—"

Sadly, the old man shook his head. "It is over, my son. I am dying. My time in this world is done. It is as it should be."

"But—"

"Be still, Eannatum." The voice strengthened just a bit. "A dying old man I may be, but I am still your king and your sire."

"Speaking will only tire you."

"There are things that must be said."

Swallowing his objections, Eannatum nodded. He reached for a drinking vessel and held it to his father's lips, lifting the old man's head. When the king finished drinking, he lay back and stared at his son.

"Upon my death, you will receive my crown, Eannatum. The kingship of Lagash will be yours. But because of your impending marriage to Puabi, daughter of Ur, you will be called King of Kish, Ruler of all Sumer. You will take your throne on the first New Year's Day after your marriage, by sacred tradition."

"I do not wish—"

"I have no care for what you may or may not wish. I am your king. I am your father, and you will do as I command. For the good of your country, Eannatum. For the sake of peace. Already you have seen the power of Ur and Lagash joined as one. From the day word went forth that you intended to make Puabi your queen, the Ummamites began to cower. When our armies, united, began to patrol the borders, those raiders scurried like scarab beetles in full sunlight. If you don't go through with your promise now, they will fall on Sumer and rip it apart. Tell me you will keep your word. Tell me you will marry Puabi upon my death."

Inclining his head, Natum sighed. It was as close as he could come to showing his consent.

"Puabi will remain in her father's palace in Ur until after your coronation. This is wise, and best for her sake as well as your own. But as soon as you are crowned king, she will join you here in Lagash, and you will take her as your wife and your queen."

"Yes." The word was wrenched from him against his will.

"Good. It is good." For a moment, the king rested, caught his breath, before he gathered his waning strength and continued. "On New Year's Day, Inanna herself will anoint you as her chosen ruler, through the ritual we call the Sacred Marriage Rite. You know what this entails."

He nodded. He knew.

His father went on as if he did not. "The High Priestess of the temple will be cleansed and purified. She will call the Goddess to come to her, to inhabit her body. And then she will mate with you, so that you will become part God yourself. Her servant always. Her consort in human form, ruling her people of Sumer by divine right. You understand?"

He nodded slowly. "It shall be as you wish it." The High Priestess . . . Lia had been elevated to that station right after Nidaba's abandonment five years ago. It would seem sinful to copulate with the woman who had been his teacher, and Nidaba's. Almost a mother to her, in fact. It would seem wrong.

"There is no time to waste, my son. Your power must be established at once. The new year is but a quarter moon from today."

A frown bent Eannatum's brow. "I assumed you referred to the next new year, my father."

Weakly, the old man smiled. "Optimist. I've not a year left in me. No, it must be now."

"But . . . Father, you yet live. I can't very well claim the crown while you . . ." He frowned, a heaviness forming in his stomach.

Closing his eyes wearily, the king said, "This night is my last."

"No . . ." Eannatum leaned closer, touched his father's face, and the old eyes opened again. "Father, how can you know this? You might live for many weeks, months, even."

"My time ends tonight, my son. Your time is come."

"You cannot know that!"

"I know. Give your solemn vow to me that all shall be as I have told you, that I might go in peace to the underworld."

"Father—"

"Give it to me!" his father demanded, his eyes flaring wider as he came off his pillows.

"I vow it. I shall do all you ask of me. But Father—"

"Good," his father said. "Good. Now, give to me the rest of my wine, and I will sleep."

Eannatum took the chalice, held his father's head up, and put the rim to the dry, parched lips. His father drank and drank, and when Eannatum tried to take the cup away, the king pressed a hand to it to keep it there, tipping it higher, draining it.

He breathed when he finished, then lay back on the pillows, and muttered, "It is done. For the good of Sumer, it is done."

Blinking, Eannatum looked from his father's face to the cup he still held, and realization flashed blindingly through his mind. He sniffed at the contents, then tasted the remaining droplets, only to draw back and grimace at its bitterness. "No!" he cried, hurling the baked clay goblet away from him. The cup hit the wall and shattered to bits. "Father, what have you done?" He bent over his father, whose face had gone lax now. Gripping the front of his robes, Eannatum shook him. "Wake! Wake, curse you! Why have you done this? How *dare* you do such a thing! Father! Father!"

The door was flung open, and then someone was pulling at his shoulders. That young priest, Eannatum saw when he whirled on the offender.

"*You* gave it to him! Didn't you, priest? *Didn't you?*" he demanded, shaking the pale, frightened man until his teeth rattled.

"*I* gave it to him," a deep voice said.

Natum released the priest, who fell into a quivering heap on the floor, and looked up to see Lathor, the detestable High Priest who was unworthy of the title, standing in the doorway. "You?"

"Yes. I. It was his final wish, and as his most trusted friend, and spiritual counsel, I had no choice but to obey."

"You murdered your king! Traitor!"

"If you go shouting that about the palace, my prince, it will be you who will be called traitor. For you will destroy what your father gave his life to protect. This kingdom. And your throne."

Eannatum stopped halfway to throttling the bastard. He was right. Damn him, he was right. But grief and fury raged in him, and he shuddered with the very effort of restraining himself. The need for vengeance warred with the knowledge of what was best for his kingdom.

His kingdom.

Turning to the bed, he dropped to his knees and folded himself over his father's prone form. He lay his head on the silent chest, and allowed the tears to come. . . .

Time passed. Hours perhaps. The two priests had left him, for how long, he did not know. His father was dead. He was to rule. To take the throne and then to marry Puabi. He lifted his head, rubbed at his eyes, and stared at his father's still, white face with blurred vision.

"Have you had enough of mourning, then?"

He turned slowly, and saw the High Priestess, Lia, standing just behind him. Swallowing hard, he let his chin fall. "I will never have enough of mourning, it seems."

"I am sorry for your loss, my prince," she said softly. "But I have come to offer words that may be of some comfort."

"What words could comfort me now?"

"Only these. I will not serve as your *lukur*, the vessel of the Goddess, for the Sacred Marriage Rite."

"How can you . . . ?"

"I have charge of the temple. And of the spiritual guidance of Lagash now that Lathor has fled."

"Fled?" Eannatum shook his head. "But he was here . . ."

"Two days ago, my prince. You have been closeted with your father's body for two full days."

Eannatum could only blink, looking around the room in confusion. He ran a hand over his chin, felt the growth of whiskers that proved the priestess's words to be true.

"Therefore, I am the highest-ranking official of Inanna's temple in all of Lagash. And I have decreed that I am unable to fulfill this role and have also set forth the solution."

Frowning, Eannatum looked at the priestess, searching her face, unable to make much sense of her words.

"The High Priestess of every temple in all of Sumer will journey here in time for the New Year's celebration. And they will dance for you, their king. They will dance the sacred Dance of the Seven Veils, in remembrance of Inanna's descent to the underworld. And when they finish dancing, my prince, you will choose the one you wish to serve as your *lukur*."

If her words were meant to offer comfort, they fell far short. "Fine," he said. "So be it."

She nodded, some secret hiding behind her eyes. But her hands on his shoulders were soft. "Come, my prince. You need to be attended. You are tired, hungry, and grieving. Let me care for you."

He turned back toward the bed. "But my father . . ."

"I have twenty priestesses waiting to attend your father, Eannatum. With tenderness, love, and deep respect. They will take care of him, I vow it to you on my honor."

He nodded slowly, knowing it needed doing, and he let the gentle High Priestess lead him from the room.

The burial passed in a blur of grief. All Eannatum wished for was Nidaba, to feel the comfort of her arms around him. And yet if she had remained here, as a priestess serving in the temple, she might have been compelled to join in the most grim portion of the burial rites. And then he would have lost not only his father, but Nidaba as well.

Bitter irony that he *had* already lost her, and yet still couldn't quite wrap his mind around the concept, much less accept it as final. Nidaba lived. So long as she did, he would never accept it as final.

He drank too much of the barley brew and paid little heed to the events of the next several days. And yet, as the only son of the king, it was required that he be there, overseeing it all. A great pit was dug, some thirty feet deep, outside the city. A two-room stone crypt was erected in the bottom, but only one of the rooms was given a ceiling. That was the room where his father's body was interred. Eannatum had to choose his father's finest robes, his favorite sword and shield. Only a few of the king's belongings could be placed with him in the small burial chamber. It was a dire task, and one Natum could perform only when he'd nearly numbed himself with brew.

A priest took his father's most precious possessions and placed them into the burial chamber beside the king. The wall dividing that room from the other was then sealed off with baked bricks as Natum stood nearby, battling his grief and a newfound sense of his own mortality.

And not only his own, but the mortality of those around him. His father had told him that death was an accepted part of life, more a change in form than an ending. But his father was a stiff corpse now, and many of the warm bodies surrounding him soon would be. He wanted to rage against the foolishness of it all. The uselessness of it. And yet it was the way of things. It had been for many generations and would be for many more.

The second room, the one beside the burial vault, was larger, and a stone ramp had been built from the sandy surface of the ground down into it. Its only ceiling was the sky, and its only contents a large pottery urn filled with poison-laced wine and fifty unadorned golden chalices that stood in a gleaming sunlit circle on the dirt floor. As soon as the burial vault's wall was sealed, the closest advisers of the king, his friends and courtiers, and several of his most devoted young priests and priestesses marched down that tiny ramp. They strummed stringed instruments, lyres and harps, they beat drums and shook rattles in rhythm with their singing. They wore their finest garments, and one by one, smiling, they walked into the pit, picked up a chalice, and dipped wine from the urn. When they all stood with glasses filled, the singing and music grew louder, faster, the drums and rattles beat an urgent tattoo, and then all at once it stopped. Silence. And every last one of them drained the golden goblets.

Then, still smiling, they lay themselves down in perfect symmetry, all save one or two who picked up their harp and lyre and began again to play music of unearthly beauty.

A shadow crossed the wall. Eannatum swore he saw her—the Dark Goddess, dancing her dance of death, sweeping her cloak of night around Her willing children. Their chalices beside them, the poison still wet on their lips, they lay there with their eyes closed, and one by one they died. The harpist fell sideways, her fingers plucking one last lingering note. The lyre fell from limp hands to the ground. And it was done.

Lathor should have been among them, Natum thought grimly. But like a coward, he'd fled. Natum doubted that any of the innocents in the pit had deserved death as much as Lathor did. Though, perhaps, Inanna's dark sister had a less honorable method in mind for that one's demise.

As Natum turned to walk away and the sun began to sink low on the horizon, eunuchs came forward and began to cover the bodies with a layer of earth. Tomorrow another room would be built atop the corpses and packed full of the king's most prized possessions. His weapons, his armor, his favorite robes, and jewels. Then that, too, would be sealed and buried, and a single marker placed atop it all.

More than fifty people followed Natum's father to the netherworld.

It was supposed to be a great honor to his father that so many wished to serve him even beyond this lifetime. But it left Eannatum with a dull feeling of sadness, and a sense of waste. Such a great, great waste.

When he died, he hoped he would have time to plan as his father had. He hoped he would sense the Dark Goddess coming for him. Because if he did, he would strip himself of his royal robes and any clue as to his identity. He would wander into the desert, alone, and lie down in a private place where no one would find him for many days. His flesh he would give, as a welcome feast for the jackals and for the crows. And by the time a mortal man set eyes upon his corpse, he hoped there would be nothing left but bones, bleached white by the sun.

He would journey alone to Ereshkigal's underworld realm.

Better than this madness, he thought. Far better.

Wakefulness crept closer, inexorably closer to Nidaba, but she fought it. It was not easy. She became more and more aware of her body. The way it ached, its stiffness. Her hunger. The pounding in her head and the dryness in her throat. The bed beneath her. The warmth surrounding her. The voice constantly speaking in her ear.

Eannatum's voice.

But it couldn't be that, for he was long dead.

Fighting still harder, knowing she could not do so for much longer, she clung to her dreams . . . her memories.

She'd been serving as High Priestess in the temple of Mari, far away in the lush and verdant northlands. But she had been summoned by the king, and his own soldiers—acting, they said, under orders of his spiritual counsel—had arrived to escort her back to Lagash.

She had never intended to set eyes on Eannatum again. They had made their painful choices long ago. The security of an entire kingdom obviously had to come before the foolish yearnings of a young prince and a young priestess in love. He had agreed to wed the spoiled and beautiful princess of Ur. And as soon as word of that impending union spread, the nighttime raids of the Ummamites came less and less frequently. When the joined armies of Lagash and Ur began patrolling the borders, those raids ceased entirely. Peace reigned in Sumer. But it was a fragile peace. The entire world, it seemed, held its breath—waiting to see if the prince would honor his word to his kingdom.

She had no idea now why she was being summoned back to Sumer. Peace had hung precariously for two years, and during that time, she had been elevated to the rank of High Priestess. But the Ummamites were growing restless. Soon they would test Sumer's unity and the king's resolve. Times were volatile. Danger and tension were everywhere.

Nidaba's journey southward was long, and never once was she told why she had been summoned. Upon her arrival in Lagash, she peered at her beloved city from the windows of the ornate sand sled in which she rode. But there was barely time to notice all the changes. She was taken quickly to the ziggurat tower, led up the outer stairs by the king's own guards, and placed in a small chamber.

For a time she paced, furious, unable to so much as look outside in this enclosed, windowless room. But finally a tap sounded at the door, and then it opened, and she saw her onetime friend Lia standing there, wearing the golden headband of a High Priestess herself.

"Lia . . ." Tears sprang into Nidaba's eyes at the sight of her beloved teacher, and she hurried forward, embraced the woman warmly, and kissed her face. She bore no ill will toward Lia. She knew the woman had done only what she had to. She'd done the same herself, so how could she blame the woman? "Lia, what is happening? Why have I been brought here?"

Lia stood back, brushed a lock of hair from Nidaba's forehead, and smiled weakly. "To serve your king, of course. Eannatum is in need of—"

"Eannatum?" Nidaba asked quickly.

"Oh, yes. Had you not heard? His father has passed, Nidaba. Eannatum is king of Lagash now, and before this New Year's Day ends, he will be crowned Ruler of all Sumer."

Nidaba lowered her gaze. "So . . . he has married her, then? Puabi?"

"No, child. He will wed her only after he takes the throne. But he cannot take the throne at all without the sacred rite."

Very, very slowly, Nidaba raised her head. "With you as his *lukur*? The vessel of the Goddess? *You*, Lia?"

"No, child. You will be your king's *lukur*, not I."

Eyes widening, Nidaba pressed her hands to her cheeks. "Never!"

"Nonsense. I have gone to great trouble to arrange this. I am convinced it is as the Queen of Heaven wishes it. You and the other High Priestesses I have summoned here will be properly prepared, and will dance before the king. The Dance of the Seven Veils, in remembrance of Inanna's descent to the underworld. King Eannatum alone will choose the one to serve as his *lukur*. And he will choose you, Nidaba."

Nidaba shook her head, backing away from her once trusted friend. "I will leave here," she whispered. "I will leave *Sumer*."

"You will do your duty as a High Priestess of the Queen of Heaven." Lia clapped her hands twice, and a dozen young men, eunuchs all, surged into the room. They came to Nidaba, even as she turned first one way, then another in sudden panic. But before she had a chance to flee, as every part of her was screaming to do, they were gripping her, holding her still, urging her with their soft voices to be quiet, to be calm, even as they began stripping away her robes and her gown.

"You will be gentle with her," Lia ordered, her voice deeper, firmer than Nidaba could remember it ever having been before. "But you will see to it that she complies. She is to be prepared in the manner I have told you. And time is of the essence. See to it."

"Wait!" Nidaba cried.

Lia was turning to go, but she paused at the doorway, stepping aside to let four more eunuchs enter, carrying a huge tub that brimmed with steaming, scented water.

"I have warned them, Nidaba, that you have a way of . . . making the earth appear to tremble when you are angered. They are not going to flee in terror if you do so. But they *will* likely carry tales of such an event beyond these walls. Simply let them carry out their orders. This is to your benefit." Her face and her voice softened. "And my way of righting an old wrong."

"I know you were forced to do what you did, Lia. Just as I was."

Lia nodded. "They'd have done far worse to you, I fear, had I not obeyed."

"I know. And I knew they would harm you if I fought them as well."

With a deep sigh, Lia said, "There was a time when a priestess wielded more power than any man, even the king himself. But that time is long past, Nidaba. Men think of battles and wealth ahead of procreation and peace these days. And the might of woman wanes."

"Like the moon, Lia, it will wax again."

"Someday, perhaps. For now, we do what we must." She nodded at the men. "Go on, do your duties."

Nidaba shook her head. "I do not want this, Lia."

But it didn't matter. Within a few moments she stood naked, her arms and legs gripped by soft hands. She was lifted off her feet, and lowered into the tub of water. Some of the men held her gently, while others ran soft brushes over her body, up and down her legs, and between them. Over her back, and her arms and her breasts. She didn't fight the attendants. It wasn't their fault, after all, and it was her duty as a priestess to comply with the request of her king. But it was Natum. It wouldn't be an act of duty—not with him.

A hand cupped her chin, lifted her face, and Nidaba blinked back her impatience to see Lia staring down at her. "I am doing this for you, Nidaba," she whispered. "Don't you see? It is the only way you will ever be able to know him."

"I do not *want* to know him," Nidaba said softly.

"Oh, but you do," Lia said. "You want it with everything in you. You know you do. You always have."

"We said good-bye," she whispered. "I can't bear to go through it all over again."

Shaking her head slowly, Lia said no more. She only backed out of the room and left Nidaba to the ministrations of the eunuchs.

They finished washing her, and she was lifted from the tub and stood on her feet, dripping. Then yet another eunuch came in,

bringing a tray filled with elaborate containers of sacred oils and per-
fumes and pots of body paint. She tugged at the hands that still
gripped her arms.

"Please, Holy Lady," the newcomer asked softly in a voice that
had never deepened with maturity. "This is no fault of ours. We do
only as we have been ordered to do. If we fail, it will be our heads."

Nidaba stopped struggling and eyed the young man. He was
slender as a *shushima* reed, his hair long and pale, for a Sumerian. A
golden-brown color that marked him as a foreigner. His eyes, too,
were tawny gold, and gentle.

"All right," she finally told him. "Do what you must."

"Thank you, *Nin*-Nidaba." She saw genuine relief in his eyes,
and he quickly backed away, setting the tray upon the floor, and
turned to fetch a robe of purest white from a peg in the wall. "Release her," he told the others, and when they did, backing away warily, he came to her and draped the robe around her. Then he
gestured toward a stack of silken pillows, nodded for her to sit upon
them, and she did.

"What is your name?" she asked him.

"I am called Aahron."

Lifting her hand, she said, "Thank you for your kindness to me,
Aahron." And as she spoke she lowered her hand to his shoulder.

A jolt of awareness sizzled through her hand and up into her
arm. It was much like the way she felt when she touched Eannatum.
She had thought it to be a reaction that could occur only with him.

Aahron's eyes widened. "By the wings of the Gods," he whispered, so softly that she was certain only she could hear him, and his
gaze fell to her legs. He clasped the robe where it came together,
tugging it to the side and baring her left flank.

She yanked it back again. "What is it you seek, eunuch?" And if
her voice suggested she ran short of patience, then it was good he
know it now, in time to save himself from her wrath.

"I . . . was told you bore a mark of some . . . uniqueness . . .
upon your left hip," he stammered.

She shook her head slowly. "You were told incorrectly," she said,
and she saw him sigh—whether in relief or disappointment, she
could not guess. "The mark I bear is on the right." Nidaba quickly
flipped the robe the other way, giving him the merest glimpse of the
berry-colored crescent moon.

He was still for a long moment. Then suddenly, he turned to the others in the room. "The rest of you may go," he said with a tone of command. "Nin-Nidaba wishes that I alone attend her."

There was muttering, a shaking of heads, until Nidaba herself spoke. "I am a High Priestess, and a powerful one," she told them. "Do not make me demonstrate the proper method of calling down a curse!"

Within seconds, they scurried toward the door, and an instant later she and the golden-haired young man were alone. Facing her, he said, "I, too, bear the mark of the crescent upon my right hip."

Nidaba stared at him in shock. "But . . . what does it mean?"

"You do not know?"

She shook her head slowly. Closing his eyes, he sighed. "A great deal, Nidaba. A great deal. But above all, it means that you are a sister of mine. Not of the flesh, but of the soul. If you wish to escape this place . . . I will help you."

Facing Aahron, she saw courage and determination—amazing in one so young—he couldn't have seen more than 17 years. Despite her desire to escape, she felt a certain protectiveness toward him. She liked him. "They would kill you," she said.

"Not an easy task, I assure you."

"You are brave . . . but foolish. No. Perhaps it is good that I see Eannatum one more time. I have . . . I have words for him."

"He hurt you once, did he not?" Aahron asked.

"He hurt me. Yes. But through no fault of his own. We . . . we hurt each other."

"He was a fool to choose Puabi when he could have had you."

She felt her face heat, and cast it downward. "Perhaps tonight he will know just once, how it could have been, had the fates smiled on the two of us." Then, lifting her chin, she glanced at the tray of pots and vessels still sitting on the floor. "Make me beautiful, Aahron. That is the task with which you've been charged, is it not?"

Aahron smiled gently. "The Gods completed that task long before I came to be in this temple, Lady." But he did fetch the tray, and bringing it back, he sat down and placed it on the floor in between them. "But I will do my best to gild an already perfect lily."

"Then do so."

Aahron brushed her hair and pinned it up in intricate loops and twists. He anointed her with holy oils that smelled of exotic fruits and herbs. He lined her eyes in kohl that extended outward from the outer corners, and painted their lids and then added a series of dots just above her brows that followed their curve. He darkened her lashes and painted her lips, and drew sacred symbols upon her breasts and her belly. Then he reached for the final pot, and she knew what it held before he said, "The honeyed wine."

Swallowing hard, she nodded. "Apply it."

Aahron knelt before her, taking the soft brush from the jar. A thick, glistening mixture of wine and honey dripped from the end of the brush. Carefully, Aahron painted her breasts with it, coating them lightly, more heavily at the tips. Then he sat back on his heels. "If you wish to do the rest yourself . . ."

"It is the custom that this be applied by a eunuch," she whispered, her voice nearly gone now. She forced her legs to part. Aahron closed his eyes respectfully as he dipped the brush again and brought it out, dripping, to stroke a path in her most private places. Three times he dipped the brush and painted her with it. And finally he said, "It is done."

Nidaba opened her eyes, felt her face burning, and was glad to see that Aahron had turned away from her. Good of him to think of doing so. He fussed with the jars on the tray, capping and righting them. And then he went to the corner, where a wooden chest sat alone, and he drew it closer, opened its lid, and said, "The costume of the sacred dance of Inanna."

She nodded, knowing the contents. She had studied the tale of Inanna's descent. She had learned the dance. As a priestess it was a part of her duties to know these things. He pawed through the box's contents as the honeyed wine that coated her slowly dried to shining hardness.

Finally, Aahron held out a hand. "Come."

She took the hand he offered and let him draw her to her feet. And when she was standing he took the items out of the chest one at a time. The crown of the Goddess, a ring of gold with elaborate stones affixed to its face, he placed upon her head. A necklace of lapis lazuli stones he tied around her throat. He encircled her waist with the girdle of purity, which was little more than a golden belt with chains of precious stones dangling from it, shorter at the outside, longer at the center—just long enough to hide her honeyed woman's charms from view. And finally, the twin *nunuz* stones. These were small oval stones, luminous and multicolored, each suspended from a tiny chain, at the end of which was a small, spring-controlled metal clasp.

Aahron looked at her wide eyes, and she saw sympathy in his. He squeezed the clasp so that it opened its tiny teeth, then placed it on his own fingertip and released it, letting it bite down. Holding his finger up, the clasp attached, the chain and *nunuz* stone dangling from it, he said, "It pinches only a little, and the weight of the stone is not so very much."

She nodded and closing her eyes held her arms out to her sides. "Affix them as you must, Aahron."

He cleared his throat and stood very close to her. She could feel him there. And then the teeth of the tiny clasp closed on her breast, right at the nipple. They bit into her enough to make her gasp, though not in real pain. But when he took his hand away, the weight of the stone tugged at her nipple, and she could only bite her lip in bittersweet anguish as he affixed the second stone in the same manner.

As she tried to accustom herself to the sudden throbbing awareness and constant tugging at the tips of her breasts, there was a voice at the door. "Time is short!" Lia called. "The others are at the palace already."

"We are nearly finished," Aahron called. "Only a moment more."

Nidaba trembled, and every movement set the stones to dancing and pulling at her. But Aahron's gentle smile soothed her. He reached into the chest to begin pulling out the multicolored veils, all silken, which he began to drape artfully about her body. "There is much I need to tell you, Nidaba. Much you do not know about yourself. What and who you truly are."

"What can you know of me that I do not know of myself?"

He arranged the first veil about her face, covering her nose and mouth. The next two he draped 'round her shoulders, to cover her breasts. "I know that you are immortal, my lady."

She blinked down at him as he bent to suspend two more veils from the girdle of purity in the back to shield her buttocks, and another in front. The final veil was knotted at her wrist and hanging freely from it. Its use would come later, should the king desire to bind her as the Goddess had been bound during her time in the Underworld.

"Immortal? There is no such thing! What foolishness."

"It's true," he whispered. "You cannot die—well, not easily, at least."

Nidaba shivered even though she laughed at his far-fetched tales. There was something about his words that touched a chord in her, and reverberated deeply. But then the door opened, and Lia stepped into the room. "It is time," the priestess said.

Nidaba hesitated, glancing at Aahron.

"It will be all right," he told her. "And we will talk again . . . later."

chapter 10

"Nidaba. Come on, now, it's all right. Calm down." Nathan watched her thrash in the bed, her head twisting from side to side on the pillows as her fists clenched the blanket and sheets and her feet kicked at the covers.

He leaned close to her and put his hand on her cheek to keep her head still, but he was careful, remembering what had happened the last time she'd become this agitated. He could see the rapid movement behind her closed eyelids, and he sensed her need to escape from the dreams that plagued her.

"Nidaba. Come on, stop fighting it. It's time to wake up."

The restless movements stilled all at once.

"Open your eyes," he whispered. "Come on, Nidaba. Open them."

The long lashes shielding her eyes fluttered, then fluttered again, and finally, slowly, they lifted. Her eyes were blank. She stared past him at some invisible spot in space.

"Look at me."

She didn't so much as blink.

"Nidaba, look at me." He held up his finger, trying to put it in the spot at which she stared so intently. Then slowly he brought his hand to his face, and amazingly, Nidaba's huge blue-black eyes followed it. She stared at him, and the dazed, unfocused quality faded as that gaze sharpened. Her brows drew together, and her lips moved, but barely a sound came out.

"It's all right," he said, and quickly filled a glass with water from the pitcher on the nightstand. He held it to her lips as he lifted her head from the pillows. She drank. And drank some more. When he took the glass away, she came off the pillows, placing a hand over his to pull the water back to her, and drank still more. Water dribbled down her chin, wet the front of her nightdress, and still she drank. She drained the glass, and only then did she release his hand, staring down at it as she did, no doubt aware of the tingle of energy that had jumped and crackled between them when they had touched.

He reached for a tissue to dry her face. But she was already wiping it dry with the sleeve of her nightgown. She sat up in the bed, looking around the room, examining every corner, every piece of furniture, every lamp and drapery and square foot of carpet, all in dead silence.

The tension stretched tighter, and finally he could take it no more. "Do you know who you are?" he asked her softly.

Her head turned, her dark gaze coming back to him. "Yes," she said at last.

"Good, good. Tell me your name."

Those eyes narrowed. "You know my name," she said in a voice so deep he thought it sounded like an echo from beyond the grave. She looked away once more, scanning the room.

"Yes, that's right. I do. I just want to be certain you do. So . . . please, tell me, who are you?"

Her head snapped back again, eyes narrow and fierce. "I am the woman you lied to. The woman you betrayed. The woman you tried to murder, Eannatum. I am the woman who will make you pay for your past sins if it is the last thing I ever do."

He recoiled instinctively, backing away as if she'd struck him. Then he stood still, not believing the power of the hatred he saw blazing from her eyes. "Then you *do* remember—my name, at least. Nidaba, I don't know what you think I did to you, but—"

"Think? What I *think?*" She flung back the covers, swung her legs out of the bed, and surged to her feet, only to sink floorward fast.

Nathan lunged forward, gathering her to him before she could hit the floor. He held her close, and she leaned into him, hands pressed to the front of his shoulders, face lying weakly on his chest.

"What have you done to me, Natum? Why am I so weak? My knees feel like water, my head . . . swimming."

His throat went dry. "You think *I* did this to you?"

Her head lifted, eyes meeting his, searching them, mistrusting him. "Is it poison?"

His hands tightened around hers. "For the love of the Gods! Of *course* it isn't poison. Nidaba, I found you in a hospital. You'd been drugged, your doctor attacked. Killed. Perhaps by someone who was after you. I broke the law to take you away from that place, and I brought you here to protect you and to try to make you well again."

In silence she contemplated all he had said before replying at last. "You're a liar."

She said it flatly, no expression on her face, no inflection in her tone. As if it were a simple fact, and one that caused no reaction at all in her. As if it were something she had accepted long ago.

He sighed in disgust and eased her into the chair where he had been sitting only moments before. "Fine. Believe what you will. Whether you like it or not, Nidaba, you're stuck here with me for the moment. Once you get your strength back, you can do what you want. But until then, you're dependent on me."

She raised her chin, her eyes narrowed to mere slits and shifted rapidly as they scanned his face. "I *always* do what I want, Natum. And I've never been dependent on anyone. Nor will I."

"I hope you're not expecting me to argue with you. You're in no shape to fight with me right now." And besides, he thought, fights with Nidaba were seldom won. He turned away from her, tugged back the covers of the bed and looked at the damp sheets. Damp with her sweat and her tears. His jaw tight, he began peeling them off the bed.

She watched him the way a cat watches a mouse as he tossed the sheets aside. They landed in a white heap near the door. Then he walked into the bathroom, feeling her eyes on his back all the way.

He took a clean set of linens from the closet and brought them back into the bedroom. Still her gaze burned into him. Ignoring it, he began remaking the bed.

"Do you think," she asked very slowly, "that all of this will absolve you of your guilt? Nothing can do that."

"You have no clue about the state of my conscience, Nidaba, so don't pretend to."

"Are you saying you *feel* no guilt? That what you did to me was not a crime worthy of hell's hottest fires?"

He looked up from the smoothly tucked sheets. "I don't believe in hell. You know that. Neither do you." He jerked the blankets roughly back into place.

"Oh, I believe in hell, Eannatum. I've *been* there."

Her froze at her words, then slowly, he turned to face her, searching her eyes. "What . . . happened to you, Nidaba?"

Her eyes were cold. Colder than he had ever seen them. "It has been over four millennia, Natum. A great deal has happened to me. But none of it more terrible than the crimes you yourself perpetrated."

"You are wrong. Whatever you think I did to you, Nidaba, you're misinformed . . . or confused."

She skewered him with her gaze. "I know what I know, *Your Highness*. I am not insane."

"I thought you were dead," he whispered. "Do you realize that? All this time, I thought you were dead."

"And I *hoped* you were. But you live." She lowered her eyes. "I had heard you were murdered in your bed, but of course, not whether the killer had taken your heart."

"She tried."

"She?" Nidaba asked, looking up at him again. Then slowly, a smile spread across her face. "Do not tell me your bitch-queen was a Dark High Witch all along?"

"No. She only aspired to be." He stared at her in silence for a long moment, seeing a surprised expression cross her face. "Nidaba . . . the Gods know we have a great deal to talk about, you and I. Four thousand years have passed, but even before, there were things you didn't know. Many, many things. Give me the benefit of the doubt, will you?"

She snapped her head away. "Never."

"You loved me once," he said, his voice soft. "And I . . . Look, I only brought you here to protect you. If I had wanted to harm you, I would have done it by now. God, when I saw you in that place where they had you locked up, I—"

She held up both her hands, and he went silent. "You are right, Natum. The past is dead. What has been done cannot be undone by telling a revised version of the tale. So let us discuss it no more. I am dizzy with hunger. I need food. This penance you seem so determined to pay, does it extend to feeding me?"

"It's not a penance," he said. "But of course I'll feed you. I'll get you something right away. But first, Nidaba, I want to know what has happened to you."

She blinked rapidly at him, brows up, a sarcastic mannerism of hers he had always found enchanting. "I will starve to *death* in the time it would take to tell you what has happened to me in the past four millennia."

"That's not what I meant." He sighed, pushing a hand through his hair. "They said you jumped from a rooftop in Manhattan, Nidaba. You revived in an ambulance, broke an attendant's arm. They sedated you, and you, naturally, became catatonic, so they transferred you to a mental hospital and kept you there, tranquilized into a state of nothingness."

Her sarcasm vanished. Her face paled. "Drugs . . . have an exaggerated effect on our kind."

"I know."

"They had me . . . imprisoned, you say?"

He bent lower to try to see her face, which was turned downward. "You were in a locked room and a straitjacket."

Her jaw tensed, and she raised her eyes. "Then I am glad I was drugged. Being held captive for the amusement of my captors has never been my favorite pastime."

"You say that as if you speak from experience."

She only stared at him, and an icy rage shivered through him as he thought of who might have held her, harmed her. He was going to have to find out exactly what had happened to her, and who was responsible. And then he was going to have to kill them. Slowly.

It felt odd, the rise of that murderous taste for blood. It was totally at odds with the man he thought he had become. Or was that simply the man he had been pretending to be? Because truly, his time without this woman in his life seemed less than genuine somehow. Like one long act, a way to kill time until she reappeared to turn his world inside out again.

Her stomach growled.

"I'll get that food," he said, and when he left the room, she didn't say a thing to stop him.

He felt as if he were escaping some new, cruel form of torture as he stepped into the hall. To see her alive, awake, alert—and to see the hatred in her eyes, and hear her accusations—it was almost more than he could bear. And there was still the question of her mental state. She seemed perfectly lucid now. Perfectly sane, despite her wild accusations. But the young blonde woman who had come looking for her had mentioned insanity. Was Nidaba truly sane? Did she really believe the things she'd accused him of or was it part of some delusion?

"You look like the very living dead, Mr. King. Has there been some change in the patient?"

He sighed wearily as Lisette walked toward him through the hall. "She's awake, and alert," he said slowly. "I'm going to find Sheila and see about getting her something to eat, and—"

His words were cut off by an ear splitting shriek from somewhere far below. Nathan's head came up fast and his heart jumped. "Gods, that was Sheila!"

He told himself as he raced down the stairs that Sheila had in all likelihood spotted a mouse in the basement. But he knew better. Sheila didn't panic at the sight of mice. And he could feel something emanating from her. Something horrible and dark.

He ran down the stairs, hit the bottom and raced through the house toward the back. The kitchen was back there, along with the nearest entrance to the basement, from whence Sheila's cry seemed to have come. There was only one other, a hatchway door outside.

He reached the kitchen, and his blood went cold because Sheila screamed again, and he felt the horror, the despair in that sound, felt it down deep in his bones. Something was wrong. Horribly wrong.

And every cell in his body told him that whatever it was . . . it was only the beginning.

Chapter 11

Eannatum was alive. And here, in this house—so close and so real and so vibrant that the very sight of him had caused her heart to pound and ache and yearn. It had been all she could do to keep from crying—from flinging herself into his arms and kissing his face. She had touched him, felt his heat. She had heard his voice, and seen the light of life in his eyes. Felt his breath on her hair, and his arms around her . . . again.

Why was it so difficult to despise him? And why had her feelings for him not died a thousand deaths by now? All this time! By the Gods, seeing him again, even now, even knowing what she knew of him . . . it was as if the years in between had never even been.

She was just as torn now as she had been before. Torn between surrender to an all-consuming, insanely passionate hunger for him and surrender to the equally insane need to crush his corded neck between her slender hands.

Nidaba sat in the chair beside her sickbed, barely able to hold her head up. Strength in an immortal never waned this low, except as a

result of some foreign substance flowing through the veins. Eannatum had told the truth about one thing, at least. She *had* been
drugged.

So she'd been drugged. But by whom? That remained to be seen.
She tried to recall what had happened to her, how she had come to
be here, or in some hospital, if he were indeed telling the truth about
that as well. But for the life of her, she couldn't remember anything
other than . . . than returning to Scotland on the four hundred
eighty-eighth anniversary of her son's death—his *second* death—and
finding his burial site defiled, his body gone. Taken.

But that had been a full year ago. How she knew that was unclear,
but she did know it. Was certain of it. And yet the time in between remained fogged, and fragmented into hazy bits that made no sense.

It hurt to see Eannatum again. It stirred to life old memories of
innocent love, freely given. Of burning passion, eagerly sated. Of
dark betrayal too vile to believe. He had taken everything from her
once. Her love, her life, her soul . . .

Her son . . .

Yes, her son. Nicky's first death, when he'd been a small, sloe-
eyed boy—that rested squarely on Eannatum's broad shoulders. And
for that, she would never forgive him.

The bedroom door opened, and Nidaba had no more time to
contemplate these things. A woman stood there in the doorway.

The woman was small, her smooth skin at odds with her silver
hair. Her eyes seemed too sharp and clear to need the glasses she
wore. And Nidaba frowned as she stared into those eyes. Because
there was something about them—something familiar. They did not
belong in that face, those eyes.

The woman smiled, but it was false. She carried a stack of towels
in her hands and came further into the room.

Nidaba got to her feet slowly, in a smooth motion she hoped did
not betray the swamping dizziness and weakness she felt. "I prefer to
be left alone for now," she said in the strongest, firmest tone she
could manage.

The woman halted in mid-stride, brows arching in surprise.
"Have your strength back, do you?"

"Every bit of it," Nidaba lied. Every one of her nerve endings
quivered with warning, and the hairs on her nape bristled. She did
not like this strange woman.

"Well, now, I'm the expert, you know. Perhaps you ought to let me be the judge of that, hmm?" The woman came closer, and Nidaba suddenly knew that her smile was false, but the hatred in her eyes . . . that was real.

And deadly.

Nathan ran through the large kitchen, nearly colliding with George as he rounded a corner.

Pale and wide-eyed, George stood staring through the open cellar door and down the stairs, obviously torn between his longtime fear of the dark and his love for the woman he'd heard crying out. "It's Sheila," George said, fists clenched, almost bouncing on his feet in his agitation. "Somethin's wrong with Sheila!"

Nathan flicked the light switch at the top of the stairs. Nothing happened. "It's all right, George," Nathan said, pushing past him and starting down the stairs. "Stay right where you are. I'll take care of this." He took the stairs two at a time, reached the bottom, tried the light switch there. Again, nothing happened.

"Sheila?" he called.

Then he listened. Soft sounds reached him through the damp darkness—ragged broken breaths, as if she were crying. "Sheila, love, what is it? What's wrong?" Stepping forward, Nathan fumbled in his pocket for a match, a lighter, anything. But he found nothing. Then he saw the small beam of a flashlight, lying cockeyed on the cellar floor, illuminating only a few bricks in the wall. Sheila must have dropped it.

Nathan picked up the pace, bent to snatch up the light, and began moving its beam around. "Sheila, sweetheart, talk to me. Where are you? Are you hurt?"

Then the beam of light found her, and Nathan halted. He thought his heart stopped beating. Sheila sat on the basement floor, cradling a body—an obviously *dead* body, already stiff with rigor mortis. It was a woman, clad only in her underclothes. Nathan swore and moved closer, kneeling down near Sheila, aiming the beam of light on the woman's face.

And then his head spun, and his chest contracted. "My God, that's . . . *Lisette!*"

"I don't understand it, Nathan!" Sheila was sobbing, rocking the body in her arms. "I was only just talking to her . . . but she's dead. She's dead, Nathan, my best friend, my mate Lisette, she's dead!"

The woman in Nidaba's room flung her stack of towels aside. In her hand a dagger gleamed. A dagger with a jewel-bedecked hilt.

Nidaba's hand shot to her thigh automatically, but her own blade was not there. And the woman who she knew must be a Dark Witch, lifted hers and charged. Nidaba reacted with the instincts of a seasoned warrior. She ducked the blade and grabbed up the nearest weapon she could get her hands on. A water pitcher. Damn! Nearly useless. The blade hissed past as Nidaba lunged to the side. Then she swung the half-filled pitcher as hard as she could, and it slammed into the woman's head. Water sloshed and splashed everywhere. But neither it nor the force of the blow seemed to faze her attacker, and within seconds Nidaba found her back pressed to the mattress by the weight of the Dark Witch.

Nidaba held the woman's wrists, fighting to keep the blade away from her own flesh. But she was so weak, and this other—an old immortal, obviously—so strong. Nidaba let go of the woman's left hand, using both of hers to grip the right one, the one that wielded the blade. The only result was that the evil one's left hand was free now, to pound and punish. It clawed, it struck, it bruised. And yet Nidaba bore it, focused only on holding the knife's razor edge away from her body. Her *heart!*

Her face split and bleeding, her body racked with pain, Nidaba broke out in a cold sweat as she lay there, locked in an endless standoff with the woman. The muscles in her arms quivered and burned with exhaustion as she held fast. Her elbows gave, and she shot them straight again. They weakened, and she forced them firm. They fell . . . and the blade came down . . .

"*Noooooooo!*"

The sound was a long, drawn-out bellow, like the blast of an infuriated, charging bull. And the next thing Nidaba knew, her attacker was knocked off of her by another body.

Eannatum's body.

The impact launched the Dark Witch through a nearby window. Glass shattered, and Nidaba jerked her head around. But all she saw was the demolished window. Then her view was blocked by

Eannatum's strong back as he looked outside, down at the ground
far below.

"Is she . . . ?"

He turned, breathless, staring at her. "Gone. Dammit, she's long
gone, whoever she was!"

Nidaba lay still, her entire body shaking with shock, adrenaline,
pain, and this damned debilitating weakness. "Is this how you plan
to hasten my recovery, Natum? By placing me in the care of Dark
Witches intent on carving out my heart?"

He came to her, and she could see the damage of her own face reflected clearly in the grimace of his. "You're bleeding." He hurried
into the bathroom and returned seconds later with a basin of water
and a cloth. Settling himself on the bed beside her, he gently
cleansed each cut, bathed each bruise.

He did not seem at all like the man she knew him to be. The man
who had tried to have her killed. Who had ordered the execution of
his own son in order to protect his precious throne, his precious
kingdom.

Even then she'd doubted he was capable of such an atrocity.
Even then. And those doubts had plagued her all this time. The mur-
derers had been *his* soldiers, *his* men—men who wouldn't *dare* to go
against his orders. And yet those doubts lingered.

She turned her head to the side to avoid his ministrations. "It will
heal soon enough. Don't forget what I am."

"I know full well what you are, Nidaba," he said, dropping the
cloth into the basin and setting both aside. "But the regeneration
process has been slowed in you. Probably because of the tranquilizers you were given, and your weakened state."

"All of which would pass quite quickly if you would stop fussing
and simply *feed me*."

He thinned his lips. "Come downstairs, then. I don't dare leave
you alone again . . . and I have a . . . situation to deal with."

"With a Dark Witch in your house, I would imagine you do."

He held out a hand, and she merely stared at it.

"In case you haven't noticed, Nidaba, someone is trying to kill
you. Now until you're back in fighting condition, you're going to
have to trust someone."

"Someone, perhaps. But you?"

"I just saved your life," he pointed out. He was still holding out his hand, staring into her eyes.

With a sigh, she took it and let him help her to her feet. "Don't think that saving my life just now even begins to make things right between us, Eannatum."

"I am called Nathan King now," he said, pulling her to her feet.

"Why?"

He lifted his brows. "It's more in keeping with the times. No one here knows what I am, Nidaba. I would like to keep it that way."

She sniffed. "No doubt. I would be ashamed too, in your place." She started toward the door, but when she would have pulled her hand free of his, he tightened his grasp.

"I am not ashamed."

She glanced back at him, at his blazing eyes as proud as if he were still a mighty king. "You should be." Then she tossed her head, even though the act made her dizzy. "As for me, I am a Witch. My name is Nidaba. I will not change it, nor will I pretend to be something else, as you do. I am no ordinary mortal, Eannatum. Don't dare expect me to act like one."

"Why would I expect that, Nidaba? You didn't *act* like one when you *were* one."

She looked at him quickly, in search of the smile she heard in his tone. But it was evident only in the slight sparkle of his eyes.

"Do you mock me, Natum?"

He shook his head slowly. "No, Nidaba. I'm just glad to see you haven't changed all that much."

"Haven't I?"

He shrugged. "You still seem to believe you're as much goddess as woman." Reaching out, he tucked a lock of hair behind her ear. "It was always one of the things I loved best about you."

She averted her eyes abruptly, and her voice became choked and hoarse. "Please . . . don't use that word when referring to me."

"What word?" he asked.

She didn't answer. Instead she moved carefully into the hallway. Her legs buckled, though, causing her to sway and grip the doorjamb. Eannatum slid his arms around her, beneath her, and swept her up off her feet.

"I can walk," she protested.

"Not unless you're strong enough to make me put you down," he said.

She knew she wasn't, so she let him carry her through the hall and down the stairs, and she tried not to notice how very protective his strong arms felt around her, or how warm and solid his chest was beneath her, or how deep his eyes were when she looked into them from this close.

But she noticed all of that anyway.

He set her down gently in a rocking chair in what seemed to be a library, and called out to someone. Soon enough a giant of a man, wearing a bright orange necktie over a yellow knit sweater came thumping into the room.

"George, this is Nidaba," Natum said.

George looked at her and his eyes widened. "You're the lady!"

She felt her brows go up.

"You got better! I knew you would. I told you she would, didn't I, Nathan? And she did! See?"

"Yes, George, you were right."

George eyed her steadily. "I'm a nice person," he said. "My name is George. Nathan is my friend. Are you going to break my arm?"

Nidaba blinked, tilting her head to one side, and studying him with a hint of amusement. "Of course I'm not going to break your arm," she said. "Are you going to break mine?"

George shook his head emphatically from side to side. "No way. I promise."

"Well, then, I suppose we should get along."

"George," Nathan said, "did you take Sheila up to her room as I told you?"

"Yeah, I did. But she's not right, Nathan. She's all curled up on her bed, and she's crying something awful. I tried to make her stop, but nothing I said made her feel any better. I never seen Sheila cry before."

"Neither have I." Natum pinched the bridge of his nose as if to pinch away some nagging worry.

"I don't like it, Nathan. I want you to make her stop. What happened in the cellar that would make Sheila cry like that?"

Natum clasped George's arm, squeezed, and Nidaba saw that the big man was quite like a child. She also saw clearly Natum's affection for him. "I'm going to explain all of that later, George. For right now, I want you to stay here with Nidaba. I don't want you to let anyone come near her. You understand?"

"Not even Lisette?" George asked.

"Especially not Lisette."

"Okay, Nathan."

Nidaba sighed, about to argue that she needed no protection, but then decided it would carry no weight, since she couldn't even get down the stairs under her own power. And Natum sent her a glance that was almost . . . kind. Warm. "I won't be long."

She simply nodded and watched him go.

"So," she said to George, who had taken a seat beside her, and was staring at her oddly, "who is this . . . Sheila?"

George smiled. "She's Nathan's friend, just like me. She lives here, does the cooking, and takes care of the flowers, and things like that. She's an awfully good cook, you know."

"Is she?" So some woman lived here with Natum. Nidaba wondered what that signified, and then wondered why she cared. "I am starving nearly to death. I would love to sample some of her cooking."

George looked at the floor. "We could . . . go to the kitchen and get some . . . but the cellar door is still open, and I don't know what happened down there."

Nidaba frowned. "Something happened in the cellar?"

Nodding, George cast a nervous glance toward the closed library door. "Sheila was down there screaming. And the lights wouldn't work. And then Nathan went down to see what was wrong. And then he came running back up, pulling Sheila behind him, and he told me to get her to her room, and then he ran up the stairs again. I don't know what happened. But something sure scared Sheila pretty bad."

"It scared you too, didn't it, George?"

He bit his lip and picked at his sweater.

"Maybe we don't need to go to the kitchen," Nidaba said, feeling sorry for him. Feeling almost . . . protective of him, if that wasn't the strangest thing in the world. It wasn't like her to go soft over mortals. But this one . . . well, he'd touched something inside her. "Isn't there any food any where else in this house?"

George's looked up and smiled. "There's a fruit bowl in the living room!"

"Then let's go to the living room," she suggested.

Still grinning, George swooped down on her like the world's clumsiest hawk, awkwardly lifting her up into the air. When she protested, he said, "Nathan said for you to stay off your feet." Then he carried her right out of the library, through a formal dining room, and into a wide parlor with a fireplace on one side and exquisite antique furnishings all around.

None of that caught her eye, though. What caught her attention was the painting—larger than life—above the mantel. An image of a woman in the unmistakable white gown and headpiece of a Sumerian High Priestess of Inanna. She stood in the desert, amid ruins of once great towers, with her arms extended up toward the giant moon. Crescent-shaped moonbeams reflected from her black eyes, and a nimbus of light surrounded her. As if she truly were some sort of divine being. "It's . . . me," she whispered.

"Yeah. I thought so too, but Nathan wouldn't admit it," George said, plunking her down into an armchair. He reached out for a bowl of fruit and set it in her lap.

Narrowing her eyes, Nidaba tried to make out the signature that was barely visible in the left corner, hidden within the swirling strands of long black hair. Eventually she saw it. But it was made up of lines in the shape of the old cuneiform script, rather than any modern alphabet, and appeared to the casual observer to be no more than swirls in the blowing sand. But she was no casual observer. The symbols stood for his name: Eannatum.

A scratching sound drew her head around. George leapt to his feet, his face lighting up as he lumbered unevenly toward the closed door.

"George, don't—" Nidaba began, but even before she could finish the sentence, George was opening the door.

Nidaba tensed . . . then relaxed as a beautiful, sleek-coated dog dove through the door, leaping on George, and licking his hands. George fell to his knees, hugging and petting the animal. "Oh, Queenie, I'm so glad you came home!" he said, laughing.

Nidaba couldn't help but smile at the two of them as she bit into a gleaming red apple. "You mean she's been missing?"

"I was so afraid she wouldn't come back!" George said in between laughter, hugging the animal, rolling on the floor with the dog.

Like a little boy and his long lost pup, she thought as she watched them.

Nathan watched her eat.

And he thought that a few days ago he had been leading a placid, calm, even respectable mortal life and had been perfectly content with it. And then, with no more than a glimpse of that face in a blurry newspaper photo, everything had changed. He had broken-and-entered, kidnapped a mental patient, fled the police, and at this moment there was a dead body lying in his basement.

He didn't know what the hell he was going to do about poor Lisette. Right now, Sheila was upstairs resting, with the help of a double dose of sleeping pills. And George was confused, frightened by all the turmoil, but thankfully distracted from it by the reappearance of his stray. The dog lay underneath the dining table at George's feet, eagerly but delicately devouring the bits of food George offered.

Nidaba, in stark contrast, wolfed her own meal as if she hadn't been fed in a month. She didn't even seem to notice that it consisted of prepackaged frozen foods he'd dug out of the freezer and heated in the microwave, with dehydrated side dishes. The stuff must have been buried in there since his pre-Sheila days. Pseudo fried chicken, instant mashed potatoes, heat-and-serve gravy. He was not untalented in the culinary arts, but he'd been in a hurry. The meal had all the flavor of cardboard, but flavor wasn't what Nidaba needed. Protein and carbohydrates were. Calories, for energy and the strength to restore her. There were plenty in the food he served her.

As she ate, he could already see the changes taking place: the color, slowly creeping more deeply into her skin; her hair, losing that limp dullness, and coming alive, thickening, shining. The changes were so gradual mortal eyes would likely never notice—not until later, when they might well look twice and wonder when she'd improved so drastically. But his eyes were not mortal. And they saw everything. The way her cheeks began to plump and fill out, the slow fading of the dark circles beneath her eyes, and of the bruises that had just begun to form on her face. The mending of her split lip and the cut in her cheek.

George, thankfully, was oblivious to all of it.

Finally Nidaba seemed to have sated her hunger. She drank two full glasses of water, leaned back in her chair, and looked at him, looking at her. Her arms no longer resembled twigs beneath the white nightgown. Her collarbones no longer protruded so sharply. He let his gaze slide lower, to where her breasts pushed at the buttons on the soft white cotton nightgown as they had not done before, making the fabric pull tight and gape slightly in between. He knew she was aware of his gaze, because of the way those breasts reacted to it—peaks stiffening as if his stare were a physical touch. And he could not help remembering the first time he'd seen them full and healthy, and aroused. For just a moment, he allowed himself the pleasure of exploring that memory. He couldn't have resisted it even had he wanted to.

Eannatum sat upon the satin pillows in the throne room, which was filled with honored guests come to attend his coronation. Platters of food were heaped on every table. Chalices were filled to overflowing, and the pleasant, excited hum of conversation filled the room. But he was hearing none of it. He had only one thing on his mind.

Nidaba. He had finally made sense of the priestess Lia's words to him just after his father's death. She had arranged it so that every High Priestess in the kingdom would come here—so that he would be allowed to choose from among them which one would serve as his *lukur*. And Nidaba, according to Natum's dying father, had been elevated to High Priestess status in the faraway land of Mari. By royal command, she had to be here.

She had left him long ago, chosen to serve her Goddess, made him realize he must serve his country. She had broken his heart, and he knew he had broken hers. But he was not the same heartsick boy now. Two years of training with his father's armies, battling in skirmishes with the Ummamites to prove the new united Sumer equal to the task, had changed him. And now . . . now he was her king. And tonight she would serve *him*, as custom and the law decreed. He could not but help come alive at the prospect. He wouldn't have been human to do otherwise. He was burning inside. Tomorrow he would marry another, but tonight . . . tonight he would know the woman he'd wanted for what seemed like his entire life. Tonight, Nidaba would be his.

He had waited as long as he could. All propriety had been observed. He clapped his hands twice, and the din turned to silence. "Begin the dance," he commanded.

Immediately the musicians began to play. The *algar* and harp players plucked at their strings in a harmonious and sensual melody while the others kept time with the jangling cadence of the *ala* and the beat of the drums. One by one, the High Priestesses entered the chamber, cloaked by veils of colorful silk that floated and swirled as they moved. Eannatum's eyes searched for Nidaba's among the women who twirled before him. But they were covered well . . . and they kept their eyes respectfully lowered.

Lia retold the tale as the woman danced and twirled.

"Long ago the Queen of Heaven turned her eyes to the Great Below. The Queen of the Great Above did turn her eyes to the Great Below. And so she journeyed there. Inanna, unafraid, peered into the darkness that so frightens us all. Bravely, she journeyed there. And at each of the seven gates, she was stopped by the guardians of the netherworld. Seven times she was stopped by the netherworld gatekeepers. And at each gate, as was the custom, she had to give over one of her garments before she was allowed to pass. For no one carries earthly costumes, nor masks, nor jewels, nor riches, nor titles with them into the land of the dead. The darkness must be entered into naked. With no pretense, no pride. Only the true self. This is what makes visiting there so frightening."

At Lia's nod, Natum clapped his hands once, and the first of the seven veils fell away from each woman. The one that had covered their hair. Narrowing his eyes, Natum got to his feet and moved among the dancers, eyeing each one closely. There were twenty women dancing for him. Twenty dropping a second veil, and a third. Twenty hoping to be chosen as the king's sacred *lukur*. But only one he wanted.

"Naked, Inanna was brought before her Dark Sister, Ereshkigal. Naked, she had to face her own Dark Sister. Her own dark side. Just as we must each face the darkness within us. But Inanna emerged from the darkness—proving that we can do the same. Meet, embrace, accept, understand, and in the end gain mastery over our own shadow side."

Natum clapped his hands again, and the fourth veil fell away. Twenty beautiful copper-skinned bodies gyrated for his pleasure. Round, delectable buttocks swung from side to side as he passed. Golden breasts bounced for him, *nunuz* stones weighing down their swollen tips. Soft bellies, dark eyes . . .

Nidaba's dark eyes.

He stilled when he saw her, and kept his gaze locked only to hers. She didn't look away, but held his eyes. Her hips rolled toward him, and away, and only three veils remained on her. The one that covered her nose and mouth from his view, the one knotted at her wrist, and the one that hung from the chain of gold at her waist, draping down to cover her center. He didn't clap his hands. Instead he reached out, and took that veil away from the chain at her waist. Then he held up his hand, and the music and dancing stopped.

The chains of precious stone that dangled from her waist concealed very little of her. Her small waist and large breasts pleased him immensely, as did the unusual length and grace of her arms, and her endless legs. He'd never seen her unclothed before. But he'd known she would be exquisite, and he was not disappointed. And with a flick of his wrist, he tugged the delicate scarf away from her face so he could watch her every expression.

"Turn around," he told her.

Her eyes widened ever so slightly. But she knew she had no choice here, and she did as her king commanded. She turned.

And he took his time. He let his eyes feast on the long curve of her spine, and the swell of her rounded buttocks, and the slight crease at the base where they met her thighs. He would press his lips to that crease tonight. He saw with some surprise the birthmark she bore. The crescent moon blazed on her thigh. Perhaps it was a sign of divine approval, for he bore the same mark himself.

"Face me," he told her.

Again, she did as he told her, her eyes defiant but full of fire. And he knew beyond any doubt she was as aroused right now as he was. Though she might have denied it, he could see it there in her eyes. Her chin was high, her stance proud. But her eyes blazed with secret longings, denied desires. He reached up to touch the *nunuz* stone that dangled from her breast, fingered the stone slowly. Each time it moved he saw the reaction in her eyes, until finally he gave the stone the slightest tug, and heard her suck her breath through her teeth. "This one," he said at last, catching the veil that was tied to her wrist and pulling her out of the group of priestesses. "This is the priestess who shall be my *lukur*. Take her to the sacred bedchamber to await the arrival of her king."

At his nod, his men-at-arms came forward and flanked Nidaba, ready to lead her away. How times had changed, he thought vaguely. Only a generation ago, it would have been the High Priestess doing the choosing. She would have had final say over whether the son of a king was worthy of the throne, and if he fell short of her standards, she would have chosen his replacement.

Now, the reality of the old ways was rapidly fading into symbolic acts with far less meaning, played out to reinforce the image of the king as supreme commander of all within his reach—even the High Priestesses of Inanna.

"Do not forget, my king," Nidaba said softly, shocking everyone in the throne room by speaking to him without permission at such a formal event. "It will be the Goddess you embrace this night. Not me. Inanna will use my body as her sacred vessel. I myself will have no part to play. But if you displease her, she may very well strike you down."

He leaned in close, and whispered in her ear, "Do you really believe that is the way it will be, Nidaba?" His cheek brushed over hers. "I do not. But we shall see. Either way, I have no intention of displeasing . . . the woman I will be with tonight."

Straightening, he commanded his men. "Go. And remember this is the body of the Goddess you have in your charge. Treat her as such. She is to have anything she desires."

She turned away from him and marched toward the door like a martyr to the pyre.

"Inanna is an impatient Goddess," someone said. "Already she lives in this priestess! See how proudly she moves!"

"Fool, don't you recognize her? She's the priestess who is half goddess already!"

"They say she has strange powers. . . ."

"Left on the doorstep of the temple by the Goddess Herself . . ."

The murmuring spread. Nidaba stopped walking and turned to

watch, as several bowed their heads in respect when she passed. A look of confusion crossed her features as she met Eannatum's eyes once more. He placed his right fist in the palm of his left hand and bowed his head. A gesture of deep respect, which he gave willingly, and meant sincerely.

Then everyone in the room followed his example, saluting her, bowing their heads. A frown creased her brow as she turned to go.

"You are staring," Nidaba said in her deep, rich voice, like honey on his senses.

Nathan blinked and shook himself out of the past. "I was . . . remembering. The coronation." He glanced sideways at George, expecting to see the man there, looking puzzled, but George had gone into the front parlor with his dog, and the two were relaxing near the fire. "When you danced for me," he said, finally.

Nidaba's thick lashes came down to veil her gaze. "I was confused when they all began to treat me as if I were the Goddess herself. As if she had already descended into my body."

He smiled very slowly. "But she had, Nidaba."

"No. She never did. She turned her face away from me that night. Abandoned me because I did not serve her well."

"You're wrong. How have you managed to live so long, and not yet come to understand your own nature? A woman like you, Nidaba, is the Goddess personified. She didn't need to take over your body. She already lived in you, from the day you were born."

That same tiny frown he'd seen in the past, marred her brow. He would have said more, but Sheila's voice, groggy and thick, interrupted him.

"Nathan, what are we goin' to do about poor Lisette?"

He stalled for a response even as he hurried to help her to the table. "Come, Sheila. Sit. Are you all right?"

"I slept some," she said, sniffling, and shuffled her feet as he led her to a chair. Then she sank into it as if boneless.

"Nidaba, this is Sheila. She's my most trusted friend."

Nidaba studied the woman, and Nathan thought she looked first relieved at the sight of Sheila and then concerned as she perused Sheila's wet, red eyes and puffy face. Nidaba glanced at Nathan then, a question in her eyes. "Is she one of —?"

"No." He said it quickly, not giving her time complete the question.

Nidaba looked doubtful. "That's what you thought about the other one, you'll recall."

"Sheila's been with me for years. The other one . . . only a day or two."

Nidaba sniffed, but eyeing the woman again, seemed to accept his word that Sheila was not a Dark Witch on the hunt.

"It's good to see you up and around, miss," Sheila said. "I only wish it had been under better circumst'nces. Not with death itself breathing down our very necks." And she shivered as she said it.

"Death?" Nidaba looked from Nathan to Sheila and back again.

"Sheila's best friend, Lisette, was a nurse," Nathan explained. "We hired her to come here, to help us care for you."

Nidaba lifted one brow in regal sarcasm. "Oh? Was she the one who tried to murder me a short while ago?"

"Tried to *murder* you? I'd like to know how she managed it when she's been lyin' dead in the basement all the afternoon!" Sheila cried, her voice breaking near the end.

"Please," Nathan said, before Nidaba could respond yet again. "If the two of you will let me speak." They both fell silent. "Good. Sheila . . . Dammit, I don't know how to say this gently."

"Say it straight, Nathan. I'm no frail flower, as you know very well by now. Or ought to."

Drawing a breath, Nathan sighed. "Your friend Lisette has been lying in that basement far longer than you realize. In fact, I suspect she was put there within a few hours of her arrival here."

"Well, now, don't be daft, Nathan! She's been right up here with us, helping to care for your ladyfriend. We've both seen her, spoken to her . . ." Sheila stopped herself when he held up a hand.

"The woman who's been walking around here with us was an impostor. Someone who killed Lisette and then made herself look just like her in order to fool us."

"Impossible!" Sheila said. Nidaba, though, remained silent.

"Remember how she lost her voice right after she got here?" Nathan asked. "So she wouldn't speak above that odd, hoarse whisper? That was because she couldn't change her voice. Only her appearance, Sheila. If you had heard her speak at full volume, you would have known it wasn't your friend's voice."

Sheila blinked. "But . . . but . . . how? She looked—it was no disguise, Nathan. She looked exactly like Lisette. Even a makeup artist couldn't have done such a convincing job of disguising herself."

"A glamourie," Nidaba murmured. "By the Gods, she must be good."

"A glam . . . what?" Sheila rubbed her forehead with two fingers. "I don't understand any of this! Even if someone *could* make themselves look that much like Lisette, why would they bother? Why would anyone want to murder her and then impersonate her? It just makes no sense!"

"To try to get to me," Nidaba said very quietly. "I'm very sorry your friend got caught up in all of this, Sheila. It seems I've brought this upon you, and for that . . . I am deeply sorry."

Sheila, though, was still shaking her head. "It makes no sense," she said again. "She looked . . . she looked exactly . . . How could anyone be that convincing?"

Nidaba's eyes met Nathan's. Only an immortal High Witch, and a very old one at that, would be likely to have mastered such an art, and Nidaba knew that as well as Nathan did himself. He could see the knowledge there. This enemy they faced could be more powerful than they had first believed.

"What are we going to do with her, Nathan? I . . . I just . . . if we call the police . . ."

"If we call the police, I'll be arrested for kidnapping Nidaba, she'll probably end up back in the mental ward, a sitting duck for this killer, and you'll in all likelihood get yourself deported. We could both easily end up as suspects in Lisette's murder, as well. I don't think that's what she would want. Do you, Sheila?"

"Well . . . well, no. I think she would want the person who did this to her caught, and . . . and punished."

"I'll see to it that they are. I give you my word on that," he said. "But not if we get the police involved." Nathan got to his feet, came around the table, and took Sheila's hands in his. "Did she have any family, Sheila?"

Sheila shook her head. "She was alone. Oh, there may have been a cousin or two, back in Queensland, but aside from that . . . no. No one." She met his eyes, and he could see that she understood. Slowly, she nodded. "I want her buried proper, Nathan. Not tossed into a swamp somewhere. She deserves respect. Words said over her. A decent resting place."

"I'll see to it," he promised, lowering his head as a heavy ache settled in his chest. "Trust me."

Chapter 12

Nidaba stood on the cliffs above the sea, with George on her right and Sheila on her left. The ever-present Rottweiler, Queenie, sat at George's feet, her gaze focused on the tiny boat, just as everyone else's was. The small craft bobbed and bounded on the waves as Natum rowed further and further out into the sea. The sky beyond him settled to a darker shade of gray, and moments later the little boat was barely visible.

"I can't see him anymore," George said, sounding scared to death. And no wonder, with the wind, the darkness, and the knowledge that a killer lurked somewhere near.

Nidaba had realized almost from the first words she had exchanged with the big man that he was a child in a man's body. Part of him—that innocent part—reminded her painfully of the son she'd had once, long ago. Her Nicodimus.

She automatically closed her hand around George's larger one and squeezed. "Don't be afraid, George. He'll light the lamp in a moment, you'll see."

"And we should light ours, as well." At Nidaba's other side, Sheila bent down to do just that, then stood, lifting the kerosene lantern so its soft golden glow spilled all around them.

The wind blew in off the sea, and Nidaba's hair snapped and danced in time with the lantern's flame. She wore a long black dress she had found in the closet. Eannatum had, Sheila told her, stocked it himself, choosing each item for her personally. This gown, a simple one of some clingy modern fabric, had a scooped neckline and long sleeves that fit her arms snugly. It hugged her body the same way, all the way to her hips. From there it flowed freely to puddle around her feet. A braided cord of silver, gold, and black served as a sash, tied loosely about her waist, the knot dipping lower in front, forming a vee. It was very much like the clothing she had worn of old, except in color. And she felt the tug, the calling of the High Priestess she had been and still was, deep inside. One of her duties had been to comfort the bereaved on occasions such as this one. She had, she realized dully, fallen into her old role with barely a pause.

Finally, in the distance, an answering light appeared on the sea. It rose, ghostlike, then moved slowly from side to side in wide arcs.

"It's time," Nidaba said.

Sheila lowered her head in silent prayer, her free hand closing around Nidaba's, though she may not even have been aware of it. She was not an immortal. Natum had assured her of as much, but Nidaba knew it for certain by her touch. And by her trembling, she knew the woman was in pain.

"Good-bye, dear friend," Sheila whispered at last.

"Not good-bye," Nidaba said softly. "She goes into the arms of the Goddess, where she will find comfort and perfect love as she adjusts to her new form. No longer physical as we are, but every bit as alive, every bit as real. Your friend is still with you, Sheila. She lives on. And she's all right. She truly is."

Blinking, Sheila turned to Nidaba. "You really believe that?"

"I do. Speak to her, if you need evidence of it. Ask her for a sign."

Sheila's face puckered with her frown. But she didn't speak. She only turned to stare out at the sea as the wind made the lamp flicker.

Nidaba closed her eyes, focused her energies, silently called on the departed soul to send comfort to her friend. As she opened her eyes again, the clouds parted, and the lopsided gibbous moon shone down on the waves for just a moment. Something arched up out of the water, moving gracefully, its skin slick and shining in the moonlight. Then it splashed down again, vanishing beneath the waves.

"Was that . . . ?" Sheila began.

The creature jumped again, and with a final slap of its tail, submerged.

"It was . . . a dolphin," Sheila said. "But it shouldn't have been. Not this far north, this late in the season."

She looked at Nidaba. "What does it mean?"

Nidaba smiled. "You tell me."

Blinking, Sheila bit her lip, but it didn't stop the tears. "When we were girls together, in Townsville, in Queensland, we used to go to Halifax Bay and spend hours just watching the dolphins." She dashed away tears. "When we were sixteen, we bought matchin' pendants." She touched the necklace at her throat, lifting it. And in the glow of the lantern, Nidaba saw the pendant, a tiny silver dolphin with a gleaming topaz eye.

"You've had your sign," Nidaba murmured. "Speak to her, if you wish. She'll hear you."

Swallowing hard, Sheila closed her hand around the pendant, and shut her eyes. "I loved you, Lisette, my friend. Like my own sister you were, and are. I'll cherish your memory always, love."

"Go in peace," Nidaba intoned.

She could not see Nathan sliding the lifeless, lovingly wrapped body into the sea. But she sensed it happening. Nathan knew the ocean here. Knew the tides. He hadn't weighted the dead woman's body, but instead had placed her into the loving embrace of an outgoing current that would sweep her quickly out into the sea's forgiving depths.

Sheila sniffled. Nidaba felt a true tug at her heart. These two people who flanked her were, she sensed, very dear to Nathan. It was not difficult to see why. Looking sideways at the woman's tear-filled eyes, she was moved to speak. No longer in the role of comforting High Priestess, however, but in that of avenging angel. "I promise you, Sheila, the person who killed your friend will pay. I will see to it."

Looking back at her, Sheila studied her for a long moment, then nodded once. "I do believe you will," she whispered.

Glancing out to sea, Nidaba saw the tiny golden light of Nathan's lantern moving slowly, steadily, back toward shore. It was done.

Still holding their hands, Nidaba led the other two away from the shore and back to the house. It would take time for Natum to make his way back to them. Sheila was exhausted, emotionally drained. And George had dealt with far more excitement today than he was used to. They entered the house through the rear door, which led into the kitchen. Nidaba released their hands and went to the stove, rummaging around in search of a pot, and teabags.

"You needn't do that, now," Sheila was saying. "You're the one who's been so . . . so ill. I ought to be fixin' tea for you."

Nidaba offered a smile. "Nonsense. You've been waiting on me hand and foot while I've been lying like a lump in that bedroom upstairs. But I'm fine now. Better every moment, in fact."

She saw the doubt in Sheila's eyes, even as the woman slumped into a kitchen chair. "It truly is amazin', how fast you seem to be recovering," she said.

Nidaba knew she was likely making conversation only to keep from thinking too much about her loss. It was natural, and she was glad to play along. "It was a reaction to the drug they gave me that made me so ill," Nidaba explained, knowing the woman might still have some lingering doubts about her mental state.

Sheila frowned. "Like . . . an allergy, Nathan said."

"Exactly like that." Locating the kettle, Nidaba filled it and set it on the burner to heat. "I was given a tranquilizer, and when I reacted the way I did, it was mistaken for a mental breakdown of some kind, and treated with more drugs, which only worsened the reaction."

Nodding, Sheila sighed. "And that's why they had you locked up in that hospital. I vow, it must have been horrible for you."

Nidaba found cups, lined three of them up on the counter, and began opening cupboards in search of teabags. "I don't remember much about it, to be honest. I wasn't even certain I believed Ean . . . er . . . Nathan when he told me that part."

"Oh, I can vouch for him on that. I was with him when he first glimpsed your picture in the paper. I thought he was goin' to faint dead away, by the look on his face. And I was with him again, the night he took you out of there."

"You were?"

Sheila rose and came across the room to open yet another cupboard, from which she took a sugar bowl and a canister brimming with assorted teas. "Yes. I was driving the car. I could scarcely believe it was our dear Nathan committing a crime like that in the dead of night, running from the police."

"I helped too!" George said from the table where he sat.

Cocking her head to one side, Nidaba studied them both. "It seems I am more deeply indebted to you two than I even suspected."

"Oh, no," Sheila said quickly, setting the sugar and the tea canister onto a silver tray. "We'd do anything for Nathan. And by the looks of it, he'd do anything for you."

"Do you really think so?"

Sheila shrugged, turned to the refrigerator and took out the cream. "Well, isn't it obvious? He's never had so much as a parking ticket, missy. Not in all the time I've known him. He takes great pains not to draw attention to himself and keeps his life so quiet and mundane that it—well, it's almost tedious. And yet, along you come. Out of the blue. And he turns everything upside down. For the love of heaven, Nidaba, have you not even noticed what he's out there *doin'* this night? Disposin' of a body, of all things!"

Nidaba paused in placing the cups on the tray. "I suppose that's true. He's putting himself and his . . . his mundane lifestyle at great risk by all of this, isn't he?"

"Ah, now, I didn't mean to make you feel badly for it." Sheila patted Nidaba's hand in a motherly fashion. "It's what he wants to do. There's no talkin' to Nathan when he sets his mind to something he wants. And I, for one, think he's doin' the right thing. It's you I'm concerned about."

"Why?" Nidaba picked up the whistling teapot and poured the three cups full of steaming water. Then she lifted the tray and carried it to the table. Sheila followed, taking a seat and helping herself to a cup.

"Well, now, do you remember what happened to cause them to give you the tranquilizer in the first place?"

Nidaba thought back, but only fuzzy bits came. "No. I guess—I think there was an ambulance, but . . ." She shrugged. "Nathan said something about a fall from a building."

"They claimed you'd jumped from a rooftop," Sheila said, dipping her teabag slowly. "Called it a suicide attempt."

"Um-hmm," George said, taking a cup himself and adding massive amounts of cream and sugar. "I remember that. Your picture was in the newspaper, and as soon as Nathan saw it, he got all quiet . . . sad, like." George stirred his tea rapidly, whipping it with the spoon as if it were pudding, then lifting the spoon out to lick the clinging bits of sugar from it. When he finished he had a wide-eyed look on his face as he said, "Hey, you won't go jumping off our roof, will you? 'Cause that might upset the birds."

"The birds?" Nidaba asked, looking from one of them to the other.

"I keep pigeons up there," Sheila explained.

"You should go up and see them, Nidaba," George began, but then he bit his lip. "But not if you think you might want to jump again."

"Don't worry, George," Nidaba said. "I promise you, I won't do that. I didn't try to commit suicide before either."

"You didn't?" George asked.

"No. I don't remember what did happen, but I know better than to think that."

"I'll wager you had some help off that rooftop, missy," Sheila exclaimed, her voice deep and angry. "This evil visitor we've had—some black-hearted murderess who wants to harm you badly enough to kill my Lisette in order to do it—who's to say this was the first time she's tried?"

"Indeed," Nidaba said. "I only wish I knew for sure." Small pieces of memory came back to her. A confrontation. Yes. A battle. Her dagger had been in her hand. There had certainly been another immortal on that rooftop with her.

"Bah. How many people have more than one enemy out to do them in?" Sheila asked. "It's rare enough to have one in a lifetime. Much less two."

Nidaba sipped her tea. Sheila couldn't know how far off base she was. Nidaba had lived far more than one lifetime, and she'd crossed blades with countless Dark Witches whose only goal had been to do her in. No matter how many she killed, she knew there were always more to come.

Always.

She sighed, truly tired of the violence of her existence. And for a moment she almost understood why Natum had chosen to live a lie, pretending to be an ordinary mortal. Perhaps the endless violence had been too much for him.

Oh, but what he'd given up to be rid of it. His identity. His nature. His freedom.

"You and Nathan . . . you've known each other before. In the past. Haven't you, Nidaba?" Sheila asked.

Meeting her eyes, Nidaba nodded. "Yes. A long time ago."

"I could tell. It's a rare kind of thing I see when he looks at you. I've seen it in him only once before. One night when I couldn't sleep, I got up and came wanderin' down the stairs. He stood there, all alone in the dark, nothin' but the moonlight flooding through the windows. He stood there, just staring up at the portrait that hangs above the hearth, and the way the moon lit it from above. And I vow, there were tears on his cheeks."

Nidaba opened her mouth but couldn't speak.

"I thought that might be something you ought to know," Sheila said with a sigh. "I'm goin' on up to bed now, love. Thank you for helpin' me through this difficult night." She patted Nidaba's hand. "And you truly did help, you know. You truly did."

"It was true, what I told you out there at the cliffs," she assured the older woman. "Your friend is still alive, just in a different way."

She nodded. "I believe it. I do."

"Take a sleeping pill," Nidaba advised, but her voice was choked and barely audible. "The rest will do you good."

Sheila nodded, leaving the room, and Nidaba turned to George. "You may as well go to bed too," she said. "You can barely keep your eyes open."

"I'll wait for Nathan," he said. "I don't want to leave you alone. What if that bad lady comes back?"

Nidaba looked around, spotted the dog lying at George's feet. "You can leave your dog—what do you call her?"

"Queenie," George said proudly.

"Well, you can leave Queenie here to protect me. She certainly looks up to the job."

"Oh, she is! She's the best," George said. He got out of his chair and crouched near the dog's head, stroking her muzzle. "You hear that, Queenie? You have to stay here and watch out for Miss Nidaba. Okay?"

The dog didn't *quite* nod, but it was close.

"Good girl," George praised. Then he drank the last of his tea, which was, Nidaba guessed, two-thirds cream and sugar. He set the cup down again. "Good night, Nidaba."

"Good night, George," she said. She watched him go, sipping her tea and trying hard not to hear Sheila's words about Natum echoing in her mind. But they echoed anyway.

To distract herself, Nidaba stared at the dog, who stared right back at her. It really was a beautiful creature, with broad shoulders, and a wide powerful chest. Feet like a bear, and a wide, untapered muzzle. She weighed close to a hundred pounds, or a bit less, and Nidaba imagined that if she turned on an intruder, she'd tear him to shreds in minutes. If she were so inclined.

The dog rose and walked toward Nidaba, her eyes piercing. The hair on the back of her neck bristled upward, and a low, menacing growl came from deep in the beast's massive chest.

Nidaba blinked, and got to her feet, taking a step backward. "What is it, Queenie? What's wrong with you?"

The growl got louder as the dog crept closer, half crouching now as if she would spring.

"There, now," Nidaba said, backing further away, edging toward the door behind her. "Don't you remember me? I thought we were going to be friends . . ."

The door opened before she ever reached it. The growling ceased, and the dog eased her stance instantly. She looked up even as Nidaba turned around. And when the dog saw Nathan standing there, she seemed to relax. Then she turned and trotted away in the direction George had gone.

Nidaba still had one hand pressed to her chest. "By the Gods, I thought the beast was going to eat me alive."

Frowning, Nathan came forward, shrugging off his peacoat on the way. "Are you all right?"

"Yes." She sighed, feeling a bit sheepish. "George told the dog to guard me. I guess the beast understands far more than I realized. She must have heard you coming before I did. She got all wrought up."

"Really?" He seemed surprised, staring after the dog. "She's never acted at all menacing before."

"Well, she certainly did just now." Nidaba shrugged. "Maybe she senses the danger in the air. That's the only explanation I can think of. Once she saw it was only you at the door, she was fine again."

Nathan rubbed a hand over his chin. "Might not be such a bad idea to have a dog like that around the place."

"No, I suppose not."

He came closer and placed his hands on her shoulders, his eyes searching her face. "It frightened you, though. You've had a hellish day, haven't you?"

Lowering her gaze from the probing power of his, she said, "I've had worse."

"I know you have."

Drawing a breath, he released her. He fetched down another cup and poured himself some tea. "I think it's time we talked, you and I. Don't you?"

"I suppose it's inevitable that we do so sooner or later."

"Come on. We'll go out onto the veranda where no prying ears will hear too much." He took her arm and led her back through the dining room, into the front parlor, toward the library off to one side. But she stopped him and turning, stared up at the portrait above the mantel.

"Do you like it?" he asked her.

She couldn't quite manage to look at him as she asked, "Why did you paint it, Natum?"

He stood motionless. "I was afraid I might . . . forget you. Your face. Your eyes. I was wrong, of course, but . . ."

She finally turned to him, but he shrugged and looked away.

The veranda was through a set of French doors in the library. It was simply a cement pad, rounded and extending from the edge of the house. A railing surrounded it, and it sported a glass-topped umbrella-shaded table at its center and benches on its sides. Natum walked past the table, stopping beside the bench farthest from the house. He stood until she sat. Then he sat down beside her.

He stared at her for a long moment, and finally said, "I hardly know where to begin. At the beginning?"

"Begin at the end," she said. "The beginning is too long ago to be important to us now."

"Not for me, Nidaba. The beginning was long ago, yes. And it's painful as hell to revisit. But to me, it's very important. Maybe . . . the most important part of my life."

She turned her head away.

"Nidaba, we have to talk about what happened between us back then," he said, touching her face, turning her to face him again. "Please."

Her eyes burned with unshed tears. "If you pound a nail into the heart of a sapling tree, it bleeds. It hurts, and it bleeds, but it survives. It lives and it grows. Layer upon layer, year upon year, until that nail is so deeply buried that it's invisible. Oh, the tree knows it's there. It's still piercing the heart, after all. It's still painful. But to remove it after so much time—don't you see? It's not possible. Not without cutting the tree down. Not without killing it."

"No. You're wrong—"

"You put this nail in my heart long ago, Eannatum. It has healed over. Don't try to pull it out, because you'll only start the bleeding anew. Leave it. Just leave it."

"*You* are the one who left *me*."

"*You* are the one who married *her*."

He clenched his jaw. "I had no choice. You were the one who made me realize that."

"I know," she said, about to argue that he did have a choice. He could have chosen her over his throne. A secret part of her had wanted him to do just that. To throw it all away just to be with her. Foolish, foolish notion. But why rake over these old ashes again? She sighed, met his eyes. "It would never have worked between us, at any rate, Natum. You obviously see things far differently from the way I do. I cherish my freedom, relish my immortality, and live fully within it. While you confine yourself, hide what you are, live as mortal."

"I'm as free as any man. I live this way because I choose to."

She shook her head. "You're a prisoner, Natum. And this house is your prison, and this persona you've created, this Nathan King, is your jailer. It's the same as before, don't you see? Only then the prison cell was a gilded palace, a royal throne. Duty was your jailer then."

"I don't see it that way, Nidaba."

"No, of course you don't."

"If you'd let me explain . . ."

"I do not care. It doesn't matter now, Eannatum. In fact, all that matters just now is the enemy who has found me here. The one who is trying to kill me."

Nathan drew a deep breath. "I think I know who it is," he said at length.

"Do you?"

"Yes. There was a woman here, looking for you. An immortal—I never touched her, but I sensed it. She claimed to be a friend."

"I have no friends."

"I thought as much. She said her name was Arianna. Arianna Sinclair-Lachlan."

Nidaba's head came up quickly. In her mind's eye, she saw her son. Nicodimus . . . and the young woman Nidaba had long blamed for his death. Her memory of the past year seemed to clarify all at once, flashing into place so brightly it was nearly blinding. Suddenly everything made perfect sense.

She had lost her son—twice—but a year ago, she had found him again. Alive, immortal, wonderful . . .

"Nicodimus," she whispered, her heart quaking at his name, tears brimming. How could she have forgotten? He wasn't dead. He lived!

"Nidaba? Is something wrong?"

She looked up at him quickly, confusion making her hesitate. Nicodimus was this man's son. Eannatum's son. And yet . . . did she dare tell Natum that he lived? He'd had the boy killed once before . . .

He couldn't have!

But what if he did? And even if he didn't, she couldn't risk Nicky's being dragged into this situation with her. Not now. Not yet. She could end up losing him yet again, to the blade of this Dark Witch, whoever the hell she might be.

If Natum knew his son was alive, he might not be willing to wait to contact him. And if he knew Arianna was a friend—Nidaba's daughter-in-law, in fact—he might contact her as well. No. She must wait. Bide her time. Make very, very sure it was the right thing to do before she confessed any of this to Natum.

Her heart doubted he had ever done anything to deliberately harm his own child. But her mind wasn't as certain. Not even for Natum would she place Nicodimus in harm's way.

A hand brushed her face. "Are you all right?"

Staring into his eyes, she nodded. "Yes. Please, go on."

"All right. Nidaba . . . for any Dark Witch to be this gifted at casting a glamour, she must be very old. Very powerful."

Nidaba lifted her chin, shaking off the remnants of her over-whelming emotions. She felt stronger now that she had remembered finding her beloved son again. "So am I," she said.

"But you're in a weakened state."

She waved a hand dismissively. "A good night's sleep, another solid meal, and I'll be back to one hundred percent. I'm nearly there now."

"Still . . ."

"Eannatum, I need a dagger. They must have taken mine from me at that hospital. And I do not wish to face this bitch alone un-armed again."

For the first time in their entire conversation, Natum smiled slightly. "Changing the subject, Nidaba?"

"No." Sitting straighter, lifting her chin, she said, "I do want to talk to you about the past. About . . . all of it." More than that, she wanted him to tell her he was totally innocent in the attack on her and her son. And she wanted to believe him when he did. "But don't you think we need to focus first on keeping our hearts in our chests where they belong? We'll talk, Natum. Soon. And I will listen to what you have to say to me. I promise you that. But right now, I need . . ."

"Some time?" he asked.

She frowned at him. "A blade," she told him.

He blew a sigh, shook his head. "You always have had a one track mind."

"A blade, dammit."

"All right, all right. Come on, come with me." He held out his hand, and Nidaba took it. Then Natum looked down, and she did too, at his large, strong hand enveloping her smaller one. He closed his eyes briefly, as if touching her were almost painfully sweet.

There were so many things he wanted to ask her. He knew she'd borne a child—but he had never been sure if that child had been his, or what had truly become of the boy. And he never knew exactly what had happened the night Nidaba and her son had allegedly per-ished in a terrible fire.

Not in all these years.

But the pain that came into her eyes at the merest mention of that time was too much for him to bear. So he told himself he could wait to learn all of those things. He could wait. Until she was ready to speak of them.

He put her into his car and drove into Boston, to his gallery, which he hadn't opened since she'd returned to his life.

"What is this place?" she asked when he unlocked the door and took her inside.

"It's my business, Nidaba. I buy and sell antiquities. And, um . . . my most private collection is here. Though I never display it. I keep it here because the security is far superior to that at home. Come." He led her through the gallery, with its swords and shields from various eras displayed on the walls. Pottery and statues lined every shelf. Tapestries and cloaks were arranged on the walls. Glass cases held chalices and spears and golden coins from civilizations long dead.

In the private display area, the small alcove he'd created for his eyes alone, were cylinder seals from the land of Sumer—one of them the very seal of the once great king, Eannatum.

His eyes stung a bit each time he visited this area, and more so this time, for Nidaba pulled him to a stop. "By the Gods, Natum," she whispered. Her fingers dragged across the face of the glass case, where slabs of cuneiform tablets stood on display stands, where headdresses and jewelry from days long forgotten decorated lifeless mannequin heads.

"It's . . . just memories. That's all," he whispered.

"But . . . but Eannatum, the *lilis* drum. It's one that was played in your own palace! And the headdress . . ."

He watched her eyes widen. "Is the one you wore when you danced for me. And the lapis lazuli necklace as well. Yours, Nidaba. I preserved them as perfectly as I could. And if you . . . *when* you leave here, you may take them with you."

Were those tears brimming in her eyes?

"You kept them—all this time . . ."

"They were all I had left of you. They and . . . and this." Reaching into his pocket, he pulled out the small bit of stone, worn with age, into which she'd carved his name, and hers, and the symbol for eternity.

Nidaba looked at it. Then at him. "This is the piece I made for you, to celebrate your initiation."

He nodded. "You gave it to me when we did the rite by the river, and filled the Euphrates with fish. My first act of magick, Nidaba. A time—and a friend—I could never forget."

Blinking, she averted her eyes. "I can't believe you've kept it all this time."

"Come." He replaced the stone in his pocket, closed his hand around hers, and led her to his office in the back, unlocking the door, and flicking on a light. Then he turned yet another key. This lock was hidden within the woodwork of a wall-sized bookcase. Only it wasn't really a bookcase at all. It was a sliding door that concealed another glass case, this one with his collection of daggers mounted inside. Dozens of them. It covered one entire wall of his office.

"Where did you get them all?" Nidaba breathed.

"Immortals. Light Witches who were murdered. Dark Witches I had to kill. I suppose "immortal" isn't exactly the word we ought to use to describe ourselves, is it? Not when every dagger in this case represents one who has died."

"Not died," she muttered. "Only moved on. Even mortals are immortal, Natum." She walked along in front of the case, examining the blades. Double-edged, single-edged, serrated and curved. Long and short. Handles of wood, bone, iron. All decorated with jewels. Sapphires, diamonds, rubies, emeralds, every stone imaginable in every possible combination and arrangement.

"Take whichever one pleases you. Hell, take several if you want them."

"I couldn't—"

"You know perfectly well you could. And you will." He watched her face as she tried very hard to conceal her delight. "You don't fool me, you know," he said. "You've always loved beautiful things. Jewels. Baubles. Enjoy this. Let me enjoy giving you pleasure, just this once."

She met his eyes, and hers were smoky and dark. "Giving me pleasure would take far more than a glittery gift, Eannatum."

His blood heated at the double meaning of her remark, the teasing warmth in her eyes. She was a heartless tease, just as she had always been. "We'll get to that," he promised her, leaning close. And when she didn't push him away, he brushed his mouth lightly over hers, lips apart, his breath fanning her.

Her breath stuttered, stopped, and her eyes fell closed expectantly. So he wrapped his arms around her waist, pulled her to him, and closed his mouth more completely over hers. He felt her lips part in invitation, and he slid his tongue between them in reply. He tasted her. Gods, he hadn't tasted her in so long!

Fire blazed between them, as it always had. The physical response when they touched, when they kissed had always been explosive, and that hadn't changed. His blood rushed and his heart pounded. Her hips arched against him, rubbing his erection to a state of painful need. His hands closed on her buttocks, tugging her harder to him, and he thrust his tongue deeper, drinking from her mouth the way he wanted to drink from every part of her.

Finally, he lifted his head, and stared down into her sparkling eyes.

And she blinked, then closed them, and turned away. "What in the names of the Gods am I doing?"

"Nidaba?"

"How could I?" She faced him again, tears brimming in her eyes. "I will not love you, Eannatum. I swear I will not love you again."

Gods, that she could still hate him this much simply because he had married another. "What I did, I did for my country, Nidaba. For Lagash. For all of Sumer."

Her face went stony and cold. "Then you admit it?"

"What is there to admit? I did it. You know I did it. And it was a sin against my own heart, Nidaba, and against you—one I have paid for ever since." Frustrated, Nathan sighed and paced away. "Choose a dagger," he told her. "You need to be armed."

"If you gift me with one of these blades, Eannatum, I'll likely use it to cut out your heart."

Spinning to face her again, he said, "All of this venom! All of this hatred, simply because I wed another woman to avoid a war that would have destroyed us all?"

She frowned fiercely. "No! For the love of the Gods, Eannatum, marrying Puabi has nothing to do with my anger at you! Are you so blind you do not realize that?"

"Well, what, then? What, tell me, am I guilty of doing to so wrong you that you would continue to hate me after four millennia?"

She stared at him in disbelief. "Eannatum, your soldiers hunted me down. Under your orders, they hounded me for years, until they finally caught up to me."

"I sent them after you because I couldn't bear to live without you, Nidaba! I wanted them to bring you back to me."

She shook her head very slowly. "And I was gullible enough and deeply enough in love to believe that, Natum. Until they finally caught up to me. Attacked me. They tried to murder me, Eanntuam. And they *did* murder my son."

She lifted her head, met his eyes. "*Our* son."

Chapter 13

He stood there staring at her, struck motionless by what she had said. *"Our son?"*

Swallowing hard, she nodded.

"And for this, you held me responsible?"

She turned away from him.

He caught her shoulders and turned her back. "Tell me. Tell me you honestly believe I could have ordered such a thing."

She couldn't even seem to look him in the eye. "I don't know what I believed. You chose Puabi over me. Your kingdom over me. Even when the threat had ended, you remained with her. I thought I knew the power of your love for me, Natum. I thought it was more powerful than anything in the world. And I knew that if you would give me up for the sake of your kingdom, there could not be many other things you wouldn't do for its sake as well."

Stunned, he released her, cut to the bone.

"An illegitimate son with a claim to the throne would have been a far greater threat to the well-being of Sumer than an affair with a temple priestess ever could have been," she said, driving the blade of her words straight through his heart.

He couldn't speak to her. He was so angry he was trembling with it.

She looked into his eyes, and when she did, she went pale.

He opened his mouth, then closed it, almost too furious to think. "I don't even know what to say to you."

Her face changed, regret swimming in her eyes, but he held up a hand, saying nothing. Instead, he reached into the glass case, drew out a gold-handled Sumerian dagger and its leather sheath. He handed it to her, closed and locked the case, and strode back through the building, out the front to his car, vaguely aware that she followed. He drove her back to the house, all without uttering a word.

He didn't dare speak. He'd have cursed her, he'd have lashed out and cut her to the quick the way she had cut him. Only when they returned to the house and he'd battled his fury into some semblance of submission did he dare to speak at all. He stopped her on the way inside. "Wait. We need to finish this."

But then the front door was flung open, and George stood there, waving his hands. "Nathan! Nathan, come, please! Sheila's crying in her sleep and I can't make her wake up!"

"Dammit, George, not now." Nathan gripped Nidaba's shoulders, but she shook her head, and her face remained stony.

"Go. See to Sheila." She strode into the house ahead of him.

He followed on her heels, having to push past George to do so. "The hell I will! Damn you, Nidaba. I'm angry as hell at you right now. You've got no right to accuse me of something that vile. All I ever did was love you, and I think you know that. Whatever you think happened—no, by the Gods no. You *can't* believe any of that. You *can't*. You don't."

A crash came from upstairs, causing them both to look up sharply. Nathan sighed. Sheila was no doubt thrashing in the grip of some nightmare. She'd stopped having them six months after coming to live with him and George, but apparently they'd come back full force. No wonder, considering recent events in this house.

"Go," Nidaba said, her voice deep, her tone firm. "This discussion has waited a long time. It can wait a bit longer."

"Not a hell of a lot longer, it can't. And it won't." He had to go.

But dammit, he didn't want to. "Come along, then," he said to Nidaba. "I'm not leaving you down here alone with this maniac on the loose."

"I won't argue with you." She preceded him and George and the lumbering, ever attentive dog through the house and up the stairs. But she stopped at the master suite's door and said, "I need to get some rest if I'm to be fully recovered any time soon. If there is anything I can do for Sheila, don't hesitate to come for me. Otherwise, though, I . . . would prefer not to be disturbed tonight."

She didn't wait for his argument, though she had to know it was coming. Instead she just went inside and closed the door on the dog that tried to follow.

Nathan grated his teeth and stalked along the hall to Sheila's room.

Nidaba closed the bedroom door behind her, leaned back against it, and covered her face with her hands. She knew, deep down in her heart, what the truth was. She had always known. But Gods, the pain had been so much easier to bear when she'd had someone to hate. Someone to blame.

He'd scorned her, chosen another woman and his royal duty over her. She had no one to blame for that but herself—she knew that. She was the one who'd convinced Natum what his duty was. But she couldn't accept that, and so she had punished him by pretending to believe him capable of the most vile crime imaginable. She may even have fooled herself into thinking she truly did believe that of him. But she knew now that she never had. She never had.

Natum had seemed truly shocked by her revelation, that her child, her Nicodimus, had been his own son. Perhaps he hadn't even known that much for certain. And yet his soldiers had hunted her endlessly, tirelessly, for years on end. And when they had finally found her . . .

She didn't want to go back to believing Eannatum's love had been real. Not when it had hurt her so to trust him with her heart, only to have it broken time and time again!

She heaved a sigh, swiped angrily at her eyes. She was too tired to contemplate it right now. Her body, still weakened, needed sleep to heal. Nidaba couldn't have fought it had she tried.

No more than she could fight the dream . . . the memory, so vivid and fresh.

She waited in the sacred bedchamber—a special room on the uppermost level of the palace. Small it was, but lined with silk pillows and spreads in rich jewel tones. Deep green and scarlet and midnight blue. Censers burned with sacred herbs, and a hundred candle flames danced, lighting the room with a soft illumination that was alive and ever-changing. As she picked her way between the pillows and spreads, it seemed she walked among a dozen living shadows that danced around her in celebration. She breathed the incense smoke, and tasted the other fragrances. Fruit and flowers. The table on the far of end of the room had no room for anything more. The most prized fruits in all of Sumer filled golden bowls to overflowing. Wine jugs and jeweled chalices stood at the ready. And blossoms littered every bit of space in between.

At the very center of the table stood a small stone image of the Goddess Inanna. She who would come to inhabit Nidaba's body this night. It was good, Nidaba thought. She would likely not even remember what transpired. She would likely not even feel it, or be aware of his touch . . . his kiss . . .

Something clenched tight in her belly.

She had no one to ask. The previous king's *lukur* was an elderwoman, an honored crone, living in a palace all her own in the mountains to the north. There had been no time to travel there, to consult with her. And no other woman alive had experienced this rite.

Kneeling before the image of the Goddess, Nidaba breathed deeply, slowly, filling her lungs with the sacred smoke and emptying her mind. Softly, she began to chant. *"Inanna me en, Inanna me en, Inanna me en. Uta am i i ki."*

Over and over she spoke the words until they became a litany in her mind, running together, and making no sense. She lifted her arms to her sides, and upward, tipped her head back, and closed her eyes. She waited for the Goddess to fill her.

"Nidaba," Eannatum said softly.

Her eyes opened. Slowly she lowered her arms and turned her head to see him standing there. The door was closed tightly behind him. His dark eyes gleamed in the candlelight. He came closer, and she wanted to tell him to stop. To warn him that she was not yet ready, that she was still Nidaba—not miraculously transformed into the Queen of Heaven. And yet to do that would be to admit that she had failed.

And even had she been willing to confess it to him, she couldn't. She couldn't form a word to save her life. His gaze moved freely over her barely clothed body, and she burned with wanting him as she had wanted him for most of her life.

She loved this man.

He came to her, standing while she knelt, and slowly stroked his hands over her hair. "So long, Nidaba. So long I have waited for this."

She shut her eyes at his touch, wondered why if he wanted her so badly, he had not come for her, even though it would have spelled disaster for everyone else in Sumer.

But it didn't matter. Suddenly none of that mattered. He was hers tonight, not Puabi's. He was hers. And she was utterly his. She leaned forward, and pressed her lips to the hard bulge between his legs, with only the royal robes between his flesh and hers. "My king," she whispered.

His fingers clenched in her hair, and he closed his eyes.

Nidaba rose slowly to her feet and stood before him. "The dance," she said softly. "Was it pleasing to you?"

"*You* were pleasing to me. I saw no others." His eyes opened, skimming her from head to toe. "This . . ." He lifted a hand, ran his fingers over her belly and the chain wrapped around her waist, with its dangling curtain of precious stones. "Is it heavy? Uncomfortable?"

"The metal is cold . . . or perhaps it is my flesh that is warm."

He lifted his gaze to lock with hers. His hands, though, remained at her waist, and he fumbled with the clasp, found its release, opened it. Then he slowly took the girdle of stones away, letting it fall with a jangling sound into the nest of pillows on the floor. "Better?"

"Yes. Better."

His eyes roamed down her body, all but naked to his hungry gaze. Everywhere he let that gaze linger, her skin seemed to heat, and tingle. "Yes," he said. "Much better." He reached out to the *nunuz* stones that dangled from the tips of her breasts, stroked them slowly, then set them to swinging with a flick of his fingers. "And these? Are they unpleasant?"

The tiny clamps bit into her nipples with minimal pressure . . .

but the weight of the stones tugged with every swing, every touch. "They pinch only a little. And their weight pulls somewhat. Though it is not . . . unpleasant, exactly."

"No. Not exactly." His smile was slight. He reached up and gently removed the stones from her breasts, but he didn't toss them aside as he had done with the girdle. Instead he tucked the clamps into some hidden place within his royal robes.

Sensation rushed into her nipples, where before the flow of blood had been pinched off. They throbbed and burned. He kept his eyes focused on her there, and she saw the blatant desire in them. Lifting his hands again, he cupped her breasts, running his calloused thumbs over her nipples repeatedly. The flicking motion over those sensitized peaks made her bite her lip to keep from crying out loud.

Frowning, Eannatum took his hands away. "You feel . . . sticky."

"It was part of the preparation," she said. "I was painted with honeyed wine for you."

His gaze snapped to hers, widening, blazing. "Well, now . . ."

Hands closing on her waist he lifted her, setting her on the edge of the table, knocking bowls of fruit aside. Flower petals were her cushion. Standing back, examining her at his leisure, Eannatum lowered his head, and she knew what he would do even before his tongue snaked out to taste her breast. "Mmm," he said, and then licked again. He caught the peak in his lips and suckled her. He took her nipple into his mouth and drew hard on it, flicking his tongue over the very tip as he sucked hungrily at her. He licked her breast clean, and continued even then, nipping with his teeth and pulling at her as if he would devour her whole.

Nidaba felt sensations she had never felt before. A sharp pleasure such as she had never imagined tingled through her. It bordered on pain and intensified unbearably when he bit down. Then he moved to the other breast, and devoured it even more frantically. And while he fed at it, he caught the other in his hand, drew his fingers together at the tip and pinched her deliciously. She braced her hands on the table behind her, let her head fall backward as her body clenched and tightened and liquified low in her belly. She arched her back and whimpered and he responded by exerting still more pressure with his fingers and his teeth.

Eannatum drew his head away then, looking into her eyes. He leaned down, kissed her long and deeply, thrusting his tongue into her mouth and lapping it as if it tasted as sweet to him as her honeyed nipples had done. She could taste the honey and wine on his tongue.

Then he straightened away and his hands crept up to her breasts again. She sucked in a breath of surprise when she felt the bite of the clamps closing once more on her nipples. The teeth felt sharper than before, their grip tighter now that those tender crests were stiff and throbbing. A cry was wrung from her.

And Eannatum whispered, "Trust me, Nidaba." Then he knelt, his hands pressing to her thighs, shoving them wide, and exposing her very center to his probing eyes. With his fingers, he parted her folds. Then he touched her, fondled her there in her most private places. He even thrust his long finger inside her, then drew it slowly out again. He brought it to his lips, tasted it. "Mmm, just as I thought. More honey."

Before she could know what he intended, he pressed her thighs wider, and buried his face between her legs. His lips, then his tongue, swept over her, flicking, licking, stroking. He licked up inside her, seeking every drop of the honeyed wine with which she'd been coated. And he laved her in places where the eunuch's brush had never dared touch.

Nidaba fell backward on the table, tipping fruit bowls over and sending their contents helter-skelter. She twisted and writhed while he fed at her. And then he found the tiny kernel of her most frenzied need and sucked at it, stabbed at it with his tongue, bit at it with his teeth. And she felt as if her body would shake itself to pieces. His hands came up then, caught the *nunuz* stones, and as his mouth worked her even more hungrily, he tugged on them. The clamps pulled painfully at her nipples, stretching them, biting deeply, and his teeth closed on that pulsing nub at her center. And her body shattered in screaming, trembling release. She cried his name, shuddered uncontrollably, and finally pushed him away from her, panting and sweating.

Natum gathered her into his arms, though, and carried her to the cushions on the floor. He lowered her into them and again took the stones from her breasts, tossing them aside this time. As she lay there, shaking, breathless, shattered, he removed his robes.

And she saw him, looking more God than man, and more king

then he had in his crown and royal vestments. "Eannatum," she whispered, "what is this magic between us?"

"This is what is meant to be," he told her. "What will be, from now on. I'll not let you leave me again, Nidaba. Not ever. Not now." He knelt over her, cupping her face in his hands. "I love you."

"I am a High Priestess," she whispered.

"And I am a king. But I love you, Nidaba." He lowered himself atop her, and she opened to him in an instinct born of nature. When he nudged himself inside her, he did so slowly, gently, kissing her face, and her neck and shoulders, whispering love words to her the entire time. She felt stretched as her body accepted his, then pain flared through her when he pressed past her maiden's barrier. She bit her lip, but it was brief, that stab of pain. And then he was moving gently, slowly, in a rhythm that made her body respond. That made her hips begin to move in answer to his call. That made the fire in her belly flare up anew. And soon she was clutching him to her while he fed at her mouth. She moved to a faster pace, and he followed. His hands slid beneath her then, closing on her buttocks and holding her to him as he thrust deeper inside her than before. And finally, his powerful movements sent her again into spasms of ecstasy. Only this time, she did not go alone. This time she felt the answering tremors racking his muscled frame. She heard that pained pleasure in his low moaning of her name. He filled her . . . and she embraced him. And then he relaxed bit by bit, slowly rolling to the side and folding her into his strong arms.

He held her for a long time, and finally, his voice still hoarse, he asked her, "Nidaba, why did you leave me in the dead of night the way you did?"

She frowned, lifting her head from his chest, and staring into his black, moist eyes. "Why does it matter? It was what was necessary. We both came to realize it, didn't we?"

He didn't reply to that. Perhaps he'd changed his mind, then? Hope flared in her breast, but she went on. "They told me you wished to marry Puabi, and do your duty as king. They told me you regretted your promise to me, but were too noble to break your vow. That you would wed me, only because you could not hurt me by refusing to do so, but that it was not what you wanted. And they made it clear I had no choice but to leave Lagash, to give you a way out. They even implied that Lia would pay the price should I disobey."

As she spoke he sat up, staring down at her in horror. "Who told you these things?"

She lowered her eyes. "Your father, Eannatum. The king told me. And Lathor. And even Lia." She felt her heart break again, and tears surged into her eyes. "I'd have doubted the others, but Lia—I knew she would not lie to me—or not unless her very life depended on it."

"By the eyes of the Gods," he said softly. "They *did* lie to you, Nidaba. And to me as well. I knew nothing of any of it. I told my father I would wed you and none other. And the next day you were gone, and I had only a stone tablet, its markings in your hand, telling me you had decided to serve your Goddess rather than your heart."

She blinked up at him. "You mean . . . you didn't want me to go?"

"I wanted you to be my queen." He pulled her to him, cradled her in his powerful arms as if he would never let her go. "And by the time I found you, you'd already taken your initiation as a priestess. Sworn to remain unwed. To break such a vow . . ."

"It would be death, Eannatum," she told him. "I would be stoned for such an offense." She kissed his strong neck, and wrapped her arms around his waist. "But it doesn't matter. We did what we did for the good of Sumer. Even if we were tricked into it, at first, we soon saw that it was the only way. And now, you . . . you are about to wed another. You have your queen."

"A woman I barely know!" he snapped.

"Oh, come now, Eannatum. You journeyed to Ur, you met the woman. The arrangements have been made. I have heard of the passionate Princess Puabi. Do not tell me her embrace left you cold."

"Her embrace only left me wishing it were yours," he told her fiercely, his voice coarse with passion.

"On the morrow," Nidaba whispered, "your queen will arrive at her new home. You will speak your vows to her. It will be her bed you share. Her face you see in the morning. . . . There is no place for me in your life now, Eannatum."

"I won't let you go," he said. "Nidaba, please, please don't do this. Don't leave me again. I cannot live if you do."

Sitting back from him, she searched his face. "What would you have me do?"

"Stay. I'll make you High Priestess of the temple here. And send Lia to take your place in the temple at Mari."

Shaking her head sadly, she sighed. "I would have to see you with your new bride every day if I stayed here, Natum. It would surely kill me."

"No. No, it will not kill you, Nidaba, because you are strong and fierce. And you will know it's you I love, not Puabi. You will know that every moment I spend with her, I wish for you. And you will know that every night, under the cover of darkness, I will come to your arms, not hers. In our secret places, we will be together. I know it is not enough. I know you deserve a great deal more. But it is all we have."

She closed her eyes. "And what of Puabi? Would her heart not be wounded by this?"

"Puabi knows I'll never love her. Our marriage is a treaty. A pact between city-states and every bit as cold as one."

Nidaba said, "You'll need to produce an heir with her."

"Perhaps. In time." He caught her face between his palms. "The king of Sumer may have any woman he desires. By law and divine right! It has always been so. Puabi knows this, and she knows too that I love another. She agreed to this arrangement with the truth presented to her. Fidelity was not a part of our agreement. And you know full well it is not forbidden for a priestess to love, only to marry. Nidaba, I thought I could live without you for the good of Sumer. I've found that I cannot. It's not possible. Please, stay with me."

She bit her lip, searching his eyes. "I may not be as strong as you think I am, Eannatum. But I do love you. More than my own heart, or my own soul."

"Then . . . then you'll stay?"

"I will try. That's all I can promise. To try. And we must be discreet. Legal or not, acceptable or not, nature is nature, Natum. I'll not be the cause of another woman's pain."

He pulled her securely against him, kissed her gently. "We'll find our happiness, Nidaba. I promise you we will."

But she knew even then that she would find only misery in being his mistress. His concubine. Only misery.

She couldn't have guessed, though, just how much.

It was no less than an hour before Sheila talked herself out, took another pill, and fell back into a troubled, restless sleep. After tucking her in, Nathan finally dragged himself back to the master suite, walked into his bedroom, and saw the door to the adjoining room closed tightly. He knew before he even tried the knob that the door would be locked. And he was right. Sighing, he rested his forehead on the cool wooden door. Dammit, he needed to talk to Nidaba, to get all of this out in the open once and for all.

She was lashing out at him. Hurting him, or trying to, because of the way she had been hurt by him. He didn't understand fully just why, but he knew one thing. She did not believe he had killed his own son. Nidaba knew him far better than that.

Or at least . . . he hoped she did.

Without bothering to turn on the light, he tugged at the buttons of his shirt and moved toward the bed, feet dragging. There was no denying it, he was exhausted. Unused to so much excitement and intrigue, he was wearing himself down emotionally, mentally . . . perhaps even spiritually. Dammit, he'd just dumped a body into the sea. How much lower would he have to sink before all of this played itself out?

Maybe this was just the price he had to pay for all these years of solitude and relative contentment. Living like an ordinary mortal man when he was anything but. He was a pretender. And now the world was extracting payment for his make believe existence.

He peeled the shirt from his body, dropped it onto the floor, heeled off his shoes and kicked them aside. His hands went to the snap and button of his jeans, freeing them, sliding the zipper down. Finally, naked, he crawled into his bed and sank almost at once into blessed sleep.

He didn't know how long he slumbered. A breath on the nape of his neck woke him, though, from the very depths of sleep.

He rolled over, groggy and puzzled, blinking in the darkness.

Nidaba lay in his bed, naked except for the sheet that came up only to the narrowest part of her waist. Her breasts swelled full and inviting, round silhouettes in the darkness.

"Nidaba," he murmured, "what are you . . ."

"Ssssssh." She held a finger to her lips and, reaching out, caught his head and tugged him forward. He started with surprise when she kissed him voraciously. And he responded at once, kissing her back. He felt himself growing hard with arousal, hungry with need . . . and yet something tickled up his nape and coiled in his belly.

"We need to talk, Nidaba," he said, breaking off the kiss, but it came out gruff. She dragged her nails over his nipples, and he lost the ability to speak at all. Then she leaned down, and replaced her nails with her lips, and her tongue. Her hand stroked a sensuous path down his abdomen. "God, Nidaba," he moaned, thoughts of discussion fleeing.

The bedroom door burst open, and Nidaba stood there, wide-eyed, staring at him and at the woman feeding on him like some succubus.

Like a dash of cold water, it hit him all at once.

He shoved the impostor away from him, and she landed on the floor. Her face rippled for a moment as the glamour she'd cast faltered, but she rolled and lunged out of the bedroom almost on all fours.

"Stand and fight if you want me, bitch!" Nidaba surged after her, and Nathan saw the glint of the dagger in her fist. He shot to his feet, tripping on his jeans, and pausing to tug them on again. Then he ran into the hall behind her, terrified that she'd be killed.

But in the hallway he saw no one other than Nidaba. Nothing. Still, she charged from room to room, flinging open doors. "Where are you? You damnable coward, face me if you dare!"

"Nidaba, stop!" He caught her from behind, closed his hands on her shoulders. "It's no use. Dammit, she could be anywhere. She could be any*one*, for that matter."

Nidaba lowered her head, her shoulders shaking. "Oh, she's not anyone, Natum. Don't you know who she is? *Don't* you?"

He frowned, shaking his head. "I—no, I—"

"How could you?" she asked, her voice laced with bitterness. "How could you do it to me yet again, Natum?"

"Nidaba, I thought it was you."

Chin lifting, her eyes locked with his. "You thought it was me? Did you not recognize her? Her voice? The feel of her lips on you? Her scent, Natum? Because I did. I did. I saw through her glamourie when it faltered for just an instant, even if you were too blinded by lust to see anything. She was your precious bride, the one you chose over me so long ago. Your queen. The bitch was Puabi."

The truth hit him like a mallet between the eyes. "Puabi," he whispered. "She lives!"

"You must have known she was immortal!" Nidaba accused.

Nathan lowered his head and, sighing, took Nidaba's arm and led her along the hall to George's room. Peering inside, seeing George sound asleep, and no one else except the dog in sight, he turned the lock from the inside and pulled the door closed. He did the same at Sheila's room, to be certain they would both be safe for the night. Then finally he led Nidaba back down the hall toward his room. "She was no immortal when I knew her," he told her. "But . . ."

"But?"

A muscle clenched in his jaw. "She knew about immortality. She sought to gain it."

"And you never warned me?"

"Hell, Nidaba, how could I? You forget, you fled Sumer long before either you or I knew what we were, or that such beings even existed at all!" He pushed a hand through his hair, shook his head in frustration. "Come. Just come with me, dammit. We're far too vulnerable to attack standing out here in the dark like this."

She stopped fighting him and let him lead her back to the bedroom, where he closed the door, locked it, and then finished fastening his jeans. The jeans had a belt in them, and a sheath hung from that belt, with his dagger inside.

Lifting the skirt of her nightgown, Nidaba sheathed her own blade, which she'd been carrying at the ready the entire time. The sheath Nathan had given her was fastened around her thigh with a red garter she must have found among the things he'd bought for her.

"It's not safe for me here," Nidaba said. "Short of killing anyone who comes close to me, I have no way to defend myself."

"You're right."

She looked up at him sharply. "I didn't expect you to agree."

"Well, I do." He looked at the bed where he'd so recently been lying naked with Puabi, and he almost gagged in revulsion. An icy chill worked its way into his bones. He turned away and went into the adjoining bedroom, holding the door open until Nidaba joined him there, and then closing it, turning the locks. "I'm sorry . . . about what you saw."

She said nothing, simply crossed the room with her nightgown flowing like ghostly tails and poured a glass of water from the pitcher beside the bed. Then she paused, glancing down at the water. "Sheila," she said softly. "Even with all that's happened, she came in here and replaced the water pitcher." She shook her head slowly. "And the broken glass . . . ?"

"I cleaned it up earlier."

She nodded, and then drank the water down before she faced him again.

"When did you find out what Puabi was?"

Pacing the room, Nathan parted the curtain and looked out the window. Seeing nothing there, he checked the closet, the bathroom, and looked underneath the bed. "Just now," he said. "I told you, I didn't know. I know she once sought it, but I had no reason to believe she'd been successful, Nidaba. Heaven knows, if she had, I'd have expected to have crossed paths with her before now."

"Perhaps you have," Nidaba replied. "Perhaps once she perfected the glamourie, she crossed your path as often as she liked, with you never the wiser."

He nodded thoughtfully. "That could very well be. Much as I hate to admit it. But I didn't know. She wasn't immortal when she came to Lagash to live in the palace as my queen," he said, speaking slowly. "But you already know that part."

"Tell me anyway. Perhaps, Natum, it's time for us to relive the hell of our past together and come at last to the truth."

He settled into a chair. "You're right. It's long past time we do that, in fact. And the way I see it . . ." he glanced at the clock, then at the darkness beyond the glassless window. He'd had to put the removable screen in to keep the insects out. The night breeze was light, but filled with the pungence of autumn. "The way I see it, we're better off staying right here until dawn. So what better time? But mark me well, Nidaba, you're going to hear the truth this time. All of it. And so am I."

Chapter 14

As he spoke, Nathan saw the past unfurling in his memory, clearly, vividly.

He could almost feel the heat of the desert sun beating mercilessly down on the lush oasis city. He could nearly smell the fishy aroma of the nearby Euphrates and feel the roughness of the bleached white stone that made waist-high walls on either side of the broad palace steps.

His bride of a little over a week, Puabi, stepped down from the litter that bore her, aided by two men-at-arms. Eannatum had known she would arrive in style, but he had not expected quite so much pomp. They'd wed in a formal ceremony only a day before, but tonight would be their first one living together as man and wife. She'd had affairs to get in order, belongings to pack and bring along to Lagash. As he stood at the bottom of the palace steps to greet her, massive stone lions on either side of him, he battled a grimace of distaste at her antics. She stepped from the litter onto a silken pillow, hastily placed beneath her feet by a young slave girl who seemed afraid to get too close. Two others, looking equally cowed, raced ahead, unrolling a carpet between them that lined the walk, then up the steps, all the way to the palace doors at the top. Eannatum had to step aside to get out of their way.

Two soldiers walked two steps behind Puabi as she started forward. The slave girls knelt and bowed. The woman—his queen— certainly looked the part. Her headdress was the most elaborate he had ever seen, made of enough gold and lapis to please a Goddess. Tiny bits of round hammered gold, like coins, layered around and around the piece, and they moved, shimmering, each time she took a step. Her gown, too, was golden, gleaming as brightly as the sun. It was made of some fabric that shimmered and shone almost as if it were metallic. Great amounts of paint enhanced her eyes—kohl lined them, and colored powders had been applied in a rainbow of stripes that covered the entire area below the brow, while tiny jewels dangled above it from the headpiece.

Behind her no less than twenty men and women awaited her word. They had all walked, while she rode upon the litter, borne by four of her strongest slaves. Across the desert they had borne her. She had refused to come by boat, as she claimed she suffered illness upon the waves. Water had to be hauled along on the journey, and she had portioned it by cruelly small amounts. Eannatum had reports that three of her slaves had not survived the journey. And he liked his new queen less than he ever had.

She reached Eannatum on the steps, inclined her head toward him, the husband she barely knew. And he bowed respectfully to her in return.

"Welcome to Lagash, Queen Puabi," he said.

"I am glad to finally be here." Smiling very slightly, she turned to face her entourage, and they all genuflected so automatically it was like a wave moving over them. "These are my people. My soldiers, slaves, and advisers. I trust accommodations can be found for all of them?"

"Of course. Had I known you would be bringing so many, I'd have had rooms prepared. They'll need rest, and a solid meal after such an arduous journey." He nodded to one of his own generals, his old friend Galor, who had been told in advance to see to it that the travelers were taken into the coolness of a nearby storage building and given plenty of fresh water to drink, beds of reeds upon which to rest, a solid meal when they were ready, and anything else they needed. Galor immediately stepped into the crowd and began speaking quietly to the exhausted men and women.

Puabi shrugged. "The soldiers are to serve alongside your own, and they will keep their rank. Except for these two"—she indicated the large men flanking her—"who are my personal guards. I want them housed in the palace."

"As you wish," Eannatum said, already disliking the thought of soldiers he did not know serving alongside his own trusted troops, much less taking up residence under his own roof.

"My astrologers, diviners, and soothsayers must be housed near the palace. I need them close to me, and they are to be given free access to my quarters as well."

Eannatum lifted a brow. "And what use have you of magicians, my queen?"

She shot him a narrow glance. "I am Queen of all of Sumer," she said. "They are my advisers."

It did not truly answer his question, but he didn't press it just then. "And the others?"

She looked down quickly, dismissively. "The slaves, you mean? Put them where you will. I've no care where, except that they be able to come quickly when I send for them."

He drew a breath, exhaled deeply. "During his reign, my father outlawed slavery within Lagash," he told her.

Her nostrils flared just a bit. "I do not come from Lagash."

"But you're here now."

Her gaze clashed with his, and Eannatum decided to let the matter rest. He would not embarrass her publicly, but her slaves *would* be freed, either to remain as paid servants or to return to their homeland with whatever compensation he could give them. He would make that clear to his arrogant new bride—later—in private.

"Let me introduce you to my closest advisers," he said at length. "My general, who is even now seeing to the comfort of your people, is Galor. The man on my right hand is my first soldier, Ris. And the woman on my left is the High Priestess of the temple, Nidaba."

Puabi nodded politely at Ris, the large soldier who was already sizing up her own men-at-arms. But when her gaze touched Nidaba's, Eannatum could almost feel the tension that crackled between them. The two women stared at each other for a long moment.

"I've heard of you," Puabi said, her face almost a sneer. "Part

woman, part goddess, they claim." She blew air through her nostrils.
"You look less goddess-like than my lowest slave girl." Then Puabi
looked at Eannatum again, having exchanged not one further word
with Nidaba. "I would go inside now," she said in a very low voice.
And without waiting for him, she moved forward, up the steps to
the palace doors. As he turned to follow, he saw her leaning close to
one of her soldiers, speaking near his ear, even as she slanted a backward glance at Nidaba. A cold feeling crept through Eannatum
when he saw that look, and when he quickly glanced Nidaba's way,
he knew she had felt it too.

A full moon cycle later, as Eannatum lay in the darkness of the
desert, wrapped in blankets and in his beautiful priestess's arms,
Nidaba whispered, "She knows about us, Natum."

"No. I've taken care, Nidaba. I never slip away until she is asleep.
I've not once been followed. I don't have to do these things. I have
every right to be with you, as king. I take these precautions only because you ask it of me. But I do take them. She does not know."

The stars sparkled overhead in a canopy wider than any in the
world. And they sparkled in Nidaba's dark eyes. Gods, how he loved
her. He hated that she insisted they see each other only in the dead
of night, that they hide their love from everyone in the kingdom.
She deserved so much more.

"You have not been followed," she whispered, leaning on his
chest, staring into his eyes. "But I have."

His frown was swift and deep, and he quickly looked around
them, scanning the dunes for prying eyes but seeing only swirls of
sand, nothing more.

"Not here, love," Nidaba assured him quickly. "No one has managed to stay on my heels through the secret passages of the temple.
But those men of hers . . . they appear wherever I go. I look up
from a table of cloths in the market square, or after blessing a boat
before it journeys on with its load of fruits or sacred herbs, and they
are there. Always. Just . . . watching me. Following me. Listening to
my every word, and often talking to the people with whom I have
had conversations."

He searched her face, knowing her too well to think she would
imagine such things as these. "Then she must suspect something.
But she cannot know about us, Nidaba."

Nidaba rolled off him, sitting up and drawing her knees to her chest, pulling the blanket more closely around her shoulders. "Those necromancers of hers, they frighten me more than her guards, Natum."

He sat up beside her, startled. "What have they done to you?"

"Done? Nothing. But they—there is a darkness about them. They've been speaking to every priestess in the temple, asking questions about me. And to the villagers as well. It's as if your queen has set out to learn all there is to know of me . . . of us. Our past. What we have been to each other, and what we are to each other now."

Eannatum felt his jaw go tight. "I'll put a stop to it. Puabi has no right—"

"No, Natum. You are wrong. As your bride, your queen, she has every right."

He looked at her sharply.

"She is your wife."

"A political alliance and nothing more. She knew that from the start."

"Nonetheless, you wed her."

"I do not lie with her, Nidaba. Or kiss those cold lips of hers. I feel nothing for her. It's you I love."

Lifting her hands to his cheeks and pressing her palms there, she stared into his eyes in the desert night. "I know, Natum. And I love you as well. But . . . but it's wrong, what we are doing."

He frowned in utter confusion. "It is my right as king! It is the way of our very culture, Nidaba. It is only you who sees a need to keep it secret."

"It's wrong because it is hurtful. I serve the Goddess, Natum, I know what I feel, and that is what I feel. I fear the price we pay will be higher than either of us can bear."

"I won't give you up, Nidaba."

She nodded slowly, then challenged him with her eyes. "Then give up the throne. Come away with me. We'll run away to some foreign land. The lost paradise of Dilmun, perhaps. Where the rivers run with honey."

"That's not real."

"It could be, for us. If you were with me, free to be with me . . . any place we were would be paradise, Natum."

He gently pulled free of her hands, stared upward at the starry sky. "Are you saying I have to choose? Is that what this is, Nidaba?

Are you forcing me to choose between the woman I love and the
kingdom I rule? Between you and thousands of my subjects? Between you and the promise I made to my dying father, to my Goddess, to myself?"

She lowered her head, licked her lips. "Yes."

"Even when it was you who made me see that I had to make this
sacrifice for the good of Sumer?"

"Yes," she said softly. "Even so. Circumstances have . . .
changed. The Ummamites have backed down."

"They'll begin again the moment they sense weakness!"

She lifted her gaze to his. "If it were only for me, I would never
ask it, Eannatum. But it has become necessary now that I think of
more than just myself. I must consider the greater good. And for me
to remain here, playing the part of royal harlot, is no longer acceptable."

"You know that is not how I think of you!" He shot to his feet,
pacing away from her as his bare feet sank in the sand.

"It is how all of Lagash is coming to think of me, Eannatum."
She got to her feet as well and came to him, placing a hand on his
shoulder. "Or do you still insist that no one knows about us? Because
they do, you know. It's obvious to any who care to wonder. When
you look at me, Eannatum, there is fire in your eyes. When you speak
to me, your voice deepens, softens. When you touch me . . ."

He spun around to face her. "I *cannot* choose. Do not ask me to
do this, Nidaba. I cannot."

Her lashes lowered, and he thought they were damp. "All right,
then, my love. I will not ask it of you again."

He sighed in profound relief, pulling her close to him. "She will
tire of Lagash soon enough," he promised. "You'll see. She'll return
home to Ur to take up residence there in her homeland, in her
palace. And I'll remain here. It will be better then."

"Yes," she whispered. "Yes, I believe you."

Tears threatened as she listened to Natum retelling the tale of
their last night together, but she blinked them away when she realized he was staring hard into her eyes.

"But you didn't believe me, did you, Nidaba? Instead, you ran
away. That very night."

Nidaba sniffled. "There were . . . things you didn't know, Ean-natum. Things . . . that made it impossible for me to stay."

He looked so pained, so hurt, even after all this time. "What things?" he asked gently.

"Puabi, for one." Her face grew hard at the memory. "She had come to me earlier that evening. In the temple. Dressed in her full royal splendor, right to the headdress, she came to me. I was in the *cella*, burning incense and praying for guidance, for I was very trou-bled, about so many things. There was a young eunuch, a servant of the temple, an immortal, like me. He kept trying to tell me about the nature of what I was, but I thought him insane. And yet his words troubled me on some level I could not understand. I finally sent him away to serve at the palace to be rid of his constant far-fetched tales. And I felt horribly guilty about that. I sensed I had done something very wrong.

"So that was one of the things that troubled me. But there was another, an even greater worry on my mind that evening. So I went to the *cella* to pray. When I heard footsteps in the rushes, I turned and saw her there. Queen Puabi, her gold baubles gleaming in the torchlight. It was just after sundown. The room was alive with shad-ows that danced over her face, over the walls. The way the torchlight gleamed in the lapis eyes of the stone gods, I almost felt they had all come to life—and had gathered there to judge me for my sins.

"'I know what you are,' she told me. 'My necromancers, my oc-cultists, they have told me your vile secret.'

"I caught my breath, and felt my heart pounding in my chest. I was certain she meant that she knew about us, about our secret meet-ings, our lovemaking. But that wasn't it at all.

"'Daughter of the Goddess, indeed,' Puabi all but spat, striding closer to me, kicking the fresh rushes aside without a care. 'Daughter of demons, more likely. You're no more divine than I am, Nidaba. You are a sorceress. A Witch!'

"When I heard the accusation, I nearly laughed, such was my re-lief.

"'Do you deny it?' the queen demanded. She stood very close to me now, and I rose, for I had still been kneeling. Standing upright, I was a good deal taller than she, and for a moment it gave me confi-dence.

"'Of course I deny it! I am a High Priestess of the Goddess!'

"'You are a priestess of darkness, born of demons. No human parents ever claimed you. No. You were left on the steps of the temple by the forces of evil, who placed you there knowing you would take over one day. Taking the name of a Goddess! Learning the sacred script when it was forbidden to women! Can you deny any of those things?'

"I stared in shock, stunned that she could know so much about me. 'No one knows who left me on the temple steps. But I can assure you, they were perfectly human.'

"'Were they? And what of your powers? Hmm? Do you deny them, as well?'

"'What powers?' Shaking my head, I took a step backward.

"'I know about them!' she cried. 'How you can make the earth seem to tremble and quake when you grow angry. How your rites and charms cause far greater effects than those of any other priestess in all of Sumer! And this!' She reached out, striking with the speed of a viper, her clawlike hand clutching at my white ritual gown and tearing it down the right side.

"Gasping, jumping back, I fought my anger. If it got the best of me, if I lost control, I would reveal the powers she accused me of possessing. And that was something that Lia—and later the eunuch with all his wild tales—had warned me never to do.

"But Puabi pointed now, at my right flank. 'There,' she said. 'It is just as my spiritualists said. You bear the mark on your thigh—the crescent moon! Demon! *Asakku!*'

"'No! I'm not!' I cried, backing away from her. But it shook me to the core, because Aahron, the eunuch, had told me of the mark's significance, and I had not believed him.

"'Yes,' she said. 'You are, and the mark is proof. If I choose to reveal your secret it will mean certain death, Nidaba.'

"I stood a little straighter, sure of myself. For I knew that my king, her own husband, bore the same mark I did. Yet something warned me not to mention that. If she had not learned of it on her own . . . I had no wish to imply that you, too, were the demon she believed me to be. 'You would not be believed!' I told her instead. 'You are a foreigner, and I, a High Priestess!'

"'I am a queen, and you an enchantress. One who has bewitched the king, stolen his seed, and even now carries her demon spawn who could well lay claim to the throne of all Sumer!'

"I fell silent, my blood rushing from my head so quickly I grew dizzy with it. 'How. . . . how could you know such a thing?'

"'My diviners, I have told you. They are not pretenders like you, Nidaba. They see the truth in the bowels of birds and the livers of beasts. And even were there doubts about my claims in the minds of the people, do you truly think they would risk it? A child is not something you can hide, Nidaba. Not for long, that is. They would never risk Eannatum's leaving the throne of Sumer to the son of the *Asakku* demon.'

"I had never believed in the divinatory powers of self-proclaimed occultists . . . but I had no choice but to believe then, for it was the truth. I was carrying your child."

Natum had sat in silence, listening to her speak until that point. But now, Nidaba stopped speaking, and looked at his face—the face she had so loved, once.

"You were pregnant. And you knew it. You were pregnant with my child."

"Yes, Natum. Your son."

He closed his eyes, and she could see his pain growing ever deeper. "I . . . I guess I knew, deep down. I just . . ."

"Puabi said she would see to it that my child was murdered at birth, unless I agreed to her terms."

Natum knelt at her feet, gathering her hands in his, his head bowed. "What did she demand of you?"

"That I see you only once more—to tell you goodbye. To end what was between us firmly, and finally. That I go into hiding, in a place of her choosing, and remain there, under her guard, until the day I gave birth. And that I then surrender the child to her."

Natum lifted his head slowly, staring into Nidaba's eyes.

"She wanted, I believe, to claim our son as her own."

"Damn her!" he spat. "I had only been with her once up to that point—to consummate the vows."

"Once . . . up to that point?" Nidaba asked, wondering if that meant he had been with the woman again later.

But Natum ignored her question and rose to pace away from her. "She likely felt that if she hadn't conceived my child that night, she might never do so." He pounded a fist onto a table. "But why? Why would she want to pretend to have borne my child?"

"She wanted a son. She wanted your love," Nidaba said, deciding that perhaps she did not want to know the rest. "And perhaps more than either of those things, she wanted to secure her hold on the throne of Sumer. With her son as heir, her own power would have been irreversible."

He nodded. "She craved power more than anything else. I knew that about her from the start." He returned to where Nidaba sat. Lifting his hands, he stroked her hair, her cheek. "So that was why you asked me to run away with you that night? To choose between you and my throne?"

"Yes."

"And when I couldn't choose . . ."

"I fled, by dead of night. I knew Puabi meant to kill me in the end, and I knew I wanted no child of mine being raised by that cold, evil woman. So I fled, to raise my son alone. You issued a proclamation far and wide that I was to be found and returned to Lagash. You sent your armies to pursue me into the wilderness."

"Because I loved you. I didn't think I could go on without you, and even if I could, I didn't want to."

"That was what I believed at first. That you sought me out of love. They hounded my every step, your soldiers. For years, my child and I knew no peace, settled in no home. And still I believed in you, in your honor, your love for me. Until they caught up to us at last."

Natum stood perfectly still. "What happened that night, Nidaba?"

Rising to her feet, she strode to the window, and gazed out, unable to face him and recall the most horrible moments of her entire existence. "They placed us under house arrest, surrounded the small hut where we had been living, far in the northlands. They stood guard all the night through, telling us not to fear. That we would be escorted back to Lagash, but were in no danger of harm. That they were under strict orders to care for us as they would for the king himself." She smiled a little bitterly as she let the curtain fall back in place. "And we believed them, my Nicky and I."

"It was the truth. Those were the orders I issued to my men."

She turned, facing him squarely. His hand was braced on the chair where she had been before. "Three of your soldiers crept into the house in the night, Eannatum. Assassins. Trained to kill and sent to do murder. Nothing less. Your son . . . oh, you'd have been proud if you could have seen him. So brave. He stepped in front of me, tried to protect me. And they ran him through."

Eannatum made a strangled sound, half cry, half shout, and dropped to his knees in front of that empty chair.

"And when I fell to the floor to cradle my dying child in my arms, they ran me through as well."

Natum's head fell forward, his eyes closed and yet a tear escaped to roll slowly down his cheek. "You . . . were immortal, though you couldn't have known it then."

She nodded. "Yes. I still didn't believe in the tales the eunuch Aahron had told me. But I would soon have all the proof I could ever need that they were true. I was immortal. But my boy was not."

"Gods, Nidaba—" Natum got to his feet, came toward her, but she held up a hand to stop him.

"You said you wished to hear all of it. There is more."

He stiffened. "Go on."

"When I revived, the hut was engulfed in flames. I knew nothing about immortality, about High Witches, Dark or Light. I could not understand why my son lay dead, his precious body already cooling, while I lived. My wound miraculously, it seemed, had healed. But his remained. Somehow I managed to escape the flames. And all the while the eunuch's tales were echoing in my mind. He had told me that the only way I could die, other than having my heart cut still beating from my chest, was by fire. And he had told me it was the most horrible death imaginable for an immortal—that the heart itself would burst into flames and burn within the body, blistering and searing the flesh from within. And even then, it was not by any sane method of calculation that I escaped. I merely stumbled out, blind and numb with grief, and half mad, I suppose. But not so mad that I was not aware that an illegitimate son would have been a threat to the throne of Sumer. Or that you finally had made that choice I had asked of you a decade before. Between me and your throne. And that you had chosen the throne."

He did come to her then, striding forward and gripping her shoulders. "My men were under orders to care for you as they would a Goddess and to bring you back to me. Nothing more." He shook her slightly. "Nidaba, by the Gods, you must believe me!"

Her own tears flowed now, slowly, like old, deep rivers. Not a ripple of a sob or a sound accompanied them. "I don't *want* to believe you, can't you see that? It nearly killed me, losing my precious Nicky. And when I finally made my way through the hell of that, there was another waiting. The knowledge of your betrayal. Because I believed in you so deeply. But I survived, Eannatum. I survived. It would be very foolish of me, don't you think, to believe in you again? To give you the same weapon that I gave you before? One that would surely kill me this time, should you turn it on me once again?"

His hands dug into her shoulders, and the expression in his eyes was fierce. "You know I'm telling you the truth, Nidaba. Deny it all you want, but you already do believe me. You know me. You know I couldn't harm my own son."

She averted her face from his probing black eyes. One finger came up to her chin and lifted it, though, so she couldn't look away and he stared deeply into her soul. "I should hate you for even pretending to believe such a thing of me. But . . . I can't hate you, Nidaba. I never could."

Then he kissed her. Long, and tenderly . . . so tenderly that her tears flowed anew. And when he lifted his head away, she knew she wanted to believe in him again more than she had ever wanted anything. And even more certainly, she knew that she already did. And always had.

But she didn't say so. Instead, she looked past him, through her veil of tears, to the orange glow painting the sky beyond the window screen, and she murmured, "It is dawn."

"I don't care."

"Yes, you do. You care about your friends. And you know as well as I do that they are not safe in this house. We need to get Sheila and George and Queenie away from here. Someplace safe, Eannatum. And we need to do it now."

Chapter 15

Reluctantly, Nathan agreed. "This conversation is far from over."

She only looked at him sadly as she got to her feet. "It's beyond over, Natum. It's long dead."

"You know that's a lie." Taking her hand, he led her through the bedroom, into the hallway, and down it to Sheila's room. Unlocking the door, he led Nidaba into the room where Sheila lay sleeping, but as he stared at her, relieved that she remained where he'd left her, Nidaba nudged him with her elbow.

"Don't be a fool, Natum. The real Sheila could be lying dead in the basement right now for all you know. Go over there . . . touch her. Make sure she isn't . . ."

He hated to admit that she could be right, but there was no denying it. Slowly, he moved to the bedside, reached out a hand, and touched Sheila's where it lay atop the sheets.

The older woman started and opened her eyes. Then she smiled at him. "Whatever are you doin' in my bedroom, Nathan?" But her smile died slowly, as memories of the day before, the night before, returned to her eyes. "What's wrong? Has something else happened?"

"No. Everything's fine. Nidaba and I simply feel it would be far safer if we took you and George . . . away for a time."

"Away? To where?"

"I'd rather not say just now."

"Rather not say what?" George said from the hallway. When Nathan turned he saw George standing there in his big checkered bathrobe, his hair tousled and feathery, sticking up in places.

"Where you and Sheila are going to go and stay for a few days."

"Oh," George said. Then he frowned. "Oh! But what about Queenie? I mean, can she come too?" As he spoke he lowered a hand as if to scratch the dog's head. But she wasn't at his side as usual, and he glanced back down the hall with a frown.

"I thought about that, but no. It won't work. You're going to be traveling, George. The dog's going to have to stay here, but I promise, I won't let anything happen to her," Nathan said.

"But . . . but . . ."

"It will only be for a couple of days, George. You know I'll take very good care of her while you're gone. Don't you?"

"Well, I . . . I guess."

"This will be like a vacation," Nathan put in. "You're going to have fun. I promise. All right?"

George smiled uncertainly. "All right."

"Good. Now the only catch is, we have to stay together, all four of us, every minute, until we get out of this house. Okay?"

George's smile died. "You think the killer's gonna get us. Don't you, Nathan?"

"I'm not going to let the killer get you," Nathan said firmly. He slanted a glance toward Nidaba, who stood silently beside him. "Not any of you. And that's why we're going to stay together while we pack and get ready to leave. Understand?"

"I guess," George said.

"It's not necessary for all four of us to remain together," Nidaba offered. "Remaining in pairs would do just as well, Natum, and speed may very well be of the essence here."

He held her gaze, nodded slowly, and knew she must be feeling the same shivers up her spine that he was. A foreboding. A threat, lingering, looming. Clapping his hands together and forcing a smile he was far from feeling, Nathan said, "Great idea. Nidaba, you can help Sheila get her things together, and I'll go with George and help him get packed. All right?"

George clapped his hands in exactly the same way. "All right. Let's go, then!"

The bags packed, Nidaba and Sheila waited in the driveway for George and Natum to go and pull the car around. It gave Nidaba time to think. To wonder. This ability of Puabi's, this astounding talent she had, just how advanced was it? What if, for example, Puabi tried to take on Natum's form? How would Nidaba know?

And yet, she thought, she *would* know. She was certain of it, in fact. Surely Puabi couldn't be *that* clever.

The question lingered though, what if she could?

Never. I know Eannatum far better than his so-called wife ever did, Nidaba thought coldly. *She couldn't fool me. Not for a moment.*

Which begged another question—how had the clever Puabi managed to fool Natum last night into believing *she* was Nidaba? Surely he knew Nidaba far better than Puabi ever had.

Then again, he likely hadn't been thinking with his mind just then.

It angered her. Infuriated her.

It shouldn't.

Gods, she still loved the man.

He pulled the car around and got out, opened the trunk and came to take the suitcases that sat at Sheila's feet.

"Do you suppose it's safe now, to discuss where we'll be going?" Sheila asked at length.

Already, Nidaba could feel the easing of the tension that had settled over them back inside the house. The gloom. The pall of death, holding them all in its grip. The tension between her and Natum, however, was still as powerful as ever. She didn't want him to know what she felt for him. It made her far too vulnerable to him to feel this way. Gods forbid he should realize it.

"There's nothing to discuss. Just get in the car and go. Don't tell me where. Don't even decide where, until you're out of here," Nathan ordered. "When you get somewhere safe, call me at home. Let me know you're all right. I won't ask you where you are, or a number where you can be reached. If I do, don't give it to me. You understand?"

"But . . . how will you know how to reach us, Nathan?" Sheila asked.

"Jot a phone number on a postcard and send it to the gallery address. Don't sign it, don't put a return address on it, and mail it from some other place or send it to someone else and have them forward it for you. I'll know what it is, and I'll call you as soon as it's safe to come home. Understand?"

"My heavens, Nathan, do you really think all this is necessary?" Sheila asked, her eyes widening.

It was Nidaba who answered the question. "You of all people, Sheila, should know that it is. This woman, this murderer, is smart. She'll use anything she can to get to Nathan and me. Including you."

Shutting her eyes, Sheila nodded. Then she opened them again and glanced at George. Nidaba did too. He looked so frightened, so pitiful. Smiling brokenly, Sheila stood on tiptoe and whispered something in his ear. His face split in an instant smile. "Can we? Can we really go *there*?" he asked, all but bouncing.

"Yes. Just remember, it's a secret." To Nathan she said, "We'll call you by six this evening. No later. I don't want you hanging about this house any longer than necessary waiting for us to call."

It seemed very odd to Nidaba that she should feel like hugging the two of them before they got into the car. Even more odd to feel tears threatening at the thought of them leaving.

And yet that was exactly what happened. She hugged Sheila tight, and the woman patted her back and squeezed her in return. "Please be careful," Sheila told her. "And don't forget . . ." Then leaning closer, she whispered into Nidaba's ear, "He *loves* you."

Nidaba had to fight back tears as she kissed the woman's cheek. Then she found herself wrapped in a powerful bear hug and picked up right off her feet. George swung her from side to side, squeezing her tight. Then he put her down and grinned at her. "Don't cry, Nidaba. We'll be back soon. Won't we, Sheila?"

"Yes, we will," she told him.

"You'll take extra good care of my dog, won't you, Nidaba?"

"You know I will," she promised, sniffling, wondering vaguely where the lumbering beast had wandered this time.

It was worse yet when she had to watch George's eyes tear up as he hugged Natum. "Please don't make us stay away too long," he said.

"I couldn't get along without you for very long, my friend," Natum replied, his voice tight.

Then Sheila hugged him, and Nidaba saw, even through her misty eyes, that she whispered something in Natum's ear, too. She wondered if it was the same thing the woman had whispered to her.

Natum looked up, caught Nidaba's eye, and said to Sheila, "Once, maybe that was true."

"Once true, always true. Some things don't die, Nathan. You remember that." Sheila kissed Nathan's cheek, and then she took George's hand and led him to the passenger side.

Nathan turned away from the car as they got in and pulled away. He lowered his head and pressed his forefingers to his temples, rubbing small circles there as if his head ached.

"You'll miss them terribly," Nidaba murmured.

"They're my family."

"I know." She lifted a hand, tentative, hesitant, and finally touched him. She stroked his hair, caressed the back of his neck in an effort to rub his pain away. "It's going to be okay. We'll make it safe for them, and then they'll come back."

He met her eyes, nodded twice, but didn't look convinced that what she said was the truth. "Let's go. We've got to pack our own things, close up the house, and collect that damned dog."

"If we can find her," Nidaba said, glancing to the left and right. "She's nowhere around at the moment."

"We'd *better* find her," Natum said grimly. "George will never forgive us if we don't."

When Nidaba came down the stairs with her few possessions packed in the carpetbag Nathan had given her, he was sitting in a claw-legged armchair, staring into the burgeoning flames of a newly built fire. In one hand he held a crystal tumbler half filled with amber liquid that turned red in the firelight.

"I thought we were leaving."

He didn't look up. "I know."

"Have you changed your mind?"

Drawing a breath, he seemed to gather himself. He turned his head slowly, faced her. The firelight painted one side of his face in orange and yellow, leaving the other side in dark shadow, so he looked like some demon prince sitting there. "I've been thinking."

She sighed, set her bag on the floor, and came closer. "Thinking about what, Eannatum?"

His gave her a thoughtful, penetrating look. "It's been so long since anyone has called me that. It almost feels like someone else's name now."

"I apologize if it makes you uncomfortable. It's who you are to me. Who you'll always be. To me, 'Nathan' is a stranger."

"Nathan is the man I wanted to be. The man I've been pretending to be for years now. I'm comfortable being him. It's safe. Peaceful. Predictable."

"And fraudulent. You're a ruler, a warrior, and an immortal High Witch, Eannatum. Not a gallery owner or an antique dealer. You're no quaint New Englander, but a Sumerian king." She drew a deep breath, sighed. "But you know all of that. Natum, you said we would stay here only long enough to gather a few things and George's precious stray, and then we'd be off again. Go someplace safe."

"I haven't found the dog yet," he said.

"Nor do you seem to be looking for her. Natum, you told me—"

"I know what I told you. It was a lie. What I told you was not what I intended to do. And it's not what you intended either. Is it, Nidaba?"

He stared at her, brows raised, eyes so piercing that she finally had to look away. "I don't know what you're talking about."

"Of course you do. You were going to go along with my plan, and slip away from me at the first opportunity, to come back here and wait for Puabi. To take her on by yourself."

She made a face. "You think you know me so well, do you?"

He shrugged. "It's what I was planning to do. We've always had certain things in common, Nidaba. Bullheadedness being one of them."

Slowly she lifted her eyes to his. "You were planning to come back here without me?"

He nodded.

"Why? She could as easily kill you as the other way around."

He smiled, very slightly, just one side of his mouth pulling upward. "Why were *you* going to do it?"

Nidaba narrowed her eyes. "I owe the bitch. Besides, I'm a warrior. It's what I do."

"I owe her as well, you know," he said softly.

"Ahh, but *you're* an ordinary antique dealer. Mild-mannered, model citizen. Boring as milk toast and content to remain that way."

His eyes seared hers with a flash of anger before he banked it again and drew a calming breath. "Sit down, Nidaba. I think it's time we finished our talk."

"I've no wish to discuss the past any further."

"You don't need to do anything but listen. Sit down."

Blinking in surprise, for he sounded just then more like the king she remembered than he had since she had seen him again, Nidaba met his eyes, searched them. "All right." She took the rocking chair and pushed it closer to the fire, closer to him, then stepped around it and sat down. "I'm listening."

He nodded, his face tight. "It pains me to think that you believe what you do of me."

"And what is that?"

He looked at her. Just looked at her. His eyes, as dark as ever they had been, and so, so intense. She could see all the way into his soul, she thought, in the power of that look. And it was obvious that he could see clear to the core of her own. She couldn't look away. Her heart seemed to shudder beneath the force of that gaze. To crack and split apart.

"You tell me," he said, his tone deep, commanding, uncompromising.

"No."

"Tell me, Nidaba. Say it."

"Don't do this to me," she whispered.

"The hell I won't. Nidaba, you *know*. You've always known. I need to hear you say it."

She jumped to her feet, turning away, but he was up in a heartbeat, gripping her shoulders, forcing her to face him. "I didn't know you were pregnant when you left Lagash, Nidaba. I didn't know you'd had my son."

"Stop."

"But even so, I turned over every rock in Sumer, and beyond, searching for you. Trying to find you."

Tears flowed down her face now. "To have me killed. To protect your throne," she whispered, her throat so tight she could barely force the lies through it.

"To bring you back to me. Because I didn't want to live without you. Because I loved you, Nidaba."

"No!" She pulled free, turned her back, and fought not to break down in front of him. But the racking sobs tore at her, straining to escape.

"Is it easier to believe it was me, Nidaba? Is it easier somehow if you can blame me, hate me? Did that make all those years of loneliness go by any faster? Did it?"

"You ordered the death of my son," she rasped. "It was your soldiers who killed him."

"No. It was Puabi who did that. I've only now come to realize that. It's the only way it could have happened, and I think you know it."

Nidaba went stiff. It was not with surprise, because he was only telling her what she'd finally begun to surmise—but refused to admit, even to herself.

"It all fits," he said. "She brought soldiers with her when she came to live in the palace. She had loyal men placed in the ranks with mine. And no doubt she ordered them to kill you both on sight. To burn your bodies in order to cover up the crime. No doubt she knew what you were, even though I did not. She knew the heat of a fire would cause your heart to explode in flames within you, destroying you utterly."

"No," Nidaba denied. "If Puabi had known what I was, she'd have wished to take my heart for herself. It's obvious now—that was her goal all along. To make herself immortal, a Dark High Witch. She needed to take the heart of a Light One to do it. So why not mine?"

"You were too far away. You'd have revived before she could have got to you."

"Then she'd have had me bound and brought to her as a captive." She'd been over all of this in her mind already. She knew all the arguments. She'd waged them with herself.

"I had dozens of soldiers there under orders to protect you with their very lives if need be," Natum said. And then he tossed in an argument she'd never thought of in all the times she had imagined this discussion. "I told my men they would pay with their lives if any harm came to you while under their care. They knew I meant it, Nidaba. So much so that over half the troop fled Sumer after that fire that supposedly killed you, rather than returning to Lagash to face my wrath. Puabi had only two or three of her own men among the troop that finally found you. It would have been impossible for them to bring you back to Puabi as a captive when my men so outnumbered them. Don't you see, Nidaba? It was Puabi, not me. I could never harm you . . . much less my own son. Never."

His hands curled around her upper arms, warming them. "Please, Nidaba, if you ever cared for me at all, tell me you know I didn't do this thing." His voice broke on the final two words.

The shield of stone she had constructed around her heart crumbled and fell to bits. And she whispered, "I know."

"Do you?"

Turning slowly, she stared up into his eyes. "I've always known, Natum. I never truly believed . . ." Fresh, hot tears flooded her eyes. "I'm so sorry. No matter what pain we've caused each other, I had no right to say what I did. I knew in my heart it wasn't you. I . . ."

He closed his eyes, pulled her close, held her to his chest and stroked her hair.

Sobs wracked her body as so much anguish finally spilled free. Her hatred released at last, there remained only pain. And her words tumbled from her lips without pause or forethought. She wasn't even sure they made sense. "I had to hate you. Because if I stopped there was nothing left but to love you, to miss you, to accept that you loved your country more than you did me. And all of that . . . was just too painful. It was easier to hate you, Natum. So I tried to do that. But I never did. Not really."

He sighed his relief, and she felt his body quiver with it. He cupped the back of her head with his hand, and she rested her head on his shoulder, her body shuddering with the emotions she'd kept pent up for so long.

"I needed you," she whispered. "Gods, I needed you so desperately. But you were with her. You were with her, and I . . ."

"I'm here now, Nidaba." His palm cradling her cheek, he turned her face until her mouth slid over his, and clung to his lips. He kissed her. Fully, deeply, passionately, he kissed her. And she kissed him back, with every bit of heartache and anguish, every bit of grief and agony she had felt for centuries spilling out and into the kiss.

His hips moved against hers, his hands curling over her buttocks to hold her tight to him. She didn't think, not now. She only felt. And what she felt was fire, the same white-hot fire that had always raged and burned between them. She tugged his shirt free of his trousers, pushed her hands up underneath it to the skin of his back, and higher, to his shoulders. His skin was warm to the touch, firm beneath her palms. She'd always loved running her hands over his hard body. He tugged at the skirt she wore, and she heard the fabric rip, but she didn't care.

Still feeding at her mouth, he pushed the skirt off her, and it fell to the floor. He shoved one hand inside her panties now, touching her, burning her, invading her the way only he would dare to do. When she moved her feet apart, they tangled in the fabric, and she stumbled backward. Her hip hit a table, and a lamp crashed to the floor. And then Eannatum was tearing her panties away, lifting her off her feet, anchoring her legs around his waist. She locked her ankles behind his back and felt his hot erection forced inside her, all the way. Her back pressed to a wall, he thrust hard against her. She clung to his shoulders as he rocked into her, over and over.

He took his mouth from hers, and muttered, "The blouse . . ."

His hands were busy, holding her backside captive, keeping her pinioned tight to him to accept every one of his powerful thrusts. With her hands, she gripped her blouse in front, and pulled it open, tearing buttons free. It didn't matter. He mattered. He wanted the blouse gone, spoke a command, and she obeyed because he sounded for once like the king she had known. Her king, for whom she would do anything. And she, his Goddess incarnate, for whom he would gladly die.

It was a powerful illusion. Even if it was only temporary.

Her breasts spilled free, and he jammed himself deep inside her and said, "Feed me, woman." Her hands rose, cupping her own breasts, lifting them to his mouth, holding them for him to suckle and bite and torment.

Then his hands closed on her waist, and he lifted and lowered her in time with his thrusts, lifted and lowered her, forced her down harder, bit down on her sensitive nipple with his sharp white teeth.

When she came, it was a searing explosion that blinded her, deafened her, so she couldn't even hear the sound of his name on her own tortured cry.

He held her close, and she felt the pulsing heat of his seed spilling into her. And then he sank slowly to his knees, cradling her in his arms as if she were a small child.

Tears. She felt them, wet on her face, but surely they couldn't be hers. She never wept. What had just happened between them meant nothing, she knew that. It was comfort, and an outpouring of long-held emotions. It was needed. It was cleansing. It was blessed release.

"Why, Natum? Why did she have to kill my Nicky, when it was me she hated?"

Eannatum stroked her hair. Gently he righted her blouse, fastening what buttons remained until she was decently covered. He reached out for her skirt, on the floor, drew it around her. When he finished, she looked as if she'd been through a battle. But she was dressed. He set her gently into an easy chair near the fire. Then he righted his own trousers and rebuttoned his own shirt.

"She was mad with jealousy, Nidaba. After you fled Lagash, your name took on the same mystique as that of Gilgamesh. You were spoken of in awed tones—as half goddess, half mortal. Rumors grew, and many spoke of the love between you and me, as well. Puabi wanted your fame, your mystery. And she wanted my love. I just couldn't give it to her."

She heard something in his voice, and swiping at her eyes, she looked up at him. "There is more," she said, her tone flat, her eyes moving rapidly over his face. "What aren't you telling me, Natum?"

He shifted away from her. "You always see the truth in my eyes, don't you? How do you do that, Nidaba?"

"Tell me," she whispered.

Sighing, he forced his gaze level with hers. "There was . . . a child."

Nidaba's heart lurched. "Yours? With . . . with *her?*"

"Though I couldn't love her, Nidaba, I was human. A man. And a king. I didn't know you'd borne my son, and I needed to provide my country with an heir."

In a pained whisper, Nidaba said, "*You* made a child with *her?*"

He nodded. "You had been gone for five years. I had little hope of ever finding you again, and I had finally come to believe that you honestly did not want to be with me anymore. It crushed me, Nidaba. But it infuriated me as well. I turned to my duty, because I had nothing else. And part of my duty was to know my queen and to produce an heir."

He pushed a hand through his tousled hair. "And maybe it was a way of . . . striking back at you for running away from me the way you did. Maybe, deep down, I wanted to hurt you back."

"You certainly succeeded, Natum. In a thousand ways you hurt me. And had I known of this, it would have hurt me still more. But I never knew."

"That's because the infant was stillborn," he said and sighed deeply. "Puabi . . . she lost whatever sanity she had at that point. Ordered the servants out of her chambers, bolted the doors and decreed that anyone coming inside would pay with his life. She locked herself in her room with that dead child for days."

"Days?"

He nodded. "I was away." He looked at her steadily. "Out looking for you, actually. On one of my endless quests, following yet another fantastical report that you'd been seen in some remote and unlikely locale. But I returned the moment word of the tragedy reached me. I had the doors broken down, the child taken from her, had it buried." He shook his head slowly. "I thought it would kill her. I honestly did. She hated me for it, and I knew she always would." He drew a breath. "It was only a short while later we began to hear rumors that you had been seen far in the north, and that you had with you a fine and healthy son some five summers old. I think that must have been what pushed her completely over the edge. She had to know your child was mine, even though when I heard the rumors I was unsure. Mostly I believed they were fantasies—so many had already been spun around your disappearance . . ." He shook his head slowly. "But Puabi believed it. And I think it was more than her grief-crippled mind could bear."

Nidaba lifted her gaze, speared him with her eyes. "I hope you're not trying to excuse what she did, Natum. A mother who knows the pain of losing a child should be damned to eternal torment for inflicting the same pain on another!"

He stared down at her. "I wasn't trying to excuse her. Your

child . . . he was my son, too, you know. And I didn't even get the chance to know him."

Nidaba rose slowly, lifted a trembling hand, touched Natum's cheek. "No. You didn't." Her own words, those she had just spoken, played again through her mind. *A mother who knows the pain of losing a child should be damned to eternal torment for inflicting the same pain on another.* Wasn't that exactly what she was doing by not telling Eannatum the truth about their son?

"I made the wrong choice when I chose my kingdom over you, Nidaba. And I made the wrong choice when I married a woman I didn't love, much less slept with her while you yet lived—it was a sin against our love. One I know you can probably never forgive. And it was my own army that tracked you down, enabling Puabi's assassins to kill our son. For that—for that I can't even ask your forgiveness. Just know, Nidaba, that I have suffered too. At least you got to know him, to be with him, for a little while. But I never did. And while our feelings for each other have . . . have changed after all this time, the love a parent feels for a child never can."

She blinked as a sudden pain struck her in the chest. His feelings for her had changed? Well. Of course they had. It had been four millennia. They couldn't have done otherwise, could they? But . . . they had made love, and it seemed as if they'd never been apart.

And yet she knew that meant very little. Physically, there would always be this explosive passion between them. But emotionally—

Besides, even if their feelings were the same, it could never be good between them. They were too different.

"I wish to Gods I had known him," he said, not even noticing her pain in the face of his own, she was certain.

"You will," she whispered.

Startled, he lifted his head, searched her face.

"For those . . . bad choices of yours, Natum, I will try to forgive you. I cannot yet say that I have, but I know that I should. What difference do they make now, anyway? As you said . . ." She swallowed, unable to repeat his words back to him. "But as for your son . . . our son . . ." She raised her chin, met his eyes. "He died trying to protect his mother from the blade, Eannatum. You *do* know what that means."

Slowly, Eannatum turned in a circle, searching his mind, it

seemed. "It means he would come into his next incarnation with the gift of immortality. But Nidaba, we'd have no way of knowing him. Of finding him."

She let her lips pull into a very sad, very slight smile. "I am a High Priestess of Inanna. I was legend in my own time, as much Goddess as woman. I am a Witch, Eannatum. Do you really think that I would not know my own son?"

He stopped turning, and stood facing her, his hands closing on her shoulders. "Do not torment me, Nidaba. Tell me straight out. My son . . . he lives? Now, today?"

As if on cue, the dog they had been searching for all afternoon, came wandering into the room, along with a cool draft, as if somewhere a door or window had been left ajar. The dog stopped walking when she stood beside them. Her head came up, ears perking as if she sensed the importance of the conversation.

"He lives," Nidaba said. "His name is Nicodimus, and he does indeed live. He's magnificent, Natum. You will be so proud."

"By the wings of angels!" Natum cried. He enfolded her in a fierce embrace, and she could feel the emotions surging in him. His entire body trembled with feeling. "Why didn't you tell me before now, Nidaba? For the love of Inanna, why?"

Sniffling, she clung to his shoulders, stared up into his face, and saw the wetness, damp and gleaming on his cheeks. "I don't know. At first my memory was so skewed that even I didn't realize I had found him again. And when I did . . . I told myself I was protecting him—from you, from this situation, from Puabi. But I knew you wouldn't risk his life any more than I would, Natum. I hope you can forgive me for waiting until now to tell you the truth."

"Of course I can forgive you. Just . . . Gods, just tell me, where is he? Is he near?"

She pulled free of him, turning away. It was too painful to have him hold her so fiercely now, when he'd only moments ago admitted that his feelings for her were no longer what they had been once. "I don't know for sure. But . . . that woman, Arianna, who came here looking for me, she is his wife. So if she is near, he must be as well. When you first mentioned her name, I was still disoriented. Confused by the drugs that were still polluting my blood and my mind. It was only much later, when I was clear headed that I remembered the rest. I didn't tell you and I should have, Natum. I just—I don't want them brought into this situation. I don't want that bitch Puabi to have another chance to take my son from me."

"She'd have to kill me first," he muttered.

Nidaba stared up at him, and a flutter of doubt skittered through her mind. What if she was wrong? No. She wasn't wrong. Eannatum would not let her down again. He would not harm her, or harm his son. Not deliberately, at any rate.

But he could still manage to break her heart. Because it was completely in his power to do so, all over again. She had been a fool then, hadn't she? She had done such a thorough job of convincing herself that she hated him, that she had forgotten to stop loving him. And now that the hatred she'd tried to make real had fallen away—as any false notion had to do in time—all that remained was the love. The desperate, hopeless love of a woman who had vowed never to feel its power again.

The problem was, she had never stopped. Not really. She had become a woman of stone. Granite-hearted and cold. Fierce and frightening. She had nearly killed poor Arianna when she perceived the woman as a threat to her son. Because her Nicodimus was the only person Nidaba had allowed herself to love. And the only part of Eannatum she had left.

But Eannatum was here, alive and within her reach. She loved him in spite of her determination not to, and in spite of her certainty that they could never make it work. Her, with her love of freedom and her need to relish her immortality to the hilt. Him, with his need to hide what he was and live a make believe life as a make believe mortal.

She had never been more afraid in her life.

The dog stretched slowly, pushing her forepaws out in front and arching her back in a luxuriant manner. Then she turned and padded almost happily out of the room.

Sighing, Nathan looked at the portrait that hung above the mantel. "Four thousand years' worth of secrets and revelations," he said. "All in the space of the past few days. Gods, but I think it's a bit much even for a once great king to deal with."

"I feel we've been weathering a storm, Natum. A fury. And this is only the eye. I fear there's far worse ahead."

"This time," he promised, "whatever comes, we'll face it together. Openly and honestly. If nothing else, Nidaba, we owe each other that. Agreed?"

She nodded. "Agreed."

"Good." Then he glanced down at his watch and frowned. "Sheila should have called by now."

Chapter 16

"How did the dog get in here?" Natum asked a few minutes later.

Lifting her brows and her shoulders at once, Nidaba shivered. "She just . . . walked in before." She smiled at the great beast, who had bounded back into the room and was dozing now near the hearth. She looked none the worse for wear.

"Or someone let her in." Bending down to the animal, Natum scratched her head. "Who was it, girl? Hmm? Was someone here?" The dog opened her eyes, and appeared to arch the brown spots above them quizzically.

"Natum, really. If there had been anyone around, this beast would have torn out their throat. I didn't hear so much as a growl."

"Do you feel that?"

Blinking, Nidaba lifted her head, forced herself to be mindful of her senses, instead of just her emotions. "There's . . . a draft."

"Dammit," Natum said, shooting to his feet. "Someone's been here!" He grabbed Nidaba's arm with one hand, drew his dagger with the other.

Nidaba yanked her torn skirt aside, and pulled her own dagger from its sheath with a deadly hiss.

"Stay behind me," Natum said softly.

Together, they moved through the ground floor of the large house. It seemed utterly empty. Utterly silent. More empty and silent than it ever had, Nidaba thought. It was a heavy silence, a living one. Like a shroud, invisible, but weighty and covering the entire place.

They walked through the dining room, stepping lightly, searching every corner, every shadow as they moved into the kitchen beyond. Nidaba sent a nervous glance toward the cellar door, recalling what had happened there so recently. But it was closed tight. Not gaping wide as it had been before.

As she turned and started forward again, though, she saw that the back door, which led outside, stood wide open. The cool autumn breeze blew in, bringing scents of the ocean, of decaying leaves on its crisp biting air.

Pulling her behind him, Natum stepped into that open doorway and looked outside. And then he went still.

"Please," he whispered. "Not this . . ."

His words jolted her, and she peered past him . . . and saw Sheila, lying on the walkway just beyond the door, a spiderweb of blood on her forehead.

"Sheila!" Nidaba shouldered past Natum, racing forward, falling to her knees beside the woman. Gently, she lifted Sheila's head and stared down at her face.

"Damn you, Puabi!" Natum roared behind her. "Damn you to hell! First my son, now my friends! What the hell do you want from me!" He was shouting at the sky, fists clenched until his knuckles were white. "I'll kill you for this, by the Gods, you know I will!" The wind picked up, and gnarled, dark cloud fingers reached in to claw at the face of the moon.

"Natum—"

"How could she have found them, Nidaba?" he shouted, slamming one of his fists into the side of his house so hard that the brick he hit crumbled with the force of the blow. "How could she have found them?"

"Natum."

"And George! Jesus, Nidaba, where the hell is George?"

"*Natum!*"

He looked down at her, his face tortured.

"She's alive, Natum. We need to get her to a hospital. The rest—we can figure the rest out on the way."

Natum scrambled down the steps, leaned over Sheila, and pressed his fingers to her throat, sighing in relief first at the warmth of her skin and then at the thrumming beat he felt beneath it.

Her eyes fluttered open. "Sheila," Natum whispered, his voice tight and hoarse. "Sheila? Can you hear me?"

"She . . . she . . . she . . ."

"All right, all right." He held her shoulders gently as Sheila struggled to sit up. "Be still now. Just relax and take a breath. Where are you hurt? Can you tell me that?"

Blinking him into focus, Sheila stared up at him. "Nathan?"

"Yes. It's me. You're safe now. Just tell me—"

"Put me . . . into the sea, Nathan," she whispered, a tear squeezing from the corner of her eye, "with Lisette."

"Sheila, no. Don't talk like that. Come on, you're going to be fine, I promise you," Natum said desperately. "Just tell me where you're hurt. And . . . and where is George?"

Sheila's eyes widened, and she sucked in a sharp, painful breath. "George! Oh, God, *George!*"

"Calm down. It's all right. Just—"

Sheila's hand closed tight around Natum's, and she pulled herself up a few inches from the concrete walk. "She . . . went after . . . George!" She managed to force the words out, each one seeming to cost her dearly. Then she let go, fell back again, exhausted.

Nidaba pressed her palm to her mouth to stop herself from crying out. Gods, not that! Not George in the hands of that horrible, cruel woman! A child. He was only a little boy, no matter what he looked like. A mere child.

And Nidaba knew how little regard Puabi had for the innocence of a child.

"*Save him.*" Sheila's words came on a long, slow breath. Her eyes fell closed, and she didn't draw another.

"Sheila? *Sheila?*" Natum's voice broke. He felt for her pulse again, searched her neck, then her wrist, then lowered his head to her chest to listen there, but the look on his face told Nidaba he heard no answering beat. "Sheila, dammit, no!" Lifting her, he held her gently to his chest, bowing over her, rocking her in his arms.

Nidaba closed her hand on his shoulder. "There's no time for this now, Natum." Her own voice was thick with tears. "She's gone. She's gone now. Let her go."

Sheila's hand had fallen open, and a slip of paper lay within it. Nidaba picked it up, and read the line written there.

"Everything you love," was all it said.

But she understood.

She crumpled the note in her fist, imagining it was Puabi's heart she was crushing.

Running back up the steps and into the house, Nidaba searched the kitchen and finally spied Sheila's old raincoat hanging from a peg near the back door. She took it, and walked outside. Natum was just as he had been before. Sitting on the walkway, holding Sheila in his arms, rocking her.

"Lay her down, Natum. We must take care of her. We don't want George to come upon her here, like this."

Nodding, Natum got to his feet, lifting Sheila's body up with him. Nidaba gently covered her with the raincoat. And side by side, they began walking, each of them knowing instinctively where they were going.

Sheila was an illegal alien with no family. Questions would be asked. It would be best for all concerned if they simply honored her final request. And that was what they did.

Her body between them in the small boat, they rowed out among the gentle swells of the sea. "Just a sheila from Down Under," Natum muttered, leaning down, kissing her cheek. "Born in the bush, and raised with the joeys."

Nidaba pressed her knuckle to her lips, but the sob escaped all the same. "You were so good, Sheila. Such a rare, and precious person. Go now, to the light. Find your peace, your friend, your purpose."

Each of them at one end, they lifted the woman's body, and lowered it gently into the water. They let go, and Sheila sank slowly out of sight.

Natum reached out, wrapped his arms tightly around Nidaba, and held her hard. She cried unashamedly, silent tears that fell softly for the sake of his pain, and for the loss of a woman she'd cared for in spite of herself. She felt Eannatum's shoulders shuddering with emotion. He held her so hard she thought if she were an ordinary woman, he would have crushed her bones.

Then he let her go, all at once, and turning, rowed rapidly back to shore. She'd never seen him look so angry. No tears. He was too furious to shed them, she thought. Perhaps they would come later. But now there was only rage. And she pitied Puabi if Natum could get his hands on her now. Because he wasn't the quaint mortal New Englander Nathan King anymore. He was King Eannatum at his most dangerous.

He held her hand as they climbed out of the boat, and even as they started toward the house, he began calling for George.

Nidaba raced along beside him, determined not to leave his side even for an instant. She wouldn't give Puabi the chance to murder him as well.

"Everything you love," the note had said.

It could have been directed at Natum. But Nidaba didn't think so. Puabi must have been watching them, somehow, when they put George and Sheila into the car, and then she followed them, just waiting for her chance. She must have seen the affection between Nidaba and Sheila when they'd exchanged that emotional good-bye. And she wanted to destroy everything Nidaba cared about.

Everything.

She intended to take away everything Nidaba loved. And she had only begun.

Something brushed Nidaba's skirt as she tramped through the woods beside Natum, and she looked down to see the big dog, loping along and looking almost concerned, if a dog could manage such a thing. Nidaba bent down and rubbed her head. The dog whined softly and nudged Nidaba's hand.

"Find George," Nidaba whispered. "I know you can do it. You find him, Queenie. Go on. Find George!"

With a soft "woof" the dog ran ahead.

Midnight.

Nathan was exhausted, filthy, damp with sweat, and chilled to the bone. His legs were scratched and bleeding, and Nidaba was in worse shape than he was. And yet they'd found no sign of George.

The dog paced the house, inconsolable, it seemed. She kept wandering from room to room as if looking for her beloved friend but unable to find him. Whining in a deep, plaintive tone, she would look from Nathan to Nidaba, as if asking what they planned to do about this. It was heartbreaking. The Rottweiler finally lay down near the fire, likely as exhausted as Nidaba and Nathan were.

"There's nothing more we can do," Nidaba told him for the tenth time. "Nothing mundane, at least. By the Gods, Natum, have you nothing in this house that we can use for divining? No cards, no board, no crystal balls?"

"No." He said it softly. "I never was much for scrying or . . . divination."

"Sorry excuse for a Witch then, aren't you?" She tried to make her tone teasing, light, he knew, but there was no lightening his mood. He sat in a chair by the fire, slumped and miserable. "If she had intended to kill him, Natum, we would have stumbled upon his body by now. Or found it awaiting us at the door. She is attacking us, trying to cause us as much pain as she possibly can. She would have made sure we knew it if George were dead."

He nodded slowly. "Exactly. And she knows that hurting him, making him suffer, will cause us even more pain."

"No. She's using him, Natum. She wants something. And all we can do is wait for her to tell us what it is."

"I dislike waiting."

"You always did."

He looked at her and realized he was being an ass. She had come to love George too, in the short time she'd known him. And Sheila as well. He stretched out a hand to touch her cheek where a long, curving scratch marred its perfection. "I'm sorry."

"Don't be, Natum. This is not your fault. It's me she wants."

But it *was* his fault, and he knew that with sudden clarity. Nidaba was right, and had been all along. He couldn't live a lie, pretend to be a mortal to escape the violence of his existence. It didn't work that way. What he was . . . followed him. And brought its violence to those he loved.

"We should shower," Nidaba said. "Clean up. Eat a solid meal. We can't sleep. It wouldn't be safe, not even one at a time. But we need to be strong. To be ready. And we need to keep busy if we're to stay awake."

"I agree."

"Then?"

He nodded and got to his feet. Taking her hand, he led her up the stairs.

There was no time for passion, nor could he think of pleasure when George was out there somewhere. Alone and probably terrified. He stood watch while Nidaba washed the briars and thistles from her hair. Then she got dressed while he took his turn in the shower. The door remained open the entire time, neither of them willing to risk the other being out of sight for a moment.

By the time they finished, their many scrapes and wounds were nearly all healed. The natural regenerative processes that were a part of their immortality had done their work. Nathan looked at the fading scratches on his arm, the one on Nidaba's cheek, now only a pale pink streak, and shook his head. "It never stops amazing me, though I should be long used to it by now."

"Being used to it doesn't make it any less amazing," she said softly as he toweled off and began to dress. "You never told me, though. How did you first discover the truth . . . of what we are?"

He hesitated for a moment. He'd pulled on a clean pair of jeans and was in the process of sliding his belt, with the dagger and sheath attached, through the loops. Nidaba had curled catlike on the foot of his bed, and a distant sadness shadowed her eyes.

"It was Puabi."

"Of course it was."

"You must understand, she was not an immortal. But she had learned about our existence." He finished lacing the belt and reached for a shirt.

"Even when we ourselves didn't know what we were," Nidaba muttered, shaking her head.

"Yes, even then. It all came out a year after your . . . your death—" He closed his eyes briefly, experiencing a stab of pain even now at the memory. "After your death was reported to me," he said, completing the sentence this time. "I had been angry at you for leaving me. I'd thrown myself into my rule, my duty, almost lashing out at you in the process. But this was different. Believing you dead was a far, far different thing."

She nodded. "You hated me for a time, or tried to. Just as I tried to hate you."

"Yes, I guess I did. But when they told me you'd burned in that fire . . . I fell into a deep melancholia. Instead of eating the meals that were served me I stared at them and felt ill. Instead of sleeping, I haunted the palace halls at night. Sometimes I would even slip away from the palace, without guards or escorts, and go to our secret oasis on the far side of the river and just sit in silence for hours."

He tucked his shirt in, fastened his jeans, buckled his belt.

She turned halfway, her face in profile, moonlit on one side and shadowed on the other. "I'm sorry you suffered because of me."

"I didn't suffer a tenth what you did, Nidaba. But I did suffer. I knew you'd had a boy with you, that he had been killed as well. And though I couldn't be certain, I suspected he was my own son. I . . . I wanted him to be. And I spent all my waking hours dreaming of how things might have been had I married you instead of Puabi. How the palace's grim halls would have been filled with the laughter of my son and my beautiful wife."

She lowered her face. To hide a rush of tears, he thought.

Reaching for her hand, he pulled her to her feet. She'd put on the black dress again. She liked the old ways, he thought. Maybe he did too. Maybe he wished he could go back in time and live it all again. Gods, but he would do things so differently this time.

Side by side, they walked into the hall and down the stairs. "When Puabi lost her child, years before, part of me . . ." He lowered his head, shaking it slowly. "Part of me was riddled with guilt— because I hadn't fully wanted the child. I wanted a son with you, not with Puabi."

She nodded slowly, her cheek brushing against his shoulder because she walked so closely beside him. If he thought for a moment that there was a chance she could ever forgive him for all his mistakes—mistakes that had cost her everything—But no. That was foolish thinking.

They stopped in the kitchen, both of them avoiding the back door. The memory of what they'd found out there, too fresh and too recent.

"It's an honest emotion, Natum," Nidaba said. "Your being less than thrilled about Puabi's child had nothing to do with its death."

"I know that. But knowing it did nothing to ease the guilt I felt." Sighing, he went on, even as he pulled out a chair, and guided Nidaba into it. "Later, when they told me you were dead, I didn't even want to live. I was glad I didn't have a child to look after, to be responsible for. I was devastated when I learned that you'd had a son, and that he had died so young, and I tormented myself with wondering if he had been my own. And even then, I didn't know it was murder. I was told it was an accidental fire."

"It is good, perhaps, that you didn't know the truth, then," Nidaba said, staring into space now, her face grim.

Turning his head, he kept his eyes fixed on Nidaba's face. "I'd have killed her if I had known. I swear to you, Nidaba, she would have paid with her life."

She cast her eyes downward, neither accepting his words nor arguing with them.

"Puabi knew how I mourned you. She couldn't help but know it. And she knew I mourned your son in a way I had never mourned hers. She thought, I suppose, that once you were gone, I would stop searching for you, stop longing for you. Perhaps turn to her, in your place. But losing you only made me realize the gravity of my mistakes. And I regretted having married her more than I ever had before. She tried to come to me, to make me love her. But I couldn't. I couldn't do it. And she hated me for that."

"Being rejected by her own husband would not have set well with that one," Nidaba said.

"No. No, it didn't. But she struck back." He reached into the refrigerator, and pulled out a covered dish, swallowing hard. "Chicken stew," he said. "Left over from the last meal Sheila cooked us."

"She's at peace, Natum."

"I know." He turned to the counter, filled two dishes with the stew, then popped them into the microwave and pressed a button.

"You said Puabi struck back at you," Nidaba said. "How did she do that?"

He watched the bowls revolve. "She began to speculate that I was cursed, under an enchantment. She whispered suggestions of black magick. Said these things even beyond the walls of the palace, and whispered accusations of all kinds against me. She thought to discredit me. But her plan reversed upon itself. The people began to talk, as people will do. But rather than condemning me, they compared my state to the madness of Gilgamesh, the legendary hero, after his best friend Enkidu was killed. I was loved more than ever before. The people said I ruled by the blessing of a real and true goddess who had for a time walked among them. They said that the mysterious High Priestess Nidaba wasn't just named for a goddess, but actually had been one. One who blessed and favored their king. But that she had died horribly, and they feared that I would soon follow, wasting away in mourning for her, unless I could be shaken free of my heartache. Gifts were piled upon the palace steps, public prayers for me uttered in the city square, musicians played outside my chamber windows. And a statue was erected in the temple in your likeness, Nidaba . . . in an effort to comfort me."

"I did not know."

"You were a true legend," he said. "And when rumors persisted that you had been seen in foreign lands, long after your supposed 'death,' the people became even more convinced of your divinity."

A look crossed her face, as if this tale pained her somehow. "Please, continue."

He closed his eyes, shook his head, took the two steaming bowls of stew from the microwave and placed them on the table, along with utensils, bread and butter, and salt. Then, sitting down, he let himself fall into the memory as he told the tale of the night his queen had killed him.

Chapter 17

Eannatam paced in his royal bedchamber. Just beyond the window, several of his most longtime advisers stood watching while a band of musicians played the lyre and harp and drums, and sang songs of the greatness of their king and the glory of the High Priestess Nidaba, who had rejoined her mother, the Goddess, and even now reigned from a heavenly throne and smiled down upon the people of Sumer.

It did nothing except etch the pain ever more deeply on his soul. Bad enough to have believed she had left him, bad enough to live without her . . . but this . . . this was surely more punishment than any man deserved to bear. Knowing he would never see her again, never touch her, knowing she had a son who might have been his own—dead, just as she was. Dead.

He threw a goblet at the wall, and the sound rang in the hollowness of the room. It was followed by another sound. That of the large oak door creaking open, of the footfalls of small slippered feet. And then of the voice of the woman he'd been forced, by circumstances and vicious fate, to wed.

"It has been over a year, Eannatum," Puabi said, her tone impatient and tinged by disgust. "Can you not let go of this mourning even now?"

He turned to look at her. She was beautiful, truly. Small and slight, with delicate features, a tiny waist, and round eyes of vivid lapis blue. Those eyes looked weary now. Nearly as weary as he felt. And yet they remained haughty, proud, and cruel.

"My mourning is no concern of yours."

"To think I hoped you might turn to me, now that your whore is finally gone," she said, bitterness overshadowing her beauty—making her seem ugly instead. "To think I had any hope at all you might do the honorable thing. The right thing for your country."

He grated his teeth and clenched his hands into fists at his sides. "You are a political ally, Puabi. You knew that from the start. It is not my fault if it pains you, now, to see me mourning another woman."

"Pains me? You think you have the power to hurt *me*, Puabi, Queen of all Sumer?" She tossed her head, stalking away from him in quick, angry strides. "It is not pain I feel, Eannatum, but humiliation. You may as well strip me naked, roll me in camel dung, and parade me through the streets. You're making a fool of me before the entire kingdom! And a bigger fool of yourself. All over some nothing little priestess who's dead and gone."

He spun on her. "That little priestess was twice the woman you'll ever be, Puabi. Speak ill of her again, and you'll regret it, I vow."

She sniffed indignantly. "Act like the king you are," she cried. "Stop wallowing in your sorrow before all the world."

He glared at her. "Perhaps you should consider returning to Ur, ruling from your palace there."

"I am queen of Sumer, not merely of Ur. Lagash is the chief city of Sumer—thanks to our marriage. It is my right to sit on its throne, and you will *not* move me from it!"

They locked gazes, hatred flashing in her eyes more brightly than he'd yet seen it. A tap came at the chamber door, and she banked the emotion, turned and flung the door open. A servant stood there, bearing a tray with wine and chalices. Puabi took the tray and then turned back again.

"What's this?" Eannatum asked, his tone sarcastic.

"Ah, but don't you see it, your highness? This is your devoted wife, playing the role you asked her to play. Ordering up wine to soothe her husband's misery." She slammed the tray down onto a nearby stand, poured wine from the jug so clumsily that it slopped over her hand, then spun and held the chalice out to him. "Take it," she snapped. "Accept a bit of comfort from the wife you never wanted. And choke on it, you bastard."

He snatched the chalice from her, sneering at her as he did, and slugged back its contents in one long draft. Then he dragged the back of his hand across his mouth and let the chalice fall from his hand to the floor. "Happy?"

Her expression changed. It darkened. She smiled very slowly. "Yes. More than I have been since I agreed to this loathsome arrangement."

No sooner did she say the words than dizziness struck Eannatum. He pressed a hand to his head. But the dizziness only grew worse. He blinked as her face swam before his eyes. "What is this, Puabi? What have you . . . ?" He tried to lunge toward the door, but stumbled instead, and found himself sitting on his own bed.

Suddenly Puabi shoved him backward, so he was lying down, and she straddled him. She tore open his robe. And he stared up at her, shivering, ill, too weak to even ask what she was doing. He couldn't fight her. The room seemed to spin around him. His hands, his arms, refused to obey his mind's commands to move, to push her off. He couldn't convince his voice to shout for help.

"I know what you are," Puabi said, her voice almost a growl. "My sages and sorcerers have told me about your kind. But you don't deserve immortality, Eannatum. You waste it, grieving over what you've lost instead of relishing what you have!" She drew a dagger from a sheath. "You don't deserve eternal life," she said. "But I do! I do!"

Eannatum blinked in shock, realizing she meant to kill him. He forced himself to move, lifted his arms weakly to fend off her attack, but his struggles were useless. "You . . . what are you . . . No!"

Puabi lifted the blade high, and drove it into his chest. It was like fire and ice all at once, splitting him. He felt the searing pain of his flesh being sliced wide, felt the blood bubbling forth like a hot scarlet geyser, and a cry was forced at last from his lips.

A cry that was heard, for even as he lay there, pain screaming through his mind, blood bubbling out of his body, the chamber door burst open, and two of Eannatum's men lunged into the room. Galor was one of them, and it was he who tore Puabi off him, disarmed her, dragged her away. But it was too late, Natum thought as he lay there. He could feel the life ebbing from his body. He was dying.

"Take her to the dungeons," Galor shouted.

"No!" Puabi cried. "He's a demon, your king. Cursed by that demoness who pretended to be a priestess. He's not human, I tell you! Mark me, you'll see! You'll see!"

Her voice faded. There was nothing more. Eannatum lay there, in a pool of his own royal blood . . . and he died.

It took a long time for him to revive. And later, much later, when he would learn about such things, he would wonder why that was. Perhaps because of the damage Puabi's blade had done to his body, his heart, or perhaps because of the sleeping powder she had put into his wine. But he truly thought that it was more likely because he had no will to live at that point. He'd been like a walking corpse ever since he'd been told of Nidaba's death. So there was no vitality in him, no life. And he suspected that was the reason he remained in the throes of death for so many hours.

When he felt that first rush of breath splitting his lungs, arching his body, jolting him wide awake, he thought he was feeling Puabi's blade driving into his heart all over again. But the pain, the shock, faded fast, and he blinked his vision clear and looked around him.

At first he saw only the earthen walls rising high on three sides, and the solid brick one at the fourth, completely finished. But he took little notice of the odd room, thinking instead of the mortal wound in his chest. He pressed his hand there, quickly, and sat up, looking down.

But there was no wound, no blood. He was dressed in his finest robes, his crown, his sword, and his dagger lying all around him. Quickly he tugged at the collar of his garment and looked inside at his chest. It was dark in this small room, but he could see, and he found that odd, disorienting. And even odder, there was no mark on his skin. No wound.

Had it been some kind of dream? A nightmare?

An aroma wafted toward his nose. He sniffed and realized it was the familiar smell of censers filled with burning herbs. Then he heard muffled chanting coming from beyond the solid brick wall.

All at once it hit him where he was, what had happened to him.

He was sealed in his own tomb, and even as he sat there, trying to understand, to make sense of what seemed impossible, he realized what was going on in the outer chamber.

Someone played a lyre. Others hummed or chanted or sang. Drummers beat a slow rhythm, a death beat. "Gods, no!"

He raced to the brick wall as the drumbeat and the chanting grew faster, louder, more and more frantic. He pounded on the bricks, clawed and kicked at them, cried out over and over, but it was all lost in the pounding beat. And when that drumming reached its crescendo, only to go silent all at once, he knew they were all out there, his advisers, his courtiers, priests and priestesses, and loyal followers . . . all of them, lifting the golden chalices to their lips, and sipping the sacred Elixir of the Dead.

"The poisoned wine," he whispered. "No! Stop, I'm not dead!"

He pounded and kicked at the wall even harder. Then he snatched the dagger from where it lay, and began attacking the mortar with its blade, fighting to loosen just one brick. Anything to get to them, to stop them in time.

Finally, he scraped and pried enough to loosen a brick. Freeing it, he managed to kick several others loose until there was a hole big enough for him to crawl through. But the moment his head emerged on the other side, he knew he was too late.

He dragged his body through the opening, but his pace was no longer rushed or frantic. Then he stood in the midst of them all, and death surrounded him. His friends, and soldiers, his priests and priestesses, and the very musicians who'd been playing outside his chamber windows such a short time ago. They lay there, all of them. Dead. Dying. Reclining on the dirt floor, looking peaceful, beautiful, serene. Some were still breathing, barely. Silver ribbons were twined in the hair of the young women. One priestess still clutched the lyre. Those golden goblets lay beside them. Toppled and empty.

God, one of the dead men was Galor!

He wanted to scream, to cry out loud and rail against the meaninglessness of it all. His attendants, his first soldier, Ris . . . all of them had died, believing they were journeying with their king, to serve him in the otherworld. Never had he known such a heavy silence. Such a weight of sadness.

But it would not last. At any moment, he knew, the procession would arrive from the temple, and they would begin throwing the first layer of earth into the pit, to cover the bodies. He had to force himself to move.

Weakly, he ran up the sloping earthen ramp that his loved ones had so recently used to walk into their own mass grave, and when he reached the surface, some thirty feet above, he ran through the night, away from the city. He vowed he would never look back.

Eannatum got to his feet, pacing the kitchen. His bowl of stew was barely touched. He filled a glass with water and sipped it slowly. "I heard what happened next only by rumor. But it seems that one of the priests, when he returned to begin covering the grave, noticed the missing bricks. And upon checking further, he realized that my body was gone. He declared that Puabi had been telling the truth when she claimed I was some kind of netherworld demon. She was restored to the throne at once."

"What became of your bitch-queen then, Natum?"

He looked down at her bowl. "Eat your stew."

"I have no appetite."

"Eat. Be strong. Better to kill her when she comes, Nidaba."

With a fierce look, Nidaba spooned some of the stew into her mouth.

Natum did as well. When he had swallowed it, he went on with his tale.

"I was confused. I did not know what it could mean, that I had somehow revived from death. I thought of going after her—had I known then that she was responsible for the attack on you and our son, I would have. But for my own personal vengeance . . . it just wasn't worth the effort. I'd had my fill of ruling as a king. I was still in mourning for you. I went away. Far, far away, to try to find the answers to what I was, what my existence meant. Shortly afterward, Puabi returned to Ur. And that was where she ruled for many years to come. She had our marriage record stricken, had every mention of any alliance between the two of us erased. Stone tablets were crushed and new ones engraved. History was changed. I was remembered as a king of Lagash and onetime ruler of all Sumer, she as the mystical Queen Puabi of Ur. But never was there mention of the two of us having so much as met. And there never will be. No tablet with our true history will ever be found."

He paused, sipped his water.

"She took the heart of another immortal, made herself immortal for as long as its power lasted," Nidaba said slowly. Then she gasped, and widened her eyes. "By the Gods, Natum, there was only one other High Witch in Lagash—Aahron! That sweet young man who tried to tell me what I was. But I wouldn't believe him. I sent him to serve in the palace." She drew a trembling hand to her lips. "I sent him to his death."

He could feel the grief that rose up in her at the thought. He couldn't bear to see her hurting so deeply. "You can't know it was Aahron's heart she took, Nidaba."

"But he was the only—"

Nathan caught her hand in his, drew it toward him, and brushed his lips over her knuckles. "He was the only High Witch you knew of, in Lagash. There could've been others. How would you have known, then? You knew nothing of our kind."

She lowered her head. "I pray it wasn't Aahron." Nathan squeezed her hand and wished he could assure her it hadn't been her young friend who'd fallen victim to Puabi's blade. But he feared that if he did, he'd be lying. "Regardless of whose heart she stole," Nidaba went on, "she killed in order to preserve her own life. And when the heart of her victim weakened, she took another, and another, and another. Do you know how many innocents she must have murdered to keep her evil alive for over four thousand years, Natum?"

"I can only imagine," he said. "But it will end. Because she will come here, in search of us. And I will kill her."

"Unless she kills you."

"That won't happen, Nidaba."

"She is clever. She even made you believe she was me."

He winced, remembering what had happened, regretting it to his very soul. There was pain in her voice when she spoke of it. Pain he'd caused, this time. "It hurt you deeply, when you saw me with her."

She shrugged, averting her eyes. "I only wonder how a man who claims to have loved me so completely could be so easily fooled."

"Because when one sees something he wants so badly to see, he tends to overlook minor details, Nidaba."

Blinking her eyes, she examined his face. "What you wanted to see . . . ?"

"Nidaba . . . when I looked at her, I saw only you. I saw your hands on me, felt your lips on me. I was helpless to resist."

"Why?" she whispered.

He smiled just a little. "Why? Because I crave you still, Nidaba. You must know that, after what happened between us earlier tonight. Neither of us can deny it, now, can we? Between us, Nidaba, the fire still burns."

Her tongue darted out to moisten her lips. "Even if the love does not. That's what you mean to say, isn't it?"

He drew his brows together. So she wanted to make sure he understood that this was no more than physical? The knowledge dug deep, confirming what he had already known. Hell, how could he have thought her love for him would survive so many lifetimes? So much pain?

"Nidaba, it's all right. Don't feel badly over that."

She returned her attention to her stew, cleaning the bowl and dropping the spoon inside. "What makes you think I feel badly? What happened between us earlier was only an explosion. An outburst of feelings held in check for far too long. And not just feelings of desire, Natum. But feelings of anger, hurt, betrayal . . . all of them."

He almost got angry. Almost. Would have, if not for the hurt he saw in her eyes and the slightest trembling of her lower lip, that suggested maybe she was being less than honest here. By the Gods, could it be? Might she still harbor some kernel of love for him? Was he a fool to even imagine such a thing were possible?

He moved back to the table, turned her chair around, then leaned over it, and braced one hand on the table on either side of her. "Then . . . what about now?"

"What do you mean?" She looked nervous. Why, he wondered.

"We've released all those pent up feelings, Nidaba. If that's all it was, between us, that must mean it's over—that you no longer feel desire for me at all."

She closed her eyes. "I burn for you, Natum. You know I do," she whispered.

He nearly closed his eyes, such was his rapture. Oh, it wasn't a confession of love. But it was a start. "Thank the Gods for that, woman, because I need to feel you tonight." He leaned closer, kissed her deeply, hungrily. She responded without reserve, her lips parting eagerly to welcome his invasion. When he finally lifted his head away, he said, "Sex without love, Nidaba? Is that all this will be?"

"Sex has many more facets to it than those of the heart, Eannatum."

She looked at him as if meeting his challenge, answering his dare. When, dammit, she was the one who had just denied having feelings for him. Other than desire, at least. But he wanted her. He was hard already, just from kissing her. And in his mind's eye, he remembered the night she had danced for him.

So many things had hit them both tonight. They'd been under attack, and the only shelter they had from the horror, the anguish, the pain . . . was each other. Maybe, for right now, that was enough.

"She may have looked like me," Nidaba whispered, "But you must admit Puabi could never give you the same pleasure I can, Eannatum."

"In four thousand years, no woman ever has."

"I would hate to think you couldn't tell the difference between her touch and mine."

"Remind me of the difference then. For just a little while, Nidaba, take me away from this nightmare we've fallen into. And I'll take you away from it too. Just for a little while . . ."

She closed her hands in his hair, and pulled his face her for a blatantly carnal kiss. She nipped his bottom lip in her teeth before she drew away slightly to soothe the sting with her tongue. "Oh, I will," she promised in a husky voice. Rising slowly from the chair, she pressed her hands to his chest, and licked his lips, pushing him backward until he was against the wall. Then she flattened her body against his, continuing to sample his mouth, and she slid her hands along his arms, from his shoulders, upward, until her fingers laced with his, and his arms stretched above his head.

One of her hands darted downward, and her dagger appeared in it. She stabbed it through his shirt sleeve, and into the wall beyond. He gave an experimental tug to test his delicious restraints, and the dagger held. Anticipation made his blood pulse hotly. His erection hardened painfully, and he bit back a groan.

Smiling wickedly she sank to her knees in front of him, and opened his jeans. She freed his erection, her very touch making him shudder. Looking up at him, staring straight into his eyes, she licked her lips, and moved them closer to him. When that succulent mouth finally touched him, it was only lightly, teasingly as she rubbed her wet lips back and forth over the swollen head. Nathan arched his hips toward her, an unspoken plea. But still she tormented him, flicking her tongue over him until he was panting with need.

Finally, she took him into her mouth. Nathan shuddered as her lips slid over him, moved up and down the length of him, and her tongue swirled and lapped at him. She used her teeth on him, making him gasp and moan. He arched his hips toward her as she suckled and teased. He wanted to tangle his hands into her hair and hold her captive, so he could thrust into her mouth, but he didn't do that. He could have torn his arms free and done just that. But he didn't. He let her play just to see how long he could bear the succulent torture. She tormented him and pleasured him with her mouth and her tongue for a long while, never letting him find release, working him into a frenzy, only to deny him the ultimate goal, over and over, until his mind spun out of control. He was quivering, sweating, moaning her name.

And finally, when he could bear no more of it, he gave a deep growl and tore his arms free, ripping the fabric of the shirt in the process. He grabbed her shoulders, and pulled her to her feet, and ravaged her mouth, thrusting his tongue into her almost viciously. He tasted her and tangled with her tongue, licking the inside of her mouth. Savagely, he peeled her dress up her body and tossed it aside. Then, lowering her to the kitchen floor, he spread her thighs wide, and knelt between them.

She moved in supplication, arching her hips off the floor, but he didn't take her. Not yet. Instead he gathered her wrists in one hand, pinning them to the floor above her head. "My turn," he whispered, determined to give as good as he got.

Using his free hand, he touched her. He slid his fingertips slowly over her chin, her neck, down her sternum. He dragged them lightly over her breasts, pausing to press her nipples just a little. A tiny pinch, only enough so she whimpered for more. Then he moved on. His finger made spirals over her belly, slid downward, over her abdomen, and then teased her center so softly she rocked her hips in search of a firmer touch. He flicked lightly, over and over until he saw the sweat break out on her forehead.

Smiling, he touched her more firmly, and then still more, sliding his fingers into her slick passage, and moving them slowly while she squirmed.

"Damn you, Natum," she whispered. "Take me now."

"Oh, I don't think so. Not just yet." He hooked his arms under her legs, lifting them, anchoring them over his shoulders. And then he bent his head, and licked a hot path over her juicy center. Using his fingers to spread her open wide, he lapped at her there. He loved her taste. He thrust his tongue inside, drew it out again, stabbed at her, sucked at her until she was writhing and screaming in ecstasy. And then he held her down, and licked some more.

"Please, Natum, please . . ."

He rose and looked down at her. Her body was flushed, her nipples hard, her face, rapturous. God he loved seeing her like this.

He caught her hands, and rolled onto his back, pulling her with him, so she was atop him. She sat up slowly, her eyes glistening, hooded, fiery. Bracing her hands on his chest, she positioned her legs outside his, and lowered her body. He felt her shudder as he slid inside her like a dagger into its sheath, and Nidaba closed her eyes and moved. She rode him, slowly at first, then faster and harder, her head tipping back, her eyes falling closed. He caught her breasts in his hands, and tormented her nipples, holding them captive in a sweet, firm pinch so that when she moved, they pulled against his fingers. She rocked even more fiercely, took him even more deeply, until his mind and body exploded in wave upon wave of unimaginable pleasure. She ground her hips against him, her body squeezing him, milking dry as she climaxed with him, murmuring his name and raking her fingernails across his chest.

Then she went limp, slumping down atop him in a boneless sprawl. He wrapped his arms tight around her waist, she nuzzled his neck with her lips. "Sated yet, Priestess?" he teased her gently.

He felt her lips smile against his skin. "I've not been with a king in over four thousand years."

"I've not been with a goddess in just that long."

"Then we've much time to make up for."

"I was hoping you'd say that." He sat up, gathered her into his arms, then snatched up her dress and her dagger. He carried her up the stairs to the bedroom, wryly amazed that he was ready for her again so soon. But it had always been this way with her. The more he had Nidaba, the more he needed her, craved her. And he knew it wasn't just sex with her, no matter what she might think or want to believe or be willing to admit. For him, it was more. Far more.

He laid her on the bed and made love to her again—Gently, this time. Leisurely. Tenderly. He kissed her, caressed her, spoke to her in soft whispers that emerged in the old tongue, as if they'd gone back in time. He tried to memorize every part of her, the way she felt against his hands, the way she tasted, the way she smelled, the way she sounded and moved and breathed in his arms. And for that short span of time, he found heaven.

Afterward, they lay sated and exhausted. Natum had opened the window to let the sea breeze in. It smelled like the ocean, like autumn, and like a looming rainstorm. Every once in a while distant thunder rumbled ominously.

Beyond the window, the ocean danced in the fall wind's touch. The scents of the sea and the fall leaves and the impending storm lingering on the air were intoxicating. And the dog, which had wandered into the room to lie down on the floor beside the window, seemed to fit the scene perfectly. "You really do love this life you've built here, don't you, Eannatum?"

He glanced at Nidaba's face and smiled. "It's been . . . a haven."

"It is a beautiful home."

"It's not just the house. Or the gallery in Boston. Or George and Sheila." He paused there, swallowing hard at the mention of Sheila's name. "It's . . . it's more than that."

"I know," she said softly. "It's a mortal's life you're living, Natum. The Dark Ones . . . they don't even seem to know you exist."

"Except for one," he said. "And who knows how many others Puabi has told about me by now? No, Nidaba, my peaceful little life has ended." He sat up in the bed, began slowly to put his clothes back on.

Nidaba shook her head, sitting up as well, and the breeze caught her hair, mussing it more than Natum had done. "I know the way that woman thinks," she told him. "She hasn't told any others. She wouldn't. She always wanted you all to herself—even now that she apparently wants you dead."

He lifted a brow. He'd pulled on his jeans, but nothing else, and he propped his shoulder against the window as he watched her with interest.

"Chances are, once we rid ourselves of her forever—you'll be able to continue on with your life just the way you have been," she said, sitting up in the bed, allowing the sheet to fall to her waist.

Even now, he wanted her. "And what about you?" he asked, his gaze taking full advantage of her nakedness.

She shook her head, got to her feet, wrapping the sheet around her sarong-style, and moved until she was beside him at the window. Turning her face into the wind, she gazed out at the whitecaps dancing on the sea. "My notoriety now is almost as widespread as it was in Lagash," she said.

"A legend yet again?"

"Among the dark ones, yes. Although it's not the kind of fame one would wish for."

"They hunt you." He caressed her jaw with a fingertip. "What has it been like for you, Nidaba?"

"Not so bad."

"No. Tell me the truth now. There's no more reason for lies between us. Not after all this." He reached for her nightgown, hanging over the chair's back, and she stood still while he pulled her sheet away, and gently dressed her in it. Then he put his own shirt back on. "Let's walk outside. You can talk to me."

Nidaba let him pull her with him into the hall, down the stairs, right at the bottom, rather than left into the living room. He took her through the library and out through the French doors onto the veranda.

She noticed the walkway, lined on both sides with late blooming flowers, that led around the house. "What's back there?"

He followed her gaze. "More flower beds, garden plots, and the stairs up to the roof." The dog got up and trotted happily at their side. "But you're changing the subject. I asked what it's been like for you."

"What is it you want to know?" She pretended great interest in the cobblestone lined flower beds that surrounded his great old house above the sea.

"You . . . said once that you had been held captive. And that woman, your—our—daughter-in-law . . . she seemed concerned about your mental state."

She shrugged as if none of it mattered. "What's on the roof?" she asked.

"Pigeons. Sheila keeps—kept—them up there. Listen, you can probably hear them."

Nidaba remembered George mentioning that there were pigeons on the roof, and she could indeed hear their gentle cooing sounds if she listened closely. "It's not natural to keep them caged. That doesn't seem like something Sheila would do."

"You're right about that. They were never caged, not really," he explained. "Sheila always left the pens open by day. They just always come back at night."

Frowning, Nidaba tilted her head to one side. "I guess they're like you. They don't mind living in captivity. Even . . . like it."

"I don't live in captivity," he insisted. He sat down on the stone wall that encircled the veranda. "What makes it seem that way to you?"

She shrugged again, and pacing to the veranda's edge, stood there with the sea wind whipping her nightgown around her legs, and blowing her hair behind her like a flag. "You aren't free to be what you are. You keep it secret, afraid to let it show. You pretend to be just another mortal. You live like one. It seems like captivity to me."

"And you . . . how do you live?"

Tipping her face up to the kiss of the wind, she closed her eyes. "Wild. Free. I travel the world. I amass fortunes and spend them at will. I *live*. I relish it." Taking a deep breath, she continued. "A long time ago, there was a man by the name of Nathanial Dearborne. He was a Dark High Witch and something of a scientist. He made a habit of taking Light Ones alive when he could and keeping them captive. Killing them in one way or another, and then watching them revive. Studying which manner of death would last longer. He even began taking their hearts . . . and then returning them to see if they would revivify."

Natum's next breath came from very close, and warmth rushed over her nape. His hands curled around her shoulders as he stood behind her. "I had heard such a thing was possible, but I never believed it."

"Believe it. It's true. I suppose that in a way I owe Dearborne a debt of gratitude. His experiments, the notes he left in his journals—they were what enabled Arianna to restore life to our son after his heart was taken." She turned and looked at Natum's startled eyes. "He laid in a grave for three hundred years. She found his heart, returned it to him, brought him back. So perhaps the torture was . . . in some twisted way . . . worth bearing."

"You were one of this Dearborne's captives?" His face seemed to pale.

She nodded. "You said you wanted to know."

"By the Gods . . ."

"Don't. It's in the past. Over. Dearborne is long dead. Nicodimus has been restored. And I . . . well, I learned how very much I value my freedom, and my life." She swallowed a lump in her throat. "Immortality is a gift, Eannatum. Why would anyone wish to ignore it—to live as if they were just like everyone else?"

"They hunt you," he said flatly. "You're forced to kill or be killed, over and over again. I lived like that, Nidaba, and I hated it."

She lowered her head. "Freedom comes with risk." She glanced up toward the roof. "I guess for some the security of domestication is worth the sacrifice." Then she stared out at the sea, spotted a gull swooping and diving. "And for others, freedom is far more important. I'd rather fight and die free, Natum, than live forever in a cage."

He looked back at his house. "This is hardly a cage."

"Yes, it is. No matter how gilded, it still has its bars."

He nodded. "We've grown very different in all this time, haven't we, Nidaba?"

"More than I ever would have guessed," she said. And she understood now why he couldn't love her anymore. He wouldn't give up the kingdom he'd built to run away with her now any more than he had been able to that night in the desert so long ago. And if he brought her into it with him—assuming that she could bring herself to live that way—she would bring battle, strife, chaos with her. And his kingdom would fall. Crumble into the sea.

It was impossible, then, wasn't it?

She met his eyes, and saw that he knew it too. And a new despair settled over her. "I used to think that a person could only live so long and remain sane. That eventually the body of an immortal would outlive the mind."

"And why did you think that?"

She shrugged. "I suppose I saw my own mind as the best example. I went a bit insane after I lost my son for the second time, in the sixteenth century when a Dark Witch took his heart. But I survived.

Eventually I returned to myself. I sought vengeance on the Dark Witch who had murdered my son, but it was I who was trapped, captured, tortured. I only escaped three years ago—both my mind, and my body were broken for a long time."

"But again, you recovered." He stroked her hair, fingertips gentle on her temples. "Perhaps the mind of an immortal heals itself just the way the body does."

"Perhaps. I recovered slowly, and only when I found my son again."

"Loss . . . has a profound effect on us, Nidaba."

Then how, she wondered, was she going to bear losing her Eannatum when this was over?

"This is a pointless discussion."

"No. I needed to know these things," he said softly.

"I can't imagine why. They have no relevance to the threat facing us now."

"Everything about you has relevance for me, Nidaba." He paused. "What happened on that hotel rooftop?"

She stared into his eyes, so filled with concern, for her. "It wasn't another bout with insanity, if that's what you've been thinking. No. It was far simpler, Natum. A simple attack by one of the Dark Ones. Something that has become routine in my life, I'm afraid. However this Dark Witch had hedged her bets. When it looked as if I would defeat her in a fair fight, she pulled a weapon—a gun. I had to either let her shoot me and carve out my heart while I waited to revive—or jump and hope to revive before the ambulance arrived. I happen to think I made the sane decision." She pursed her lips in thought. "Though had I known what would follow, I think I'd have taken my chances with the gun."

"Gods, when I think what you've been through . . ." He leaned closer, kissed her cheek. "You're getting cold. We should go back inside." One arm around her, he urged her through the French doors.

She shivered, realizing only now how chilled she was, and started toward the living room, moving ahead of him. She was eager for the warmth of the fire. Natum followed her, then headed back into the library. "I'll be out in a moment," he called.

Nidaba kept walking, rubbing her chilled arms and thinking about how differently they saw things now. She touched the long, thin nightgown she wore, and it reminded her vaguely of the sacred white gown she used to wear in the temple. She wasn't wearing anything else, except, of course for the dagger at her thigh.

It hurt, very deeply, to know that he felt only desire for her. That the love he had professed of old had not been as immortal as they both were. But he had made love to her as if nothing had changed. And for now she would have to be content simply to pretend. It was painfully obvious they could never go back to the way things had once been.

Nidaba stopped short when she stepped into the living room and saw the dagger that pinned a scrap of parchment to the wall beside the mantel like a butterfly's wing.

"Eannatum!" she cried.

He appeared a moment later, a blanket in his hands, which he draped over her shoulders. "Right here," he said. "I just wanted to grab this throw out of the library for you to . . . Nidaba? What's wrong?"

Lifting a finger, she pointed.

Natum followed her gaze. She heard the hiss of his dagger sliding free of its sheath. "Stay close to me," he whispered, moving around her, clasping her hand behind him.

Nidaba drew her own dagger, its golden hilt cool in her palm. Slowly they moved across the room, looking all around them, listening, every sense alert. Even the dog looked uneasy as she lifted her head and looked around.

Natum reached up, yanked the note from the dagger's blade, leaving the blade where it was. And then he read it aloud.

"A trade," he read. "George for your son."

Chapter 18

"How could she know? How?" Nidaba sank into a chair, the blanket around her shoulders, her head in her hands. The skin around her eyes was already stinging from the drying salt of so many tears. But she was angry now. Frightened for George and furious for his suffering, and for Sheila. But this was more. This was her son.

Natum's face was cold and grim. "She . . . must have overheard us talking when you told me he was still alive, that you knew where he was," he said. "I just don't understand how. There was no one here, but us, and the dog and—wait a minute. Wait a minute, that's it! The dog."

Nidaba shook her head even as Natum started looking for the dog. "No, it's not her, Natum. I've touched her. I would have known."

"Wait, here she comes," he warned. "Come on, Queenie. Here, girl."

The big Rottweiler trotted up to him, and when he reached out to stroke her head, she turned it and licked his hand. No sparks. Damn.

The dog went to the door then and scratched it with a forepaw. Absently, Natum opened it and let her out. "I was so sure."

"She can't take my son from me again, Natum. I won't allow it."

"Of course you won't. Nor will I!"

"But George—she has George," Nidaba muttered.

Natum stopped pacing, looked slowly from the note to Nidaba. "What if she doesn't?"

"What do you mean? Her note says—"

"Never mind what her note says. She's evil, Nidaba, she'd certainly have no compunction about lying to get what she wants. All we have is her word that she has George."

"And Sheila's," Nidaba reminded him.

"No. No, Sheila said, 'She went after George.'" He turned to the windows, pushing the curtains back, staring out into the ever thickening darkness. The storm was rolling closer now. The thunder was closer, louder, and Nidaba could feel the static in the air.

"What if George saw her attack Sheila and ran away?" Natum said.

Nidaba sat up straighter in her chair. "Then Puabi would have gone after him."

"She'd never have found him. Not if he made it to the woods before she caught up."

Sighing softly, Nidaba got to her feet. She went to where he stood and put a hand on his shoulder. The familiar tingling jolted through her hand at the contact, then faded to warmth. "Natum, I know you love him, and you want to believe he's all right. But Puabi is a High Witch over four thousand years old. George is just a simple mortal. Besides, we searched the woods. There was no sign of him anywhere."

He nodded slowly. "I know. George loves those woods. He used to vanish for days at a time. And damned if I know where he hid, but wherever it was, he got there by way of the woods." He let the curtain fall, turned to face her. "I used to search—hell, the neighbors and the volunteer fire department even got involved one summer. We turned those woods inside out. But we never found him. He showed up safe and sound when he was ready. I got so worried I had to ask him not to go out there anymore. And when he saw how upset I was, he promised he wouldn't."

Nidaba blinked. "Do you really think there is a chance George could be so well hidden that even Puabi cannot find him?"

"I think there's a chance, yes." He closed his eyes. "Gods, please let there be a chance," he whispered, and she knew it was a prayer, heartfelt and potent.

"I don't think we should count on it, Natum."

Drawing a long breath, he expelled it quickly. "Maybe . . . it's time we call Nicodimus."

Nidaba's head came up sharply. "What do you mean?"

"We have the name of the hotel, the number. The woman, Arianna, left it with me. We should let our son know what's going on."

"Why?" Her brows bent deeply as she searched Natum's face in horror. "He would only come rushing out here to help us, Natum!"

"Which would force Puabi to show herself."

"You want to use my son as *bait*?" Nidaba's eyes narrowed on him, and she looked more closely. At his skin, its texture, his eyes, their color.

He held up a hand. "Just hear me out. You said yourself Nicodimus is a powerful immortal. A strong warrior. We'd never let him out of our sight, Nidaba, and when Puabi came for him, she would have all three of us to contend with."

She shook her head in disbelief. "You would risk him that way? Your own son?" She backed a few steps away from him.

Natum frowned. "No. No, Nidaba, you're misunderstanding me. There would be no *risk* to it. Puabi would have to go through me to harm him, and that's not going to happen." He took a step toward Nidaba.

She took a step back.

Natum stared at her, his eyes widening. "Nidaba, don't look at me that way. If Nicodimus is half the man I think he is—I know he is—then he would want to make this decision for himself. He would want to be here to help me protect you from Puabi."

"My son died protecting me once. It will not happen again. And if you can even suggest what you just have, then you are not worthy of calling yourself his father."

The dog came wandering in from the kitchen then, halted halfway across the room, stared at Natum, and suddenly began to growl deep in her throat.

Nidaba shot a panicked look at the animal, then back at Eannatum again. "Oh Gods, no," she murmured.

He held up a hand. "No, Nidaba. Don't . . . don't think what you're thinking. It's not—"

"Stay away!" She took a step backward for every one he took forward and yanked her dagger from her thigh, holding it up between them.

"Don't do this, Nidaba."

"The dog knows you're not Eannatum," she whispered. Her breaths came faster, shorter. She told herself to lunge at him, to drive her blade into his chest, but for the life of her she couldn't do it. Even though she knew he must be Puabi. Otherwise, why would the dog behave that way? Growling at him, hairs bristling. He'd been out of her sight when he got the blanket for her from the library. Only for a moment, but still . . .

He just kept shaking his head, staring at her and shaking his head. "It's me, Nidaba. I only want to keep you alive, protect you. I only want . . ." Then he reached out for her, and in her panic she jabbed her dagger at him. He swung one powerful arm, delivering a blow that sent the dagger flying out of her hand. Left with no other choice, Nidaba turned and ran from the house. And even as she lunged into the night, and fled at top speed, he gave chase.

"Stop! Dammit, Nidaba, wait!"

Thunder clapped loudy, and Nidaba turned to look behind her as she raced around the house. She saw the dog launch itself at Natum—or at the person who *looked like* Natum—and send him face first to the ground. His head connected with a rock. She saw blood, and he went still, not moving again. Good. Then the dog raced onward, as afraid, Nidaba thought, as she was.

What the hell had that bitch done with the real Eannatum?

He couldn't be in the house. He'd have cried out. And now that the stormclouds had rolled in, it was too dark to see outside as well as she would have liked. Still, her night vision was far better than that of a mortal. Dammit, the storm was going to break any moment. Again thunder clapped, and this time the wind whipped with it.

She rounded the corner to the rear of the house and saw the stairway there, hugging the back wall, angling sharply upward to the flat roof. The dog raced ahead, pausing on the bottom step. Even as the wind whipped harder and the first few fat raindrops smacked her in the face, Nidaba nodded. "Yes, the roof. I can see all around from up there."

Mounting the steps, she started up them. The wind whipped her hair, and her white gown snapped around her ankles. Bowing into it, she gripped the slender rail and made her way to the top, the dog right behind her.

Finally, she reached the flat, tar-coated rooftop and looked around in the darkness. The moon was blotted out now by dark clouds, and the sea in the distance roiled with whitecaps and froth. The wind was treacherous up so high, and getting worse by the minute. She staggered forward against it, squinting in the darkness to see the large square structure in the center. Cooing and scratching sounds told her what this was. The pigeons. Sheila's precious pigeons.

Lightning flashed, illuminating the night, and two things became visible, and invisible again, in that one blinding moment. The form of a large man, curled up, shivering and lying on his side next to the giant coop, and the body of the huge Rottweiler lying close beside him.

"George?" Nidaba cried out, and she started to move forward, but stopped in her tracks when the deep-throated growl came from behind her.

"Nidaba? Is that you?" George asked in a frightened voice.

Going utterly still, she swallowed hard and her mind raced. *But the dog was in front of me, lying beside George . . . so how is it behind me, snarling at me? Oh, Gods—two dogs. Two dogs. One, George's best friend . . . and the other . . .*

The beast behind her growled more loudly. Nidaba turned to face it, and she saw its eyes come alive, glowing with an unnatural yellow light.

"I always said you were a bitch, Puabi," Nidaba said. "But I didn't expect it to be literally true." Her hand touched the sheath at her thigh, but the blade was not in it, and her heart sank as she recalled that Natum had knocked it out of her hand. Natum—lying down there with his head split open, bleeding. The sky burst open with an explosion of thunder. Icy rain fell in sheets as the beast crouched and attacked. Teeth tore through flesh, giant paws knocked her flat. George cried out, and she heard the other dog— the real dog—snarling. The dog-Puabi leapt onto her chest, and even as she clasped its big head to hold the beast off, she knew she couldn't win.

When the powerful jaws locked on her throat, and the incisors ripped into her jugular, Nidaba knew it was over.

But even as her blood pulsed out of her, and her life force weakened, the lightning flashed. The killer beast rose away from her. She saw the other dog, the real dog, lunge at it, only to stop short and cower in fear. The beast was changing, morphing, right before Nidaba's eyes. And the shape it took this time was her own. A Nidaba look-alike, white gown intact, throat unmarred, Puabi knelt over her. And she lifted a blade, held it poised above Nidaba's chest.

"Know before you die that I will take Natum and your son next. Know it. Feel that pain. I want you to suffer the way I have."

And then there was a deep menacing growl. Nidaba turned her head weakly, and saw George's dog flying forward, having overcome her fear in order to protect Nidaba. Queenie's powerful paws hit Puabi squarely in the chest, and the Dark Witch sailed right over the edge of the roof.

Squinting through her fading vision, Nidaba turned her head toward the place where George crouched with his knees to his chest, rocking in abject terror. She tried to call out to him, but her throat had been too torn apart to allow speech.

The dog—the real dog—leaned over her, licking her face, as death swept her into its cold prison once more. She could only pray that the healing would take place in time to save Natum. And then there was darkness.

"Nathan? Oh, Nathan, are you all right?"

Nidaba had not once called him by his modern alias. Until now.

Nathan blinked the dizziness away, tried to shake off the pounding in his head, and managed to sit up. Nidaba leaned over him, cradling his head, speaking in an unnaturally hoarse voice.

"That dog—that damned dog—" Nathan began.

"It was no dog, Nathan. It was Puabi," Nidaba whispered, her voice far too soft. "I'm so sorry I doubted you, my love." She rubbed her throat and Nathan saw bruises there in the shape of hands.

"Are you all right?" he asked her. "What happened to you?"

"She attacked me. Choked me, and my vocal cords are slow in re-pairing themselves. But . . . it's all right, Nathan. I—I killed her. She's dead."

Nathan sighed and closed his eyes. Reaching out, he wrapped his arms around Nidaba, held her tight. "Thank the Gods. It's over. Fi-nally, over. God, if only we could find George."

She nodded, sniffling and snuggling her head into the crook of his shoulder. "Well . . . for that we can get some more help. If . . . if you're up to it, Nathan, I think it's about time we made that call. You've waited far too long already . . . to meet your son. Don't you think?"

He brushed her hair away from her face, smiling at her. "Yes. Yes, I have. Go ahead, and call him, Nidaba. The number is in the drawer of that small table beside the fireplace," he told her softly. She looked toward the house. "Go ahead," he told her. "I'll be along in a minute. My head is already on the mend." He lifted a hand to rub at the spot on his skull and sent her a sheepish grin. She returned the smile, and ran into the house to search for the phone number.

Nathan managed to get to his feet, though his head throbbed and dizziness swamped him. He drew his dagger and steeled himself against the gut-churning fear. He didn't know where the hell Nidaba was . . . what the bitch had done to her, or to George, but he knew one thing without a doubt. *That* hadn't been Nidaba. Nidaba had not once called him Nathan. And her touch had never been cold, her voice soft, her demeanor hesitant.

He made his way to the front door, his dagger behind his back. He walked quietly inside, step by step, closer and closer to the woman who leaned over the small table rummaging through the drawer. He brought the dagger around, lifting it above his head.

Behind him someone screamed.

He whirled in time to see the blond woman, Arianna, in the door-way, pointing at him and yelling, "I *knew* it! I *knew* he was lying!"

And then a handsome, powerfully built man, with russet hair and midnight eyes surged past her, landed a blow that slammed Eanna-tum into the wall. His already injured head cracked against the plas-ter, and exploded in new pain.

"Nidaba! Gods, are you all right?" Arianna Sinclair-Lachlan asked, rushing forward to spin the impostor around and embrace her.

Eannatum fought to stay conscious, to keep from sliding to the floor, as the man strode up to him, gripped the front of his shirt, and held him upright.

"Are you Nicodimus?" he managed to ask, before the man could pummel him again.

The man nodded once and bared his teeth. "Yes, I am. And might I ask who the hell you are, before I put you into the ground for good?"

Nathan nodded weakly. Blood was running from his nose, and this man knew by now that he was an immortal from the shock at contact. Probably didn't know if Eannatum was Dark or Light, and even more probably didn't care.

"I'm Eannatum," he said. "I'm your father."

Nidaba dragged in her next breath, her *first* breath, the breath of life itself. It jolted through her, arching her back and filling her lungs to near bursting with storm laden air and rainwater. Someone leaned over her, patting her face.

She opened her eyes.

"George. Oh, George, you're really okay!"

"So are you," he said. Beside him his dog wagged her tail, and for a moment she went stiff with fear as memory surged.

The roof.

The pigeons.

Eannatum . . . the dog . . .

"*Natum* . . ." Her voice was raspy. She wondered why. And then she knew, even as she struggled to sit up, to stand. Still weak, not yet healed, she staggered to the edge of the rooftop, looked down over. The car in the driveway hadn't been there before. But it was a familiar model.

"Nicodimus! Oh, Gods, he's here."

Her hands went to her throat, and she felt the gaping wound. At least it was no longer bleeding as it slowly healed itself. But the damage within still made every breath a tortured wheeze. It hurt to breathe. Hurt more to call out. Yet she tried all the same. But the sound that resulted was barely as loud as the contented chuckling of the pigeons.

"It's okay, Nidaba. Come on, I'll help you down."

George pulled one of her arms around his shoulder and held her as she made her way toward the stairs. Stumbling, she fell to her knees once, but he pulled her right back up. He was not, she realized, in much better shape than she was—he was dripping wet, freezing, probably suffering from exposure, as well. He was cut and bruised and scared to death. "What happened after you and Sheila left here, George?" she asked as he slowly helped her down the stairs.

"The bad lady . . . she must have followed us. She ran us off the road and made us get into her car and come right back here. We never even got to go to the beach like Sheila said we could. And then . . . oh, it was bad. It was so bad, Nidaba. That lady, she said she was gonna take us into the house, so you and Nathan would know she meant business, and Sheila, she tried to get away."

"And Puabi killed her," Nidaba said. They had paused in the middle of the stairway.

"No. Sheila tripped, and she hit her head." His face contorted. "And then she just didn't get up anymore. Did she . . . did she . . . die?"

Nidaba pressed a hand to his cheek. "I'm so sorry, George. She did. She went to be with Lisette."

"I wanted her to stay with us," he said.

Beside him the dog whined softly, as if she too were mourning Sheila's death.

"I was scared," George said. "So I ran. I went and hid in the woods, and then I sneaked back here. Because I knew Sheila wouldn't be able to take care of her pigeons."

"So you came to take care of them for her."

He nodded and went back to helping her down the stairs. "Then I was too scared to come down. But I thought the bad lady would never find me on the roof."

They finally reached the ground, and the doorway. She peered inside, and saw someone holding Natum against the wall by his shirt and pounding on his face. "George, the bad lady's in there, and she has made herself look just like me. You stay away from her."

"How will I know which one of you is which?"

"Code word," she told him. "I'll know our secret code word."

"What is our code word?" he asked, wide-eyed.

"Sheila. It's Sheila."

He smiled, nodded, and Nidaba threw open the door and rushed inside, pouring every bit of strength she had left into her attack. She reached out, grabbed Nicodimus by the back of his shirt, and yanked him off Eannatum with so much force that he lost his balance and fell on his backside. She looked down at her son and said, "Hello, Nicky. I see you've met your father."

He stared up at her in shock, then turned his head to look across the room. When she followed his gaze, she saw the impostor, looking just like her, with her arms around Arianna.

Chapter 19

Nidaba stared at Nicodimus. Then at Natum, who was fighting to remain conscious as blood ran from his nose and split lip. He'd sunk to the floor, where he kept blinking, shaking his head.

But there was no time to help either of them, because Puabi was already in motion.

"Arianna, look out!" Nidaba shouted, but it was too late. Even as Arianna sent a confused look her way, the false Nidaba swung her clasped fists as one, clubbing Arianna on the head so hard she went down at once.

"What the hell!" Nicodimus leapt to his feet and lunged toward her, but Puabi was faster. She snatched up a paperweight and hurled it at him with deadly precision, and then he was on the floor too.

And it was down to the two of them. Nidaba and Puabi. Nidaba focused, knowing she could not match this woman alone, in her weakened state. She was still not fully recovered from Puabi's most recent attack. She needed help. And as a High Priestess of the Goddess, she knew where to get it. Nidaba focused her energy, drawing it up from the earth below and down from the sky above. Feeling the power pulsing in her body, she mentally contained it, directed it, forced it upward, to her eyes, and to the spot above them in the center of her forehead. "First sight, second sight, third eye, never lie."

She opened her eyes, and saw the vision, the glamour, begin to ripple. Like heat waves shimmering over the false face Puabi wore.

"You'll never make it work, Nidaba. I'm far more powerful than you will ever be," Puabi taunted.

"It's my face, you foolish sow," Nidaba whispered. "You might have been able to sustain any other form but this one. I know myself too well not to see the truth beyond the glamour."

"Then why are you still squinting so hard?"

Beyond the ripple, Puabi's hand swam higher, lifting a dagger. Nidaba was still unarmed. Her own dagger lay on the floor ten feet to her left. She took a step toward it, but Puabi moved into her path.

Nidaba eyed the woman coolly. "You cannot hope to defeat me, Puabi. Dagger or no. I am a High Priestess of Inanna!"

"Your Goddess turned her back on you long ago, when you betrayed her by falling in love with her chosen king, Nidaba. And you know that as well as I."

For a moment Nidaba's will weakened. And Puabi's glamour solidified again before her eyes. But then she glanced sideways at Eannatum, and his eyes met hers, though they were slitted with pain and he was barely conscious. She saw the love in his eyes, and she knew. She finally understood what he had been trying to tell her before. Her Goddess had never abandoned her. And neither had her Natum. Nidaba, had never done anything wrong. She and Eannatum were simply meant to be.

Nidaba lifted her hands and her head, closed her eyes, trusting utterly. She heard Puabi rushing forward and yet she didn't move. She only chanted the sacred words she'd learned at Lia's feet so many years ago. *Inanna me en, Inanna me en, Inanna me en!* I am of Inanna, I am of the Goddess, and she is of me. We are one, and you cannot stand against us."

The blade came down. Nidaba heard it slicing the air close to her body. Calmly, guided by a force beyond her, she brought her hands down, palms outward, and opened her eyes to see the blade stop in mid-air. As if it had hit a brick wall. She saw Puabi as she truly was. Small, slight. Short dark hair framing her pixie-like face. Her round lapis blue eyes gleamed with hatred as she tried to force her blade to move, and looked stunned and confused when it wouldn't. Her fisted hand gripped the dagger more tightly, and her face contorted as she drew back and swung the blade again. But it was blocked by an invisible shield.

"Be gone!" Nidaba commanded, guided by a force that was beyond her. A bolt of pure energy burst from her palms, slamming into Puabi. She flew backward, airborne, her blade sailing harmlessly across the room. Her body crashed into the wall and she slid to the floor. But she scrambled to her feet almost immediately. Nidaba was so stunned by the power she had just channeled, that she was not ready for the second attack. She stood looking in awe at her hands, half expecting to see burn marks in her palms from the searing force that had burst from them.

Puabi bent low and charged, driving into Nidaba headfirst like a rampaging bull. The two rolled in a tangle of arms and hands and clothes. Furniture crashed to the floor, knickknacks shattered. Queenie raced around them, barking and growling.

They pounded, kicked, clawed, beat one another, until finally, Nidaba landed a roundhouse blow that sent Puabi reeling. In the split second before she attacked again, Nidaba scrambled to grab a dagger from the floor, and sprang to her feet again, crouched and ready. She glanced down at the weapon in her hand. Puabi's jewel encrusted dagger.

Puabi, too, had used the opportunity to arm herself. She squared off, facing Nidaba, and in her hand, she held the gold-handled dagger that Eannatum had given to Nidaba.

The two faced each other, panting, breathless, daggers at the ready. A flash of movement caught Nidaba's eye, and she glimpsed Nicodimus, Arianna, and Eannatum standing together, staring at them. George cowered in a corner, apparently too afraid to watch. Nidaba realized that to their eyes, she and Puabi still looked exactly the same.

"My Goddess, what's going on here?" Arianna asked. She drew her dagger, eyeing the two women who circled each other amid the rubble of the room.

"Her name is Puabi," Eannatum explained slowly. "She was responsible for your first death, Nicodimus, some four thousand years ago. And she's come back now to try to kill you again."

"I can't imagine why she would want to," Nicodimus murmured, his gaze darting from one of the women to the other. "I don't even know her."

"Mostly, she just wants to hurt your mother," Natum told him grimly. "But she's also a Dark High Witch, so I suppose your heart would be an added bonus."

"So which one is she?" Arianna asked, looking from one woman to the other in bewilderment.

Eannatum frowned, his eyes sliding to the Nidaba on the left, as she sent him a pleading look, brimming with love, begging him to recognize her. He then turned to look at the Nidaba on the right. Her eyes met his only briefly, and if looks could kill, he figured he would be breathing his last about now.

Eannatum nodded toward her with a slight smile. "That one's your mother. She's mad as hell because she thinks I don't know which is which."

"Be gone," Nidaba said in an intense, resonant tone that filled the entire room with an unnatural reverberation. She held her palm out toward her enemy, her dagger clasped in her other hand. "Be gone, Puabi."

Puabi shrieked and drove forward with her blade, but again, it hit that unseen resistance. Eannatum blinked and looked again, because for a moment it seemed there was another woman in the room, larger than life, her form like an aura around and above Nidaba's. Her eyes were like winking bits of lapis, and the rest of her as faint as a breeze. Her hand seemed to meld with Nidaba's as she held it out, palm facing her attacker.

There was a blinding flash of light that seemed to emanate from Nidaba's palm, and Puabi flew backward as if hit by a wrecking ball. Her blade flew from her hand, and landed in the fireplace, burying itself amid the coals. Puabi slammed into the wall with such force the plaster crumbled as she sank into a broken heap on the floor.

As her hold on the spell weakened, the glamour faltered, and Nathan saw Puabi for the first time in well over four thousand years. Ever young, beautiful, selfish and utterly ruthless.

Her dazed eyes met his for an instant. "I only wanted your love," she whispered. "That's all . . . that's all . . ." And then those vivid blue eyes fell closed.

Nathan turned away from her and sought Nidaba. She was standing on the other side of the room, her body nearly limp with exhaustion, bruised and bleeding. He rushed to her, caught her up in his arms, and held her tenderly against him when it seemed she could barely stand on her own.

"You were right," she muttered. "About the dog. There were two—part of the time, at least. George was on the roof, and I went up there. One dog attacked me . . . and the other . . . she saved me."

She sagged against him, stunned, he thought, at the events that had just transpired. Finally, though, she steeled herself, stood straighter, and looked up at him. "Tell me you knew which was really me?"

"I knew, Nidaba. From the very start. If you doubt me, you can ask your . . . our son." He offered a small smile, which died at Arianna's cry.

"Nicodimus!"

Nathan turned and for an endless moment, could only watch in horror. Puabi had roused unnoticed, and retrieved her blade from the coals of the hearth, where it had landed. Its blade glowed red-hot as she rose slowly, drew back her arm, and flung it at Nicodimus. It seemed to happen in slow motion, and yet too suddenly to prevent. Nic, hearing Arianna's cry, turned as the fire red blade whirled end over end toward him, and Nathan knew it would set his son's heart aflame if it pierced his chest—destroying him utterly.

Reaching out for his son, Nathan shoved Nicodimus away, stepping right into the path of that blade to do so.

It sank deeply into Nathan's chest, burning, searing him. He dropped to his knees as a cry of undiluted agony burst from his lungs. Flames leapt from the fabric of his shirt, from his skin. From inside him! Puabi's eyes widened. "No! No, not you, Eannatum! Not you!"

Arianna backhanded the woman, and her head connected with the hearthstone. Then she slumped into silence.

Nidaba jerked the knife from Nathan's chest, and tossed it aside. It hit the floor near the window, still glowing red. Ignoring it, Nidaba pressed her hands to the blazing wound, but the flames kept coming. And then a large, hulking form lifted Nathan away from her. She looked up. "George! No, George, you mustn't—George, wait!"

But George was hearing none of it. It looked bad, Nathan thought, as he clung to consciousness despite the screaming pain in his chest. His skin blistered and bubbled and he could smell the stench of his own burning flesh. George was scratched, bruised, his clothing torn, and soaked through. And he was limping even more badly than usual. But he shrugged off all the hands trying to hold him back, and loped toward the open door, and through it.

Nathan heard the others rushing out right behind them. George stood in the pouring rain, and lifted Nathan in his arms like an offering to the heavens, as the deluge came down.

Blessedly cool rainwater pummeled him, soothing the burning in his chest. Cooling the pain. Nathan opened his mouth to cry out in mingled anguish and relief. And the tongues of flame on his body hissed out their final breaths, and died. Nathan closed his eyes, certain he was about to do the same.

Nidaba raced forward, gasping at the sight of the thin spirals of smoke rising from her beloved Eannatum's chest. She stared aghast at his scorched shirt, the blistered skin and gaping wound with its blackened edges.

"Put him down, George. Right here in the rain."

"Did I . . . did I help him?" the big man asked, dropping to his knees to lay Natum down on the wet grass. He leaned over his friend, his face contorted with worry. Beside him the dog, Queenie, looked nearly as worried as George did.

"Yes. You helped him more than any of us could," Nidaba said. She knelt on Natum's other side and framed his face with her hands. "Live, Eannatum," she whispered. "Live. Damn you, you must. Do you hear me?"

"Nidaba . . . Mother . . . ?" Nicodimus knelt beside her, encircled her shoulders with his arm. "He saved my life."

"He only wanted a chance to know you. He's your father, Nicodimus. Or he was . . . in the lifetime before."

"I know. He . . . he told me."

"Live, Natum. Please, please, live. I can't bear this to be the end, do you understand me? I can't."

She pressed her hands to his chest, wishing with everything in her that she would feel his heart beating strong and steady. There was silence, utter stillness, but Nidaba then felt something else. That sensation of another person embracing her. Another hand, surrounding hers. Another force moving though her.

Her hand grew hot, and a soft white light came from her palm, suffusing the entire area of Nathan's wound in its glow. The heat intensified, grew, nearly scorched her, but she didn't move. She just let it happen.

And then the light faded, and her palm cooled . . . and she felt the beating of Natum's heart against her hand.

"Oh, my Goddess," she whispered as tears streamed down her face.

Exactly. The word echoed in her mind.

Eannatum's eyes opened. He stared up at her, lifted a hand, curled it around her nape and drew her face down to his. He kissed her, gently, softly.

"Oh, no, the house!" Arianna cried.

They all turned to look. The living room was fully engulfed in flames, and the fire was spreading rapidly, licking its way toward the roof.

"Puabi?" Natum asked.

"She was still inside." Nidaba spoke the words with a hint of regret, even though she knew Puabi probably deserved no sympathy, given all the harm she had done in her lifetime. She also knew that she and Eannatum were partly to blame for what the woman had ultimately become.

Natum closed his eyes, bowed his head. "I wish . . ."

"I know," Nidaba said softly. "I know." Drawing a breath, she looked up at her son. "Nicky, we need to get some help. The fire department. This is Natum's home, he loves this place. We have to—"

"No." Eannatum sat up slowly and reached up for a hand. Nicodimus closed his hand around his father's and helped him to his feet. For a moment, the two remained that way, standing there, face-to-face, hands clasped. Natum looked into Nicodimus's eyes, and his became moist. "Good to meet you . . . Nicodimus. At long last. You make a hell of a first impression, you know." As he said it, he rubbed his nose, which was already healing.

"So do you," Nicodimus said with a grin. "Saving my life, I mean."

"Natum . . . your house!" Nidaba tugged him around to face her, trying to get him to pay attention to his home. But he only looked at George, and smiled broadly.

"You okay, my friend?"

"I'll be okay, Nathan. I'm just glad I left the pigeon coop open." He looked up and pointed. The pigeons were already fleeing into the night, vanishing instantly, swallowed up by the darkness.

Natum turned to Nidaba. "We need to talk."

"But Natum, your house!"

He glanced toward Nicodimus. His son gave him a nod. "Hey, George, what do you say you come with Arianna and me? We'll fix up your scratches, get you something to eat, some dry clothes, okay?"

George looked down at the Rottweiler by his side. "Can Queenie come with us, too?"

"Sure."

"Just a minute," Nidaba said, and she moved forward, put a hand on the dog's head. No tingling jolt rushed through her. She nodded, satisfied this one was the real dog, and gave her a loving scratch between the ears. Then she nodded her assent. "It's okay. She's the real Queenie, not the impostor."

The imposter . . .

Nidaba glanced toward the flames and felt a heavy sadness for Puabi, in spite of herself. They'd had a lot in common, the two of them. Both willing to fight and die for the love of one man.

Natum gave George a nod and George walked with Nicodimus and Arianna toward the car the two had arrived in. Queenie ran along beside him. Nic called back, "There's an inn nearby. The Hampton. You know it?"

Natum nodded. "We'll be along. Later."

"Natum?" Nidaba whispered.

"I know, I know. My house. Come on, love. We still have not finished our conversation. I had no idea I had so much more to say to you, but I find that I do. Besides, we have a proper farewell to say. To Sheila."

"But the house . . ."

"Let the damned house burn. I don't need it anymore. What I need, Nidaba—*all* I need—is for you to come with me. Let me say what I need to say to you before you walk away from me again. I'm not going to let you go this time until you've heard everything I have to tell you. Everything I'm thinking and feeling. And until you've told me everything you are thinking and feeling in return. You understand?"

She nodded, looking into his eyes, and seeing a familiar gleam there. He radiated a familiar power. He was himself again, she thought. At last. She had located her long missing king.

As the dawn broke over the waves, Eannatum and Nidaba sat in the small boat, staring down at the still water. It was the same spot where they'd lowered Sheila's body, and while the currents had long since carried her away, they returned to this spot to honor her. Nidaba had chanted long prayers in Sumerian, and Eannatum had joined her. There hadn't been time before for more than a hurried farewell. So now they said their good-byes, wished her soul well on its journey, shed their tears. Looking back at the shore, all Eannatum saw was a pile of smoldering wreckage, charred beams, refuse where his house, his haven, his make-believe world, had once stood.

"You were right, you know," he said very softly.

"Was I?"

He nodded. "I've been living a lie, Nidaba. I'm not an ordinary man. I'm not a quiet antique dealer from New England. I am Eannatum. Immortal High Witch. King of the greatest nation of its time."

She smiled. "You're more than that, you know. More than even I realized. We both are." She clasped his hands in hers and stared into his eyes. "We've been given this gift for a reason, Eannatum. Not just so we can live forever, grow more powerful, battle the Dark Ones. There's more to it. There has to be."

He hesitated for a moment. "I saw . . . something back there at the house. A being . . . surrounding you like a nimbus."

"It was . . . something greater than any of us," she whispered. "A force beyond what I understood before. Beyond any God or Goddess I know by name . . . more like . . . All. Like All that ever was or ever will be, combined into one being that is you and is me and is . . . everything. Even Puabi."

He stared into her eyes. "And what does this being want from us?" he asked, his voice touched with wonder.

"I don't know. I only know . . . there's more to this than I have understood. We need to find out what, and set about the business of doing what we were put here to do."

"It has taken me four thousand years to understand one of the most important things I was put here to do, Nidaba. But I know it now. So perhaps we can start with that."

She nodded slightly. "Yes. Of course we can. What is it, Natum, that you believe you should be doing?"

He lifted a hand, cupped her cheek. "Loving you. Endlessly, deeply, passionately loving you, my beautiful priestess."

A joyful smile spread across her face and her eyes gleamed. "Eternity is a long time to love one woman."

"You are more like . . . like a collage of all womankind. Far beyond one woman. And I have already loved you for an eternity. If I couldn't stop in four thousand, five hundred years, even when I tried, why should I expect it to change from now until forever?"

"I cannot live as a mortal, Natum."

"And I cannot live without you, Nidaba." He smiled very slowly. "We should marry. The way we should have long ago. In fact, we should marry a hundred times, in every form of wedding rite that exists. We'll have a Christian ceremony, and a Buddhist one, a Wiccan handfasting, a Sumerian marriage rite, and everything else we can think of. Just . . . just tell me you still love me, Nidaba. Even if it's only a little bit. I know I've hurt you deeply, but I swear—"

"Shh." She pressed her lips to his and kissed him tenderly. When their lips finally parted, he was stunned to see tears in her eyes. "I have loved you for all my lifetimes, Eannatum. And for all those yet to come, I will love you still."

He looked at her beloved face, into her beautiful, dark eyes, and he knew she meant it. They were meant to be together, had been from the very first day they had met, a young prince and a precocious little priestess who wanted to learn to write her name. Chosen and placed on this planet for some purpose, yes, but one they could find, and understand, and ultimately accomplish only if they were together. This was their destiny.

"Gods, but we've wasted so much time," he said, pulling her close, savoring the miracle that was Nidaba.

"Yes, we have, my love. But we aren't going to waste any more."

Immortality

Prologue

❦

For the first time in four thousand years I was ready to die. And it looked as if I would get my wish. For the flames surrounded me, searing my flesh, and every breath I drew burned in my throat and lungs. And yet I could see them. Beyond the smoke and dancing tongues of ravenous fire, I could see them. My husband, the man I had loved, and his mistress wrapped up tight in his arms, safe, outside, bathed in the cool night air while I roasted. Through the window glass I watched them, beyond the flaming draperies and through the thickening smoke—and then the window exploded, and the fire filled the open space. Even my preternatural eyesight couldn't pierce the wall of flames then.

It was over. He'd left me for dead, likely relieved to be rid of me. He would probably celebrate my demise.

The hell he would.

Something rose up in me. I was tired, tired of living, tired of fighting to stay alive, and tired of hating. I told myself to just close my eyes. Just lie there and let the hungry fire do its work. But something inside me fought back. It made me struggle to my feet, that insistent something. It forced me to drag myself through the inferno, toward what I sensed was the rear of the house. My dress caught fire. My hair smoldered and smoked, and my skin blistered. I would have screamed in anguish had I a voice, or even a breath left in me. But I didn't. If I'd been an ordinary woman, I'd have been dead at that point. But I wasn't ordinary. I wasn't mortal. So I stumbled onward, a living torch, and I tasted hell. Finally I fell, unable to go any farther.

But it was cool, damp ground beneath my body. It was blessed icy rain that pelted down on me from above. Lifegiving rain.

And still that something inside, whatever it was, pushed me onward. Urged me irresistibly onward. I tried to get to my feet but couldn't rise even as far as my knees. So I dragged myself forward. I clawed my fingers into the wet soil, and I pulled myself inch by agonizing inch, onward. I suppose I couldn't bear the thought of *them* coming upon me this way. Seeing me with my skin charred black and my life force ebbing low. They would finish me off, if they found me.

Natum had taken everything from me. *Everything.* I wouldn't let his be the hand that took my life as well. No, I would die on my own terms.

And so I crawled . . . inched, toward the cliffs. "To hell with him," I whispered when at last I reached ahead of me to find there was no more ground to grasp. I opened my eyes and saw yawning darkness and far, far below, the boiling white froth of the sea. "To hell with both of them. And to hell with the world."

With one last effort, I, Queen Puabi, the darkest of the Dark Witches, pulled myself over the edge and into oblivion. And as I plummeted I wondered how many times I would drown and revive and drown again before my power ran out. And what would become of me then?

Could there be peace for one as purely evil as I? Or would I remain trapped in some semblance of awareness even while the sea creatures fed on my flesh? I didn't know. I didn't care.

I didn't care.

Anything was better than the anguish I left behind.

Or so I thought until I smashed through the surface of the sea, like smashing through concrete, and into its briny depths, which burned far more than the flames had done.

Chapter 1

He thought his heart stopped cold when he saw the dead woman floating in the sea. At first he'd glimpsed only color and shape. Something white and oval hovering beneath the jewel-blue ripples of the ocean. He'd stopped rowing then and leaned over for a closer look. Her pale, lifeless face bobbed up, broke the surface.

"Jesus!" Matthew jerked away so fast he stumbled and fell, nearly tipping the small boat over. Then he sat there on the floor of his rowboat, stunned and gaping like the fish in his pail. His heart hammered. Squaring his shoulders, he got up onto the seat, slid to the side, and looked again.

She was still there, still dead, and she still looked startlingly like Gabriella. Dark, dark lashes rested eternally against her sculpted cheeks. Her lips were tinted blue and full, her nose, straight and small. Her arms were unclothed, hands delicate and lily white.

Water lapped over her face. Tiny waves, flinging themselves onto her lips, her eyes, as if in an effort to claim her.

Hell, he couldn't just leave her there.

Matthew told himself to buck up and do the right thing. If he had come to one conclusion during his temporary retreat from the world, it was that from now on, he would make an effort to do the right thing. So he would haul the dead beauty to his island, keep her there until the impending storm passed, and radio the authorities.

Sighing deeply, he knelt in the bottom of the small boat, leaned over, and managed to get hold of one of her arms. Then he frowned. She wasn't cold. Cool, yes. But not cold. He drew the woman closer, until he could get his hands beneath her shoulders, and then he pulled her up and inward. Her head cleared the boat's side and lolled backward. Her neck and shoulders were above the water level, and he bent to get a better grip, putting her face directly below his, upside down and void of expression. He did not like being this close to a dead person. He'd been spending far too much time contemplating death lately.

Suddenly the pale lips opened wide, and the dead woman sucked in a desperate, strangled breath. Her body arched backward so forcefully that he almost lost her to the sea. He was so startled by her sudden animation that he damn near let her go.

He rapidly regained his hold on her, tugging harder now that he realized he wasn't recovering a body but saving a life. God, he'd been so certain her chances were nil. Her eyes flew open, looking wild and dangerous, electric-blue—too vivid to be real, and flecked with gold—and she began to twist and struggle.

"No!" he barked. "Settle down, woman, or you'll drown yourself. I'm trying to save your life here."

She stilled instantly, maybe startled by his tone. It had startled him, too. He hadn't barked at anyone that way in almost three months. Hell, he'd probably scared her half to death, he thought. She seemed totally disoriented. He pulled her mostly nude body out of the water, into the boat, and she let him. Then she just lay there between the seats, water sluicing off her skin and her short, dark hair soaking his sneakers, his feet. Her clothes, what remained of them, were in tatters. Rags that might once have been a skirt clung to her from the waist down. From the waist up she was completely naked, and apparently unconcerned by it. She didn't try to cover herself. Then again, she'd nearly drowned. Having a stranger see her breasts was probably the least of her worries. And yet he did see, and he did notice. She was very cold. So it was tough not to notice.

She shivered, and he dragged his gaze away from her breasts. "What do you want of me?" she whispered.

He narrowed his eyes on her, gave his head a shake, and started to peel his sweater off. As he pulled the sweater over his head, he caught the glint of sunlight on steel. Looking up fast, he saw her dainty, waterlogged hand clutching a deadly-looking blade—and bringing it down fast. He flung up an arm just in time to deflect hers. Then he caught her wrist in his hand, exerted pressure, and eyed the double-edged dagger she'd damn near plunged into his chest just now.

"Drop the knife, dammit!"

She shook her head, her eyes flashing with life, with anger, with violence, though only moments ago they'd been lifeless and dull. They were like lapis stones, her eyes.

"Crush my wrist," she all but growled. "Go ahead, mortal, and see how fast it heals again."

He stared at her, and wondered how someone could look so much like Gabriella and yet be so completely different. This woman personified rage. "You're delirious. Put the knife down before you make me hurt you."

She shook her head. Matthew squeezed her slender wrist in his hand until she cried out in pain and the blade clattered to the bottom of the boat. He eased his grip, set her down again. She slumped against the side of the rowboat, looking at her wrist as if confused.

"I'm weak," she muttered. Then she closed her eyes tiredly. "You should have left me in the sea."

"You try anything like that again, I'll throw you right back in."

Those blue eyes opened, and she glared up at him.

He glared back. Then he bent to pick up her blade, looked it over. It was a nice piece. If the stones embedded in the handle were real, it was worth some money, too. "I'll just hang on to this for you," he told her, tucking it into his belt. Then he retrieved his sweater from the seat where he'd dropped it and handed it to her. "Put this on."

She looked at him with fury in her eyes. But she took the sweater and pulled it over her head, thrust her arms into the sleeves. "Where are you taking me?"

He nodded at the tiny island in the distance. "There."

"And what is there?"

"Nothing much, besides my villa. It's a private island. *My* private island." He sat facing her and bent to the oars. He saw the way she looked toward the west. On a clear day, the ghostly shape of St. John's would be visible in the distance. Saba was closer, and you could almost always see its distinctive volcano-shaped cone, but not today. It was far from clear in the distance today. "There's not time to go any farther," he told her, and nodded toward the darkness far in the distance. "Storm coming."

She narrowed her eyes on him in suspicion.

"What, you think I'm lying? That I *want* a psychopathic drowned rat in my only haven? Trust me, lady, I'd take you to one of the big islands if I could. But I can't, so unless you think you can swim that far in a storm, you're stuck with me."

He thought those laser-blue eyes would burn him, they grew so fiery. "If you think I am *stuck* anywhere, you are sadly mistaken." Then she leaned back in the boat, closed her eyes, and there was not another sound from her.

He wasn't sure if she'd passed out, died, or was just ignoring him. He rowed faster. It didn't take long before he was out of the boat, tugging its nose up onto the sandy shore of the small island. Then he scooped her up and saw with relief that she was still breathing. She was light in his arms, limp in them, her body leaning into his chest as he carried her inland, over the sand to harder ground and then along the barely discernible path through the palms and tropical plants, to his home away from home. It wasn't much, his island villa. Not compared to his seaside mansion back home. But it served him well when he needed to escape. And he had needed that. Badly.

It was as if the fates didn't *want* him to escape, though. How else could he explain what had happened here just now? Finding this woman—a woman who, aside from her vivid blue eyes, could have been his wife's evil twin.

What the hell did it all mean? Who was she? And why would she want to drive her pretty dagger into her rescuer's heart?

Puabi woke to softness and a surrounding warmth that had worked its way into her body. She opened her eyes with a start, her fingers curling, clawlike, into the surface on which she lay. She'd expected water. Water had been her entire world for so long . . .

But that man had pulled her from the sea.

Sighing, she eased her grip on the mattress beneath her, tried to focus her vision, and took stock. She was alive. But far from strong. Her head still pounded. Her lungs ached. Her skin and eyes burned and felt raw. This tiredness clung to her, and her vision wasn't good even by mortal standards. It was blurred and dull.

The room around her seemed bright, sunny. She made out windows, and rich dark wood furnishings. A fire danced warmly in a freestanding fireplace. And the bed in which she lay was huge and soft. Fit for a queen, she thought, almost smiling at the irony.

"Awake, are you?"

She turned her head slowly and saw the man sitting in a rocking chair near the bed. He set aside the book he'd been reading and leaned forward, elbows resting on his knees. He was a big man. Broad-shouldered. Very dark. His skin bronzed by the sun, and his hair as black as her own. He had the thick, dark brows of a Sumerian, but aside from that she could make out little of his face.

"How are you feeling?"

"Why do you want to know?" Her voice emerged rusty with disuse.

He got to his feet, poured water into a glass, and offered it to her.

Puabi blinked at the large, blurred hand that held the glass.

"You're dehydrated," he said. "You should drink all you can stand."

She had never liked being told what to do. She liked it even less when the man doing the telling was correct. Sitting up with no small effort, she accepted the glass, tipped it to her lips and drank. She drained it, despite his protests, which began halfway through, then set the glass down. The cool water hit her stomach like a brick. For a moment she thought the liquid might come back up, but she quelled the sick feeling with a hand to her belly and slowly lay back onto the pillows.

"Probably a little at a time would have been better," he said. "Your stomach's been empty for a long time."

"How would you know that?" she asked, her eyes falling closed.

"Your hair is like straw, your skin is burned from the sun and

chapped from the salt water. Your eyes are so bloodshot I'd be surprised if you could see straight."

"I can't."

He sighed and set the glass aside. "How long were you in the
water?"

There was something about his voice. Its deep timbre had a con-
trolled quality to it. As if he were keeping it level only with great effort. And there was something else, something that tickled her nerve
endings with a static charge.

"I don't know," she answered.

"How did you get there?"

She opened her eyes to look at him, but as before, he was unclear. Dark hair, longer than was fashionable in men of consequence
today. And he was one of those, she knew that much. He'd called
this his island. He spoke with an air of authority and command. And
something else. Pain.

He was waiting for her answer, she realized. She didn't give him
one.

"There must have been a fire," he said. "What remained of your
clothes had been burned."

"I don't want to talk about that."

He blinked slowly. She couldn't make out his eyes, but she knew
they were focused on her face, and she felt their intensity. "Then you
do remember."

"I remember. I wish I didn't. Either way, it's no concern of
yours."

"You're right, it's not." He shrugged as if he could care less about
her trauma. "There's a lukewarm bath waiting for you in the next
room. Soak in it for a while. It'll soothe your skin."

Puabi tilted her head to one side and frowned at him. "I
don't . . . understand."

"A little oatmeal in the water," he said. "An old trick my father
taught me. Good for everything from sunburn to poison ivy." She
thought he might have smiled slightly, but sensed it wasn't a real
smile. "Go ahead," he said. "Take your time." He started toward the
door, then paused, turning back. "Uh . . . there's a bell on the nightstand to your left. Take it with you into the bathroom, just in case."

She blinked through her swimming vision as he left her alone.

What was he up to, she wondered. Why was he bothering with her comfort? Bringing her water, running her bath? She got to her feet, but her head swam with dizziness. Gods, things were not right. Not with her—and even more clearly, not with the mortal. He was up to something. She felt it right to her bones.

Chapter 2

Puabi lay in the cool, soothing water, head tipped back, eyes closed. The mortal had been right—though his actions were suspect. In her experience no man was this kind without some hidden motive. Still, whatever he'd put into the water did ease her burned skin. But her eyes . . .

She lifted a soft washcloth, dripping wet, and laid it gently over her closed eyes. No doubt the salty seawater had done some harm. But her body ought to have healed itself by now. It was taking an unreasonably long time. Ah, but then again, she had died and revived countless times at the whim of the sea. Her power must be waning very low indeed. And there was only one way to restore it, to prolong this hideous existence. To find another immortal High Witch—one of the Light Ones—and kill her.

The idea held little appeal, oddly enough. And the mortal had taken her dagger. That did not bode well, and only added to her suspicions about him.

Sighing, she dunked her head beneath the water to rinse away the conditioner that had been soaking in her hair for several minutes now. She'd had all she could bear of lying up to her neck in water, after so many days surrounded by the stuff. Tiredly, her muscles protesting in pain, she got to her feet, stepped out of the tub, and used a thick soft towel to gently dab herself dry. Then she rubbed her hair down as well.

Her vision was still blurred, but it was slightly clearer than before. She could see more of the room's details. The tub was free-standing and claw-footed. The walls and ceiling were white, and bamboo mats were scattered around on the floor. Large, arching windows let sunlight flood the place, and she glanced through one of them for a moment. She glimpsed palm trees, blue sky, a sandy beach with waves lapping at it. Then the brilliance hurt too much, and she had to look away.

Hadn't the mortal claimed there was some horrendous storm looming? That yellow sunlight didn't look stormy to her.

So she'd caught him in a lie already. That confirmed her opinion that he was up to no good.

Sighing, she continued her inspection of the room. Aside from the porcelain fixtures, everything in the room was rattan—from the cabinets on the walls to the towel racks to the frame around the full-length mirror. She paused there and squinted at her hazy reflection. Her skin was still an angry red color. Tender to the touch, and warm. Her hair stuck up like black feathers, but it felt softer than before. Slinging the towel over her shoulder, she found a comb lying on a stand and pulled it through the short black layers.

"Everything all right?" His voice came from beyond the door, and again the sound of it made her skin prickle with some kind of awareness.

Looking toward the door, she noticed a large white article of clothing hanging from a hook there. "Fine. I'll only be a moment." She dropped the towel to the floor and went to retrieve the white clothing, which turned out to be a large cotton robe. Its touch was cool and delicious on her skin as she pulled it over her arms, around her waist, and tied the sash. It hung well below her knees. From what she could tell, she was decently covered—not that she particularly cared, but she was in no shape to gut the mortal should he try to assault her, driven to violent lust by a glimpse of her flesh. It wouldn't be the first time, she mused. She opened the door and stepped back into the bedroom.

And she smelled food. Her stomach growled loudly even as her eyes sought the source. There, beside the bed, was a tray that emitted aromatic steam. The man stood near it. She sent him a suspicious look. "Why are you being kind to me?" she asked him.

"This isn't kindness," he said slowly. "It's decency. I'd do as much for a stray dog."

"And likely get your hand bit off for your trouble," she snapped, even as she walked quickly forward and climbed onto the bed, curling her legs beneath her and reaching for the tray of food. Drawing it into her lap, she leaned over it and sniffed. She smelled meat, vegetables, seasoning, toasted bread, melted butter, cheeses.

"How are the eyes?"

"Fine," she lied as she moved her hands around on the tray trying to identify the items. There was a bowl, and hot liquid. Soup. And a small plate held some kind of a sandwich. And a cup . . .

"Careful, the tea's hot," he warned.

She ignored him, picking up the sandwich and bringing it to her mouth. Grilled cheese. It was far from the finest meal she'd eaten in her lifetime, but she thought she enjoyed it as if it were. The soup turned out to be chicken broth with noodles, vegetables, and hunks of meat. She devoured the entire sandwich and drained every last drop of the soup. Then as she lifted the mug of tea, the man took the tray from her lap.

She looked up quickly, having nearly forgotten his presence. It was unusual for her to let her guard down with a stranger—especially one who had taken her dagger and lied to her in order to keep her here.

He set the tray aside. "I have some eyedrops here. They might help."

She shook her head, not trusting him. "I don't need them." Instead she sipped the tea.

"All right." He sighed and took a seat in the chair beside the bed. "So why don't you tell me who you are?"

"I am Puabi."

She could see well enough to know when he tipped his head to one side. "Just Puabi?"

"No, not *just* Puabi. Queen Puabi. I am of royal blood."

The flash of white told her he smiled. "Queen, eh? And what are you queen of?"

She averted her poorly functioning eyes. "A land that no longer exists. A world that is no more." Slowly, she closed her eyes. "You think I'm insane, no doubt."

"I didn't say that."

She took a fortifying sip of tea, but truly her head was feeling heavy on her shoulders. "Where am I?" she asked him, suddenly overwhelmed with the urge to go home, even though she knew there was no such place. She wouldn't recognize Sumer now. It was buried beneath the sands of four thousand years. New civilizations had covered over her own. They called it Iraq now, and it was peopled by children of Muhammad, not of Inanna.

"You're near the Virgin Islands. Roughly between St. John's and St. Kitts. The nearest inhabited island to us is called Saba. It's just five square miles—but it has a small airfield and a medical clinic."

She swallowed the lump that had formed in her throat. "I went into the Atlantic off the coast of Maine. I emerged in the Caribbean, in the tropics. Gods, how long must such a journey have taken?"

He was silent for a moment. When he spoke, he spoke softly. "I think you're still a little . . . disoriented."

"I came through the Triangle, didn't I?"

"The Bermuda Triangle? Yes . . . I suppose you could have."

"Perhaps that's got something to do with the way I feel."

"And how do you feel?"

She shook her head, searching for words. "I don't know. Odd. Different." She lifted her chin. "I want to leave here," she demanded. "I want to go to the mainland. The States. Now, today." She set the teacup on the nightstand, but it landed so near the edge that it toppled to the floor. She ignored the sound of the porcelain shattering, turned in the bed, and swung her legs to the floor.

"You can't leave yet," he told her.

"I can, and I will." She surged to her feet. Dizziness welled up like a tidal wave in her head, and her knees dissolved. Arms came around her, strong, fast, and firm. And there was something—some moment of déjà vu. A sense of odd, niggling familiarity about the man, even as he held her against his powerful body.

"Gods," she whispered. "Something is wrong with me. I feel . . . so strange."

"A few days in the sea will have that effect on a person," he said, and he lowered her carefully to the bed again.

"It's not that. It's more than that." She squinted up at his face, hovering over hers. "I know you," she whispered, the words dripping with accusation. "Who are you?" Why the hell wouldn't her eyes focus and allow her to see his face? She would know it. She was certain she would.

"Easy, Puabi. Come on, take it easy." His hand still cradled the back of her head, lowering it to the pillow before moving away.

"I want to leave," she said, but the words came weakly, softly.

"You can't. Not until the storm passes."

"There is no storm. You lie."

"I don't lie. There's a tropical storm stalled a hundred miles out to sea," he said. "The longer it sits there, the stronger it becomes. It could start moving in at any time, and I don't intend to be caught out there in a small boat when it does."

She let her eyes fall closed. It made her head hurt to strain them so hard in the effort to see him. "Then tell me your name. For I know we've met before."

"My name is Matthew. And we've never met. You're not the kind of woman a man would forget."

And that was all. She was out cold.

Matthew stared down at her, shaking his head in complete bewilderment. Who the hell was she? And just how much brain damage had she suffered? He sat on the edge of the bed, threaded his fingers into her hair, and probed her scalp. He took his time, felt every bit of it, but found no sign of head injury. That didn't mean much, though. The sun, the heat, the dehydration—she could have suffered a stroke or some kind of mental breakdown. Any number of things could be causing her delusions.

First she'd tried to kill him. Then she'd claimed to be a queen. And now she thought she knew him.

Hell, she certainly played the part of royalty well. She hadn't so much as thanked him for the food. Or for saving her life, for that matter. And a glance at the condition of the bathroom—towels on the floor amid puddles of water, tub still full—suggested she expected to be waited on.

But that wasn't fair, was it? She wasn't exactly in peak condition right now.

Asleep, it was stunning how much she looked like Gabriella. Awake, she couldn't have been more different. And the last thing he needed here was her face reminding him of his wife. Sweet, shy, lonely little Gabriella. She'd been lost. She'd foolishly thought he was her salvation. She said she loved him. And died because of it.

Hell. He closed his eyes, fought the regret that rose up. Gabriella was gone. The woman in the bed had nothing to do with his young wife. The resemblance was a coincidence. And she, Puabi, was a mystery. One he didn't need or want to solve.

Sighing, he reached for the bottle of eyedrops and leaned over her. With his thumb, he pulled one eyelid upward. "Trust me on this, your highness." He squeezed a few drops into her eye, then repeated the process on the other side. "I want you off my island just as badly you do."

Her eyes flew open and rolled back into her head. She thrashed, her arms flailing wildly. The lamp on the nightstand flew. Then she hit the stand itself, toppling it. She twisted and arched on the bed as he tried to catch hold of her, keep her still. God, she was burning up with fever. It had come out of nowhere. She kicked, then sat up, and though he tried, he couldn't hold her to the bed. How the hell could she be that strong? When she flung herself backward again, she slammed her head into the headboard. One hand slashed across his face and then raked her own chest. Trails of bright red blood beaded on her pale skin in the wake of her clawlike nails and trickled downward.

My God, she was strong! And she was hurting herself. She was like a wildcat, lashing out, convulsing, and he was damned if he knew what to do to keep her from harming them both. He caught one flying arm, then the other, and held on while she thrashed. He could only pray that she would wear herself out soon.

Chapter 3

When Puabi woke again, she moaned softly and arched her back in pleasure even before she opened her eyes. She was lying facedown in the warm, downy-soft bed, and something cool and wonderful was stroking her back. Over and over, it moved soothingly, leaving blessed relief in its wake.

Then her mind cleared, her memory returned. She tried to roll over, even while reaching for a blanket to cover herself as she realized she was naked and fully exposed. But her hands didn't move. Frowning, she lifted her head, and tugged at the soft strips of cloth that bound her wrists to the headboard above her.

"You *dare* . . ."

"What, now you're complaining?" he said in that rich, velvet tone that stroked every nerve ending to life.

She couldn't see him. Could only hear his voice, and feel his hands smoothing something creamy and cool over her flesh. "A few seconds ago you were damn near purring."

"Take your hands off me," she commanded, and even to her own ears, the order lacked any real power.

"In a minute. Your skin is so burned it's blistered in places. This stuff will help."

"I don't want your help."

"You're not exactly in any condition to know *what* you want. Much less what's good for you, so I've taken the decision out of your hands."

His hands smoothed a path over her buttocks. Cool, clinical, so soothing she wanted to sigh in relief. She twisted away from his touch, but she couldn't go far. "I knew you couldn't be trusted," she seethed. "I knew you were up to something."

"The only thing I'm up to is keeping you from killing yourself, or me, or both of us."

His hands moved down the backs of her thighs, spreading that coolness to the creases behind her knees, and lower, over her calves.

She relaxed in spite of herself. "I reacted the way I did when you pulled me from the sea out of sheer instinct. If you'd lived the life I have, you'd have done the same. And it's moot, anyway, because you took my dagger from me. I'm no threat to you now."

"Somehow I doubt that." He was massaging her feet, gently working the salve, or whatever it was, into them. But he stopped, and moved into her line of vision, and then he knelt beside the bed, looked her in the eye, and pointed to his face. Red scratches marred it. "You did this without any help from your fancy knife."

She flinched when he said it. She hadn't meant to. Her vision was significantly clearer than it had been earlier, and suddenly she wished it wasn't. "I did that?" she whispered hoarsely.

"Is that remorse I see in those strange eyes of yours, Puabi?"

She frowned at him, but she was no longer looking at his neck. Instead she'd turned her vision inward, searching her mind, her self, for the source of this uncommon emotion. "Yes," she said. "I think it may be. Incredible."

Blinking, she focused on his face, seeing it more clearly now than before. Brown eyes, hard eyes. Lines at the corners, small ones, frown lines. Wide jaw. Lips and nose both full. Sensual. By the Gods, he was handsome.

"You sound incredulous that you're capable of feeling sorry for having attacked me."

She nodded. "I am. Why should I be sorry? Your injuries are minor, so why should even the slightest remorse plague me?"

His brows rose as one. "Maybe . . . because I saved your life?"

"You underestimate me. I was still a long way from dead when you found me. Though I suppose I might have expired, eventually, had you not."

He studied her, shaking his head. "Here I thought the big question was why you'd want to kill me after I took you in, fed you, tried to help you . . ."

"I told you, instinct. I've had to fight to stay alive for a very long time. It's my nature to attack before the attacker has the chance. Strike fast, strike first, live to strike again."

"That's a pretty brutal philosophy." Then he tilted his head. "Actually, it sounds a lot like my own."

"Really?"

He nodded. "Yes. Really. Until recently."

"Then you've changed your mind? Why?"

He averted his eyes as she searched them, and she knew she had hit on something sensitive—some tender spot. He was vulnerable there. It was good to know a man's weakness early on.

"Roll over. The ointment's pretty well soaked in on this side."

Pursing her lips, she thought about refusing. She considered snapping the bonds that held her, which she was certain she could manage with minimal effort, even in her weakened state. The one thing she could be certain of, however, was that her back felt a great deal better than before, while the front of her still burned and stung as if she'd been dragged naked over sandpaper. The man hadn't tried anything inappropriate yet. If he did, she would kill him. Perhaps. Or perhaps not. It wasn't a complicated matter at all.

She rolled over, the strip of cloth that held her wrists twisting easily.

The man went still, his gaze sliding slowly down her body, lingering where it shouldn't, heating with desire.

"Look your fill and let's get on with this, shall we?"

He let his eyes slide up her, from her toes to her eyes. "Pretty full of yourself, aren't you?"

"You're the one who tied me up and stripped off my robe."

"*My* robe," he corrected. "And I only tied your hands because you went wild on me. Look at your chest."

She lifted her head from the pillows and saw the marks she'd dug across her own chest. "Point taken. But just why am I bound now, Matthew Fairchild?"

He frowned at her. "How did you know my last name?"

"I assume you told me."

"I didn't."

She frowned in thought, but quickly dismissed the question with a shake of her head. "I'm in significant pain, mortal. Would you apply your lotion already?"

He nodded, reached for the cloth that bound her wrists. She shook her head. "Leave it."

His eyes flew to hers, flaring slightly.

She met his gaze without blinking.

"I'm not into playing bondage games."

"Oh, come now. Have you ever tried?" She taunted him with her eyes. Then she shrugged. "Besides, I can pull free of your little knots easily. Remind me to show you sometime how to properly restrain a subject."

Matthew shook his head and kept his eyes averted. As if he thought she might not see the animal desire in them that way. Much less the guilt that came with it. She did, though. She saw it all. He might be an amusing distraction, this handsome mortal.

He sat on the edge of the bed, and dipped his fingers into the jar on the nightstand, and they came out dripping with a clear, gel-like substance. He moved his hand toward her, and she stiffened in anticipation. The cold stuff touched her heated skin, her shoulder, and slowly he smoothed it down her arm.

"What is it?" she asked.

"Aloe, mostly. It's working wonders on your back already."

"I'm a fast healer," she said softly, her eyes riveted on his hand as he dipped it into the jar, drew it out again, and spread more of the stuff over her neck, and then gently upward, following the line of her jaw, sliding over her chin. His fingers moved against her face, her cheeks. She closed her eyes, and he touched her forehead, her nose, the bit of skin above her lip. There was something in his touch . . .

His hand was trembling.

The moment she noticed it, he drew it away, and she opened her eyes to look at him. "What is it?"

He shook his head, but there was pain in his eyes. "You . . . remind me of someone," he said at last. Then the emotional look left him, and the more cynical one returned to his eyes. "At least you do when you aren't bitching at me or trying to kill me."

She tilted her head, ignoring his barb. "Who?"

"No one." He coated his fingers again and returned to his work, spreading the stuff over her other arm, all the way to her wrist, skipping only the part covered by the strip of cloth. He moved on to her hands, her fingertips, which he did one by one. Then he went to the foot of the bed, and started at her ankles, smearing ointment up her shins, over her knees, and along her thighs. He didn't shy away when he neared their juncture. He kept going, painting her pelvic bones, hips, lower abdomen. He only skipped the dark curls. Then he was at her waist, her belly. Her rib cage and sides. His hands worked some kind of magic, soothing away her pain and leaving a cold fire in their wake. His touch felt good. Like the caress of a lover. And she was too much a woman not to be aroused by it.

He took his hand away, gathered more aloe from the jar. Came back. She couldn't help it. As his hand neared her breast, she closed her eyes in anticipation. And then that coolness touched her, and she let her breath whisper out of her. As his fingers neared the center, she knew her nipples hardened expectantly. She didn't care. And then his fingers were there, softly, gently rubbing the cold gel over her nipple. Too soon they moved away. But he began again at the other breast, and she thought she would die if he didn't touch her more thoroughly. When he got to the nipple this time, a soft cry was wrenched from her. His hand stilled, fingers on her hard nipple. She arched her back to press herself against his touch, and he responded with gentle pressure. Too gentle. And then he swore softly and moved his hand away.

"Don't stop," she whispered. She opened her eyes, met his, and saw a flicker of desire in his velvet-brown gaze. "You may take me if you like."

His eyes flared wider, slid down her body again, and he licked his lips.

"It's been a very long time since a man's touch has felt the way yours does," she whispered. "We're both adults, Matthew."

He turned his head away from her, forcing his eyes elsewhere. "As I said before, you're in no condition to know what you want right now."

She set her jaw, and with a deep growl, tore free of the fabric that bound her wrists. "To hell with you, then."

He looked back quickly, eyes sharp on her. She thought he expected another attack. But what kind, she wondered. Was he afraid she would kill him or ravage him? Then she looked at his eyes, and she knew he wasn't afraid. Not at all. He stood there expectantly, watching her, and waiting. Fully ready to deal with whatever she might attempt to do.

She narrowed her eyes on him. "This woman I remind you of," she said softly. "She was your lover?"

"She was my wife."

"And you wronged her in some way?" she asked, certain that he had. It was the only explanation for his having shown any tendency at all toward kindness to her—the only reason he hadn't throttled her by now, or tossed her back into the sea where he'd found her. And the only reason he hadn't taken her up on her offer of sex. Guilt. She could smell it on him.

He was stone silent for a long moment, and then, his face stark, he said, "I killed her."

Chapter 4

Night fell, and the strange woman slept. He sat in a chair beside the bed and wondered what the hell he was going to do with her. She didn't look *exactly* like Gabriella, he mused as he studied her face. In fact, the more time he spent with her, the more different she seemed. Gabriella had been fragile, and frail. She'd been clingy and dependent. She'd been hollow and empty inside. She'd been quiet and shy.

Puabi was the opposite in every way. She was fire to Gabriella's ice. She was technicolor to Gabriella's pastel. She was aggression, and sexuality and danger.

Hell, the two women looked less alike by the second.

She dreamed. She hadn't dreamed in so long, she couldn't even remember the last time. She'd thought once, that perhaps when one became immortal, one lost the ability to dream. But she'd never been sure.

The dream was not a good one. She was floating, tossed up and sucked down by the icy sea. Gods, she was so cold. It was as if she would never be warm again. And it was getting colder. She spun, caught as if in a whirlpool, sucked deeper and deeper into the frigid hubs of the sea. And then she was floating there, freely floating, not struggling to breathe. The water looked like sky. The fish, like stars, and she was no longer certain where she was. Around her, she saw other forms floating. Faint, misty shapes, some more distinct than others. And she wondered who they were.

Souls. The word whispered in her mind. *I'm in the Hall of Souls.*

Blinking, she tried to see them more closely, but this damn blurred vision wouldn't allow it. She realized she was in the Devil's Triangle. And somehow, she was seeing things that were not real.

But they are real, that voice said in her mind. And she realized suddenly it was not her own voice. Not some inner knowing. It was coming from without.

"It's not real," she cried aloud, but her words were only bubbles in the waters. "I don't have a soul."

You gave it up, Puabi. You gave it up when you made yourself into one of the Dark Ones. But now you'll have the chance to get it back again.

"How?" she asked, breathless, desperate, close to death.

You have a mission, Puabi. A job to do.

"What?"

Suddenly she was being pulled upward again, spiraling back to the surface before she'd received her answer. "No! No, not yet! Not yet! You have to tell me what I have to do! What am I supposed to do?"

"All right, all right, it's okay."

"No, no, no." She was shaking, freezing, shivering so hard her teeth chattered. And then he was beside her, around her, holding her to him. Gods, he was strong, and warm. His chest was firm and his arms powerful. He wouldn't let her fall into that cold sea again. He wouldn't.

Slowly his warmth seeped into her, and she stopped shivering. But his arms never eased their grip. "I loved you so much once. Why couldn't you love me?" she whispered, her voice weak, breaking. "All I ever wanted was for you to love me."

She felt him stiffen against her, and for a moment she wondered if she was speaking to Natum or to the stranger, Matthew. But it made no sense. She'd never loved Matthew. She snuggled closer and fell into a deep, dreamless sleep. Once she heard him speak to her softly, but she couldn't respond. "Who the hell are you?" he whispered. "Where did you come from?"

(Dhen Puabi woke, there was sienna-colored light infusing the place with a muted glow. She studied it, wondering why she felt there was something she had to do today. A . . . mission. Something . . . there had been a dream . . . or was it a memory?

Warmth, heaviness, against her and around her.

Matthew.

She rolled over carefully. The man, the stranger who had pulled her from the very mouth of death, was holding her close to him. He lay on his side, facing her now, his mouth only inches from hers. His legs were entwined with hers, and his arms held her close. It was as if she were his beloved.

She almost laughed, a bitterness welling up in her belly. To think that she could ever be that important to anyone. It had taken her more than forty lifetimes to finally figure it out. No one would ever love her. And why in hell would they? She closed her eyes as the memories of the things she had done came crashing in upon her like waves on the shore.

Why? What the hell was the matter with her? After all this time, had she suddenly developed a conscience? Gods, it made no sense! What was happening to her?

Lips touched her mouth. Lightly, very softly. A hand gently cupped her head, fingers sinking into her hair. His mouth was warm, and moist, and tender as it tasted hers. Oh, God, it felt good to be kissed by a man this way. She parted her lips and kissed him back. His arms tightened around her, and she slid hers around his waist, hands splayed on his muscular back. The kiss deepened then, as he came slowly awake. He moaned, and his tongue slid into her mouth to taste deeply, as if she were some luscious confection that he craved. He licked at her mouth, suckled her tongue, fed on her lips, and she relished every second of it.

And then he drew away and opened his eyes. Fiery eyes, passion-filled. His voice gruff, tense, he whispered, "Tell me your name."

"Puabi," she said. "I'm Puabi."

He nodded, closing his eyes slowly. Then he rolled over and sat up in the bed, lowering his feet to the floor, holding his head in his hands. "You said something last night. In your sleep. You said, 'Why couldn't you love me?'"

She closed her eyes. "I don't know why I even care."

His head came up slowly, but he didn't face her. "About who?"

Swallowing hard, sensing he had a reason for asking that went beyond anything obvious, she saw no harm in speaking of it, even though she recalled feeling confusion at the time—naturally there was only one man she could have been speaking to in her troubled sleep. "My husband. Natum—Nathan is the name he uses now. He never loved me. Every time I needed him, he was with his lover. When I lost our child, when I was left for dead in that burning house, when I was swept away by the sea. All he could think of was her."

Matthew turned slowly, a look of pain etched on his hard face. "You lost a child."

She lowered her head. "A son. Stillborn." Her heart constricted. "It destroyed me."

"I'm sorry. And . . . sorry about your husband, too."

"Don't be. I've wasted far too much time fighting for a man who never wanted me."

"You deserve better."

She closed her eyes. "I deserve exactly what I got. You don't know me, Matthew. I'm . . . evil."

He looked down at her, his eyes intense—she didn't have a clue as to why he always seemed so intense when he looked at her. But it wasn't the first time she had noticed it. "He did that to you, and you think you're the one who's evil?"

"You don't know the whole of it."

"I don't want to know the whole of it," he said, walking to a chair and picking up some clothes she hadn't seen before. A pair of shorts with a drawstring and an oversized tank top. He handed them to her. "Do you feel up to breakfast?" he asked, changing the subject.

She nodded, sitting up in the bed. "The more I eat, the faster I'll mend."

He let his eyes move down her body, and a frown darkened his brow. "You mend any faster and I'll wonder if you're even human."

She glanced down at her chest, where he was looking. The scratches she'd put there herself were completely healed. And her skin looked as smooth as a newborn's.

"Yesterday you were burned so badly you were blistered. Today your skin looks as if it's never even seen the sun."

Puabi shrugged. "Who knew aloe was so powerful?"

She felt his eyes on her, probing, so she forced herself to meet his steady gaze head-on. He knew she wasn't telling him something. And she knew he knew it. "Matthew—there are things about me that you are better off not knowing. For now, suffice it to say that I'm not like other women."

"I'd figured that much out, Poppy."

She lifted her eyes to his. "Why do you call me that?"

Matthew shrugged, getting to his feet. "Puabi is a mouthful. Poppy—suits you. Beautiful. Deadly. Mysterious. Occasionally mind-boggling and quite possibly addictive." He said it playfully, teasingly, but there was a serious undertone to his words.

He inclined his head and led the way out of the room. She quickly pulled on the makeshift clothing he'd brought to her and followed him, relieved that he didn't push her for any more information.

The living area of the villa was huge, and took up most of the front of the place. Wicker furniture was scattered sparsely in the high-ceilinged rooms beneath giant fans that spun in perpetual slow motion. The place was not all that large or fancy, but you could feel the money behind it all the same. It took wealth to make a place look this casual. This comfortable. This effortless.

"The kitchen's this way," he said. "What would you like for breakfast?"

"What do you have?"

"Everything," he said, leading her through to a smaller room equipped with spotless white appliances. Marble tiles lined the walls and the floor. "I had a full supply flown in so I wouldn't have to leave until I was ready."

She narrowed her eyes on him. "Just how long have you been out here?"

He looked away. "Two, almost three months."

"Alone? All this time?"

His shrug pretended to be careless. "For the most part."

"Why?"

He didn't answer her. "Bacon and eggs sound good?"

"Sounds fine."

He nodded and turned to the refrigerator. Left with nothing to do but wait, Puabi wandered back into the living room, and then she caught sight of something so surprising that she made some sound of alarm without meaning to.

Matthew came to her, asking what was wrong. Then he followed her gaze to the photograph that hung on the wall and swore softly. "I'm sorry. I forgot it was there," he said.

"My God, who is she?"

Drawing a breath, he sighed deeply. "Gabriella. My wife."

Puabi stepped closer, eyes riveted. "She could be my twin. No wonder you look at me the way you do." Turning to him, she saw the pain in his face, in his eyes. "You loved her very much."

"No," he said. "I should have loved her. But I didn't. And she died because of it."

Frowning, she tilted her head to one side. "She's the reason you're out here, hiding away from the world? Because you should have loved her, and didn't? How could that kill a person?" Then she blinked slowly. "Was it suicide, Matthew?"

He met her eyes and she knew she was right. "I'm not a good person, Poppy. I'll tell you that much. I'm a bastard, to be honest. A lot like your own husband, I imagine, which makes it even more ironic that you ended up here. Only in my case, it wasn't another woman I preferred over my own wife. It was my business, and my freedom."

She shook her head. "I don't believe you. My husband was relieved by my death—or, my presumed death. You . . . you've exiled yourself from life to come here and grieve for her. It's not the same at all."

"No? Well, she's just as dead, Poppy. And so is the child she was carrying." He spun on his heel and returned to the kitchen.

Puabi let him go, her knees trembling so much she had to sit down in a big wicker chair before she fell down. Her gaze was drawn irresistibly back to the photograph of the woman who was her mirror image except that her eyes were black as night. Ebony eyes that, for a moment, seemed to stare right back at her. "Gabriella," she whispered. "A child. Gods, a child." Her own pain, old, but so very sharp still, cut again into her heart and clutched tight in her barren womb. Nothing had ever hurt her so much as losing her baby, so long ago. Nothing ever would. It had been the end for her. Part of her had died with her tiny stillborn son.

Gabriella's face was softer than Puabi's. The lines of jaw and cheekbone, less harsh and drawn. And her eyes were jet, while Puabi's were blue with flecks of gold.

Puabi stared at her, anger rising up. "You're nothing like me," she whispered. "I'd have given anything to save my child. If you were anything like me you couldn't possibly have taken yours with you into death."

Pans banged in the kitchen, and Puabi looked that way. Matthew was hiding here, punishing himself for not loving his wife. How could he blame himself for that? You couldn't force yourself to feel something that simply wasn't there.

She lowered her head, bit her lip. By the Gods, neither could Natum.

Oh, what the hell is this? I'm feeling sorry for Natum now? I'm pitying him and understanding why he wronged me so? What the hell is this?

Why couldn't she have stayed the way she was? Hating, raging against everything and everyone, acting without conscience or consequence, despising her husband and his lover for betraying her. It had served her well for more than four thousand years. Why should it begin to change now?

One thing was sure. No matter how many deaths Matthew Fairchild claimed—he couldn't come close to the blood that stained her hands.

Smells reached her from the kitchen. Coffee. Bacon. They made her stomach growl. Then there was something else that distracted her from those smells. A sound, like a deep, droning buzz, that grew louder. She rushed to the window and looked out to see a small yellow airplane descending on the island.

Chapter 5

"What the hell is she thinking?" Matthew hurried to the doorway when he heard the familiar sound of the pontoon plane's motors. Poppy was there ahead of him.

"Who is it?" She looked nervous.

He opened the door impatiently.

"Matthew, give me my dagger."

Frowning, he looked at her. "You expecting some kind of attack, Poppy?"

Licking her lips, she averted her eyes. "You never know."

He took her hand in his and started for the door. They were outside and halfway down the path by the time he realized he was still holding it. It had been an impulse, grabbing her hand that way. It had been automatic. And it still felt right, her small hand in his. He stopped walking, looked down at their joined hands, then at her face.

She met his eyes briefly. Something unspoken moved between them, some palpable, electrical charge. And he didn't know what the hell it was, but he decided not to let go. Then her eyes seemed to shutter themselves, as if in defense, and she tugged her hand free. "I'm not Gabriella," she told him.

"I know that."

"Do you?"

He felt his lips quirk upward at the corners. Not a smile, but close to one. "If you'd ever met her, you wouldn't ask, Poppy."

"It's Puabi."

She was still damned bristly. Almost hostile. He had yet to figure out why, but then again, he hadn't figured out anything about her. How she managed to heal at the speed of sound being at the top of the list. And now was not the time. He turned and continued to lead the way. The path was a winding one, shaded by palms even on the brightest days. This was not one of those. It was damned ominous outside today. Still. Utterly still, with that odd heaviness to the brick-tinted atmosphere.

They emerged from the trees near the horseshoe-shaped inlet where the yellow pontoon plane was just now skiing to a halt. He stopped where he was and waited for the engines to shut down, the hatch to open. Finally, Murial hopped out onto the pontoon nearest her. She reached up to close the hatch, then turned and stepped off the floating ski and onto the sand.

Matthew waved and moved toward her, and when she caught sight of him she waved back, but then she froze, her hand in midair, her eyes fixed on a spot beyond him.

He glanced sideways, but Puabi wasn't there. She'd stopped walking a few steps back and stood now staring at Murial.

"What's wrong?" he asked. "Come on, it's all right. She's a friend of mine."

Poppy met his eyes. "A friend?"

He nodded. "Murial works for me. Has for years. I'd trust her with my life."

Her eyes narrowed on his. "And I suppose you think that means I ought to trust her with mine?"

"Come on, Poppy. Look at her." Murial was willowy, pale, and with her ready smile not at all menacing or frightening.

Puabi breathed slowly. She still seemed exceedingly wary. "All right, then. If you trust her."

"I do." He started forward again, and this time she came with him. When they reached the point where Murial stood, they found her gaping. Murial was tall and slender as a reed, with long, perfectly straight blond hair and the sun-kissed face of a girl half her age. Pale lashes and brows, light blue eyes, a killer smile. She wasn't smiling now, though. She looked stunned, and Matthew felt a twinge in his gut. He should've left Poppy behind at the villa, so he could have prepared Murial for her appearance.

"It's okay, Murial," he said softly. Waves lapped against the pontoons, making slapping sounds. Other than that there was dead silence.

"But . . . but how . . . how could she . . . ?"

He reached out and clasped Murial's hands in his. "This is Puabi," he said. "Not Gabriella. Although I understand your reaction. Mine was pretty much the same."

The woman frowned, her eyes dragging themselves away from Puabi to meet his. "My God, the resemblance is . . . but what's she doing here, Matthew?"

"I'm stranded here," Puabi answered. Matthew knew by her tone, regal and impatient, that she resented Murial's asking him instead of her. "Until the storm passes."

Murial looked at her, studied her, her gaze intense.

"Exactly," Matthew said. "And speaking of the storm, what the hell were you thinking coming out here today, Murial? Do you know what a risk you're taking?"

She seemed to shake herself out of her inspection of Puabi. "I come out with the weekly reports every Friday."

"But the storm could have kicked up while you were in the air."

"It didn't," she replied.

"It wasn't worth the risk."

She rolled her eyes. "You're as overprotective as always, I see." Then she slipped her arms around him, hugged him gently. "How are you, Matthew?"

"Better," he said. And he glanced at Poppy and realized he wasn't lying about it. He'd given Murial the same reply every Friday for more than two months now, and this was the first time it had actually been true.

Poppy had something to do with that. He wasn't sure what. Maybe she'd just given him something else to think about besides his own guilt. Right now, though, Poppy looked even bitchier than usual.

Murial released him, and he said, "Let's get you back to the house. We were just about to have some breakfast."

"Great. You know I never turn down a meal."

You wouldn't know it to look at her, he thought idly. "Murial is my executive assistant," he told Poppy as they headed back along the path to the villa. "But she's more than that, too. Frankly, I don't know how I'd have made it through the last few months without her." He shook his head slowly. "I couldn't have left the business to anyone else. I'd have had to stay myself."

"Are you sure that would have been a bad thing?" Puabi asked.

Her tone startled him, and he shot her a look. "I needed to get away, to grieve in private, and try to heal. It was Murial who made me see that, and by stepping in for me, she gave me the means to do it."

Puabi sent Murial a saccharine smile. "You must be a very kind and generous soul."

Murial's expression was just as sweet, though more genuine, Matthew thought. "I care a great deal about Matthew."

"And Gabriella, no doubt," Puabi put in.

Murial nodded. "I was her best friend."

Puabi glanced pointedly at Murial's hand, which was on Matthew's shoulder, and said, "I can see that."

Whoa, what the hell was up here? He could feel the tension emanating from Puabi, and she was definitely firing rounds at Murial, but he wasn't sure why. He picked up the pace, and the two women kept up.

"I apologize for staring at you back there," Murial said after a moment. "You look so much like her—I thought I was seeing a ghost at first."

"Real people are far more frightening than ghosts," Puabi replied, and the words had an undertone that was almost threatening.

Back at the villa, the moment Murial went into the bathroom to wash up, Matthew took Puabi by the arm and drew her into the kitchen, closing the door behind them.

"You don't like her," he said. "Why?"

"I don't like anyone," she responded.

"You like me."

Her gaze raked him. "You're confused, Matthew. I have a compelling urge to have every imaginable form of sex with you. Repeatedly. That does not mean I like you."

His throat was suddenly very dry. To have her put it so bluntly . . . hell.

Poppy smiled wickedly at him. "I've rendered you speechless?"

He shook his head and tried not to visualize her words quite so clearly in his mind. But for a moment all he could see was a vision of tangled, sweaty limbs, and moist lips, and . . . hell. "I just want to know why you took such an instant dislike to Murial." He frowned then as a thought occurred to him. "Is it . . . jealousy?"

She tipped her head to one side. "I suppose it could be some form of that. But if it is, it's based on simple animal instincts. I haven't had my fill of you yet, so I resent the competition of another female." She seemed to mull that over for a moment. "Yes, that could be it."

He closed his eyes. "Murial is not interested in me in that way. Gabriella was never the least bit threatened by her."

"Gabriella was a naive, trusting, needy little girl."

He frowned, hard. "How do you know that?"

Blinking, Puabi looked at the floor and shook her head. "I'm not sure. I just do. I knew it as soon as I saw her photo." Lifting her eyes, she said, "Am I right?"

"Yes. About Gabriella, at least."

"About Murial, too. I don't know what she wants from you, Matthew. Whether it's the same thing I do or not. But regardless, she wants something. And whatever it is, she's not telling you. I dislike games and hidden motivations. I prefer people who say what they mean and mean what they say. Even an honest enemy is preferable to a dishonest ally."

He turned away from her, faced the food that was even now cooling in its pans on the stove. "You're honest, I'll give you that." He reached to the cupboard over his head, and took three plates down, then turned and handed them to her. "Here, put these on the table, will you?"

She lifted her brows, looking down at the plates with disdain.

"Oh, come on, don't give me the royalty routine. You're obviously feeling better. So pull your weight." He put the plates in her hands, and as she carried them out of the room, he tried very hard to erase the images she had painted in his mind. She wasn't delirious anymore. She wasn't sick or feverish or in shock. And she openly admitted to wanting to—how had she put it?—have every imaginable form of sex with him. Repeatedly. But she didn't like him.

Hell, did he really care? He didn't like her all that much either.

The lovely, lithe Murial spent most of the morning ensconced in a sitting room with Matthew, on the pretense of discussing business. Puabi listened at the door a few times, and each time she did, that was precisely what they were doing. Discussing business.

Maybe she'd been wrong about the woman. Murial seemed kind, concerned. She spoke softly, smiled easily.

But how was she, Puabi, to believe she could be mistaken about the woman? She'd been the ruler of Ur, most powerful city-state of Sumer. She did not make mistakes.

She used the time when she was left alone to snoop through Matthew's villa, where he had come to lick his wounds after his young wife's death. At Murial's urging, Puabi reminded herself. Interesting. It wasn't a large house, but every inch was spotless, neat, organized. No television or radio anywhere to be found, other than the shortwave radio she located in a small room in the back. She couldn't have operated the thing if she'd wanted to, and had no interest in it anyway. What did interest her were the items she found in the bottommost drawer of the stand on which the radio rested.

Inside were things she knew instinctively had belonged to the dead Gabriella. Photographs of her with Matthew on their wedding day. Clippings announcing the marriage. A dark, blurry ultrasound printout, showing the tiny pollywog-shaped fetus she had carried.

Something hot stabbed at Puabi's belly.

At the very bottom of the drawer there was a diary.

Puabi reached for it, then hesitated, her hand hovering a hairsbreadth from the tiny book. She glanced behind her, into the hallway, but no sounds reached her. Matthew was still occupied with Murial. She would have time.

She picked the diary up, opened it, and began to read. And very soon, she was engrossed. All sense of time deserted her as she fell into the pages, because the story that unfolded on those pages could easily have been her own. The only difference was that Gabriella had grieved while Puabi had raged. Gabriella had given up where Puabi had fought. Gabriella, in the end, turned her pain inward. Puabi had turned hers outward, unleashing it on everyone she encountered.

As she closed the book, Puabi was stunned to feel dampness flooding her eyes. She lifted a hand, touched her fingertip to her cheek, and drew them away staring in disbelief at the teardrop she had caught. She was even more stunned to hear Matthew's deep voice from the doorway, saying softly, sadly, "So now you know."

chapter 6

꧁꧂

She looked up quickly, no doubt startled to have been caught red-handed with his most private possessions. No matter. It seemed perfectly logical to Matthew that Puabi would find and read Gabriella's diary. He felt almost as if he'd expected it.

What he hadn't expected was to see tears on her face.

She dashed them away with an angry swipe of her hand and got to her feet. "I'm sorry. I . . . couldn't help myself."

He nodded. "I didn't think any sad story would be enough to melt that hard, practical heart of yours, Poppy. But it looks like Gabriella's did."

She shook her head slowly, then turned and tucked the book back into the drawer. "Not her story. Mine."

"Yours?"

She faced him again, sliding the drawer closed. "Almost word for word."

He glanced behind him, into the hallway. He'd left Murial in the study, where she'd been making notes of his instructions for the coming week. She would be busy for a moment. And this was a side of the mysterious Puabi that he hadn't yet seen. He wanted to probe it—in private. He closed the door softly, then turned to face her again, and he said, "Tell me."

She shook her head slowly.

"Come on, Poppy, you owe me. You violated my privacy. You read my dead wife's most intimate thoughts. You know my worst secrets. Now tell me yours."

He saw her face change, saw the capitulation there. He hadn't expected that either, not without more persuasion than he had yet applied. Maybe . . . maybe she needed to talk it out as much as he needed to hear it.

He watched her sink back into the chair where she'd been sitting. Her eyes focused not on his, but on some spot beyond the wall. "You already know most of it," she said, her tone gruff. "My story is Gabriella's. I married a man as a matter of convenience. Although in my case, unlike Gabriella's, it wasn't a one-night stand or an accidental pregnancy. It was a treaty between nations. But the results were the same. I fell in love. He didn't. Not with me, at least. And it wasn't enough for me."

He nodded, not moving from his spot, afraid to jar her out of this revealing mood. "He was a fool, then. As much a fool as I was."

"No, Matthew. He couldn't force himself to feel something he didn't. No more than you could. I see that now. I just . . . I don't know why I didn't see it then." She drew her focus back in, from wherever it had been. She looked at him now. And her eyes were clear and sharp. "I think what pushed me beyond the edge of my endurance was the day I lost our son. He was stillborn while my husband was out searching for his mistress. I just couldn't forgive him. After that, hating came easily to me. I made it my life's work, in fact."

Sighing deeply, Matthew moved toward her, unable to stop himself. He reached down to brush a tear from her cheek with his thumb. "I'm sorry, Poppy. Losing a child—that's a hurt no one should ever have to know."

"On that we agree."

"Obviously the outcome was different for you than for Gabriella. You're still alive."

She nodded. "For now."

"What's that supposed to mean?" He tried to search her face, but she lowered her head. Matthew dropped to one knee and pushed her hair aside, trying to read her.

She refused to look at him, and changed the subject. "Gabriella's response to rejection was despair. Mine was rage. I lashed out against them—my husband, his lover. In the end, they escaped un-scathed and my rage rebounded like a boomerang, coming back to harm only me. The house burned. I was trapped inside, and they left me there, left me for dead."

"How did you manage to escape?" he asked, his gut churning be-cause he sensed that every word she spoke was true.

She shook her head. "I don't know. Something in me made me keep fighting. I dragged myself out of the fire, to the cliffs, and fell into the sea. I honestly didn't expect I'd ever emerge again. Not alive." Looking deeply into his eyes, she said, "And the rest you know."

He nodded slowly. Then he swallowed hard and decided to say what he was thinking. She'd been bluntly honest with him, after all. "It . . . has crossed my mind that you didn't end up here by accident. That maybe you're . . . some kind of chance at redemption for me."

"*Me?* Your *redemption?*" She smiled bitterly. "No, Matthew."

"I couldn't save Gabriella. But I could save you."

She shook her head again. "By saving my life, you cursed hu-mankind to suffer my existence a bit longer."

"Don't say that, Poppy. It's bullshit and you know it. You're no more evil than I am."

She looked as if she were about to argue, but stopped herself. "Tell me what happened to Gabriella. I feel . . . I feel as if I know her, somehow."

Drawing a breath, he sighed deeply, rose to his feet. He couldn't get through this if he had to look her in the face. Instead, he paced a few steps away as he spoke. "It was a one-night stand. She worked in the mail room, and she caught my eye. I had too much to drink one night and . . ." He sighed. "She got pregnant. I married her. I said it was because of a takeover in progress with a Christian book pub-lisher whose owners placed a high value on morality. But, hell, it wasn't that. There was something about her that just—I don't know—drew me." Looking at the floor, he paused for a moment. "I didn't intend to, but I became . . . fond of her. She was such a tender thing. So needy. She took my kindness for more than it was and began to imagine a happy ending for us. We'd agreed to a quiet divorce once the child was born. I'd promised her a generous settlement. She knew I would provide for her and the baby. I thought it would be enough."

"And it wasn't," Puabi said.

Having reached the far end of the room, he turned. "No. It wasn't enough. She confessed her love for me one night, told me she didn't want to go through with the plan. I was shocked . . . I reacted badly. Reminded her she'd signed an agreement."

Puabi closed her eyes, gave a little sigh.

"I know, I know. She was furious. We argued, and she took the car and left. I was going to go after her, but Murial called with a business emergency. She convinced me to give Gabriella time to calm down, and talk to her later, when we were both more settled."

"But later never came."

He met Poppy's eyes. "No. She drove the car off the road and over an embankment. It plunged eighty feet to the ground. The gas tank exploded and . . ." He looked at the floor as the memory of what had remained of his naive little wife floated through his mind.

Puabi came to him, and her hands curled over his shoulders. Her breath fanned his face when she spoke. "I'm sorry, Matthew."

"So am I. Sorry I wasted so much time. I could have had a devoted wife who loved me unconditionally. I could have had my child, safe and healthy and wonderful. Instead, I have my precious freedom and my all-important business." Lifting his head, he met her eyes. "And I don't give a damn about either of them anymore."

Their gazes locked. He saw the pain in hers, and recognized it. Knowing its source made it even more powerful to him. And she drew him suddenly, like a magnet. He leaned nearer. Her eyes fell closed, those thick lashes caressing her cheeks. And her lips parted expectantly. He closed his hands on her waist and bent his head. His mouth brushed over hers, and he could feel her breath on his lips.

"Matthew?" a voice called.

Jerking his head up quickly, he glanced toward the door. Then he looked at Poppy. She lowered her head and turned her back on him. One hand was pressed to her forehead, the other, braced on the nearby table.

"Are you all right?"

She nodded, but didn't face him.

"Poppy, what is it?" He clasped her shoulders from behind, felt them trembling just slightly. Was this a reaction to that almost kiss? It seemed like far more.

She stiffened her spine and turned to face him with a smile painted on her face. "I'm fine."

The door opened. Murial stood there, looking from one of them to the other with innocently curious blue eyes.

"I'm ready to head back," Murial said. "See you next Friday?"

Matthew turned, forced his attention on his friend. "Oh, no, you're not."

Murial frowned at him. "What do you—"

"You're staying right here, Murial. It's already late enough that you'd be flying in the dark, and that storm could easily hit before morning. I'm going to have to insist that you stay. And when you do go back . . . Poppy and I will be hitching a ride."

Murial's eyes flared wider. "You . . . but, Matthew, you aren't ready."

"I wasn't." He looked at Poppy and she met his eyes. "I think maybe I am now. Either way, it's time."

Paabi wasn't sure what brought on the rush of weakness that nearly put her on her knees when Matthew had been about to kiss her. Or what brought on the other feelings. Feelings that were utterly foreign to her. Her heart had twisted for Gabriella. And she'd felt Matthew's pain as well. Why? How could she feel for him when he'd treated his wife almost exactly the way her own husband had treated her? And when she'd anticipated his kiss, it hadn't been animal hunger alone burning in her. It had been something more. Something she . . . and her kind . . . did not feel. Were incapable of feeling—or so she had always believed.

The rush of dizziness that had followed, though, that was physical. Her legs had turned to water, her stomach had knotted up, and she would have fallen if she hadn't had the table for support.

Whatever it was, it passed quickly enough. But it left her weak and shaken. And wondering just how much life remained in her. If she suffered another mortal death—would she revive again? Or had she used every life she had ever stolen, during her endless months at sea?

They sat outside that night. Despite the storm so nearby, the sky was clear, and stars dotted it everywhere. Matthew had suggested a walk along the beach, since Puabi hadn't seen much of the island yet, and so the three of them walked barefoot in the sand between the shore and the villa. It honestly was beautiful here, Puabi thought. Like a small, lush oasis in a vast desert. Only the desert was sea.

"What's that?" she asked, pointing to a charred circle in the sand.

"They used to build bonfires there, I think."

"They?"

"The people I bought the island from."

"But you never have?" Puabi asked.

Murial clapped a hand over her own mouth to stifle a bark of laughter, but it escaped anyway. Matthew looked at her. "What?"

"Just the image of you, Mr. Tycoon, building a bonfire . . ." She shrugged. "Then again, I wouldn't have pictured you walking barefoot in the sand, either."

"No. Neither would I a short while ago."

Murial's smile turned softer. "This place is good for you, Matthew. It's healing you, I can see it."

"And I have you to thank for that."

A twinge of something that might have been jealousy nipped at Puabi's gut when Matthew reached out a hand to touch Murial's face. But it was brief. He dropped his hand to his side again quickly and said, "Let's build a fire."

"You're kidding," Murial said, and she shot Puabi a smiling look of disbelief. "He's kidding, isn't he?"

"Sit, both of you. I'll do the honors."

Puabi shrugged and looked around, spotting a hollow log that looked as if it had served as a bench in times past. She walked to it and sat, surprised when Murial sat on the other end. Matthew hurried into the woods, and came back moments later with an armload of twigs, dried leaves, and other debris. Then he vanished again, and returned with more sticks, larger ones. He arranged the kindling as carefully as if he were building a bridge, then headed back for more wood.

"A few weeks ago, I was afraid he would never bounce back," Murial said softly.

"It's like you said—the island is good for him."

Murial tilted her head to one side. "Maybe you're what's good for him."

Blinking in surprise, Puabi searched the woman's face. "I'm surprised to hear you say that."

"Why?"

A soft breeze kicked in from the sea, and Murial's blond locks danced in its touch. Puabi studied her face and saw nothing sinister there. "I guess I thought . . . you might have some romantic interest in him yourself."

"No, Puabi. I don't. I work for him. And I care for him, but only as a friend. Obviously, though, things are different between the two of you."

Puabi shook her head. "They can't be."

"Why not?" Murial asked.

Looking out toward the sea, Puabi was silent for a moment. The moon was just rising now, far out over the distant edge of the water. It sent silver ripples toward them. "There are reasons," she said at last.

Murial sighed, nodding to herself. "Puabi, you care about him. I can see that much." Puabi met the woman's eyes, but didn't reply. "Try to talk him into spending just a little more time out here. You don't know what he was like before. I was afraid for his life, I truly was. He'll listen to you. He needs more time. He's not ready to face those memories—not yet."

Before she could reply, Matthew was back, carrying logs this time. He arranged them near the fire and finally searched his pockets for a match. Murial got to her feet and offered him a lighter.

"Always prepared for anything," he said. "Aren't you?"

"I try to be," she told him.

Matthew knelt down and lit the fire.

chapter 7

Puabi was in Matthew's bed. She'd realized that only today. It was where he'd put her that first night, and where she'd been ever since, despite the fact that there was a guest room in the house. She knew there was, because that was where Murial was spending the night. Matthew had taken the sofa. She wondered about that. His putting her in his own room that first night, rather than the guest room. What did it mean? Or did it mean anything at all?

Better question, she thought, suddenly scowling into the darkness, *why the hell do I care?* She was not the sort of woman who spent her time musing over a man's motivations. Then again, she wasn't an empathic sort, either, most of the time. But there was no question she was feeling empathy for Matthew's suffering, and for that of the ill-fated Gabriella. Gods, Gabriella. She couldn't seem to go five minutes without thinking of the woman, seeing her in her mind's eye, like a younger, sweeter, innocent version of herself. Like a little sister.

"Sickening," she muttered, rolling over and punching the pillow into a more comfortable shape. And her mind was so occupied with all of these new and inexplicable feelings, that she was sure she was missing something else. Something vital. Her powers were weak, yes, but not gone. She sensed something afoot here. Unseen forces were stirring in the astral. Magick was at work. She could feel it, almost taste it in the air. But she couldn't identify it or pinpoint its source, much less its intent or nature. It was more an inkling on her part. A static charge and a whisper she couldn't quite hear.

What did it all mean?

She tossed and turned for hours, and when she finally did begin to drift off, it was only to be shaken awake again by that ghostly memory—or was it a vision? She was in the water, and the water turned to sky, and someone had spoken to her in a voice that sounded like her own—told her she had a mission, a job to do.

Sitting up in bed, shivering and sweating at once, she pressed her hand to her forehead, closed her eyes on hot tears. "What is it?" she whispered. Gods, her stomach was churning, her head awash in questions. "What the hell am I supposed to be doing?"

But no answer came. She listened, looked for signs, and heard only the soft whisper of the wind on palm fronds outside, and the occasional cry of a night bird.

Sighing, she flung the covers aside, and rose from the bed naked, warm, welcoming the kiss of that dark breeze coming in through the open windows. A walk, she thought idly. To clear her head. She pulled on Matthew's white cotton robe, cinched the sash at her waist, and padded quietly out of the bedroom and through the villa. She tiptoed through the living room, careful not to disturb Matthew, who she assumed was curled beneath the mound of blankets on the sofa. The door didn't squeak when she pulled it open, thank goodness. And then she was outside.

Closing her eyes, she hurried away from the house, along the path through the lush growth. Most of the plants were foreign to her. She heard scurrying in the brush and wondered what sorts of animals dwelled here. And then she didn't care. She emerged on the beach and stood there for a long time where the waves washed in, lapping around her ankles, covering her feet, muddying the sand that oozed between her toes. The breeze here was stiffer, cooler, invigorating somehow. She found herself closing her eyes, opening her arms to it. As if in response it blew harder, buffeting her body, tousling her hair. It was damp, that wind. It kissed her face with moisture, tasted of salt and seawater.

"What am I doing here?" she whispered. Opening her eyes, she searched the distance, the dark sea, and the black velvet sky. Its starry face was streaked with dark, clawlike fingers of cloud. "I don't understand."

"Maybe you're not supposed to."

The voice, soft and deep, came from very close to her, and she didn't need to turn to recognize it. Matthew's hands curled around her waist, and he drew her backward until her body pressed to his. "Maybe it doesn't matter."

Her head tipped back against his shoulder, and he bent his, so his lips touched her neck lightly, softly, then lingered there.

"There's some reason, Matthew," she whispered. "You were right about that. None of this is coincidence, and I should know . . ."

His whiskers rasped over her sensitive skin, and she sucked in a breath.

"Right now," he said. "There's only right now. This moment. What came before, what comes later, those things don't exist."

"But they do—"

"Not if we say they don't. Try, Poppy. We deserve this moment. We need it."

She did try. She felt the waves wash over her feet, and as they retreated, she imagined them taking time itself away with them. Her past, her crimes, the blood that stained her hands, all washed out to sea. Yes. Gods, yes, to be free of all of it.

She broke away from Matthew, running forward until the depth stopped her. The white robe dragged, wet and heavy, and still she moved forward, dragging her legs through the cooling water, deeper and deeper. The water reached her chest, and a wave broke over her head, soaking her and driving her to her knees. Then it surged back, lifting her, tugging her into its embrace.

But there were other hands. Human hands. Matthew's hands and his arms locked around her. His body melded tight to hers, and his mouth claimed hers. The tide washed back out to sea without her. She was anchored to him. And he was carrying her toward the shore, carrying her in his arms, kissing her, and there was nothing else. There was only here and now. This moment, just as he had said.

She clung to him, tasted the seawater in his kiss, and more. Her fingers tangled in his wet hair as he dropped to his knees in the sand. Still kissing her, he laid her down, and stared down at her hungrily, eyes blazing, as he untied the sash and flung the robe open wide. Then he bent over her and drank every drop of seawater from her skin, kissing her dry. It seemed to Puabi that his lips left fire in their wake, heating her flesh beyond endurance.

Then rising above her, he looked deeply into her eyes. "Don't love me," he said. "I don't deserve to be loved. I destroy what loves me."

"Don't love me," she told him in return. "I destroy all that I touch. And I will break your heart in the end if you let me."

He held her eyes for a long moment, and when he kissed her again, any hint of restraint washed away in with the waves that ebbed and flowed around them. Puabi pushed at his jeans, until he helped her to strip them away. And then he bent over her, nursing at her breasts, one, then the other. She arched toward him as his mouth moved over her body, in a useless effort to quench the fires he'd ignited in her skin, her belly, her thighs. And when he tasted more of her, she twisted her fingers into his hair and held on. The wet sand was cool beneath her back. The water washed over them in an ever more urgent rush. His hot mouth, demanding and hungry, fed at her. Pressing her wider, he delved inside with his tongue, sucking at her as if she were a ripe fruit oozing juices he craved. He pinched gently, deliciously, with his teeth, as if he could squeeze out more, then lapped up every drop, and demanded more.

She screamed aloud when she came, and her entire body shuddered with the force of her climax. And even then, he was sliding his wet, warm body up over hers, higher, covering her, spreading her, filling her.

It had been so long since she'd held a man inside her. So long. And her orgasm never stopped. It eased only slightly before beginning to build again as he moved deeper, drew back, and thrust into her again and again. Her nails raked his back. She whispered words of old, in a tongue long forgotten.

Again the peak burst upon her, and shattered her very being. This time he was there with her, grating his teeth, moaning her name—the name he'd given her. Poppy.

Slowly, their bodies uncoiled. Matthew rolled to the side, pulling her into his arms, holding her against him. She felt his heart pounding in his chest. Powerful and strong. Her own beat rapidly, too. But it wasn't as strong. She could feel, more than ever, the flaws in its imperfect rhythm. The weakness in its most powerful beat.

He stroked her hair. "What language was it that you were speaking to me, Poppy?"

She lay against him, loving the feel of strong male arms around her, no matter what else was wrong in her world. "Sumerian," she told him. "It was spoken four thousand years ago, in my homeland."

He nodded. She felt the movement of his head. "Oh, I get it now. That's where I've heard that name of yours before, isn't it? You're named for some ancient queen, aren't you?"

She shook her head slowly. "No, Matthew. I'm not named for anyone."

Rising up on his elbows, he studied her face, a hint of humor in his eyes. "You mean you actually are some ancient queen."

"Of course I am."

He bent and kissed her shoulder. "And what were you saying, my sexy, crazy, Sumerian queen?"

"It was a bit of ancient poetry, part of a song they say the goddess Inanna sang to her husband. 'Your kiss is like honey. Touch me and I tremble, my strong, powerful lion. Your kiss is like honey sweet. Kiss me again.'"

He lifted her chin and kissed her lips, as if in response to her request. But when he lifted his head away again, his eyes were serious. "It wasn't a mistake, what just happened, between us."

She shook her head. "No. It can't have been."

He nodded. "I don't want to hurt you the way I've hurt others in my life, Poppy. Don't let me."

She let her gaze roam his face, his stubbled chin, strong jaw, full lips. "I'm not the one in danger of getting hurt here." She lowered her lashes. "Don't get attached to me, Matthew. I don't have that much more time."

"You've said that before. I'm going to have to insist you tell me what the hell you mean by it this time. Because if you're thinking about—about—"

"Suicide?" she asked. "No. I just . . ." She looked at his face, at the sudden intensity in his eyes, and she couldn't tell him the truth—that she probably wouldn't live very much longer. She knew it, though. Sensed it with every breath she drew. Better to spare him that knowledge. "When we get back to civilization, Matthew, I'm going to leave. You need to know that. Be aware of it. And prepare yourself."

He stared at her. But finally he licked his lips and nodded. "All right. If that's what you have to do, then . . ." Lowering his head, he shook it slowly. "I don't want to think about it, to tell you the truth. Here and now, remember? That's all I want to think about."

She smiled very slightly. "That's good, Matthew. Because here and now is all we have."

He frowned, searching her face, but she said no more. Instead she rolled to her feet, ran into the waves, then dove into the water.

Chapter 8

Something was wrong with her, he knew it with the same uncanny clarity with which he knew other things about her. He knew, for example, that she was not an ordinary woman. There was something otherworldly about her. Something older than time. He knew, too, that she hadn't come here by accident. That it had been predestined. That he was supposed to help her in some way. To save her—from what, he wasn't sure. Maybe from whatever it was he sensed was wearing her down.

She wasn't getting stronger here, as he'd expected, but weaker. Day by day, weaker. Sure, she'd recovered somewhat from her ordeal at sea. But this was something else. Something he felt, more than saw. It did show, physically. It showed in how easily she could become breathless. A short walk would do it. It showed in how she grew paler all the time, no matter how much sunlight she got. It showed in her eyes, which revealed pain she wouldn't admit to feeling. But he sensed it even more powerfully. He sensed something in her slowly fading. Like a bright light growing gradually dimmer as its fuel burned away.

They made love, and slept, and woke and made love again, until finally Poppy fell into a deep, heavy sleep. Sensing she wouldn't wake again until morning, he wrapped her in the nearly dry robe, and carried her back to the villa. She never stirred. And maybe it was his imagination, but she seemed lighter than before. Frail and light and cool in his arms. Less substantial than the last time he'd carried her over the same path.

He tucked her into his bed and brushed her hair away from her face. Her skin was cool, and he thought he detected the bare beginnings of shadows beneath her eyes. She was sick. He would lay odds that she'd been sick long before her time in the ocean. She might even be dying.

And she seemed to have accepted it. But she hadn't counted on him. She had no clue as to what the kinds of things a man with his power, his wealth, and his connections, could accomplish. He hadn't been able to save Gabriella. But he would damn well pull out all the stops to save her dark sister.

Her dark sister. When had he begun to think of Poppy that way?

Smiling very slightly, he bent to press a kiss to her forehead. "Don't you worry, Poppy. I'm going to fight this thing. And you're going to fight it with me. I'm not giving you any choice in the matter."

Dawn broke in neon. Blazing orange and glowing yellow painted her eyelids from beyond the windows and burned through them until she awoke. The light made her head ache, and she immediately turned away from it and groaned.

Then she realized she was in bed. She'd expected to wake up on the beach. In Matthew's arms.

Gods, last night . . . She closed her eyes, remembering. She'd never felt that way before. Not even with Natum. How was that possible? Natum had been the love of her life . . . hadn't he?

She heard voices then and, frowning, got to her feet. Her legs were oddly watery and her head heavy. Still, she moved closer to the door, listening as the voices outside rose.

"It's too soon, I tell you! Why are you so damned stubborn, anyway?"

"I have my reasons, Murial. And since when are you my keeper?"

"Dammit, Matthew, that hurts. I'm your friend. You know that."

His tone was softer when he replied. "I know that. I'm sorry. But I don't want to argue about this anymore. The Weather Service says there's still time. So we're going back—this morning."

There was a long pause. Poppy opened the door a crack and peeked out. She could see down the hall, into the living room where the two stood facing each other. Matthew had a cup of coffee in his hand. Murial looked close to tears.

Backing inside, Poppy gathered her strength and quickly showered and dressed in some of the too-large clothes Matthew had found for her. By the time she joined them, Matthew was putting plates of food on the table and refilling his coffee cup.

He smiled when she came in, pulled out a chair for her. "Morning, Poppy," he said. Gods, if she went by the look in his eyes, she might think he was speaking to someone he cherished. "How are you feeling?"

Odd question, she thought with a frown. "Fine. I'm feeling fine." She slid a glance toward Murial as she sat down. "In fact, I think this island air is good for me. A few more days out here and I'll be as good as new." She forced a bright smile as she spoke the lie.

Matthew set a plate of food in front of her that could have fed three grown men. "I wish I could agree with you, there, but as I've already told Murial, I think we need to get back."

She lifted her gaze to his. "But why? I thought we were going to wait out the storm here."

He shook his head, then took his own seat. "No, that's impossible. For one thing, the Weather Service says the storm is close to hurricane force now. It's moving in, but slowly. They expect it to hit us by nightfall, and it's just not going to be safe here."

She nodded, sliding a surreptitiously apologetic glance at Murial, who was so deep in thought that she didn't even notice. "So it would be too dangerous to stay," she said, looking at Matthew again. "I'm confused, Matthew. Just yesterday, you thought it would be too dangerous to leave."

"We have better information today. There's plenty of time to make the flight back to Miami. We'll be flying away from the storm, and, as I said, it's moving slowly. At this point, it would be far more risky to stay than to go."

Again she nodded. "And what's the other reason?"

"Other reason?" He leaned over to fill her cup with coffee. She hadn't asked. She'd barely glanced at the cup, thought of coffee, and he'd acted. It was as if he could read her thoughts. Or maybe he was just watching her that closely.

"You said, 'for one thing' before you mentioned the storm. That implies some other thing."

He averted his eyes, gave his head a shake. "I'm just ready to go back. I think it's the best thing."

He was keeping something from her. She could barely believe it. She sighed impatiently and ate a few bites of the food, but her stomach didn't receive it well. "You're just going to leave the place to the storm, then?"

"This place isn't that hard to button up," he said, looking relieved at the change of subject. "It's not as if hurricanes are a rarity out here. I'll have the barriers on the windows and doors inside an hour. So finish up your breakfast and grab what you want to take with you." He glanced at his watch. "We'll leave at nine. All right?"

It seemed there was no talking him out of it. And who was she to try, if this was what he felt he needed to do? Maybe it would be good for him to go back, to face his past and deal with his ghosts, despite what Murial thought.

Something twisted into a tight, hard little knot inside her, and she hated to admit that the idea of leaving him, as she knew she would have to do when they arrived back in the States, was painful. Almost unbearable.

She hadn't arrived on the island with much. Her dagger and her tattered clothes. So there wasn't much for her to throw into the small bag that Matthew gave her, but she managed to find a few things. The toothbrush and hairbrush he'd given her. The white robe—she'd grown rather attached to the silly oversized thing. And Gabriella's diary. She didn't intend to keep it, of course. But she couldn't bear the thought of leaving it here to be washed away by the storm. She would give it to Matthew before she went on her way to face an uncertain future alone.

Murial climbed into the plane first. She started its engines, and the whir of the propellers sent sea spray flying in a fine mist that dampened anyone who came near. Matthew stood near the front end of the pontoons, untying the rope that held the plane to the island. "Go on, Poppy, climb aboard." He had to shout to make himself heard above the roar of the engines. "I'll have to give this baby a push to get her into the water and turned around."

Nodding, Poppy went to the open door, gripped a handle, and put her foot on a step. She looked up, met Murial's eyes, and returned her ready smile. Then she reached out a hand.

Murial clasped it.

The jolt that rocked through her at that touch would have knocked her down to the sand, if the other woman hadn't held on so tight. Murial tugged, and Puabi found herself pulled right into the plane's cockpit, shoved through a doorway into the rear section, then down into a seat.

She blinked up at Murial, her heart racing. That jolt of contact could only mean one thing. "You . . . you're an Immortal High Witch!"

"A Dark One," she whispered. "Just like you. It took you long enough, Puabi. I was beginning to think you'd never figure it out."

"But . . . but I don't understand. What do you want with Matthew? He's a mortal. He's just an ordinary man."

"Oh, I think we both know there's nothing ordinary about Matthew Fairchild," she said with a slow, wicked smile. "But it isn't him I want. And I'm afraid you aren't going to live long enough to learn any more than that. Neither of you is."

Puabi reached for her dagger, her hand shooting automatically to her thigh. Years of battle had made the reaction a reflex. But her dagger wasn't at her thigh—it was packed in her bag. She'd thought she wouldn't need it at hand at least until they reached the mainland. Gods, when had she become so complacent?

"What's the matter, Puabi? Do you think I want your heart? You know perfectly well that the hearts of the Dark Ones are weak trophies at best, and yours is all but used up. Tell me, Puabi, why haven't you killed one of the Light Ones to rejuvenate yourself? I just can't figure that out."

Puabi surged to her feet, balled up a fist, and swung at her, but Murial ducked the blow and easily shoved Puabi down on the seat again. "I don't want to fight you, Puabi. I just want you out of my way."

She brought her hand around, and Puabi glimpsed the object in

it. Large, metallic, red. She ducked fast, then drove her head toward
Murial's belly. But the other woman was faster and stronger—in
peak condition, while Puabi was running on empty. Murial simply
dodged the attack and swung again. The small fire extinguisher
smashed down on Puabi's head, and lights exploded in her eyes.
Then one by one, they blinked out. The last thing she heard was
Murial's voice, cruel and deep. "You're going to die, Puabi. For
keeps this time, if you ask me."

Matthew waded into the surf, tugging the plane easily around to
face away from the island. Then he used the pontoon as a step,
climbed in, and pulled the hatch shut behind him. "All set," he said,
turning to Murial.

She sat at the controls, smiling at him, her light blue eyes
sparkling. "Great. We're on our way. Go on, now, go buckle up."
Even as she spoke, she set the thing in motion. Matthew turned
toward the rear and made his way back, through the small doorway
toward the set of passenger seats, smiling as he caught sight of
Poppy relaxing there. The warmth that moved through him whenever he saw her was amazing. He wasn't a fool. He knew damn well
that part of the attraction was her resemblance to Gabriella—the
woman he'd taken for granted and lost. But it wasn't only that.
There was something more to Poppy.

Moving nearer, he felt his smile freeze in place and then slowly
change into a frown. "Poppy? Hey, what's wrong?" She was
slumped against one side of the plane, eyes closed, body limp. He
knelt in front of her, gripping her hands, touching her face. "What is
it? Poppy?"

"Anything wrong?" Murial called. "What's going on back there?"
The plane was banging against the incoming waves now, shuddering
a little, but then it lifted off and left the choppy waters behind.

"It's Poppy. She's out cold." He checked for a pulse, watched her
chest, and held his breath until he felt hers whispering from her lips
to bathe his face. Finally, he detected the soft thrum of the blood
rushing through her veins. "She's alive," he said, as much to confirm
it to himself and the universe—to make it so—as to inform Murial.
"What the hell happened in here? She seemed fine . . ."

"Damned if I know." The plane was banking now, settling into flight. "She was okay when I helped her aboard. Gee, maybe she's sicker than I realized. I mean, I sensed she wasn't quite well, but I had no idea she was seriously ill."

He sank into the seat beside Poppy, pulling her into a more comfortable position with care. "She is, I'm afraid. That's why I wanted to get back today, Murial. I want her to see the top specialists in the country. The world, if necessary."

"You know what's wrong with her, then?"

"No. I think it may be her heart, but she hasn't told me." He frowned then, as the clouds parted briefly, and the sun slanted through the window. It reflected on something shining or wet in Poppy's hair. Bending closer, he probed with his fingers, and then found the small cut, and felt a knob the size of a goose egg forming around it. "For the love of . . ." He got to his feet and laid her on the seat, then pried back one eyelid with his thumb, trying to check her pupils. "She has a head injury!" he shouted. "Jesus, Murial, something must have happened in here!"

"Oh, no!" Murial said. "You know, I heard her fall, when she was getting into her seat, but she said she was fine. I should have checked."

Matthew grimaced, then went for the first aid kit mounted to the wall nearby. He took out a cold pack and crushed it to activate it, then laid it on Poppy's head. "Hard to believe she could have fallen hard enough to do this much damage," he muttered.

"Look, I'll have you in Miami in under two hours. Just hang in there, okay? She'll be fine."

He nodded. And he sat with Poppy for a time, holding her, speaking softly to her.

It kept getting darker by degrees. It didn't register right away, but when it did, Matthew feared the storm may have picked up its pace. Maybe it was coming in faster than predicted. Hell, that was all they needed.

"Better get a weather update," he called to Murial. "I don't like the looks of this." She didn't answer, and he turned to shout toward the front. "Murial, did you hear me? I said you ought to get a storm advisory in case . . ." As he spoke he glanced out the window, and he was briefly disoriented because the storm clouds were on the wrong side of the plane. "Jesus, Murial, where the hell are you taking us?"

Still no answer, and his stomach clenched. "Dammit, Murial, answer me!" A rush of air and sound came then. Matthew made his way forward, only to see Murial vanish through the open hatch. He reached for her but grabbed only air, and he watched her plummet with a sense of horror before he realized that she was wearing a parachute. It bloomed far below, and beyond it he saw the familiar shape of Saba. Then he yanked the hatch closed, his mind racing with questions.

"She's trying to kill us, Matthew. Both of us."

He turned to see Poppy, clinging to the walls to hold herself up, leaning into the cockpit. She looked so weak. "But I don't understand. Why?"

"There's no time now," she whispered. "Look."

He looked out the windshield, and what he saw made his heart flip over. The whirling, swirling black sky. Murial had pointed them directly into the hurricane before bailing.

"Do you know how to fly this thing?" Poppy asked weakly.

He met her eyes, his own grim. "No."

Chapter 9

The engines coughed as if to punctuate his answer, and he scanned the panel to try to figure out why. It wasn't a difficult puzzle. The needle of the fuel gauge pointed to Empty. "She must have dumped the fuel. She wasn't taking any chances." One last sputter, a cough, and the craft began to descend.

"I won't give up without a fight, dammit." Matthew got himself into the seat, took the controls. He'd been in the plane with Murial often enough to have picked up a few things. He found the lever that would lower flaps and, he hoped, slow their airspeed. He used the stick to keep the nose from dipping too low as the plane's engines died all at once. And then they drifted on the air, and he could hear the wind all around them. It was damned eerie.

"Where did she go?" Poppy asked. "How could she jump into all that ocean?"

"Island," he said, his attention on the controls, on the plane, on the water rushing up at them. "Saba. Back there." Faster and faster the sea rose toward him. "Sit down, Poppy! Brace yourself!"

He didn't know if she did or not. They hit, a wing dipped, and the plane cartwheeled. Matthew was tossed around violently as water rushed on him from all directions and his body smashed into hard objects.

And then there was only water. Stillness, and water, all around. He didn't know which way was up or down. So he struggled toward the light. It was all he had to go by.

His head broke the surface. He sucked in a breath, and a wave slapped his face and crawled down his throat. Choking, gasping, and spitting, he tread water, sought air.

Poppy! Jesus, where was she? "Poppy! Poppy, where are you?"

He couldn't see her. God, he couldn't see her! "Poppy!" More water down his throat, in his lungs. Hell, where was she? The sky was black, the wind picking up. A huge wave broke over his head and drove him under. When he tried to struggle to the surface, something bumped his leg.

Shark. The word whispered through his mind like a razor-edged blade.

Then the thing bumped him again, its body hitting his. And the next thing he knew he was on the surface, sucking in air.

The animal circled him, arched out of the water, and vanished again. Not a shark. A dolphin.

The clouds burst, and rain fell in a deluge, powerful drops driving into him like icy pellets. He searched for Poppy, screamed her name until he was so hoarse he could barely speak. The waves increased, and he was thrown under again, and again, but each time the dolphin pushed him back up. He was barely conscious the last time it happened, and his hand closed around the dorsal fin.

And suddenly the animal shot forward, cutting through the waves like a knife through butter. He held on for dear life—that was all he could do.

Matthew coughed, rolled onto his side, choked and gagged. Water trickled out of his mouth, and he rose up onto all fours, arching his back as his lungs expelled more salt water.

When the spasm ended, he rose to his knees in the black sand, wiping his mouth with the back of his hand. "Poppy," he whispered, staring out to sea. "God, did you make it?"

Something moved in his peripheral vision, and he swung his

head around. There, farther along the beach, tangled in seaweed was . . . something. The dolphin?

The tail rose and lowered again. The woman moaned softly. He blinked, and rubbed his eyes. And there was no tail. No mermaid lying there in the sand. There was only Poppy.

He ran forward, fell to his knees beside her, and lifted her slowly. "Baby, Poppy, are you all right?"

Opening her eyes very slowly, she nodded. "I have . . . to tell you . . ."

He pressed a finger to her lips. "No. No, you're too weak. I need to get you to a doctor." He looked around him, frantic. "Wait a minute, this is a black sand beach. And there, there's the crater. See it?"

She looked where he pointed. The peak of the tiny volcano island rose into the storm clouds.

"This is Saba," he told her, scanning the place to get his bearings. "Yes, there's a road off this way. And there's a town a mile farther. God, I hope they haven't evacuated the entire island."

He scooped her up into his arms and carried her. "How did you get to shore, Poppy? God, I was so afraid. I couldn't find you. How did you do it?"

She opened her eyes and stared up at him, her vision unfocused. "I swam. And I pulled you with me."

He frowned, wondering if her fever was back. She'd been through so much. "No, baby. A dolphin towed me in. But it's okay, I understand—"

"It was me. I only made you think I was a dolphin. It was easier than answering all the questions you would have . . ." she turned her head to the side, and coughed.

"But, Poppy, that's impossible."

"No. It's a spell. The *glamourie*. It's only a trick of the mind."

He kept walking, kept carrying her. "Even if you could make me think you were a dolphin, you couldn't swim that fast," he said.

"Yes, I could. Faster, if I were at full strength. But I used up almost every bit of power left in me, Matthew. And I won't last much longer now."

"Yes, you will, dammit. I'll find a doctor. I'll save you, somehow, I swear."

She smiled weakly. "We haven't much time. I must tell you now, what I am. I'm a witch, Matthew. Not an ordinary witch. I am an Immortal High Witch. I've been alive for more than four thousand years. I survive by taking the lives of others like me. Taking their hearts—"

"No."

"Yes, it's true. Just listen to me, I beg of you!"

He swallowed hard, tried to walk faster. The village he sought was in sight now. The road was muddy and slick, the rain coming down in sheets. "If you're immortal, then you can't die. Yet you keep telling me you're not going to live much longer."

"We die. And we revive again. Over and over, but only so long as our stolen power holds out. At least that's how it is for the Dark Ones, like me. I could make myself strong again by killing another. But . . . something has changed, Matthew. I can't do it anymore."

He closed his eyes briefly. It was insanity, she was talking insanity!

"Murial is what I am. She's the same. And she wants something from you. I don't know what. I cannot even guess, but there's something. You have to kill her, Matthew. You have to kill her, and there are very few ways you can do that."

His jaw was clenched, rain streaming down his face. Her hair was plastered to her head, her clothes to her body.

"You need to cut out her heart. And when that's done, you must burn her body, and her heart as well. That will release her spirit. And Matthew . . . you must do the same to me."

"This is ridiculous! You're talking crazy. You aren't going to die, Poppy, you—"

"Please," she whispered. "Promise me you'll see to it that my wishes are carried out."

He stared down at her as he trudged onward, through the rain. "All right. If . . . if the worst should happen, I'll see to it."

She nodded slowly, relaxing in his arms, and he figured it was worth it, making that ridiculous promise, if it eased her mind. He'd be damned before he would do it, though.

"You were right, you know," she murmured. "I did wash up on your island for a reason. I think it was to save you from drowning, and now that I've done that, I probably won't live much longer. It doesn't seem like enough—to redeem me, I mean. But it's something, anyway."

She closed her eyes then.

Matthew stopped walking. Her head tipped back and hung limply. He shook her. "Poppy? Poppy, dammit, don't you go! Not yet, not like this. I love you, do you hear me? I don't give a shit what you did in the past, or what kind of monster you think you are. I love you. Dammit, Poppy, I love you!"

No response. He looked up, and saw a miracle standing in front of him, in the form of a sign carved in wood, with an arrow pointing to the right. The sign read, SABA MEDICAL CLINIC.

Chapter 10

The clinic was in a large house in the middle of a banana planta-
tion, and he guessed the doctor who ran it likely lived in it as well.
He hoped desperately that someone was home, as he carried Poppy
to the door and pounded on it.

A light came on within. Footsteps. Then a tall, almost regal-
looking dark-skinned woman opened it. She wore white, and her
name tag called her Aliyah. "Please," he said. "She needs help."

"Of course! Come in! What's happened to her?" She barely
glanced at Poppy as she led them quickly into a room and pointed to
a bed. "There, lay her down there. I'll call Dr. Sloane."

Matthew laid Poppy in the bed, noticing that she wasn't the only
patient. There was another bed in the room, a curtain drawn around
it, in typical hospital-room fashion, to block it from view, but he
could hear the steady beep of some kind of monitor. The nurse had
depressed a button on the wall and was now leaning over Poppy,
one hand to her cheek.

But then she sucked in a breath and jerked backward, her eyes
widening. "I don't . . . I don't understand . . ."

Poppy drew a shuddering breath and opened her eyes. "I'm so cold," she whispered.

Shaking herself, the nurse pointed at the closet. "There are dry nightgowns in there. And blankets. Get them. Go!"

He did, and by the time he came back with the requested items, she had efficiently stripped Poppy of her soaking-wet clothes and dried her with towels. She dressed her quickly in a white flannel nightgown, then had Matthew lift her up so she could strip away the wet bedding and briskly put warm, dry sheets on the bed. Then he laid her down again and tucked blankets around her.

The nurse stuck a thermometer into her mouth and was taking Poppy's pulse when the sound of shuffling steps alerted him, and he turned to see an aging man with skin so tanned it stood in shocking contrast to his snow-white hair. He was in his seventies, easily. "Well, now, what have we here? A couple of refugees from the storm? Should have evacuated with the others, son."

"We were in a small plane that veered off course and went down," Matthew explained. "We were lucky to make it to the shore."

The old man arched his brows in surprise. "My God, you're lucky to be alive!" He nodded to the nurse. "Go on and find this fellow some dry clothes. I'll see to the girl."

"A moment, please, Dr. Sloane?"

He glanced up at the nurse, who stood beside Poppy's bed, leaning over her. She sent him a look filled with meaning, and he frowned and went closer. Aliyah nodded at Poppy, and the old man looked down. Then he blinked, and his brows drew close. "How in the . . ."

"Why do you both keep looking at me so strangely?" Poppy asked, a hint of her former haughty attitude making its way into her tone. It did Matthew a world of good to hear it.

"I . . . well, I . . . you look very much like . . . someone."

"Yes, she does," Matthew said, coming closer. "She looks like my late wife, Gabriella."

"Gabriella," the nurse whispered, and she crossed herself. "Jesus, Joseph, and Mary."

"What the hell is the matter with the two of you?" Matthew demanded.

"Go on, Aliyah," the doctor said. "Get those dry things for the young man." She left, and the doctor seemed to square his frail shoulders as he faced Matthew. "I'm Alan Sloane," he said.

"Matthew. Matthew Fairchild. Now, can we skip the part where we discuss the weather and get to the point here? I can see something isn't right."

Dr. Sloane nodded slowly. "You're quite right about that. You see, about three months ago a patient—a young woman who looked remarkably like this one," he said with a nod at Puabi, "was transferred here to this clinic. Brain-dead, but on full life support. Her sister paid us a generous amount—enough to keep the clinic running for years—to keep her here, and care for her until—"

Matthew turned slowly, his eyes moving from the doctor's to that closed curtain that surrounded the other bed. Another patient. She looked like Poppy. And she'd been here for three months. His knees jelled, and Poppy reached out from her bed to clasp his hand.

More clearly than before, now, he heard the steady beeps and the pumping and hissing of the machines that kept someone alive according to some warped definition of the word. He pulled free of Poppy's hand and walked toward the curtains.

"There's more," the doctor began.

But he tugged the white curtains open. There, in the bed, lay Gabriella, her skin pale and waxy. Her hair neat and short. They'd cut it, probably to make it easier to care for her. It was as short as Poppy's now. But the biggest difference in his young wife, was the swollen mound that was her belly, expanded to the size of a beach ball underneath the sheets. And even as he stared at it in utter shock and total disbelief, the child inside her moved. He saw it.

"Sweet Jesus," Matthew whispered as he dropped to his knees, unable to hold his emotions in check any longer.

Puabi ignored the sudden skipping of her heart, like a motor working to keep from stalling. She couldn't focus on herself now. Not with Matthew on his knees, his entire body shaking with the force of his emotions. She glanced at the doctor. "Give us just a moment, will you?"

"No, not yet. You need medical attention, and I need answers."

He moved toward Matthew, clasped his shoulder from behind. "As no doubt, you do as well. Is this woman your wife?"

"Yes." The word was stark, and Puabi felt the pain in it. She struggled to sit up in the bed.

"And what happened to her, so far as you knew, I mean?"

Swallowing hard, Matthew lifted his head, but his eyes never left the body of that small woman in the bed. Puabi understood that, because she couldn't take her eyes off the woman either. So like her. And yet, softer somehow. And the fact that her belly was swollen with a child she would never know seemed like a twist of fate too cruel to bear. Why? "She could be my sister," Puabi heard herself whisper. "My small, frail little sister . . ."

"She was in a car accident. Her body—someone's body—was burned beyond recognition. We . . . we thought she was dead. I buried her, I—God, Gabriella . . ."

"And her sister? The one who brought her here to us, made these arrangements for us to keep her on life support until the baby was born—she never told you?"

He finally looked away from his wife, his head turning slowly to face the doctor. "She doesn't have a sister."

"Murial," Puabi whispered. "It had to be Murial." Her heart shuddered, and she tried to catch her breath without letting on that she was in distress. Short, shallow, openmouthed breaths were all she could manage. She got to her feet, somehow, moved until she was at Gabriella's bedside. And once there, she reached out and touched the face of the woman in the bed, the woman who looked so very much like her.

"You really could be my little sister."

Matthew lifted his gaze to the doctor's. "The baby? It's . . . all right?"

Puabi glanced downward at the swollen belly and lowered her hand gently to it. She could feel the life force inside, powerful and strong. "Fine. The baby's fine," she said, a little louder now, a smile pulling at her lips.

Dr. Sloane clasped Matthew's hand and helped him to his feet as they both looked at Puabi. The doctor seemed puzzled, but he nodded. "Yes, you're right. The baby appears to be perfectly healthy in every way. In fact, we'd originally scheduled the C-section for tomorrow. Though we may very well have to put it off another day if this storm hits the way they're predicting it will."

Matthew's eyes turned bleak. "What about that, Dr. Sloane? The storm, I mean. If the power goes out—"

"We're prepared for that. We have a backup generator. It kicks on automatically, son. The baby will be safe until its birth, we'll see to that."

Matthew nodded, seeming relieved, but only for a moment. Then he looked grim again. "And then what?" he asked.

Puabi returned her hand to the woman's face and stroked her hair, feeling an odd ripple of emotion that she had never felt before. *Never.*

Dr. Sloane looked at Gabriella, his expression sad. "She's not going to come out of the coma. She's brain-dead, son, she has been for months. The kind thing to do, the only decent thing to do, would be to take her off the life support. Let her go."

As had happened before, Puabi's heart seemed to skip, leaving her short of breath. Then it contracted—as if being slowly squeezed by a large, powerful hand.

The steady, monotonous pattern of the beeps emanating from the machine behind her suddenly changed. Rapid-fire, then slowing.

Matthew looked up sharply, and Dr. Sloane literally lunged toward the bed. Puabi stepped away to give him room as he put his stethoscope into his ears and pressed it to Gabriella's chest.

"What was that, Doctor? What happened?" Matthew asked.

The doctor held up a hand, frowning, listening. He shook his head. "Her heartbeat is fine. Must have been a glitch in the monitor." But he still looked puzzled.

Puabi was too dizzy by now to stand up without giving herself away, so she sat down in a chair in the corner. The nurse had gone to get those dry clothes the doctor had requested for Matthew. And the two men seemed too busy fussing over Gabriella to notice her.

The nurse returned, her arms full of clothes for Matthew. She handed them over, then frowned at Poppy. "You ought to be in bed. We haven't even examined you yet."

"I'm fine," she said. "Really, I'm feeling much better." She couldn't lie down. Not yet. She was too tired, and she was afraid— so afraid—that if she rested, she might slip away. She might die, for the final time. And now—now she sensed that her mission, her reason for washing up into Matthew's life—was not yet complete. There was more. It had to do with Gabriella. And her child.

Dr. Sloane said, "I'll leave you alone for a minute or two now. But not long. I want to examine you, young lady." He nodded to Matthew. "I'll be nearby. Call if you need me."

Matthew nodded, never opening his eyes until the doctor left them and closed the door. Then, he went to Poppy in the chair, knelt in front of her, clasped her hands. "Are you all right?"

She smiled through moist eyes. "Me? Matthew, how can you think of me when you're going through so much?"

"Because I care about you, as much as you detest hearing sappy emotional garbage like that. And I can see you're feeling like hell right now. And because I know what a shock all of this is to you, walking in here, seeing her for the first time. The baby . . ." He looked toward the bed.

"It's a boy, you know," she whispered. "A son, like the son I carried, and bore. Only yours is strong and healthy."

He sighed deeply, shaking his head. "Why is fate so damned cruel, Poppy? Why did a healthy, loving mother like you have to lose her child? Why does a strong, healthy baby have to lose his mother?"

She shook her head slowly. "I don't know. I only know that you need to grab on to whatever joy you find in life. And you've just found some, Matthew. You have a son on the way. You won't be left alone. You'll be a father. That's what you need to focus on here. Not losing Gabriella. Not even losing me. But the joy of this gift. This miracle." Her eyes seemed too heavy to keep open. She was so tired all of a sudden.

She expected him to look toward the woman in the bed again, as she did, but instead he frowned. "Poppy?" His palm pressed to her cheek. "Poppy, what is it? Dammit, you're in trouble, aren't you? Poppy?"

But she only smiled weakly at him and slipped into sleep as Matthew shouted for the doctor.

There was chaos. Dr. Sloane, Matthew, and Aliyah surrounded Poppy's hospital bed.

"I called for more help, Doctor," Aliyah said. "They're on the way."

"We're losing her," the doctor yelled.

Aliyah raced into the hall, and when she came back three other strangers followed, two women and a young man. Aliyah pushed a large box with ominous paddles attached.

"Oh, God, no . . . no, please." Matthew's heart was breaking. Jesus, this couldn't be happening.

"What the . . . what the *hell*?" The nurse beside him exclaimed.

He glanced at her, saw her gaze riveted on Gabriella's monitor. And when he followed that gaze, he saw erratic spikes and valleys in the lines on the screen, heard its frenzied beeping, totally out of rhythm.

"Doctor!" the nurse shouted as she rushed to Gabriella's side.

"Not now," the doctor yelled. Then he shouted, "Clear!" and Matthew saw Poppy's body arch off the bed.

"No good," someone said. "Hit her again."

"For the love of God, Dr. Sloane!" the nurse near Gabriella said.

The doctor looked up, started to say something, then stopped as his eyes raked over Gabriella's monitor. Frowning, he handed the paddles over to a nearby set of hands. "Keep working on her, Sally. I'll only be a sec."

Sally took the paddles. "Let's try again," she said. She nodded to the woman who was slowly squeezing air into Poppy's lungs, even as Dr. Sloane crossed the room to Gabriella.

"Clear!" Sally yelled.

This time, Matthew was looking at Gabriella. And he saw *her* body arch off the bed in response to the electric shock jolting through *Poppy*'s heart.

Dr. Sloane froze in his tracks and crossed himself.

Sally said, "Wait a minute, wait a minute—"

"We have sinus rhythm, Doctor," a nurse said from near Poppy's side. "She's back."

Dr. Sloane turned to Gabriella's monitor, and Matthew saw it was again bleeping in normal time, with regular patterns in the lines on the screen. "My God, I've never . . . my God!" Sloane looked from one monitor to the other.

So did everyone else.

What they saw, Matthew realized, was two women who looked damn near identical to one another, and two hearts beating out an identical pattern. The beeping of the machines sounded like one louder beep. The patterns on the monitors were a perfect match.

Dr. Sloane said to a nurse, "I want printouts of both EKGs over the past"—he glanced at his watch—"ten minutes." Then he turned to Matthew. "You said Gabriella didn't have a sister. Are you sure? Could these two be sisters—twins?"

"I don't know."

"Hell, even if they were, it wouldn't explain . . ." He looked at the nurse who had first alerted him to Gabriella's condition. The one he'd called Sally.

"Yes, Dr. Sloane," she said. "I saw it, too."

"So did I," Aliyah said.

Dr. Sloane shook his head slowly. "Let's just see to it that they stay stable until we can figure this out." He looked at Matthew. "Son, do you know anything at all about your . . . Poppy, you call her?"

"Her name is Puabi. Poppy's . . . just a nickname."

"Do you know anything about her medical condition?"

He shook his head. "I think she believes she's dying. That her heart is wearing out and that nothing can be done."

"Do you know where she's from? A family doctor? Anything?"

"No. No, I'm sorry. She came here from Maine, but that's not where she's from. She . . . told me once that she was born in the desert. I think it's Iraq nowadays, but . . ." He stopped, unsure of whether to continue. She'd also said she was four thousand years old, an ancient queen, a witch, and some kind of shape-shifter. Was he supposed to tell the old doc all of that, too?

Frowning, Dr. Sloane squeezed his shoulder.

"The baby's still fine," Sally announced, removing her stethoscope and smoothing the blankets gently back over Gabriella.

"Thank goodness," Aliyah said, as she ever so carefully taped Poppy's IV in place, her eyes tender and caring.

"Good. That's something to cling to, then, isn't it?" Sloane said. "I've got tests to run. Calls to make while we still have phone lines. We may need more expertise than I have to figure this out, young man, but I promise you, I'm going to give it my best shot. For now . . . well, you need to get into those dry clothes. Get warm, and get some rest."

"I'm not leaving them."

Sloane sighed. "I figured you'd say something like that. Stay in here, then, but the rest still goes. I'm going to have nurses watching them both round the clock. Once we get through this damned storm, we'll bring in cardiologists to examine . . . Puabi. Okay?"

Matthew looked at Poppy in the bed, nodded slowly. "Okay."

Dr. Sloane turned to leave. Then he turned back. "Puabi. Wasn't that the name of some ancient queen of . . . Babylon or something?"

"Sumer," Matthew said vaguely. "Four thousand years ago."

"Right. Sumer." He clapped Matthew on the shoulder. "Let's just get them through the storm, okay? Let's just focus on that, and we'll move on from there. All right, Matthew?"

Matthew nodded. But somehow he didn't think there was going to be an aftermath to the storm that approached outside. He felt certain it would sweep down and swallow up his entire world.

Chapter 11

Hours later, Matthew sat in a chair against the rear wall, with his dead—or was she only partly dead?—wife on his right side and the woman he loved on his left. His child's life seemed to hang in the balance. No matter how often Dr. Sloane assured him that his son would be fine whatever else might happen, Matthew found himself doubting it. How could anything be fine? The two women he'd cared for more than anything else in his life were dying, as if in some twisted brand of cosmic synchronicity. God, it was as if the two were connected somehow, the way their hearts seemed to beat almost as one.

No. Not almost. Not almost at all. He was freaking trapped in some esoteric *Twilight Zone* episode, with no script and no control. Jesus, it was maddening!

Outside, the storm unleashed its full might on the tiny island. It raged. It clawed at the windows and pounded on the walls as if determined to get inside. It didn't take much imagination to think of the storm as some dark-robed angel of death, storming the gates—on its way here to collect a soul or two.

Or three?

"You're not taking them," Matthew whispered. "I'm not gonna let you take them, dammit."

But the storm raged even harder. Something smashed against the windows—a limb, or perhaps a sign ripped from some nearby business. The safety glass shattered but didn't break apart. A corner of something wooden stabbed through, then the wind tore it free, and the rain and wind sluiced in through the hole. Matthew was on his feet instantly, even as one of the nurses rushed in to help. He balled up a spare blanket from the foot of Poppy's bed and crammed it into the hole. The wind stopped rushing in. The rain was blocked out. He lowered his head in a bone-deep sigh of relief . . .

. . . and then the lights went out. The steady beats of the heart monitors stopped, and their screens went dark. The machine that had been pumping air into Gabriella's lungs stopped its hissing.

"Gabriella! God, the baby!"

Immediately, even before Matthew finished shouting in alarm, the lights came back on, as the backup generator kicked in. So did the monitors. But their tones were long and steady, and the lines on their screens, flat.

The life-support machine did not come back on. The nurse, Aliyah, started hitting its buttons, her eyes growing more and more desperate as she tried to make the machine work. Then suddenly the control panel popped and sent a shower of sparks out from it like a fireworks display. Aliyah backed away, shielding her face with her arms.

"Dammit, do something!" Matthew cried. He turned to Poppy, fell to his knees beside the bed, and gripped her cool hand. Her monitor was flat-lined as well, he realized in horror, droning its steady death tone. "Don't go! For the love of God, don't do this, Poppy, please . . ."

"Start CPR!" Sloane shouted. Sally, one other nurse, and a young man crowded around Poppy and followed his instructions. Pumping her chest. Forcing air into her lungs by squeezing a bag. The doctor turned back to Aliyah, who was doing likewise to Gabriella. "Keep her oxygenated or we'll lose the baby!" he shouted toward the door. "Get a surgical tray in here!"

Matthew didn't know whom he was shouting to. The old guy

must have rounded up a few more volunteers, or he'd had others here that Matthew hadn't yet encountered. Within seconds an older, white-haired woman was wheeling a tray into the room. She might even have been Mrs. Sloane.

"What the hell is wrong with the machine?" Matthew demanded, still clinging to Poppy's hand, his own tears streaming freely now as he watched Aliyah and Dr. Sloane working frantically on Gabriella. "Why isn't it working?"

The older woman bared Gabriella's belly and was swabbing it with horrible-looking reddish-brown disinfectant. The others still worked over Poppy, stopping every few seconds to try to find a pulse—only to go right back to pumping her chest again.

"Try to stay calm, Matthew," Dr. Sloane said, his voice loud to overcome the noise in the room and the storm raging outside. "We have to take the baby now, and a C-section is a remarkably fast procedure." Sloane looked across the room. "How's Poppy doing?"

They paused in working on her and checked again. "We have a heartbeat, Doctor," Sally reported, with a sigh of relief. "Weak but steady."

"Thank God," Matthew muttered, his head falling forward, his neck like water.

The curtain around Gabriella was pulled shut, and Matthew had no choice but to let them be. Let them work to save his child. He focused his attention on Poppy, sitting close to her, right on the edge of her bed, holding her hand, stroking her hair. "If you can just get through the storm, Poppy. Things will be better then. We're going to find you the best specialists there are. You're going to be . . ."

"We're losing the fetal heartbeat, Doctor!"

The voice from beyond the curtain made Matthew's own heart stand still. Then suddenly Poppy's hand tightened on his. He looked at her, saw her eyes open and clear. She smiled gently at him. "Don't worry about the baby, Matthew. I'm not finished yet."

"God, Poppy," he whispered. "Honey, it's all right. You're going to be all right."

She shook her head slowly. "I'm done, either way. What power I have left . . ." She stopped talking and stared past him, her gaze turning more intense than he'd yet seen it. He followed her gaze and saw the slight gap in the curtains, and Gabriella's lifeless face visible there.

"Scalpel," the doctor said from beyond the curtain. "Hurry, dammit!"

"The baby's back," Aliyah said. She sighed and even laughed slightly. "Must have been a glitch in the monitor."

Poppy's hand on Matthew's went slack. He turned back to her. Her eyes were still open. But she was gone. He knew it in that single glance. The life was gone, the light in her eyes extinguished. Matthew heard her heart monitor's tone turn to a steady drone once more. "No," he cried. "Oh, Poppy, no."

"Keep the oxygen coming," the doctor said. "Stop CPR so I can make the incision."

"Doctor . . . wait. Don't make that cut!" Aliyah said.

"Why the hell not, Nurse?"

"I . . . I'm getting a pulse."

Minutes ticked by, and the storm raged.

Sally and the others at Poppy's bedside worked on her as before, pumping her chest, but it was different this time. Matthew was holding her hand, and he felt the truth with gut-wrenching clarity. This wasn't Poppy anymore. It was as if she'd pulled her tender hand away and left him holding an empty glove. It was just like that. She was gone. God in heaven, she was gone.

Kneeling on the floor beside the bed, he tipped his head skyward. "Why? For the love of God, will somebody please tell me why? Poppy, Poppy . . ." He lowered his head, sobbing now, unashamed. He loved her. And she was gone.

Behind him, the nurse put her hand on his shoulder, and he heard her breath hitch in her throat, as the others who were crowded around Poppy seemed to realize the futility of their desperate attempts to revive her. "I'm so sorry," someone said.

Brushing the tears from his cheeks, he managed to pull himself to his feet again. Leaning over Poppy, he kissed her gently, and then with hands that trembled he closed her lapis-blue eyes.

His stomach in knots, he turned, wondering if he would come away from this night with anything but loss and heartache. His entire body ached with the loss of the only woman he'd ever loved. He parted the curtain, and no one tried to stop him. He looked at Gabriella on the table. At the others standing around her, just staring at her, and at the heart monitor, which was beeping, showing spiked lines instead of a flat one, even though no one was doing CPR, and the life-support system was a smoking, burned-out wreck.

"What's . . . going on?" he asked, unable to speak above a whisper. And then, suddenly, Gabriella opened her mouth and sucked in a harsh, desperately sharp breath, as her body arched itself off the bed.

Then she relaxed again, falling against the pillows.

"Normal sinus rhythm, Doctor." Aliyah said the words, but they were a bare whisper, and her eyes registered sheer disbelief.

"My God," Sloane said, "she's breathing on her own." He turned to the others. "She's *breathing on her own.*"

Matthew stared at Gabriella's face, rubbed his eyes, and stared some more. He didn't understand what was happening.

"The heartbeat is getting stronger, Doctor," another nurse said.

Sloane said, "I can't believe this."

Then the impossible happened. Gabriella opened her eyes.

But they were not Gabriella's eyes. They were not ebony. They were a startlingly bright blue, flecked with gold, like lapis stones. "Matthew?" she whispered, and her voice was harsh with disuse.

There was stunned silence in the room. Then a burst of activity as they all bent toward her, whipping out penlights and stethoscopes. Matthew shoved them all away. "Please, please, just . . . just for a second."

They backed away mere inches, Dr. Sloane never taking his eyes off the monitors. Matthew bent toward her, frowning as he searched her face, not seeing Gabriella—seeing Poppy instead. He didn't know how, he didn't know why, he didn't even believe it fully. He glanced toward the bed on the other side of the room, but he could make no sense of it.

He turned back to the woman in the bed, fixed his gaze on her eyes once again. "Tell me your name," he whispered.

She frowned at him. "You know my name. It's Puabi. Even if you do refuse to use it." And her smile was weak. "To be honest, I like when you call me Poppy." Her gaze slid lower, then suddenly widened when she saw the shape of her belly under the blankets. "What—Matthew, what's happening? Why am I . . . where is . . . ?"

She lifted her head from the pillows, glancing across the room to the body in the other bed. "Gabriella?" she whispered. Then she looked up at Matthew again, her eyes round and confused. "Why did we change beds?" she asked. Then she frowned. "Why did we change *clothes?*"

Then slowly, her brows lifted and she met Matthew's eyes. "Oh, by the Gods, Matthew . . . I think I'm in Gabriella's . . ." But she didn't finish the sentence. Instead she grimaced and grabbed her belly.

"What is it? What's wrong?"

Poppy looked back at him. No doubt about it. It was Poppy, not Gabriella. And she said, "I think I'm in labor."

The labor hit hard and fast, and Puabi was already dizzy with confusion. It was as if she were trapped in some kind of dream where everything she had known was changed. Altered. Her senses seemed dulled, as if she were seeing and hearing everything through a filter. Gone were the sharply honed senses of four thousand years of living as an immortal. Gone.

And her heart . . . it beat in her chest powerfully. She'd become adept over the centuries at feeling her heart, knowing its condition. Moments ago, she'd known it was weak, winding down like an old clock, and probably beating its last. She'd known she had very little power or magick left in her, and she had willed every ounce of it to Gabriella's unborn child. Whatever strength she had, she'd consciously sent to him, realizing at last that saving Matthew's son was the mission she'd been meant to accomplish. And that it would be her last deed on Earth.

Now, though, she felt a strong, steady beat in her chest. A healthy heart.

A healthy *mortal* heart.

And with it, an iron manacle of pain, tightening around her belly and lower back. She gritted her teeth and came upright in the bed, and Matthew held her hand and stared at her in shock and wonder. Gods, he must be as confused as she was by all this!

The doctor and his nurses swarmed, and argued. She was too weak for a natural birth. It was too risky. She was too weak for surgery, it could kill her. And the contractions came hard and fast, and one of the nurses nurse said, "Doctor, this baby is coming. Now!"

Matthew leaned closer, his hand fisted around hers, his face close to hers. He couldn't seem to take his eyes off her, kept checking and rechecking to be sure she was who she was. Hell, *she* wasn't even sure who she was anymore. He stroked her hair, bathed her face with cool water. Talked to her as she struggled to give birth, while the storm outside raged on and on. And mingled with the pain were memories, images, and sounds floating through her mind of a past that was not her own. She remembered the day she had told Matthew she was pregnant. She remembered the day they'd been married.

How could that be? She wasn't Gabriella!

Then she was pushing, and all her attention was focused on the task. Nothing else dared distract her.

Finally, what seemed like hours later, she felt the pressure ease in a rush. She fell backward onto the pillows, her hair damp with sweat, her new heart pounding fiercely in her chest, breath rushing in and out of her lungs.

And then a sound, soft and congested, rose up like the most fragile bleat of a newborn lamb. A sound she had longed to hear for longer than any woman ever had. Her newborn child's first cry.

Puabi blinked and met Matthew's eyes. They were wet and locked on hers. And he tore them away only when Aliyah came between them to lower the baby, wet and slick and wrapped in a tiny blanket, into her arms. The nurse said, "I've seen a lot of things. But tonight, I've witnessed my first honest-to-goodness miracle." She smiled, tears rolling down both cheeks. "Welcome back, Gabriella."

Puabi frowned at the name. "But I'm not . . ." she began, but Matthew shook his head at her. She licked her lips. "Thank you."

The nurse backed away, and Matthew leaned close to her, bent to kiss her forehead, and then the baby's. "Our son," he said.

"Our . . . but . . . ohhh," she whispered, losing track of her confusion when she looked at the tiny face, the wrinkled little nose and hazy blue eyes. "Oh, how can this be real?" she whispered. "How can this be real?" Her own tears flooded, and though she tried to contain them, they overpowered her. Her entire body shook with the force of the emotional storm raging inside her every bit as powerfully as the one outside. Sobs bent her over her child, and her tears rained down on his beautiful face.

Aliyah reappeared, easing the baby from her arms. "It's overwhelming, I know. It's all right, honey. We'll take the baby just for a few minutes. The doctor needs to be sure he's a hundred percent. I'll bring him back all clean and dry for you soon. You rest with your husband now. You two have so much to talk about."

Puabi nodded, still sobbing, and Matthew put his arms around her, pulled her close to him, and just held her while she cried.

Chapter 12

Everyone left the room, though she doubted they had left the clinic, since the storm still threw its temper tantrum outside.

"Matthew," a voice said from the doorway. "My God, I can't believe you survived it."

Poppy looked up and saw her. Murial, standing there, wet from the rain, and vicious. "I see your girlfriend wasn't so lucky," she added with a nod toward the body on the other side of the room. The body that had housed Puabi.

"Think again, Murial," Poppy said. She pushed back the covers, darting a quick glance around the room and seeing the stainless-steel surgical tray, which had been pushed aside but not yet removed.

Murial frowned at her. "Gabriella? But you were brain-dead."

"You made sure of that, didn't you!"

Matthew rose, standing between Poppy and Murial. "What do you mean by that?"

"Oh, it was no accident that night, Matthew. And it wasn't a suicide attempt, either. This bitch ran me off the road. She pulled me out of the wreckage and bashed my head in with a tire iron. She had a life-support unit in the back of a van, ready and waiting. This was all planned."

"Honey," he whispered. He was facing Murial but darting odd, worried glances at her. "How can you know this?"

"I don't know. But I do. I remember it very clearly. Just as clearly as I remember my days on the throne of Sumer and my time on that island with you." She fought the confusion and went on, letting the words come as they would. "She tossed some other body into the car, torched it, and brought me here, claiming to be my sister. She asked them to keep my body functioning until I could deliver the baby—and then to pull the plug."

"Very good," Murial murmured, stepping forward. Matthew moved toward her, but Poppy got to her feet and stepped around him.

"This is my fight, my love."

"You're weak," he said.

Murial smiled. "Not to mention mortal. Don't bother sacrificing yourself, Gabriella." Then she frowned and looked more closely. "Or is it Puabi?"

"I have a feeling it's both," Poppy replied. "And we'd both die happily before we'd let you touch our child."

Murial looked confused, but only briefly. She kept glancing toward the other bed, with the sheet-draped body, then back at Poppy again.

"What do you want with my son, Murial?" Matthew asked. "What the hell can you possibly want with him?"

She lifted her brows. "I'm sure by now you know what I am," she said. And when he nodded, she continued. "Every witch has a certain gift. It's enhanced to incredible degrees in Immortal ones. Hers used to be the *glamourie*," she said, with a nod toward the bed. "Oh, yes, she could make you see her any way she wished. Mine was the gift of prophecy. I see into the future. Not everything, but certain things. I knew your son would be born with a very special power— one I want to make my own. And there's only one way to do that."

"Over my dead body," Poppy said, and she reached out and snatched the scalpel from the tray. She lunged past Matthew as Murial crouched and whipped out her own dagger.

Footsteps came from the hallway. Poppy saw Aliyah step into view, the baby in her arms.

IMMORTALITY

Murial laughed aloud, the sound long and low and evil. "Ahh, my delivery is here." She clutched the dagger in her fist, lifting it high, and turned toward the baby.

Poppy screamed and launched herself, even as Matthew did the same.

But at that very instant a horrendous crack and a terrible roar split the air. The entire ceiling came down on them all, leaving a cloud of dust and water. Rain flooded in, and the wind whipped, roared, tore through the place. Curtains flew, objects went sailing around the room, crashing into walls.

She pushed the debris off her. She hurt everywhere, but nothing seemed broken. She got to her feet. Matthew was beside her, his arms around her. And Murial? Poppy glimpsed one pale, bloody hand, sticking out from beneath a massive beam.

She didn't even spare the woman a moment's attention as she climbed over the rubble in search of her child.

Aliyah was still standing, several feet away. She'd turned her back to the storm and was hunched over the baby protectively, and the others were even now rushing to her. Matthew took his son gently and held him very close. He held Poppy to his side with his other arm. "We need to get out of here."

Dr. Sloane gestured them toward the exit. "My truck is right out front. We can make it into town, to the shelter. It'll be safe there."

Matthew nodded, and they all started toward the front door.

Poppy stopped herself. Then she turned back toward the rubble, beneath which Murial lay. "Go on, take the baby," she shouted above the wind and rain. "I need to finish this."

"I'm not going anywhere without you, Poppy. Your son needs you now."

"But—"

"You're finished with that, Poppy. That part of your life is over. Now, come on."

She blinked, and swallowed hard. Could it be true? Would she never have to kill another being again? Never have to carve out a heart to ensure her own survival? Was it even possible?

She didn't have time to find out. More of the roof came down, and Murial was buried under so much rubble that Puabi realized heavy equipment would be needed to dig her out. The house shuddered under the force of the storm, and Matthew pulled her outside.

He held her tightly as they raced for the doctor's SUV. Then they all crowded into it, and Dr. Sloane drove them over the muddy, rutted roads and through the fury of the storm toward town.

Dawn broke, and Poppy stood in the warm sunshine and the slight tropical breeze, surveying the rubble that had been the Saba Medical Clinic. She held her son in her arms, and Matthew stood beside her.

She'd slept like a rock last night, her husband and child snuggled close. But so far she hadn't so much as changed the darling baby's diaper. Too many willing volunteers at the shelter were loathe to see her lift a finger after her ordeal. She had become a local celebrity—the comatose woman who had given birth during a storm and somehow returned to life.

"She's gone," Poppy said softly, staring at the collapsed house, knowing that Murial was no longer trapped beneath the rubble.

"How can you be so sure?"

"I don't know. I feel it."

"I thought you weren't a witch anymore, Poppy."

She smiled up at him. "I'm not an immortal anymore. There's a difference."

He led her to a large rock and helped her to sit down on it. Soon the boat he had sent for would be arriving to carry them back to Miami, and Poppy would begin her new life—as a mortal woman, wife, and mother. It would be odd. And yet, she thought, it was a dream come true.

"Why did she want the baby?" Matthew asked. "I just can't understand why she would think he would have any kind of . . . power she might be able to steal."

"I don't know. I don't understand it." The baby whimpered, and Poppy unfastened the front of the borrowed blouse she wore, held him to her breast, and watched him suckle with a sense of wondrous ecstasy enveloping her entire body.

Close by her side, Matthew stroked her hair and watched his child take nourishment. "Poppy, what do you think happened here last night?"

She sighed deeply. "It goes back a lot further than last night," she whispered. "Matthew, when I lost my first child, I think a part of me died with him. The good part. I went mad. I turned into . . . something else. Something dark, without any light at all in me. It was something I was never meant to be. By using the foulest black magic, the darkest of the dark arts, I kept myself alive. For four thousand years I lived on, at the expense of the lives of others. But in all that time, part of me was gone. Part of me, the good part, had moved on without me."

She ran her fingertips over the baby's face. Gods, but it was so soft.

"It was Gabriella," he said softly. "It was her, wasn't it?"

"I think so. I think she was the part of me that moved on. You said yourself that she never seemed whole. That she craved something she couldn't seem to identify, much less obtain. And that resonated so well with me, because I'd always felt the same. She was lightness without dark. I was darkness without light. I think we were reunited last night—somehow, we melded."

He nodded, staring into her eyes. "Two halves . . . of the same soul? The dark and the light?"

She nodded slowly. "Somehow we were put back together. I have my memories now, but I also have hers. I feel complete—for the first time in, in forever."

"But how did it happen?" he asked.

"I don't know. I knew I was dying. I lay there, trying to will my remaining strength and life force into her, to help save your son. I didn't realize it was possible to will my soul to heal and to rejoin its other half as well."

"This is all just . . . it's so . . ."

"Far-fetched. I know. But it's true. I feel it, Matthew, it's all true. I felt it when I set eyes on her. In a way, she truly was my sister. And a part of me."

She could sense him trying to deal with this knowledge. "So are you Gabriella or are you Puabi?"

She shook her head slowly. "I like to think I was reborn last night. You named me, when you pulled me from the sea. Poppy. That's who I am now."

He smiled gently, stroked her hair and kissed her mouth. "I love you. I love you by any name. Whole and well. You're my wife, you know. Legally, you're my wife. Gabriella Fairchild. And the mother of our son." He looked down quickly. "We need a name for him."

"Gabriel," she said. "After the best part of his mother."

He nodded. "I like it."

The baby released his hold on her breast, and Poppy turned him toward her, resting him against her shoulder and patting his back so he would burp. As she did, he squirmed and the blanket fell away.

Poppy looked down—and went still.

On the baby's right hip, clear as day, was a small, berry-colored birthmark in the shape of a crescent moon. The right side. Not the left, but the right. She had given birth to one of the Light Ones. An immortal High Witch. Not a Dark One, as she had been. He would never need to kill to sustain his life. He'd received immortality as a gift. And suddenly she knew why Murial had wanted him. His heart must be a powerful one, indeed. He was special. And destined for great things.

"It's a miracle we've been given, Poppy," Matthew said, leaning close, replacing the blanket around the baby.

"Oh, Matthew," she whispered. "It's only just the beginning."